THE AMISH NANNY

MINDY STARNS CLARK
LESLIE GOULD

HARVEST HOUSE PUBLISHERS

EUGENE, OREGON

Scripture quotations are taken from The Holy Bible, New International Version® NIV®. Copyright © 1973, 1978, 1984, 2011 by Biblica, Inc.™ Used by permission. All rights reserved worldwide.

Cover by Garborg Design Works, Savage, Minnesota

Cover photos © Chris Garborg; Bigstock / Denis Pepin

The authors are represented by MacGregor Literary.

THE AMISH NANNY
Copyright © 2011 by Mindy Starns Clark and Leslie Gould
Published by Harvest House Publishers
Eugene, Oregon 97402
www.harvesthousepublishers.com

Library of Congress Cataloging-in-Publication Data
Clark, Mindy Starns.
    The Amish nanny / Mindy Starns Clark and Leslie Gould.
       p. cm. — (The women of Lancaster County ; bk. 2)
    ISBN 978-0-7369-3861-7 (pbk.)
    ISBN 978-0-7369-4160-0 (ebook)
    1. Amish—Fiction. 2. Nannies—Fiction. 3. Lancaster County (Pa.)—Fiction. I. Gould, Leslie. II. Title.
    PS3603.L366A85 2011
    813'.6—dc22
                                                        2011007092

If I rise on the wings of the dawn,
if I settle on the far side of the sea,
even there your hand will guide me,
Your right hand will hold me fast.
PSALM 139:9-10

ACKNOWLEDGMENTS

Mindy thanks

My husband, John, for love, support, advice, brainstorming, editing, creating, sharing, and more. From beginning to end, I could never get through the book-creating process—nor, indeed, through life—without you!

My daughters, Emily and Lauren. Whether here at home or away at college, you are both always there with me every step of the way.

Author Sicily Yoder for clarification and advice on the Amish, and Aaron Jarvis for help with the German language. Any errors are purely mine.

Vanessa Thompson, Stephanie Ciner, Kendell Weland, Brian and Tracey Akamine, Brad and Tracie Hall, and Fanus and Mariette Smith.

Leslie thanks

Peter, Kaleb, Taylor, Hana, and Thao Gould for their love, support, and encouragement; my siblings, Kathy Fink, Kelvin Egger, and Laurie Snyder; and my father, Bruce Egger.

Libby Salter and Taylor Cavestri for input in the early stages of the story.

Tim and Leslie Boettcher for sharing their expertise on traveling in Europe (any inaccuracies are mine), and my cousin Robert Germann for his hospitality in Switzerland years ago. That trip was vividly in my mind through the development of this story, especially the scene in the castle in Thun (although I took some liberties with the timeline of that historical site).

Mindy and Leslie thank

Our agent, Chip MacGregor, for his vision; our editor, Kim Moore, for her dedication; and the exceptional folks at Harvest House Publishers for giving such care and attention to every detail of the publishing process.

Also, thanks to Dave Siegrist for his expertise; the Mennonite Information Center in Lancaster, Pennsylvania, for their invaluable resources; and Erik Wesner, author of amishamerica.com, for his insightful view of the Amish.

PROLOGUE

The mailbox was hot, so I yanked the door open and gingerly fished my hand around inside, pulling out three identical square envelopes. That was all. My heart sank. I'd been hoping for a big packet, one containing the acceptance letter and related information about the teaching job at the new school a district away, in Willowcrest.

Teaching was what I wanted to do, and though my acceptance hadn't yet been made official, the president of the school board had already assured me that the position was mine. I knew I had the rest of the summer to get ready, but I'd been so excited after he told me that I had come straight home and started planning lessons and activities for my future scholars. I'd also subscribed to *Blackboard Bulletin* and had even made arrangements to attend my first teacher training class. All that was left now was to receive the official confirmation from the school board. Instead, the mailbox held just three little envelopes, one addressed to my grandmother, one to my parents, and one to me: *Miss Ada Rupp*.

My disappointment quickly evaporated once I realized these were from my sister, Lexie. Her Oregon address was on the back, printed in fancy lettering near the top. Slipping my index finger under the flap, I carefully opened it and pulled out the contents: cream-colored paper tied with a pink ribbon to a larger, dark-brown card.

An invitation.

Standing there at the mailbox beside the empty highway, my eyes skimmed the elegant printing on the front. It read:

THE HONOR OF YOUR PRESENCE
IS REQUESTED
AT THE MARRIAGE OF

Alexandra Clarissa Jaegar

To

James Patrick Nolan

THE FIFTEENTH OF AUGUST
AT THE FAMILY FARM OF THE BRIDE
3214 ORCHARD ROAD
AURORA, OREGON

RECEPTION FOLLOWING
PLEASE RSVP BY AUGUST EIGHTH

So Lexie was finally to marry her one true love, James. Eyes filling with sudden tears, I held the invitation to my face. The paper felt cool against my skin. The ribbon was soft. The smell of the ink was faint but noticeable. *God's blessings on you both.*

Blinking away my tears, I looked up the highway in each direction. With not a buggy or car or truck in sight, I began crossing the hot pavement back toward the house, my bare feet sticky against the blacktop.

Though Lexie had been raised Mennonite, she seemed to do things pretty much the way any *Englischer* would—which meant as different from here as could be. No doubt her wedding would be nothing like the ones I was used to. For starters, couples in my community wouldn't send out paper invitations like this. Instead, following a formal announcement in church, know as a "publication," guests would be invited verbally.

At least I was familiar with the term "RSVP" thanks to my cousin Ella, who had found out about Lexie's engagement a month ago and had chattered endlessly about *Englisch* wedding traditions ever since. The last time I saw Ella, she had pulled me aside to show me a magazine made especially for brides that she'd bought in town, one with photos of beautiful dresses and handsome grooms and elegant cakes. We had flipped through it together, Ella obviously enthralled with every page, though I wasn't sure what to think. All I knew was, Amish or *Englisch*, the sacredness of the commitment was what mattered. My sister was getting married, and more than anything, I wanted to be there with her when she did.

Reaching the other side of the road, I paused at the head of our driveway, looking again at the words on the invitation and doing the calculations in my head. August fifteenth was four weeks away, plenty of time to make some sort of travel arrangements. Plenty of time.

But who was I kidding? It would never happen.

In the field to my right, a hot breeze began to rustle the green, waist-high stalks of corn. Standing there, I watched the thick leaves as they fluttered and swayed, feeling on the inside much like those cornstalks, as if my very soul were rustling and shifting in response to some deep, internal force. I had no word for that force, though I tried several. Want? Need? Hope?

Desperation, perhaps?

So much had changed in my life recently. So many things were so completely different than they had been before. Some days, I wasn't sure who I was or what was to become of me.

For one thing, there had been changes to my health. Thanks to a medical condition that caused a rare type of anemia, I had spent my life on our farm living under the constant hovering of my worried mother and quiet father, feeling too weak to do much more than get through each day as best I could. But recently we had learned more about my disorder and had taken the needed steps to correct it. Now, thankfully, I was no longer impaired to any real extent, my sick days all but gone.

There had also been big changes in my family. After years of silence, half-truths, and out-and-out lies, my parents and several other close relatives had sat down in April with Lexie and me and come clean about the circumstances of our births. Lexie had always known she was adopted, but I never knew I had been adopted as well, the two of us raised by different families at opposite ends of the country, completely unaware that the other even existed. All of that information had helped Lexie to find healing, but for me it had done the exact opposite, creating within me new questions and doubts and confusions about who I was and where I belonged.

Changes had even come to my relationships—well, one relationship in particular. Will Gundy. The handsome young widower with three small children. The man whose glance could set my hands sweating and my heart pounding. All my life I had dreamed of being a wife and mother, but because of my condition I wasn't sure those were roles I would ever have. Then, once I had come to understand my disorder better and how to manage it, I had begun to feel as if marriage might be a possibility for me after all. I started to dream—not just of marriage, but of marriage to *Will*. I knew how I felt about him, and I just knew I could be a loving wife to him and a kind mother to his children. I thought he had feelings for me as well, but then I learned through the Amish grapevine that he was courting Leah Fisher, the bishop's daughter.

If that was really true, then I had no doubt the battle was already lost. I was no match for Leah and never could be. For one thing, my looks were far too ordinary—flyaway blond hair, angled face, dull brown eyes—especially compared to Leah, who was a striking beauty. More than her glossy hair and red lips and sparkling green eyes, though, was the very vitality of her demeanor, the musical sound of her laughter, the way she flounced around and flirted with almost everyone she met. I couldn't compete with that, couldn't even try. Instead, I would quietly bow out. Will and Leah would marry.

And I would end up alone, after all.

Suddenly, a sob gurgled from my throat. Pressing a hand against my mouth, I held it there until the urge for tears had passed. In their wake I could feel a familiar, deep ache rising up inside of me, and I knew that eventually my heart would heal and my confusion would be sorted out, but what would remain was *this*, the ache of yearning that plagued my thoughts and fueled my dreams and sometimes threatened to suck the very breath from my lungs. I was twenty-four years old but, thanks to my medical condition, had done and seen less than most children half my age. Bottom line, I wanted to *live*, to *experience*, to *explore*. Yet here I remained, still on the farm, still utterly sheltered, still sitting on the sidelines of my own life, just as I had sat out nearly every softball and volleyball game throughout my school years.

I knew without asking that my parents would never allow me to go to Oregon for Lexie's wedding. Though I was certainly old enough to make such a decision for myself, the truth was that I lived under their authority. Yearnings or not, desperation or not, this decision was theirs to make, not mine.

Turning away from the cornfield, I looked toward the pasture to my left, where a cluster of Holstein cows was standing near the fence line, calmly chewing their cud. As I stood there watching them, one gazed up at me, still chewing, her moist brown eyes lazy and content.

Slowly, I began walking up the driveway toward the house, the invitations still clutched in my hand. As I went, images of my long-lost sister filled my mind. Lexie and I had only just found each other last spring. Before then I hadn't even known she existed. But now that I did know—now that I had met her and come to know her and learned to love her—I wanted more than anything to be at her side on her special day. But how could I ever make my parents understand that?

Blinking to ward off a fresh threat of tears, I spotted a morning glory vine trying to wind its way up a fence post. Sliding the invitations into the pocket of my apron, I went over to the fence, bent forward, and yanked the vine from the ground. Standing, I wrapped it up in my hand, letting the roots trail along behind me as I continued.

Ella was no doubt facing this same dilemma across town—or she would be, as soon as her invitation came. Like me, she had grown very close to Lexie, and I knew she would desperately want to go to the wedding, even though she couldn't afford it, not to mention that she was only sixteen. At least Ella was Mennonite, which meant that her mother, my Aunt Marta, might be more agreeable to the idea than mine would be. As a general rule, Mennonites traveled more than we did.

But the Amish traveled too, sometimes. Silas Yoder, a boy I went to school with, had been out to Oregon several times with a group and even once by himself. He was planning to go alone again in a month or so. I knew lots of people who had been to Florida. One young couple had gone to California on a wedding trip.

But then there was my family. Once they moved to Lancaster County from Indiana many years ago, they had never gone anywhere since.

The pines stirred ahead, the breeze high in their branches. Sweat trickled down the backs of my knees. The front door to the house fell shut, and in the distance I could see my *mamm* headed toward me. She'd been happier lately than I'd ever seen her, with a little bit of a bounce in her step. It seemed that almost everyone had benefitted from our family's truth-revealing session last April—everyone except me.

I stopped on the front lawn, in the shade of the pine trees, and she met me there. Without speaking I handed over her invitation. She opened it and read it slowly. Then she looked at me.

"I got one too," I said. "So did *Mammi*, though I'm sure Lexie knows our grandmother wouldn't be up to making such a trip."

Mamm looked down at the envelopes still in my hand and then back up at my face again.

"You want to go," she said, more of a statement than a question.

I nodded, knowing it didn't matter what I wanted. Still, I asked, "And you?"

She shook her head. "No. I need to take care of *Mammi*."

Of course. And now here would come her reasons why I too had no choice but to stay home.

"It would be expensive," she added. "For you to go."

Expensive, yes. That was one reason, a legitimate one.

"Then again," she continued, "*Mammi* could help out with the cost."

I swallowed hard, my eyes wide. What was she saying? That she would actually consider it? My grandmother was occasionally a source of money, if the purpose for it was deemed worthy, but I couldn't imagine my mother allowing it in this case.

Her gaze drifted off to the pasture and she bit her lip. Without looking at me she added, "You could take the train."

Gasping, I shook my head, not wanting her to say another word unless she really meant it, unless this was an actual possibility. I swallowed again and waited until she met my eyes with her own.

"I think it would be good for you, Ada."

I took a step back, afraid I was dreaming, afraid she would change her mind before I could even respond.

"What about my teaching?" I whispered.

"School doesn't start till September. You would have time to get ready once you got back."

"And a chaperone?" Before she could answer, I offered, "How about Silas Yoder? He'll be going to Oregon in August."

She laughed. "Silas is younger than you are, Ada. No, we were thinking of the new couple in our district, Samuel and Lizzie. They are riding the train out to Montana to visit relatives of hers, and they agreed to make—"

"Wait. What? You talked to them?"

Mamm grinned, and at that moment I realized this actually might happen, that it wasn't a dream, that she wasn't going to change her mind.

"They agreed to make their trip in August," she continued, "so that it would coincide with the timing for Lexie's wedding. They will chaperone."

Understanding suddenly flooded my brain. "You knew already."

She nodded. "We've been talking about it for weeks, trying to decide how it could work. Marta would like to go but can't because of her patients. Your *daed* considered it, but he'll be too busy with the farm. And, like I said, I have to be here to care for *Mammi*. Given all of that, I think Sam and Liz are the perfect solution, even if they aren't quite going all the way to Oregon. You'll only be by yourselves for a day each way. Plenty of *youngie* travel, and we think it would be a good experience for you. For Ella and Zed too."

I stood there, dumbfounded. Zed too? Zed was Ella's younger brother, and only thirteen. "He's so young."

"Yes, but you aren't. Not anymore."

I knew that, but was it possible she had begun to understand it as well?

"Marta checked the train schedule and talked to Lexie," *Mamm* added. "She and James can pick up the three of you in Portland, no problem."

She stopped talking, waiting for me to absorb all of the information.

"And you're thinking—really thinking—we can go?" I asked finally, my heart pounding so loudly I was certain she could hear it.

She reached for my hand then and gave it a squeeze. "You've been restless, *ya*?"

I nodded. More than restless. Desperately so. I thought I'd hidden it well, but obviously I hadn't, not completely.

"A trip would be good for you, Ada. Time with your cousins. And your sister. Then you'll come home. Teach. Join the church. Settle down." She didn't say *Get married and have a family*, but of course that was what she wanted. She smiled again. "I think it's exactly what you need." Gesturing toward the barn in the distance, she added, "Your father is waiting for me to help him clean the tanks, but maybe later we could go over to Marta's to discuss things further. I imagine Ella and Zed are going to be quite excited."

My mother tried to release my hand but instead I squeezed it harder. Then, impulsively, I brought it to my face, pressing her palm against my cheek.

"Thank you, *Mamm*," I whispered, my eyes brimming with fresh tears. I blinked them away.

Eyes twinkling, she nodded as I released her hand and then she stepped away, crossing to the fence and letting herself into the pasture. Watching her clutch her skirt as she moved through the grass, a huge grin began to spread across my face.

Oregon. Could it really be true? I couldn't wait to talk to Ella, to share this incredible excitement swelling inside my chest.

After my mother disappeared around the far side of the barn in the distance, I strode to the fence, climbed up onto the bottom rail, and called out to a nearby cow.

"I've never even been out of Lancaster County!" I told her loudly.

In response she merely bit off a fresh clump of grass and began to chew.

"Well?" I asked, crossing my arms. "What do you think of that? Little ol' me, going to Oregon!" Then I laughed, fully aware I was talking to a cow. "Never mind."

Jumping down from the fence, I decided to go check on *Mammi* and deliver her invitation as well. Before I even reached the garden, however, my cell phone rang. It was Ella.

"Ada!" she shrieked. "Can you believe it? We're going to Lexie's wedding!"

ONE

Four weeks later

Lexie was a beautiful bride. Her white gown had little cap sleeves, which was modest, I knew, for an *Englischer's* wedding dress, but it looked a little like a summer nightgown to me. While Ella and I sat side by side on the bed and watched, one of Lexie's friends fixed her hair, artfully piling blond curls atop her head and pinning them in place along with her veil. Once they were finished, Lexie stood and spun around. We all cheered, Ella's elbows bumping mine as we clapped.

The first time I met Lexie last spring, I thought she was beautiful. Later, she and I stood in front of a mirror, side by side, and I'd been surprised to realize that we looked a lot alike. Same blond hair. Same brown eyes. Same tilt to our noses. That didn't make much sense, for I knew I was merely average while she was stunning. Perhaps it was her glow, her vibrancy, that set her apart. Either way, today she was positively radiant, and even more beautiful than I had ever seen her before.

"Breathtaking," Sophie pronounced from her perch on a stool in a corner. As one of Lexie's closest friends, Sophie had declined the request to be a bridesmaid as well, insisting she was far too old. Instead, she had been serving as a sort of fill-in mother of the bride, something needed here, given that neither of Lexie's parents were still alive to share this day. Her mom had been dead for many years, but her father had passed only six months ago, and I knew his absence was being sorely felt by Lexie—and by everyone else who had known him.

"You look like a princess," Ella gushed at Lexie as she completed her spin.

"Thanks, cuz," Lexie replied, giving Ella a wink and a loving pat on the knee before returning to the mirror for a final touch-up on her makeup.

I glanced at Ella in time to see her looking down at her own outfit and then over at mine. I could tell she was feeling quite dowdy by comparison, as though Lexie were Cinderella at the ball and we were the scullery maids. Ella and I were dressed Plain, of course, in white *kapps* and aprons over dark brown dresses. Being Mennonite, Ella could have worn a print but opted to match me instead, although with her auburn hair, ivory skin, and lively eyes she was far prettier. At least we both fit in with the wedding's color scheme and with the other two bridesmaids, who wore the same brown color, though in dresses far more stylish and made of a silky, shiny material. At weddings back home, the bride and her side sitters would all have dresses out of the same fabric, usually blue or purple. But this was an *Englisch* wedding, which meant attendants in coordinated colors and a white gown for the bride.

A soft rap interrupted us, followed by a voice asking, "Lexie? Are you ready? The guests are seated." The door opened and Mrs. Glick, who had to be older than *Mammi*, stuck her head inside. Looking at her, I realized that even she, with her simple calico dress, looked more stylish than Ella and I. At the sight of Lexie in her gown and veil, Mrs. Glick's face broke into a broad smile. "Oh, you look lovely, my dear. Just lovely."

"Thank you, Mrs. Glick," Lexie replied, standing up straight and smoothing out the skirt of her gown. "Everybody ready?"

We all stood, adjusting our skirts as well. Lexie thanked the two bridesmaids for their help with her hair and makeup and then flashed Sophie a grateful smile, no doubt for all the many ways she'd been helping out as well, not to mention her quiet, calming presence. Finally, Lexie turned to Ella and me and opened up her arms. We stepped into them for a hug, careful not to pull the back of her veil or crush the lines of her dress.

"Have I told you how much it means to me that you guys came all this way?" she asked.

We laughed. She'd told us multiple times since we'd arrived five days before. When we pulled apart, her eyes were full.

"Don't cry!" Ella said. "You'll ruin your makeup."

Lexie shook her head, blinking away her tears as Sophie turned toward the tray on the dresser and began handing out the flowers we would all carry—tiny bouquets of pink roses trimmed with white, pink, and brown ribbons. Lexie's bouquet was a bigger, fancier version of ours, with added greenery, baby's breath, and extra ribbons woven among the flowers. We didn't use flowers like this in our weddings back home, but I thought it made a nice touch here.

"They have started the music," Mrs. Glick told us from the doorway.

"You lead the way," Sophie instructed the older woman, who started down the hall to the stairs. Sophie followed, and after her went the two bridesmaids and then Ella.

I started toward the door next, but Lexie grabbed my hand and squeezed it, hard. I turned toward her and gave her a final hug, and then with tears stinging my eyes headed through the hall and down the stairs. As I went, I couldn't help wondering what my life would have been like if my family had kept Lexie and given me up for adoption to the Jaegers instead. I probably would have gone to college, and though I wouldn't have become a nurse-midwife, I could have become a teacher. By now I would probably have a classroom in an *Englisch* school. Perhaps, even, I'd be the one wearing the Cinderella dress, ready to unite with my own Prince Charming.

I shook my head as I paused at the back door and watched Ella start down the aisle between the folding chairs in the yard. It was wrong to covet. God had given Lexie the life He'd chosen for her and given me the life He wanted for me. I would be grateful for what I had been given and trust that He knew what was best for each of us.

When Ella was halfway toward the front, I started down the back steps just as we had practiced, careful to hold on to the rail. I didn't recognize the music coming out of the portable sound system in the back, but it was slow and soothing and pretty. Zed, with a goofy grin on his face and his blond bangs hanging low over his eyes, already stood at the front with the three other attendants and James. They all looked handsome in matching black tuxedos and dark-brown "cummerbunds," a term Ella had been using with authority, having picked it up from her bridal magazine. I was so pleased James had included Zed in the wedding party. He was a great kid and Lexie's cousin, but James hardly knew him except from the short time he'd spent in Pennsylvania earlier this year, when he'd come out to join Lexie. Including Zed here now was a nice gesture, one that made me appreciate James's sweet heart all the more.

The guests, mostly older, smiled in encouragement as I made my way toward the front. Before I got there, I knew the groom had spotted his bride waiting in the back for her turn, because his eyes grew wide, his lips curving into a tender smile.

I took my place beside Ella. Then the guests all stood and turned to watch as Lexie started down the aisle, her veil flowing out behind her on the gentle breeze. Her gown hung flawlessly as she walked, her carriage regal and tall. She came alone, her gaze fixed on James, her eyes filled with love. Still, something about her expression seemed almost melancholy, and I knew she was missing her late father now more than ever.

Suddenly, a breeze caught the spokes of the windmill high above our heads and sent it twirling. Lexie looked up, and it seemed a gasp caught in her throat as she froze in place. Watching the windmill spin, a beautiful smile illuminated her features. When finally she began moving forward again, gaze once more on her groom, I realized her sadness seemed gone. In its place was the joyous expression of one fully at peace, almost as if the windmill had signaled a greeting from heaven itself, a blessing on this special day.

When Lexie reached us, I took her bouquet and she joined hands with James. Facing each other as the pastor began to speak, it was as if they disappeared into another world, lost to the rest of us. I sighed inside. Would I ever experience that kind of love? Not from Will Gundy, that was certain. Not now that he was courting Leah. At least I would have my teaching. That was where I'd find my calling.

After all, what other choice did I have?

The service was short and sweet, not like the weddings back home that went on for hours and hours. There were no stories from the Bible here about Abraham and Sarah, Isaac and Rebecca, Jacob and Rachel. No songs from the *Ausbund* lasting twenty minutes each. Instead, the pastor simply read from 1 Corinthians 13 and spoke about love and submission, including submitting to each other and making sacrifices in marriage.

After that, he led the couple in exchanging vows, and then he declared James and Lexie husband and wife.

"Now you may kiss the bride," he added, grinning.

I blushed at the sight of their enthusiastic kiss. At our weddings, there was nothing like that in the service itself—though it would not be unusual to see the couple stealing a kiss or two later as the day went on.

Another song began, this one louder and faster than the one we had walked in to. Clasping hands, James and Lexie moved back down the aisle, grinning widely at each other and at their assembled guests. After a beat I took the arm of the best man and we followed, with the other members of the bridal party also pairing up and coming along behind us. Except for Zed, James's attendants were all married, so once we reached the back of the crowd, we reshuffled a bit so husbands and wives were together. Then we headed for the orchard to take some pictures.

I had discussed with Lexie the fact that I was uncomfortable having my photograph taken, but she had convinced me to participate in just one shot as a favor to her: a picture of the two of us. Now, posing in the shade of the graceful hazelnut trees, Lexie and I stood together arm in arm, laughing even as we were trying not to cry.

As I stood there with my sister, waiting for the photographer to take our picture, my heart began to soar with such a joy I could barely contain it. Lexie and I may have spent the first part of our lives far apart and unaware that the other even existed, but once we had found each other, the bond we had formed was instant and deep. God had blessed us in abundance, and I knew that neither my sister nor I would ever take each other or our relationship for granted.

After the photo had been taken, I hugged Lexie before excusing myself to go help in the kitchen. There I found Sophie and the other women from the church carrying out stacks of plates to the long table in the yard, so I jumped in as well. On one trip I glanced over toward the orchard to see that Zed had something in his hand—more than likely Ella's cell phone—and he was using it to film the various attendants as they continued to pose in different groupings for the pictures. Zed was obsessed with moviemaking and had been driving Ella and me crazy with his nonstop filming since the trip had begun. I could only hope he wasn't in the way out there among Lexie and James and their friends.

The other women and I continued to put out food and see to all the details of the reception. As we worked I couldn't help but compare how much simpler this was than the way we did things back home. For weddings, the norm there was three hundred guests or more, with two full meals being served, both lunch and dinner. By comparison, this one meal for Lexie's eighty wedding guests seemed an easy task indeed.

The next time I emerged from the kitchen, I noticed the members of the wedding party wandering back from the orchard, and it looked as if everyone except for the bride and groom had finished with their part of the photo-taking. Ella was walking with purpose toward the house, no doubt so that she could go inside and tend to the wedding cake. A gifted baker even at sixteen, Ella had been obsessed with this cake for days, decorating it in secret and not allowing any of us see it in its finished form.

Zed still had her phone, only now he was coming toward me with it, trying to get up close as he filmed. He knew I didn't want to be caught on camera, but he was so persistent that finally I turned my back on him and strode to the house as well, closing the door in his face.

It was time to bring out the roasted chickens, but when I got to the kitchen I stopped short at the sight of Ella's beautiful cake in the corner, which she had finally unveiled. It was three layers high, each one decorated with swirls and patterns in white frosting, accented with delicate, edible gold balls. This fancy cake would never do for a Plain wedding, but here it seemed just right. I knew Lexie and James would be thrilled.

Several of the other women had also noticed the gorgeous cake and paused to compliment Ella on her artistry. But she was so focused on adding the last few finishing touches that she barely acknowledged them. Grabbing the platter of roasted chickens, I decided to give her a little room to work. I would tell her later how pleased I knew the happy couple would be.

Stepping outside, I soon realized that Zed hadn't given up—and that now he was adding narration as he filmed.

"Here's my cousin Ada again," he said, "carrying the roasted chickens she made for the bride and groom. Are you the roast cook, Ada?"

"*Englisch* weddings don't have roast cooks," I replied, wishing he would be quiet and go away. Back home at our weddings, the couples in charge of roasting the chickens were known as the "roast cooks." We also had "potato cooks," who made all of the mashed potatoes.

"Wow!" Zed exclaimed suddenly, interrupting my thoughts.

I turned to see what he was looking at and spotted Ella just emerging with the finished cake, carefully balancing it on a board covered with paper. Immediately, Zed zoomed in on her and continued his narration.

"And now we have Ella, my sister and a cousin of the bride, carrying the cake she spent the last three days making. Tell us, Ella, did you set some sort of record, taking that long to make one cake?"

"Knock it off," Ella said. Tightly gripping the board holding her creation, she went down a step, the tall cake tottering slightly as she did.

"Oh, my." Zed held the phone closer to his face. "It looks as if a catastrophe's looming."

"Put that thing away and help me." She took another step, but the cake wobbled again, leaning even further this time. "Zed! Please!"

"Oops, incoming text." He turned the phone and flipped it open.

"Don't you dare read it!" Ella took another step, and this time the board tilted enough for the cake to slide a little.

But Zed had his hand out in half a second, steadying it as he slipped the cell phone into his pocket. "Whoa, easy does it."

Together they stabilized the board and then carried the cake across the lawn. Once they finally eased it onto the center of the dessert table, she gave it a few last adjustments and then asked for her phone. Zed gave it to her, announcing the text was from Ezra, as if any of us would be surprised. Ezra was Ella's beau—not to mention Will Gundy's little brother.

I set the chicken on the main table between the stuffing and creamed celery, glad that I'd thought to gather the recipes from *Mamm* before I left for Oregon. The other women brought out the last of the dishes and added them to the table, things like relish trays, hot potato salad, and little sausages. Stepping back to survey the entire spread, I realized that it was quite the mix of Amish and Mennonite "cuisine." I smiled. That was yet another word Ella had picked up from her bridal magazine and used as often as possible.

Glancing around for Ella, I saw she was standing away from the crowd just a bit, furiously texting away on her phone. She needed to be done with that and focus on matters closer at hand, but before I could get over there to tell her, I was sent back inside for more serving spoons. By the time I returned and had finished distributing the utensils among the various platters and bowls, a few minutes had passed. Yet Ella was still standing in the same place, focused on her phone.

I walked over to her, realizing as I got closer that instead of texting, now she was talking—or rather listening, the phone pressed tightly to her ear, her lips pursed shut.

"Ella, you need to get off the phone," I whispered.

She looked at me, eyes wide, and shook her head no. Glancing toward the orchard, I saw that Lexie and James were still posing for the photographer. Though Lexie wasn't the type to embarrass easily, I didn't want her guests, especially the older ones, to think that Ella or Zed were typical American teens, obsessed with a cell phone at the expense of the people around them.

Ella whispered something into the receiver, turning slightly so that her back was to me. Stepping around in front of her, I softly repeated my request.

"I can't," she said, covering the phone with her hand. "This is important. It's about Alice. Alice Beiler."

My eyes widened. Alice was Will and Ezra Gundy's grandmother, one of my own grandmother's dearest friends and a woman I absolutely adored. Though Alice and *Mammi* were about the same age, Alice was in far better health than *Mammi* was. When Will's wife died, Alice was one of the women who had taken over most of the daily care of his children so Will could keep working.

Fearing that Alice had now fallen ill or perhaps become hurt, I took Ella's arm and led her around to the side of the house, where we could deal with this call more privately. Except for a few marriages between distant cousins, Ella and I weren't related to Alice or her family in any way, but we certainly considered the Beilers and Gundys to be treasured friends, and Alice in particular. Had Will and I married, they all would have become my in-laws. Even though that was never going to happen for me, I was aware that they could still become Ella's in-laws someday if she married Ezra.

"What's wrong with Alice?" I pressed, and when Ella didn't reply, I spoke more loudly, "Is she sick? Did she break a hip or something?"

Ella put her hand to the phone. "No, it's nothing like that. You're not going to believe it, Ada. Alice is going to Europe!"

TWO

While the thought of Alice, an older Amish woman, going to Europe was, indeed, big news, it was nothing compared to the dreadful possibilities my mind had been dredging up. I exhaled slowly, relief flooding my veins.

"Europe?"

"Yeah. She and Will are talking about it right now. It has something to do with a legal matter."

A legal matter? In Europe? "Says who, Ella? Who are you talking to?"

"Ezra. It's not gossip, I promise. He heard it with his own two ears."

In that case I'd be interested to learn all about it. But later. Right now, Ella's communication with the people back home was bringing a distraction to Lexie's big day. But before I could speak, Ella continued.

"At first Will and Christy were planning to go with her. He even applied for their passports. But now he's decided he can't leave the twins for that long, so he and Christy aren't going after all."

Ignoring the flutter in my stomach from the mere mention of Will's name, I said, "Poor Christy. She must be so disappointed."

"I doubt it. You know how she is these days. She doesn't seem to care much about anything."

"Ella!"

"Well, it's true. The kid is pretty messed up."

Will's daughter Christy had been just ten years old when her mother died. The fact that the girl was still having trouble grappling with that death less than a year later was not our business to discuss.

"Hang up, Ella. This doesn't include us."

"No, wait. It does," she said, grabbing my arm before I could walk away. "Guess who else is going to Europe with Alice?"

I hesitated, waiting for her to answer her own question.

"Either your mother or mine," she said, almost triumphantly.

I blinked, shaking my head. "What?"

"Ezra heard Alice say she has to bring along either Klara or Marta."

Klara and Marta were sisters, Klara being my mother and Marta being Ella's mother. Regardless of whatever legal matter was involved here and what on earth it had to do with going to Europe, there was no way on earth either of our mothers would be willing to go somewhere so far away. Marta was a midwife with a thriving practice and tons of patients who could go into labor at any time. She'd sooner die than abandon them, even for a short while. As for my mother…well, I'd be less surprised to hear a cow speaking back to me in Pennsylvania Dutch than I would to find out Klara Rupp was planning a trip to Europe.

"Oh no!" Ella hissed suddenly into the phone. Looking at me, she whispered, "Ezra almost got busted."

Busted? At that moment I realized the full scope of what was going on.

"Ella, is Ezra eavesdropping on a private conversation between Will and Alice? Is that how he knows all of this?"

She nodded, and then after a moment of listening she told me, "It's okay. They didn't spot him."

I closed my eyes and spoke, trying not to raise my voice.

"Hang up right *now* or I will take your phone away for the remainder of the trip."

Opening my eyes, I held out my hand, palm up, waiting, and told her she had exactly ten seconds or it was bye-bye BlackBerry.

"I'll have to call you later," Ella whispered into the phone. Then she disconnected it, thrust it into her pocket, and snipped, "It's not a Black-Berry. It's a Vio4G. If you weren't *Amish* you would know the difference."

She spun around on her heel and marched away, heading toward the clusters of guests on the lawn.

I stood there for a long moment. I loved my cousin dearly, but she still had a lot of growing up to do. Silently, I said a quick prayer for patience, and then I began walking toward the others. I reached them just as James was clapping his hands to get everyone's attention and asking us to join him in prayer. Before bowing my head, I glanced at Ella, who was standing with one of the bridesmaids and pointedly ignoring me.

Closing my eyes, I took in a deep breath, willing my mind to turn toward God as James began to pray aloud. He thanked the Lord for his beautiful bride, Lexie; their friends and family; and their future as husband and wife. His "amen" was followed by a hearty echo all around—except by me. Not that I didn't affirm his prayer. I just wasn't used to people praying out loud and didn't know we were supposed to do that at the end.

Then James directed all of us toward the buffet. I followed Zed, not surprised to see Ella moving in far behind us, her face deliberately turned away. It was just as well. I didn't feel like dealing with her any more right now anyway.

Across from us was a little girl who had gotten in line without her family. She looked to be about six or seven and was wearing a pink dress trimmed in lace, her hair pulled neatly into twin braids. When she had trouble getting the potato salad off the serving spoon and onto her plate, I leaned forward to help her.

"Thanks!" she said, looking up at me and flashing a semi-toothless smile.

"You're welcome," I replied. After a moment, I added, "And thank you for thanking me. You have excellent manners."

Reaching for a warm roll, she was quiet for a moment and then spoke. "Well, thank you for thanking me for thanking you."

She and Zed and I all laughed. What a cutie-pie.

Zed and I ended up sitting by Mrs. Glick, at her invitation. While we ate I marveled at how everyone was able to enjoy the meal together, explaining that at our weddings back home, the diners had to eat in shifts because there were so many guests. We also didn't serve our food "cafeteria style" like this. Instead, guests sat at the tables and aunts and uncles of the bride would bring food to them, with single girls often helping during the first meal.

"Fascinating," Mrs. Glick said before biting into a fluffy roll slick with butter.

I didn't add that if Leah married Will, she would probably ask me to serve at their wedding. If she did, I would never accept, afraid my emotions might get the better of me.

Once the conversation turned from Amish wedding practices to Lancaster County in general, Mrs. Glick mentioned that she had always wanted to visit there, so I encouraged her to do just that, inviting her to stay at our home if she did.

She reached over and took my hand. "Ada, I might just take you up on that." Her pale blue eyes grew misty. "It's such a blessing that you have been able to share this day with our Lexie. I'm so thankful she has you and her cousins." Her fingers were bony. Suddenly I missed *Mammi* and wished she could be here for Lexie too.

"Speaking of Lexie's cousins…" Mrs. Glick said brightly, looking up over my shoulder.

I turned to see Ella standing behind me, her earlier anger gone, her eyes now aglow with some new excitement. Oh, the ups and downs of a sixteen-year-old girl! Our earlier conflict apparently forgotten, she motioned for me to come with her. I excused myself, stood, and followed as she led the way inside the house and into the kitchen. Once there, she simply handed me her phone and directed me to read a series of text messages, every one of them from Ezra.

The first one read: *Sorry I got you in trouble. I'll keep you updated via text. Right now they're talking about Frannie, that it's a shame she's not healthy enough to make the trip herself. They mean your grandmother, right?*

I glanced at my young cousin, appalled that she and her boyfriend were still at this. "Ella, I thought I made it clear I don't approve of Ezra's eavesdropping. This is none of his business. Nor ours." I handed her the phone and moved toward the door, reaching for the knob.

"Just keep reading, Ada. *Please.* They talked about you."

I hesitated, the door half open. Then, against my better judgment, I accepted the phone from her and read through the next several messages. Sure enough, Ezra had written: *Will said it should probably be Ada. Unlike*

Marta, she has no job to worry about, and unlike Klara, she doesn't have a husband to take care of. Alice agrees, says that out of everyone, Ada's probably the only one who is free enough to go.

My eyes filled with hot tears, the lines on the screen growing blurry. I didn't need to see Will's words to feel them driving the knife into my heart: *She doesn't have a husband to take care of.* Is that really how he thought of me? As an unattached, unloved girl free to take off on a trip at the drop of a hat? At least he was wrong about the job. Obviously he hadn't yet heard that I was soon to be a teacher in his very own district and that, in fact, I would have his daughter Christy as one of my scholars.

"Keep going," Ella prodded, oblivious to my misery.

Shaking my head, I couldn't even bring myself to speak. She reached out and took the phone from my hand, skimming the words on the screen and launching into a recap of the remaining messages. I was only half listening, but the one thing that came through loud and clear was that whatever this trip to Europe was regarding, it involved both the Beiler family, specifically Alice, and the Lantz family, specifically Frannie, and some legal matter that would require the presence of both women, in person, to straighten out. If either one was unable to go, a family member could serve in their place. That was why our various names had come up. Obviously *Mammi* was in no shape to go anywhere, much less to another country, so she would need a relative to represent her.

"That's about it," Ella said, still looking at the screen. "The twins came in, so Alice and Will agreed to finish their conversation later."

I was trying to think of a reply when Ella surprised me by apologizing for her earlier behavior.

"I really am sorry, Ada, especially that crack about you being Amish. I don't even know where that came from."

Ella's lack of maturity was the least of my problems. I had already forgiven her, of course, but right now my mind was on more important matters. Clearing my throat, I looked at my young cousin and said, "Actually, Ella, I would like you to send one more text. For me."

"Sure," she replied, her eyes sparkling with new interest.

"Tell Ezra that contrary to what his brother believes, I am not, in fact, without a job. I'll be starting as the teacher at Willowcrest in just a few weeks." That the confirmation packet still hadn't shown up by the time we left for Oregon was beside the point. I had stopped at Levi Stoltz's the day before our trip started, and he had assured me, again, that the job was mine.

I doubted Ezra would pass along that message to Will, but he'd likely find out soon enough on his own. I may not have a husband to take care of, but soon I would have an entire classroom full of children who would be looking to me for their educations. Once school started, I wouldn't be free or unencumbered anymore, not at all, regardless of my marital status.

Ella's thumbs were tapping away at the tiny keyboard as I went back outside and headed across the lawn. When I walked past the table where the little girl with the braids was sitting, she smiled and gave me an enthusiastic wave. As I waved back, I could feel my tension ebbing. Will hadn't intended for his words to be cruel, just factual—to the extent of his knowledge, at least. Besides, what right did I have to be hurt by a comment made in private and never intended for me to hear in the first place? My pain now was a direct result of my own actions, not his.

I reached my seat just as Zed returned from the buffet with what looked like a second helping of almost everything. For some reason, the sight of his eager, innocent face grinning proudly at his overloaded plate made me smile.

"Take all you want, but eat all you take," I told him, echoing one of our grandmother's more frequently used proverbs. Across from us, Mrs. Glick chuckled.

Sliding into my seat and reaching for my fork, I dug into the delicious meal once again, thinking about Will and Alice as I ate. I'd met anyone who had been to Europe, at least not anyone from the Amish community, so just knowing they were considering it astonished me. Beyond that, the fact that they had discussed having me go along as well was so mindboggling I couldn't even begin to comprehend it. Regardless of whether my teaching job prevented me from going or not, I still wanted to know more. Unlike Ella and Ezra, however, I would wait until someone was ready to tell me about it to my face.

"Zed, I can't imagine where you're putting all of that food," Mrs. Glick said, gesturing toward his plate, which was already almost half empty.

"My mom says there's a two-hundred-pound construction worker living in my stomach," he replied between bites, causing us both to laugh.

Soon, we were back into our conversation, with Mrs. Glick peppering me with questions about Amish wedding traditions. She asked how we managed to handle such a massive onslaught of guests, and I explained that the mother of the bride would usually make up a list of all the help the family would need, and then she would recruit friends and relatives to work through that list by butchering the chickens, cooking, setting up, ushering, serving, cleaning, attending the horses, and more.

"My, my," Mrs. Glick said. "This is all so fascinating. And I have to say, Ada, you certainly have a knack for relaying information."

"It's her inner teacher," Zed managed to say, just before he took another bite.

I turned toward him. "My what?"

"Inner," he began with his mouth full, but then he thought better of it and swallowed before continuing. "Teacher. Inner teacher. It's like you can't turn her off sometimes."

I wasn't quite sure that Zed meant it as a compliment, but Mrs. Glick seemed to think that was the case. "That's exactly right!" she said, placing her frail hand on my forearm, directing my attention back to her. "So tell me, Teacher, how does it work to have all of that cooking going on when the wedding ceremony itself takes place in the same house? It sounds awfully busy."

"Sometimes a kitchen housed in a trailer is rented and delivered to the home of the parents of the bride a week before the wedding," I explained. "It's equipped with stoves and refrigerators that run on propane, and stocked with all the needed pots and pans. Other times an extra kitchen is set up in an outbuilding of the home or in the basement."

"Sounds like a good system," she replied, smiling, "as long as you have enough friends and relatives to pull it off."

"True," I replied.

Taking a bite of salad, I looked around at all of the guests here, my gaze finally landing on James's mother, Mrs. Nolan, who was sitting not too far away. As far as I knew, out of all the people at this event, she was the only blood relative in attendance other than Ella, Zed, and me. I found that astonishing. Our weddings back home were filled one end to the other with siblings, aunts, uncles, cousins, and more. Thinking of that, I felt doubly glad the three of us had been able to be here for Lexie.

I was about to ask Mrs. Glick if Lexie's parents had any siblings still living when I felt a warm hand on my arm. Turning to my left, I realized Ella was kneeling at my side, the expression on her face one of concern—and pity.

"I have to tell you something," she said softly.

Glancing toward the others around me, I asked her if it could wait until later.

"I don't think so," she replied, shaking her head slowly from side to side. "Probably the sooner you know, the better. Don't you think?"

That all depended on what she had to say. I squinted and pursed my lips, not sure how to respond.

"I'm so sorry, Lexie," she persisted. "I sent the message to Ezra, like you said. About the teaching job."

"And?"

Ella took a deep breath and let it out slowly. "And he texted me back. He said...well, here. I'll let you read his response."

"Please, just tell me what he said."

"Okay." She swallowed hard, meeting my eyes. "He said you didn't get the teaching job at Willowcrest. It's not yours after all. The school hired somebody else."

THREE

And just like that, all of my plans, all of my dreams, began evaporating into thin air.

I didn't ask Ella if her boyfriend knew exactly what had happened or why. I simply apologized to Mrs. Glick and asked her to excuse me yet again.

"Of course, dear. Is everything all right?"

"Everything's fine," I lied. Then I got to my feet and began walking away.

Didn't get the job? Levi Stoltz had promised it to me several times, including right before we had left Lancaster County. I'd sat on his front porch, held his five-month-old baby, and heard him say he'd have the confirmation packet ready for me when I returned from Oregon.

"Ada?" Ella said, moving to catch up with me. "Ada, wait!"

Looking around, I realized I had walked halfway to the orchard. I stopped, my feet feeling strangely unsteady beneath me.

"Did you hear what I said?" Ella pressed. "You didn't get the job."

"Yes, I heard you, but I'm afraid you're wrong. There has been some sort of mistake."

"That's what I thought, but Ezra says it's true." Ella reached for my hand. I pulled away, shaking my head. I wanted to take off running through the orchard. If not for all of the people who would see me and think me mad, I would have.

"Who did they give it to instead?" I rasped, closing my eyes. "Is the teacher someone we know?"

She reached for my hand again and this time held it. "He didn't say, but I can find out if you want."

Opening my eyes, I looked back at the table, where Mrs. Glick and Zed were both watching us with concern.

"Look at it this way, Ada," Ella continued. "At least now you'll be free to go to Europe with Alice. Whatever that's all about, it has to be more exciting than being in charge of some dumb classroom full of kids back in Pennsylvania."

I sucked in a breath, aware that others were starting to look our way now as well. Whatever was going on with Alice and Europe was beside the point. I wanted to teach.

But I hadn't been given the job.

Staring vacantly at the crowd, a flash of white off to one side caught my eye. Focusing in, I realized that it was Lexie, who was at her husband's side, still circulating among the guests. She and James had been making the rounds since the meal began, moving from group to group and chatting with everyone in turn. Soon they would probably be cutting the cake, and then it was only a matter of time before they would leave on their honeymoon and this whole big party would be over.

"I'm not going to talk about this right now," I said to Ella, my heart filling with sudden resolve. "We're here for Lexie. Everything else can wait."

With that, I returned to the party. Putting on my best smile, I approached my sister and asked if she and James had been able to eat yet. She said no, so I offered to put a plate together of finger foods for them so they could easily eat as they continued chatting.

"Good idea," James said, grinning at me, though Lexie said she wasn't hungry just yet.

Grabbing a plate, I went down the buffet line and loaded it with everything that looked as though it could be eaten without utensils. As I did I tried to act as if my entire future wasn't crumbling before my eyes.

How could this possibly be true?

Maybe it wasn't, I decided as I squeezed small dill pickles onto the plate between some little sausages and a buttered roll. Continuing down the buffet, I thought about the possibility that Ezra's text had merely been based on a rumor. I knew how these things went back home. Someone would express an opinion or an idea, and the person they had said it to would pass that along to someone else, and as it continued to move on down the line, that opinion or idea would slowly transform into fact. That's probably all that had happened here, a rumor that started going around, solidified, and then ended up making it all the way out to Oregon. Just a rumor.

Not even looking in Ella's direction, I carried the plate to James and stood chatting with him and Lexie for a while as he ate. They both seemed so incredibly happy, and their joy was infectious. By the time they were ready to move on to the dessert table, I had nearly forgotten about Ezra's message and the teaching job entirely.

As James and Lexie cut the cake, Zed filmed them on Ella's phone, adding commentary all the while. After just one bite, James began to praise the cake effusively, causing Ella to beam from ear to ear. Together, she and I served the guests, with a little help from Zed.

All too soon it was time for my sister and her new husband to leave on their honeymoon. As Lexie hugged me goodbye, she made me promise to stay in touch faithfully once I got back home. "And give my regards to Will Gundy," she added, lifting her eyebrows and poking me on the shoulder.

"If I happen to see him, I certainly will," I replied, blushing in spite of myself.

"Mm-hmm," she teased, eyes sparkling.

"I told you that he's courting someone else."

"Perhaps, but just remember, Ada," she replied sagely, holding up her index finger, "it's not over till the fat lady sings." I had no idea what she meant, but the way she said it reminded me so much of our grandmother spouting one of her proverbs that I couldn't help but laugh.

"You sound just like *Mammi*. I suppose it's true what they say, that the apple will not roll far away from its tree."

That made Lexie laugh as well, though I wasn't quite sure why.

"The saying is about family," I started to explain, but she just nodded and smiled, saying she knew what it meant. Flushing with heat, I realized that my inner teacher really did come out a little too easily, even when she wasn't needed at all.

"Speaking of family," Lexie added, lowering her voice, "have you thought any more about going to visit Giselle?"

I studied my sister's face, startled by the question. Giselle was our birth mother, and though we had communicated with her via email this past spring, neither Lexie nor I had met her in person. The problem wasn't just that Giselle seemed reluctant about connecting with the two daughters she'd given up for adoption all those years ago. The situation was made infinitely more complicated by the fact that she lived very far away—across an ocean, in fact—in Switzerland.

Which was in Europe.

At the very thought, it was as if a light had suddenly turned on inside my head. *Is this what You are up to, God? Is this why You have closed one door, so as to open another?*

"I'm not sure," I finally managed to utter to Lexie. "There may be a slight possibility..." My voice trailing off, I didn't elaborate. This wasn't the time or place for this conversation.

"Well, keep me posted, okay? And if you have the chance to go, promise me you'll take it."

Eyes welling with sudden tears, I couldn't reply but instead simply gave her a nod and another hug. She squeezed me back, hard. We both knew that, eventually, a trip to Switzerland to see Giselle would be in order by at least one of us, her two daughters. The thing was, Lexie was much freer to go than I, but she didn't want to. I wanted to, but I was far less free to go. Ordinarily, *Mamm* would never even consider allowing me to take a trip to Europe, nor was there any way I could afford it even if she did. But now that something was afoot with Alice, something about Europe, who could say for sure? At this point all I could do was keep it in prayer, trusting that God knew the deepest desires of my heart and would work out everything in accordance with His plan.

The happy couple climbed into James's old car and drove off as we all waved goodbye. Lexie had told me that many *Englisch* couples honeymooned in places like Hawaii or Mexico or the Caribbean, but that with James still in school they had neither the time nor the money for anything so elaborate. Instead, they were heading to the San Juan Islands, near Seattle, where they would stay for a week before returning home to Portland.

Eventually, this farm her father had left Lexie would become their home. But that wouldn't happen for a while, not until James was finished with school and they both managed to find jobs close by. I thought that was a wonderful plan. The old house needed a lot of work, but it had enormous potential. And James was a resourceful, industrious man who, with Lexie's help, could turn this place into something very nice indeed.

"Do the Amish take honeymoons?" Mrs. Glick asked, interrupting my thoughts. The woman next to her seemed interested as well.

I explained that we had no such thing as a honeymoon, although some couples might take a wedding trip later on. Generally, a newly married couple would spend their wedding night at the home of the bride's parents. The next morning they would rise before dawn along with everyone else to continue their share of the cleanup from the previous days' festivities.

"But don't they want privacy?" the other woman asked. "Wouldn't they rather be alone?"

I shrugged, never having thought of it that way before. "I think being with the family is more important," I said finally. "This is how we learn to be good husbands and wives, by watching our parents and spending time with them once we are married as well."

I went on to explain that a newly married couple would likely live with one side of the family or the other for a while, sometimes for months, after the wedding. During that time they would visit relatives each weekend, receiving their wedding gifts visit by visit, until eventually they were ready to set up housekeeping on their own.

"Fascinating," Mrs. Glick said, using her favorite refrain for the day.

Once the crowd had disbursed, Ella and I joined up with the remaining women to clean the yard, put away food, and wash the dishes. Zed helped the men fold up the tables and chairs and load them onto the beds of several waiting pickup trucks. As we worked, Ella kept asking if I was "going to be okay" or if I needed "to talk about it," but I said no and then avoided the subject entirely, feeling far too confused and vulnerable to bare my soul to her or anyone.

At dusk I finally managed to slip off to the orchard. I walked down one of the wide paths between the trees, forcing myself to breathe. I'd seen

Lexie out here just this morning, standing statue still, her head turned up to the canopy of leaves. I was sure she was missing her dad and mom, and my heart had ached for her. It was at times like that I felt ashamed of coveting her education and opportunities. Having a *mamm* and *daed* alive and well, as I did, was worth any cost, any sacrifice. Perhaps I would remind myself of that the next time my yearnings for something more began to rise up and choke the very life from my soul.

A late afternoon breeze wafted through the branches, stirring the leaves and cooling the earlier heat from the day. The orchard was such a peaceful place, very quiet and soothing. Hazelnuts didn't grow in Pennsylvania, at least not that I knew of, and as I walked along I tried to think of how I might describe this place to everyone back home. The nuts themselves grew in pairs, bigger than acorns but still small. The trees were odd but strangely appealing, with a gray and gnarly bark and scraggly, ancient-looking branches.

After a while, as I walked, I thought I could hear the sound of a voice, a male voice. Stopping to peer through the rows of trees, I finally spotted Zed up ahead and to the left, babbling out loud even though he was alone. I realized that he was filming, focusing up close on a hazelnut tree trunk while narrating in a nonstop commentary. Not wanting him to see me, I turned around and went back the way I had come.

Retracing my steps, I thought how surprising it was that Ella had let Zed get hold of her phone again. That cell was her lifeline to Ezra, after all. More than likely, Zed had asked to borrow it for just a moment and then slipped away into the orchard where she couldn't find him to retrieve it.

As I neared the house I found myself wondering if Ella and Ezra would end up marrying in the end. They were certainly crazy about each other, and I thought their personalities made a nice fit. Unfortunately, such a union would be tremendously problematic for religious reasons, given that Ezra was Amish and Ella was Mennonite. Because of that he would have to make a choice: marry her or join the Amish church. He would not be allowed to do both. Surely she understood that.

Then again, maybe she was planning to join the Amish church with him. That was one option if they really did want to marry, though I couldn't imagine Ella trying to become Amish and living our lifestyle. She was Mennonite, yes, which meant she knew how to live Plainly in some aspects. But she was also used to cars and computers and an education past the eighth grade. It didn't seem likely she would be happy to give all of that up—at least not over the long term.

I reached the house and went inside, feeling much better for having taken a walk. I found Ella in the bedroom busily packing up her things, and I was relieved when she didn't ask me where I'd been or bring up the teaching job. Instead, she just started talking about Lexie's wedding and how beautiful it had been. I agreed, and soon she and I were rehashing the day's events, from the clothes to the conversations to the look in James's eyes whenever he gazed at his beloved.

I decided to pack up as well, and we continued talking as we both folded clothes and sorted belongings for the long train ride home that would begin tomorrow afternoon. After a while she started waxing romantically about her own future nuptials and what they would be like. From the way she talked, it didn't sound as if an Amish wedding was what she had in mind, not at all.

"Do you plan on marrying Ezra?" I asked casually, seizing the opportunity to bring up the question as I folded a pair of stockings and tucked them into my bag. Back home such an inquiry might be considered offensive and inappropriate, but I'd asked it anyway, feeling justified by my concerns for my cousin.

"Who knows?" she replied. Her voice was light, but when I glanced her way I could clearly see the longing in her eyes.

We grew quiet after that, each of us lost in our own thoughts. I decided not to say anything about the religious issues at play, but I couldn't help thinking about Ezra's family and how they would feel if their youngest son declined to join the church when the time came. I thought of Will, and it struck me again that if Ella and Ezra did marry, she would then have a direct connection to Will and to the whole Gundy family, something I would never have.

Even as Ella's first cousin—and therefore vaguely related by marriage—I'd still be, in the end, just poor, single, unconnected Ada, the girl who had never gone anywhere other than here, never done anything, and most of all never been loved by the only man who had ever captured her heart.

FOUR

Ella and I spent the next morning giving Lexie's house an extra-good cleaning, and even Zed seemed happy to pitch in. Sophie would be driving us to the train station in Portland, and she showed up at 2:30 p.m., exactly as planned. Our train wouldn't be leaving until almost 5:00, but we were eager to get there, check our bags, and find our departure gate with plenty of time to spare.

The route she took kept us on back roads, winding past farms and alongside woods. As we went Sophie told us this was real "Oregon country," the place where many of the pioneers who followed the Oregon Trail had settled. I hadn't heard much about all of that, so I asked her a lot of questions.

"No offense, Ada," she said finally, "but didn't they teach you any of this in school? It's basic American history."

"We touched on it, I suppose," I said, startled by the bluntness of her words. "But not so much in depth."

"The Amish might be big on their own history as a people," Zed added, speaking to Sophie, "but they are not nearly as concerned with the overall history of the country."

She nodded thoughtfully, without judgment, but at that moment I felt strangely embarrassed.

"Actually," she said, slowing to make a turn, "once you start teaching, I would imagine a class discussion of the Oregon Trail might make an excellent jumping-off point for your students. You could talk about what might compel people—all sorts of people, including the Amish—to leave their homeland and make a new start somewhere else far away."

"True," I replied, heat suddenly rising in my cheeks. In the backseat, Ella and Zed grew conspicuously silent.

"Have you finished putting together all of your lesson plans yet?" Sophie continued, unaware of the hornet's nest she was stirring. "If not, maybe you could find a way to slot it in. Children love to hear stories of the Oregon Trail, and I think knowing that you've actually been to this area and seen the region firsthand would make it doubly fascinating for them."

Even if I had known how to reply, I don't think my voice could have made a sound. Fortunately, Ella cleared her throat and spoke on my behalf.

"Ada won't know for sure whether or not she got the teaching job until we get back home," she said.

"Oh, well. A mere formality, I'm sure," Sophie replied, accelerating as she merged into a line of cars. "Those people would be fools not to hire you. Anyone can see you're a natural. You've been teaching us about Amish life all week."

"Thank you, Sophie," I whispered, and then I looked away, my face turned to the side window, praying I wouldn't start to cry.

I thought of the text message Ezra had sent to Ella yesterday. Had he been reporting rumor or fact? I still didn't know, but in the light of this new day I was starting to fear that it was, indeed, the latter.

I kept reminding myself of my only consolation, that something else was brewing back home, something that had to do with going to Europe, and maybe that would end up being even better than the teaching would have been.

Still, vague possibilities from a situation I didn't even understand paled in comparison to the certainty of a confirmed teaching job. I kept wondering what was wrong with me. Why didn't they want me? Did they think I wasn't good enough to teach their children?

Ella spoke from behind me, interrupting my thoughts. "Ada would be, like, the best teacher *ever*," she said emphatically. "They would be lucky to have her."

I could see Ella's reflection in the car's side mirror. As if sensing my gaze, her eyes suddenly met mine, and I knew *she* was the one who was starting to cry. After wiping away her tears with her fingertips, she gave me an encouraging smile and then followed it by reaching forward, placing a hand on my shoulder, and giving it a squeeze.

Ella could try my patience sometimes, but her heart was good.

Though the rest of the drive was uneventful for us, Sophie received several calls from a patient who seemed to be moving into the first stages of labor. The woman was a month early, and I could see the concern on Sophie's face as she talked to her over her speaker phone. When we reached Portland, I told her she could just drop us off at the station and go, that we could find our way inside and onto the train ourselves. She did not protest.

Traffic near the entrance was heavy, so she pulled to the curb half a block away and we jumped out, quickly unloading our things onto the sidewalk. After a quick hug and round of goodbyes, she was gone.

Gathering up our belongings from the ground, I was feeling somber and very quiet, but Ella and Zed were the opposite, babbling excitedly about the train trip ahead. We walked toward the station, and as we neared the entrance, I noticed a familiar figure coming toward us from the opposite direction: Silas Yoder.

Growing up, Silas was the kind of boy who had never been any good at baseball or volleyball, but when it came to wilderness-type activities—hunting, fishing, hiking, and camping—he had turned out to be a natural. I had known he would be out here on his own Oregon adventure, so prior to the trip my mother had given his parents our travel dates and times, saying that Silas would be welcome to join us for the return home if things worked out that way for him. I hadn't expected to see him at all, but now that he had come, I was glad.

"Silas!" I called out, waving.

He looked up, squinting through his glasses, and then he hurried toward us, the pack on his back bouncing up and down as he came. "Ada! Hi! I'm so glad to run into you folks out here. I was afraid I'd have to search the whole station."

Grinning, we greeted each other, and though Ella and Zed vaguely knew Silas already, I reintroduced them just to be polite.

I had always thought of Silas as the reserved, quiet type, but soon he was acting the very opposite, chatting excitedly about his wilderness adventure and emphasizing his words with broad, sweeping gestures. He kept talking as we all moved into the building, got in line, and checked our bags. As we followed the signs to our gate—Zed and Ella walking ahead and the two of us falling into step behind—Silas's nonstop chatter continued. He quieted briefly as we found the waiting area and sat down, but then Zed asked Silas if he'd seen any bears while he was hiking, and Silas was off again, telling us a long story about how he'd woken up one morning and come out of his tent to find fresh animal tracks not five feet away from where he'd been sleeping.

"I think they were bear prints," he told my wide-eyed cousins, "and there's likely nothing I could have done to protect myself if the animal had decided I'd make a tasty breakfast."

"You're so brave," Ella gushed, but Silas merely shrugged.

"'Courage is merely fear that's said its prayers,'" I told them, echoing a proverb familiar to all four of us.

Nodding solemnly, Silas continued the saga of the animal prints and then went on to explain what he would have done if he'd come face-to-face with a bear. I tuned them out after a while, keeping my eyes on the wall clock and the sign that was to tell us when we should head to the tracks.

That time finally came, so we all stood and gathered our belongings and fell in step with the crowd filing toward the door. Our little group of four was separated in the confusion, but we managed to find each other again once we reached the boarding area outside. There, I expected Silas's chatter to resume, but instead he surprised me by taking my elbow and apologizing for his verbosity, his cheeks blushing a vivid pink.

"It's just that I've been alone for so long, up on Mount Hood," he explained. "Except for a few polite exchanges with other hikers, I've barely spoken to another living soul for more than a week."

Poor thing, he really did seem embarrassed. "Then it makes perfect sense," I replied reassuringly. "You have lots of words stored up that just needed to come out somewhere, *ya?*"

We both chuckled. It struck me that I was relieved to have someone along for the ride home who was closer to my own age. On the trip out

I'd had the company of our older chaperones, of course, but they had kept to themselves for most of the trip, barely interacting with us at all. As for Ella and Zed, though they were quite mature for their ages—and I did love them dearly—there was still a big difference between thirteen, sixteen, and twenty-four. Silas seemed older than his twenty-two years, probably because his many travels made him so worldly-wise.

I didn't explain any of this to him. I simply told him that I was glad he'd been able to wrap up his trip in time so he could join us for the ride home.

"We were hoping you'd make it, but we didn't think you would," I added.

"Me either, but I finished early. The trail was in good shape, so that last leg didn't take nearly as long as I'd thought it would."

I was about to reply when I heard someone gasp. Startled, I looked up to see an older, well-dressed woman standing nearby, gaping in our direction. Glancing around, I realized a lot of people were watching us, whispering to each other behind their hands, some also openly staring. Though this had happened a lot on our trip out, there hadn't been as much of it for the past week. In Lexie's small town, people had been polite enough not to be so obvious, not to mention that practically everyone knew who we were anyway and why we were there. Now that we were back in a more populated area, among strangers, their attention had caught me by surprise, even though I knew it shouldn't have.

"Welcome back to the zoo, fellow animals," Silas muttered under his breath. I nodded, and the four of us exchanged knowing glances.

As we stood there stoically waiting for the train, a man sidled over and asked if we were Russian Orthodox. Everyone else within hearing distance seemed to perk up their ears so they could hear our answer as well.

"No," Silas replied evenly. "She and I are Amish and they are Mennonite."

The man nodded politely and stepped away, but to my surprise, the woman who had gasped earlier now snickered rudely behind one hand.

I glanced at Silas, who was working his jaw but remained silent. None of us said much after that, not until the train arrived and we had climbed aboard and found four seats together. After putting our things in the overhead racks, Ella and I sat side by side with the boys directly across from us and facing our way. Once we were all settled, we relaxed a bit, putting the incident behind us.

The train pulled out of the station and quickly gathered speed, the city of Portland flying past. Soon we were rumbling alongside the incredible Columbia River Gorge, Silas acting as our own personal tour guide as he pointed out Mt. Hood and Beacon Rock and told us all sorts of interesting facts about the region.

Though he was obviously more familiar with the geography of the area than the three of us were, we all knew what to expect on the trip home, which would be a reverse of the trip out. After crossing Washington and a little ribbon of Idaho, we'd reach West Glacier, Montana, by morning, where Sam and Lizzie would be joining us. After that, we would continue on through the rest of Montana, North Dakota, Minnesota, Wisconsin, and Illinois, finally getting to Chicago by tomorrow afternoon. There we would change to a different train and spend our second night passing through Indiana and Ohio, reaching Pittsburgh by the next morning. Then we would change trains one last time for the final six-hour leg across Pennsylvania, all the way to our final destination of Lancaster. We would arrive there in the early afternoon, three days from now.

If our ride home was anything like the trip out, then what remained of our voyage would be by turns fun, irritating, fascinating, boring, and exhausting. Along the way we would relax in our big, comfy seats in the passenger car, spend hours playing board games in the lounge, eat as inexpensively as possible in the dining car, and try to sleep through the nights back at our seats, which never seemed nearly as comfortable once bedtime rolled around. Still, it was worth all of the trouble, especially when the sun would come up to reveal the vistas outside of rolling plains, city skylines, and endless trees. I wanted to savor every minute of what was left of our trip, but something about moving eastward, toward home, felt completely different than had moving westward, toward Oregon. In a sense, if the ride out had been like one long, extended intake of breath, the return home was its exhale.

I thought about all of this as Ella, Zed, and Silas continued to babble almost nonstop. They seemed so happy, but I continued to grow more melancholy. I was eager to get back, yes, but I was also sorry our trip was ending. Mostly I was afraid to face whatever news awaited me in Pennsylvania, terrified that once I got there I would learn the horrible truth: I wasn't wanted, wasn't needed, and wasn't going to be of any use to the school after all.

At one point Zed asked Ella for her phone so he could show Silas the film he'd made, explaining he'd titled it "Lexie and James Get Hitched."

Silas laughed, taking the phone in his hand and holding it close to his face so that he could watch the tiny screen. As the movie played, he seemed to enjoy it, laughing in all the right places. Zed's face beamed with every reaction that Silas gave.

I had never really considered Silas Yoder to be attractive—had never thought to look at him that way at all—but seeing him now, so relaxed and engaged, his ruddy cheeks sporting such a healthy, outdoorsy glow, there was something appealing about him in a brotherly sort of way. He hadn't joined the church yet either, but from what I'd heard he planned to soon. I couldn't imagine he'd stay single long after that. His family was wealthy, with enough land still available for parceling out into a second farm, a rarity in our area these days. The rumor among the youth was that once Silas married he would be getting not just the land but a house to go on it as well, which made him a vital marriage prospect indeed.

Rumor also had it that he wanted to court Leah Fisher, though I didn't imagine he'd make much progress there. Leah had obviously set her sights on Will Gundy, and we all knew Leah Fisher got what she wanted. If Silas pursued her, he would end up in the same boat as I, rejected and alone. Too bad he and I had no interest in each other, at least not in that way. We might have made a good life together—one that could even include travel. But I knew without question that such a union would not include love, and if that were the case, what would be the point? Some of my friends wanted marriage at any cost, but as far as I was concerned, I'd rather grow old all alone, a spinster to my death, than live out life with a man I did not love and who did not love me.

Feeling weary to the bone, I leaned my head against the seat and closed my eyes, glad when it sounded as though the little wedding movie had finally ended and Ella was taking back her phone. Soon my seatmates began to quiet down, leaving me with only the rhythmic rattle of the rails to punctuate my thoughts.

More than anything I wanted a husband, some children, and a home of my own, but I couldn't imagine anyone other than Will Gundy as the man in that scenario. If that really was not to be, then I would have to learn to fill my life in other ways, with teaching, with serving the community, with caring for my parents as they grew older. Surely God in His wisdom would eventually still the yearnings of my heart and help me find some sort of peace in such a life. Teaching would be the best, first step toward finding that kind of happiness.

Unless even my dream of teaching was not to be. Rumor or truth? If only I could know for sure. When I got home, I would visit Levi Stoltz immediately and find out exactly what was going on and why I had not been given the job he had promised me, if indeed I had not. I was eager to have that conversation and get this whole thing straightened out once and for all. But that couldn't happen for another two and a half days, so I decided that between now and then all I could really do was to plan out exactly what I would say, enjoy the trip while it lasted, and spend much time on the matter in prayer.

Across from me Silas was busily texting away on his cell phone. Zed and Ella were resting, their heads lying back against their seats. Zed was fast asleep, judging by his snores, though Ella was not. She, too, was texting with someone, though at a much slower pace than Silas, stirring every few minutes to read her screen and type something in response before again closing her eyes. At one point, she held the phone in her lap with its screen facing toward me, and though I knew I shouldn't, I stole a peek before it went dark. No surprises there. She was communicating with Ezra, her last text declaring that she was "literally counting the hours. LITER-ALLY!!!" until she would see him again.

Turning my attention back to Silas, I watched him type for a moment, his dirt-stained fingers clumsy on the tiny keys. Eventually he glanced up at me, as if sensing my gaze.

"Someone special?" I teased, gesturing toward the phone.

His face broke into a grin. "How did you know?"

"Your eyes are twinkling."

He laughed, his cheeks flushing a bright pink. "*Ya*, I suppose so. It's Leah. Leah Fisher."

I gave him a nod and a smile, though I hoped the pity I felt didn't show on my face. Didn't he know Leah wasn't interested in him that way? Didn't he realize her plan was to become the wife of Will Gundy, the handsome widower with the three adorable, motherless children—and that when it came to what Leah wanted, no other man stood a chance?

Before either of us spoke again, his phone dinged, and when he looked down at the screen, the grin on his face widened. He didn't bother to share what he read, and suddenly I was feeling quite left out.

"So what's the news from home?" I asked, wondering if I might be able to interest anyone in taking a walk to the club car soon for a game of Rook or Uno. "Anything earth-shattering take place while we were all away?"

After he finished returning her text, Silas shifted his attention back to me.

"Not sure about anyone else," he said, "but Leah has big news."

"Oh?" I asked, something shifting inside my chest. Surely that news wasn't about her and Will. Couldn't be. If it was, Silas wouldn't be sitting here acting so relaxed and happy. "What is it?"

Beside me, Ella got another text. She raised her head and opened her eyes to read it, and then a small moan suddenly escaped from her lips.

"Well?" I pressed Silas, ignoring Ella and her teenage dramatics beside me. "What's Leah's big news?"

"Silas, don't—" Ella began, but he was already speaking again, saying Leah had just gotten a job.

"There was an opening for a new teacher," he added, glancing at Ella and then back at me.

I nodded, swallowing hard. "And?"

"And she got it."

"Got it?" I managed to squeak out.

"Yes, the job. She got the job. It's official. Leah Fisher is the new teacher at Willowcrest School."

FIVE

Ella gave me a sympathetic look as I excused myself and headed toward the restroom, my heart racing. If Silas had said anyone besides Leah Fisher had been given the job, I wouldn't have believed it. But I had to be honest, at least with myself. Now I was worried. There was no doubt in my mind that if Leah had wanted this job, it was hers.

As the train rumbled along, I braced myself against the counter in the tiny bathroom and called the phone in the barn at *Mamm* and *Daed's*, leaving a message that everything was fine and I was on my way home, but I had a question for them and could they please call me back as soon as possible.

Ordinarily, of course, they might not even check for messages for several days, but I had a feeling they were keeping a closer eye on the machine while I was gone. I was hoping to hear back from them by nightfall. In the meantime, the only choice I had was to ignore Ella's dramatic version of what she thought was compassion and distract everyone from the subject of Leah entirely with some board games in the club car.

That and dinner got us through the rest of the evening, but by the time we were settling back into our seats for the long night, I was frustrated that my parents still hadn't called. Somehow I managed to fall asleep anyway, and in my dreams the steady *click-clack* of the rails became the clomping of cows' hooves against long, wooden walkways that had no end.

After a restless night of tossing and turning and trying to get as horizontal as possible in the angled seat, I was finally awakened in the early dawn by an odd sensation against my hip. As I struggled toward consciousness, I realized that what I was feeling was my phone, vibrating silently in my pocket. Pulling it out, I managed to rise and make my way toward the end of the car as I answered in a hushed whisper. Fortunately, the bathroom was empty, so I slipped inside where I could have a conversation without waking up my fellow passengers.

"What time is it?" I asked softly, closing the door and leaning against the narrow counter, my stocking feet cold on the metal floor.

"Almost eight thirty," my mother said, which meant it was five thirty here, unless we had already crossed into Mountain time. There was no window in the bathroom, but I could tell from the soft gray glow that had lit my way in here that the sun was just coming up outside.

I removed my *kapp* and ran a hand over my hair, trying to smooth it into place as best I could. It was no use. I would have to take it all the way down and start over.

My mother was anxious to hear how I was doing, so I assured her everything was fine. Once I felt awake enough to converse coherently, I came right to the point. "I heard Leah Fisher got the teaching job. Is it true?"

"Talk to your father about that," she said, and then after a moment my *daed* came on the line.

I repeated the question, pulling bobby pins from my hair as I did, soft blond waves falling loose against my shoulders.

"I'm very sorry, Ada, but it is true." His voice sounded so timid and far away, and for a moment I felt bad for him, that he had to be the one to confirm this rumor for me. "Bishop Fisher told us just last night."

"But Levi Stoltz promised me the job!"

"It wasn't his to promise." *Daed* explained Levi was new to being the president of the board and hadn't realized the others might end up outvoting him.

"But why?" I demanded, my voice sounding bitter. "Just because Leah's the bishop's daughter?"

"Now, now, Ada, don't cast aspersions. There were legitimate reasons for the board's decision."

"Such as?"

"Concerns about your health, for one thing."

"My health is fine."

"And some felt Leah was…better suited for the position."

"She's *not*," I answered. For years everyone had always said how good I was with children. I was a born teacher. Leah, on the other hand, was far too focused on herself and her looks—not to mention whatever man she happened to have in her sights.

We both knew it was true, but my father chose not to respond to my statement. He'd never said a negative thing about a soul in his entire life. I shouldn't expect him to start now.

"Another job could come up," he said instead, and I knew that was true. With so many children and schools in Lancaster County, some years there were more jobs than teachers. But at this point it was likely too late to secure another position for this fall. If only Levi had been honest with me from the start.

"Ada." It was *Mamm* again. "How have you been feeling? Have you gotten enough rest? Been careful not to overdo?"

"Yes, Mother, I've been careful. I'm perfectly fine."

If there was one thing that drove me almost to insanity, it was *Mamm*'s hovering. I'd put up with it my entire life, but suddenly I felt as though I couldn't tolerate it a moment longer.

"You're sure?"

"Yes," I said, sighing. "I'm sure."

My condition, hereditary spherocytosis, had caused me to suffer for years, off and on, with haemolytic anemia. Occasional blood transfusions had provided the only relief—until Lexie showed up this past spring, that is. Lexie was a nurse, and after learning of my condition, she had suggested I start taking certain supplements, primarily folic acid, which had been known to have a profound impact on my condition. Sure enough, since the day I started taking them I hadn't had to have a single transfusion. In fact, I felt better than I had in years. Other than following several important precautionary measures in the future, such as getting an annual flu shot, I didn't even see my health as an issue anymore, thanks to my sister, who I hadn't even known existed until she showed up and changed my world, inside and out.

"Well, we're looking forward to you being home," *Mamm* said quietly. "You've been gone so long."

Cradling the phone to my ear with my shoulder, I reached up and used both hands to pin my hair back in place.

"I've really enjoyed traveling," I answered.

"Oh."

"A lot," I added, feeling a little guilty for the emphatic tone of my voice.

After a long pause, *Mamm* said simply that *Daed* would meet me at the station in Lancaster tomorrow afternoon. It was obvious she was ready to get off the phone. I was too.

"Please tell him thank you," I said, heat suddenly rising in my cheeks. I wanted to add that I appreciated it, I really did. But after having been snippy with her I knew that such words would sound disingenuous. "I'll see you soon, *Mamm*."

"*Ya*. See you tomorrow."

After finishing with my hair as best I could and pinning on my *kapp*, I made my way back to my seat, relieved to see that Ella, Zed, and Silas were still asleep. As quietly as possible, I dug out my carry-on bag and returned to the bathroom to brush my teeth, try again with my hair using a brush this time, and clean myself up for the day.

After I was finished, I looked and felt much better. Returning again to my seat, I put away my bag and tried to get comfortable, knowing I was too wired up for any more rest. I wanted to watch the misty landscape roll past as the sun continued to rise, but my seat was on the aisle, and Ella had closed our curtain.

Shifting, I accidentally kicked Silas's leg. He half opened his eyes, looked at me, and then let the heavy lids lower again before I even had a chance to whisper an apology. I remained perfectly still for a long moment after that, willing him back to a deep sleep, wanting suddenly more than anything else to be alone.

I needed to think.

After checking my pockets to make sure I had my wallet, I made a bold move by slipping on my shoes, quietly standing up, and heading toward the dining car. I couldn't remember if the restaurant would be open yet, but if it was, I intended to have breakfast there, by myself, despite the stares I would get from the other passengers or the fact that my traveling companions might become worried if they woke to find that I was gone. I also wasn't going to think twice about the expense. On the trip out we had brought along several insulated bags full of sandwiches and snacks, and thus had managed to avoid the expensive onboard meals entirely. But the dining car had been so lovely, so inviting, that I had been strangely tempted to splurge. Now I was going to do that very thing. This breakfast would likely cost a fortune, but I didn't care. I had the cash, and for the most part I'd been frugal on the whole trip.

When I reached the dining car, I saw that the tables were all empty save for one, and I was afraid they were still closed. But then a man in a crisp uniform appeared, gave me a nod and a smile, and asked if I would be dining alone. I told him yes a little too emphatically, but he didn't seem to notice. Instead he simply grabbed a single menu from the shelf and led me to a nearby table. I took the chair closest to the window and sat, feeling oddly invigorated by this small act of independence. I accepted the elegant leather menu he handed to me before he walked away to greet another incoming guest. As I studied the choices, a second man came and introduced himself as my waiter. After pouring ice water into my goblet, he asked if I would be having coffee or juice.

"Yes, please."

"Which?"

"Which what?"

He smiled, but there was something patronizing in his expression.

"Which would you like," he said more slowly, "coffee or juice?"

I met his eyes and replied, "I want both, thank you."

He cleared his throat, obviously realizing that I was neither stupid nor obtuse, despite my strange clothing.

"Very good, ma'am," he said, and then he disappeared again into the back.

Ma'am. I liked being addressed that way. Though my mother would have found it rather silly, I thought it was polite, not to mention it made me feel more like an adult.

More *like* an adult? I *was* an adult. Contrary to the way my parents treated me or the school board thought of me, I was an intelligent, capable, fully grown adult. And yet...

And yet, at twenty-four years old, the most rebellious, independent thing I could think of to do was eat by myself in a fancy restaurant? How pitiful this moment would seem to my friends back home. Some of them were already married, for goodness' sake, with babies on the way. And here I was, feeling at best like an awkward little girl trying to play dress-up in her mother's big shoes. What was wrong with me?

Eyes on the menu but my mind far away, I thought about that for a bit. Basically, I decided the problem had to do with my own perception of myself. How could I make the transition from child to adult, not just on the outside but on the inside? I knew my number, the count of years since I'd been born, but other than my age, what was going to tell me when I was finally a real grown-up? Did that happen at marriage? At childbirth? If so, and if I never experienced either, would I go through life feeling always like this, like some sort of overgrown child stamping her foot and trying futilely to declare her independence? Maybe that was one reason I'd wanted the teaching job so badly, because I knew it would help confirm that I was a mature, responsible adult.

My thoughts were interrupted by the waiter, who brought my beverages and told me about the chef's morning special. I realized that more people had been coming in, and that almost half of the tables were now occupied. A different waiter moved past carrying two small bowls of fruit, which he delivered to a couple who had been seated directly behind me.

Though I had no idea yet what I wanted to order, I handed back the menu and said the special would be fine. As various conversations slowly grew in volume around me, I ignored them all and instead focused on stirring cream and sugar into my coffee and then sipping it slowly as I looked out the window at the passing landscape. We were in Montana now, I felt sure, and would likely be reaching West Glacier in an hour or so. There, our chaperones would come aboard and join us, one big happy group of weary Amish and Mennonite travelers rattling across this vast country together toward home.

I heard the people behind me say something about a "horse and buggy," and from their hushed tones I realized they were talking about me. As they conversed, the woman's voice grew louder and soon the man was shushing her. She replied that he needn't worry. She said she'd heard me and my whole group talking earlier and we used some other language. "She probably doesn't even speak English," she concluded.

"Well, either way," he whispered in return, "I'm surprised to see them on a train. I didn't think they were allowed to use anything but a horse and buggy, nor go so far from home."

"Sure they can," the woman replied softly, with authority. "Judging by their ages, they are probably all on their ringalingas."

As she went on to explain to the man what a ringalinga was, I couldn't help but roll my eyes. She meant my *rumspringa*, the running around period all Amish kids went through, starting in the mid- to late-teens and lasting for a year or two, sometimes more. *Rumspringa* was a time when we were given extra freedom and privacy, a welcome loosening of the rules as we transitioned into adulthood.

To hear her description of it, however, it sounded more like some sort of parentally sanctioned free-for-all, an easy excuse for wild, drunken, promiscuous behavior, the chief aim of which was for all of the girls to land themselves hearty Amish husbands, most often by "accidentally" getting themselves pregnant.

Trying not to listen, my jaw clenched tighter and tighter as she went on. But then I decided this was a teaching moment I couldn't pass up, and I spun around in my seat and spoke, looking from one to the other as I did.

"Actually," I told them in a calm and pleasant voice, "I do speak English. The word you're looking for is *rumpsringa*, not ringalinga. Despite popular opinion, the point of this practice is to allow those of us who were raised in Amish homes to understand fully the choice we'll be making if we decide to join the Amish church."

Both of them sat there gaping at me, grapefruit-laden forks frozen in midair, halfway to their mouths. I continued, keeping my voice even and low.

"The good Lord has given every human being free will, you see, but if we were ushered straight from a sheltered, Amish childhood into the commitment of full church membership without any real perspective or knowledge of the world, we wouldn't actually be making a free and informed decision at all, now would we?"

The man was still frozen, though the woman had recovered enough to lower her fork and shake her head no.

"That's right," I went on. "*Rumspringa* allows us the opportunity to gain that perspective. It's a time of growing up, of gaining a clearer understanding of what a life lived outside the church would really be like. And though it's true that a few individuals use it as an excuse to be foolish, most kids take it quite seriously and behave themselves in a godly manner throughout. Believe it or not, pregnancy prior to marriage is actually quite rare among the Amish, especially when compared to the rest of the world."

Still no spoken response from either of them, so I couldn't resist adding one more thought.

"Statistically speaking, you know, the majority of us *do* end up making a decision to join the church. Obviously, then, the practice of *rumspringa* does work. I'd say it's a very necessary and useful phase of life. I just wanted to make sure you knew that it has nothing to do with wild parties or illicit behavior or trapping husbands and everything to do with building a solid, obedient, mature church body. I hope that clears up any misconceptions you may have had on the matter."

My lesson finished, I gave them one last moment to reply, and when they didn't I simply turned back around and gulped down some juice. But then my heart began to pound and my cheeks began to burn as I realized what I'd just done. These weren't little children, my teenage cousins, or even elderly Mennonites interested in the Amish way of life. These were *Englischers*. And I'd been rude. I wanted to get up and run out of there, but instead I forced myself to stay, feet crossed under the table, hands shaking only slightly when the waiter brought my food and I reached for my knife and fork.

The couple behind me, however, didn't last nearly as long. Before I'd even finished choking down my first slice of bacon, they were asking for the check and preparing to leave. I thought I could hear the man say something to the waiter about me, and suddenly I was afraid I might have blown the whole trip for everyone. Was I crazy, speaking to a pair of total strangers like that? What would happen if my companions and I were kicked off the train because of my behavior, way out here in the middle of nowhere? So much for being an adult! Right now I felt more like a toddler who had just thrown a big tantrum than a teacher educating others.

Once the couple was gone, I found that my appetite had left as well. Putting down my fork, I motioned to the waiter and told him I was ready to pay.

"No need, ma'am. It's been covered."

"Excuse me?"

He pointed toward the now-empty table behind me.

"The gentleman who was sitting there with his wife said to tell you that your breakfast is on him." Looking at me quizzically, he added, "Oh, and also that they were sorry for having been rude."

After a long moment, a smile began to spread across my face. I told the waiter never mind, that my appetite had suddenly returned after all and I wouldn't be leaving just yet. He offered to refresh my coffee and then wished me "bon appétit" before walking away.

I scooped up a big bite of eggs and popped it into my mouth. Imagine that! Here I had confronted an *Englisch* couple and basically told them off, yet *they* ended up apologizing to *me* for having been rude—and paid for my meal besides. Shaking my head, I honestly couldn't decide if my actions had been right or wrong. As a Christian, I was to be *in* the world and not *of* it, after all, and by allowing their conversation to get my hackles up, I had been concerning myself with the world and its silly misconceptions. On the other hand, with so much misinformation about my people floating around, how could it be wrong for me to have corrected such an embarrassing assumption, as long as I had done it respectfully?

I still wasn't sure how I felt about what I'd done, but either way, my unintended tirade had earned me a free meal and an apology. Though I doubted I'd ever tell the full story of what had just happened to a living soul, I couldn't wait to share the term "ringalinga" with someone. But who? Maybe Silas, who was currently on a ringalinga of his own.

As was I, actually, now that I thought about it.

At that moment I realized something, and it caught me with such force that the smile faded from my face entirely. Of course. How could I have missed it before? No wonder I didn't feel like a real grown-up much of the time. I'd never had the chance to go through *rumspringa* and experience that transition time from child to adult. Now that I was twenty-four, my loved ones were getting impatient for me to go ahead and join the church, to bring an end to my *rumpsringa*.

But how could I bring to an end something that had never really begun?

I sat back in my chair, thinking of my teenage years as I watched rolling fields, tall trees, and white-capped mountains go by. I'd always been too weak and too tired to make it to most of the group sing-alongs, volleyball games, and picnics with my friends. Sometimes I'd wanted to give participating a try, but I always held back, knowing that the danger was too great, that such activity could cause irreparable harm. I knew there was some big secret about my condition, something my parents were aware of but had chosen not to tell me. Knowing that terrified me, sometimes with a paralyzing fear. In my heart I just knew I was sicker than they let on. Whenever I engaged in any sort of physical activity, I expected the worst, that I might drop dead at any moment.

What else could the secret be, unless it was that I would never be able to teach or to marry or have children—a life sentence almost as scary as death itself. Whatever the secret was, it had to be pretty bad for them not to have told me.

Then this spring I found out exactly what they had been keeping from me all these years. Much to my astonishment, the big secret had nothing to do with my medical condition and everything to do with my parentage: I was adopted. *Mamm* was not genetically my mother and *Daed* was not genetically my father. Instead, my birth mother had been *Mamm*'s sister Giselle, the aunt I'd never met. When I was still a newborn, Giselle had given up both me and my older sister, two-year-old Lexie, and fled to Europe. Lexie had been adopted by a Mennonite couple from Oregon, but I'd been adopted by my *mamm* and *daed* and kept right there at home in Lancaster County.

Lexie had been raised knowing she was adopted, but I'd never been told a thing, not until this spring, when she showed up asking questions about the identity of her birth parents. Ultimately, she had received the answers she'd sought, and the secrets of our whole family's past had finally been brought out into the open. Lexie had gone home with a real sense of closure, her lifelong quest to find her birth parents finally satisfied.

I, on the other hand, had been left with this bizarre knowledge about my biological mother and a trillion new questions. At least I'd also been given new insight into my health and a more realistic perspective on the seriousness of my disorder. As soon as I understood that I wasn't going to drop dead at any moment, that I actually could have a chance at a normal life, my health began to improve. The folic acid and other supplements went a long way toward my recovery, yes, but I knew that my mind-set had much to do with it as well. Once I realized that the big secret wasn't about my condition at all, I started forcing myself to do more even when I didn't feel like it. As my body grew stronger, I even began to allow myself to dream. I started thinking of the future.

And those new dreams and hopes were making me feel restless, incredibly restless, for the first time in my life.

My mother had thought this trip would settle that restlessness, but in fact it had served to do the exact opposite. Now that I had seen what I was capable of—that I could get on a train and go across the country, spend a week without the hovering concern of my parents, walk into a dining car, order a meal, and scold two total strangers in a way that ended up gaining me a free breakfast—I wanted to experience even more, not less. I wanted my *rumspringa*.

I had no need for silly teenage games, of course, no flirting or sneaking around or partying. I didn't even want a hidden pair of jeans or a stash of makeup or a driver's license, as many of my friends had. What I wanted was freedom and the opportunity to understand what that meant. I wanted the full knowledge of what was out there, of who I might be should I choose not to follow in my parents' footsteps and commit myself to the Amish faith.

I had a feeling I would eventually make that commitment, but for now my heart swelled with the desire to live as I wanted, go where I wanted, and see what I wanted whether my parents agreed with it or not. Closing my eyes for just a moment, I prayed that God would show me if I was wrong in this, and if I wasn't, that He would bless me with even greater adventures ahead.

"There you are," a voice said suddenly, startling me so much that I dropped my fork. I looked up into the face of a smiling Silas, who slipped into the seat across from me.

"You scared me to death," I scolded. I bent over to pick up the fork and set it at the end of the table.

"Yeah, well, Zed and Ella are about this close to calling the police," he said, holding up a thumb and forefinger about an inch apart. "They are convinced you were so upset about not getting the teaching job that you got off a couple of stations ago and are currently wandering around somewhere out in the middle of Idaho."

I could feel my face flush with heat.

"Well, for goodness' sake text them right now and tell them you've found me."

He chuckled as he pulled out his phone.

"Just don't tell them where we are," I added softly. "I don't need them bursting into here and embarrassing me in front of the whole dining car."

"I hear you," he said as he began going at it with his thumbs.

"Why would they make such a ridiculous assumption anyway?" I asked, dabbing at my mouth with my napkin. He was too busy typing to reply.

No matter, I thought, as I waited for his back-and-forth flurry of communications to end. They had overreacted because of exactly the same things I had been thinking about here. Ada Rupp was not the kind of girl who ever acted on her own accord, who would ever strike out from the group with any measure of independence or self-determination—not even if all that meant was to walk alone to the dining car and order a meal. She was neither child nor adult, but neither was she a young woman on a *rumspringa*. At least not until now.

"Okay, crisis averted," he said finally, setting the phone onto the table. "I told them everything is fine and we'll meet them in the club car by the time we reach West Glacier."

"Thank you, Silas," I said softly, still mortified.

"Which, judging by my phone, will be in about ten minutes."

I nodded, glancing down at my food, which was only half finished. Dirty fork or not, I wouldn't be eating any more. He, on the other hand, was eyeing the leftovers hungrily, so I slid the plate across to him and offered up my spoon.

"Thanks, Ada."

As he ate I thought about telling him of the incident with the *Englisch* couple, but for some reason I decided not to bring it up at all. Instead, I gestured toward his cell and asked him how he would survive without it once he got ready to join the church and would have to give it up.

He shrugged. "Small price to pay, don't you think?"

"Good answer," I said earnestly, suddenly envying him and all of his travels more than I ever had before. When he finally made that leap and joined the church, it was going to be with the full perspective of a *rumspringa* well spent. Were I to make that decision now myself, I certainly couldn't say the same.

"So you'll be joining the church soon, then?" I asked.

He nodded, biting down into a triangle of buttered toast.

"And if Leah won't consent to be your bride?" My question was bold— to be honest, it was downright rude—but this seemed to be a day of speaking my mind.

"Trust me," Silas replied after taking the final swig of my juice and swallowing it all down, "she'll come around eventually. I'm not worried. She's already taken the classes, so I know she's done with her running around time. All I have to do now is take the steps to join as well, and then convince her I'm the perfect fellow for her."

I fell silent after that, wondering how much longer he was going to persist in his delusions. Didn't he know that Leah wanted to be Will Gundy's wife? There was nothing Silas or I or anyone else could do about that. Leah was already bound to marry the one man I cared for the most in this world. Did she really have to take my job from me now as well?

Tomorrow afternoon I would be able to speak to Levi Stoltz in person and find out what had happened. But in the meantime, I still had a country to get across, still had traveling companions to placate, still had more than twenty-four hours left of quiet conversations, endless board games, and magnificent, sprawling vistas outside every window.

Eager to embrace the freedom of each mile that we had left, I placed several dollars on the table for a tip and then rose, falling into step behind Silas as we made our way toward the club car. I'd make the most of every moment. Then once this trip was over and I was safely back at home, things in my life were going to change.

Regardless of the scheming Leah Fisher or the easily-manipulated Levi Stoltz or even my controlling mother, I still had a life to live.

It was time to declare my independence.

SIX

The next day we stepped off the train, bleary-eyed and stiff, into the bright Pennsylvania sunshine. Between the suffocating heat and sweltering humidity I realized I missed Oregon already.

Our little group moved along the platform and into the station, where light from the tall windows reflected off the shiny yellow floor. I squinted, searching the room for *Daed*. Ella spotted him first, or at least she spotted Ezra standing next to him. She squealed and rushed past me, throwing her arms around the tall young man. I glanced at Lizzie and Sam, our chaperones, watching for their reactions. They both shook their heads, just barely, and then continued on toward the baggage claim area.

I greeted my father with a surge of emotion, surprised to find myself blinking back tears at the sight of his kind gray eyes. A quiet man, he was also good and gentle and sweet, someone who had always been there for me and no doubt always would.

"Thanks for coming to get us, *Daed*."

"Of course, Ada. I trust the trip home went well?"

From the bemused expression on his face, I had a feeling that my hair and *kapp* were probably askew. At least that would make them the perfect match for my wrinkled dress. Two and half days with nothing but a tiny bathroom had left us all looking a bit bedraggled.

"Where's my mom?" Zed asked, craning his neck in search of my aunt Marta.

"She planned to come along," my *daed* answered, "but she had a patient in labor."

Zed seemed disappointed, though Ella barely acknowledged her mother's absence. She and Ezra were gazing giddily at each other, their hands clasped firmly together.

Silas's brother showed up just as we'd grabbed the last of our bags. Sam and Lizzie would be riding with them, so we all walked to the parking lot together and then said our goodbyes there.

In the vehicle *Daed* had hired, Zed sat up with the driver, *Daed* and I took the front bench seat, and Ezra and Ella climbed in behind us. As we wound through the busy streets of Lancaster toward Aunt Marta's house outside of Willow Street, Zed turned around in his seat to tell *Daed* all about our trip. Soon Ella joined in from behind, the two of them going on and on about the countryside, Lexie's farm, the little town of Aurora, and Portland. They described Lexie's wedding and how beautiful she was, although they left out the part about Zed making a film of it. They recounted almost every aspect of the train travel, out and back, though I noticed they both omitted any mention of my disappearance yesterday morning or the distress it had caused them. Feeling weary and distracted, I sat there in silence all the way to their house, simply listening to their words and enjoying my *daed*'s reactions.

When we got there, he climbed out and walked to the back of the vehicle to help with the bags, which gave Ella and Ezra a quick moment to steal a kiss.

"Thanks for being at the station," Ella whispered, kissing Ezra again and then reluctantly climbing out of the van. After a beat I followed, giving Zed a hug goodbye and then taking Ella's elbow and nonchalantly pulling her aside.

"I know you are caught up in the moment," I cautioned her softly, "but now that you're home, you and Ezra must be very careful about how you conduct yourselves—both in public and in private. Missing someone can make you do things you absolutely should not be doing." Looking intently into her eyes, I prayed she would hear my words as coming from a wise older friend rather than some parental authority figure.

Instead, she barely seemed to have heard me, so caught up was she with the drama of gazing over my shoulder at her true love, who was still sitting in the backseat of the vehicle gazing back at her. Under Zed's direction, my *daed* and the driver were rooting out one last bag from the bottom of the pile, so I reached up with my hand, gently turning her face toward mine.

"Ella Bayer," I said softly, locking my eyes on hers. "I know you missed him, but your behavior borders on inappropriate. Mind yourself."

It took a moment for my words to sink in, but when they finally did, Ella's reaction wasn't at all what I had expected. She seemed neither embarrassed nor resentful. Instead, her eyes filled with pity and compassion as she whispered, "Oh, Ada, someday maybe you'll fall in love too and then you'll understand."

I stepped back as if struck, her words piercing my heart. If she only knew how much I loved Will Gundy and always had! Oblivious to the emotions threatening to overwhelm me in that moment, Ella simply threw her arms around me and gave me a tight squeeze.

"Thanks for an amazing trip, cousin!" she cried happily. "I'm going to miss the sight of your face every morning."

I was saved from having to reply thanks to Zed, who called out for Ella to help him bring in the bags.

Soon we were back on the road minus our two passengers, the van nearly silent now as we covered the final ten miles to our house. On the way I refused to dwell on my feelings for Will, so I put him out of my mind, forcing myself to focus on the scenery instead. As we rode along, I realized how strange it felt to look at Lancaster County through the eyes of one who had been away. Silas had talked a lot about the perspective he always got from travel, and at that moment I understood exactly what he meant. Almost as if it were all new to me, I could see the incredible beauty of the rolling pastures, the crispness of the stark white homes and barns, the colorful contrast of freshly washed clothes hanging from the lines and flapping in the breeze.

No wonder tourists flocked to Lancaster County. It wasn't mountainous, like Montana, or all lit up, like Chicago, but it had a beauty completely its own. Perhaps the next time I found myself clucking in disapproval at the cars lined up behind my buggy waiting to pass or the tour buses that drove slowly down our lane so their passengers could snap pictures through the windows, I would remind myself that God had blessed me greatly in allowing me to live here year-round, and that the least I could do was to show some grace to those who only wanted to share it for a while.

As we turned into our own driveway, I allowed my eyes to linger on the beauty here as well. The tall, abundant stalks of corn. The black and white cows grazing contentedly in the grass. The line of neat, white fencing that delineated the pastures. The driver pulled to a stop near the house, and my father was swinging open the door just as my mother came rushing out to greet us. As I stepped from the van, she reached out for a hug, and I realized I was seeing her through this traveler's perspective as well. The lines of her aging face. The widening of the part in her hair. The redness of her hardworking hands. Closing my eyes, I moved into her embrace, feeling an odd detachment from the moment even as I hugged her tightly in return.

While *Daed* settled up with the driver and Ezra started carrying my bags to the house, *Mamm* linked an arm in mine and walked me toward the front steps, peppering me with questions all the way. She seemed excited but also nervous, as if she were afraid something had fundamentally changed somehow. Perhaps she was more intuitive than I'd given her credit for.

When we reached the door, I hesitated, looking toward the *daadi haus* out back.

"I should run and speak to *Mammi*," I said, detaching myself.

"She's not home."

"Not home?" *Mammi* never went anywhere anymore, at least not without me or *Mamm* close by her side. For a moment, my mind conjured up the worst images imaginable: tubes, machines, a hospital bed. Then I realized what it must be instead.

"She's over at the Gundys'. Will and Alice came by this morning and picked her up."

Will and Alice. Just as I'd thought. This was about Europe.

Keeping my voice casual, I said, "Really? What for?"

Mamm shrugged, an odd expression on her face. "I have no idea. Something to do with the old family property back in Switzerland. I'm not real clear on the details."

At the word Switzerland, my heart skipped a beat.

Giselle lived in Switzerland.

Did Alice and Will's legal issue over in Europe have something to do with Giselle?

I swallowed hard, knowing that the subject of my birth mother was a touchy one for *Mamm*. I usually accepted her attitude with varying degrees of irritation and compassion, depending on my mood and the situation. At the moment I chose to tread very carefully, lest my words mess up any sort of plans that might have been forming over at the Gundys' even as we spoke.

"I thought *Mammi* sold that property years ago," I said evenly, taking *Mamm*'s arm again and steering us into the house. She fell right into step beside me, pushing open the kitchen door and motioning for me to go through first.

"She did. Well, most of it anyway. Apparently, this has to do with an important historical site that's been discovered on the piece that's left, something related to the early Anabaptists."

My eyebrows lifted. Of all the possibilities I'd been rolling around in my mind, that certainly wasn't one that had occurred to me.

The term "Anabaptist" referred to the Amish and other groups, such as the Mennonites and Hutterites, who believed in adult baptism. Early Anabaptists had been baptized in the state church as infants, so when they chose to be re-baptized as adults, they had become known as "again baptizers," or Anabaptists. Though we all connected deeply to our Anabaptist heritage, I couldn't imagine what that had to do with *Mammi* and Alice going to Europe.

"I don't know much more than that," *Mamm* continued. "I haven't really paid too much attention. But for the past week, she and Alice have been scheming and whispering right and left. It's actually kind of cute. It reminds me of when they were younger."

I understood what she meant. When I was a little girl, *Mammi* and Alice were together often, usually for canning or quilting or some other task easier done with two pairs of hands than one. *Mammi* had no sisters, so in a way her good friend Alice had become that for her. But *Mammi* had a stroke, limiting her mobility, and then just last year Will's wife, Lydia, had died. These days Alice was so busy helping to care for the three children that visits from her here were rare.

"So what do the Gundys have to do with this?" I asked, still keeping my tone nonchalant as I kicked off my shoes under the coat rack.

"Truly, Ada, I have no idea. All they told me was that they wanted *Mammi* to come over to their house to meet some man who was visiting, a historical expert of some kind."

She seemed so nonchalant about it that I decided she surely hadn't got wind of any connected travel plans, either for her or me or anyone else in the family. She wouldn't be acting so calmly if she had. I decided to keep quiet about it for now.

Without asking if I was hungry, my mother pointed toward the kitchen. I hesitated, eager to head upstairs instead. Then I looked toward the table and saw that a late lunch had been all laid out for me there. Unfortunately, eating was the last thing on my mind. At the moment all I wanted was a shower, a fresh set of clothes, and a horse and buggy at the ready. Now that I was back, I had places to go and people to see.

Ezra came clomping down the stairs at that moment, having delivered my bags up to my bedroom. My mother thanked him for his help, chatting warmly as she walked him back outside. As she did I walked over to look down at the meal she'd prepared, wondering how to get out of eating it without hurting her feelings. It wasn't lost on me that she'd made all of my favorites: sliced turkey on homemade bread, sweet pickles, and macaroni salad with fresh broccoli. Then I saw it, there at the center of the plate: a circle of cottage cheese, decorated to look like a person. Just as she'd done when I was a small child, she'd used carrot curls for hair, pineapple segments for ears, raisins for the eyes and nose, and an orange segment for the smile.

I sat, my mind swirling. *Mamm* hadn't made a cottage cheese lady for me in years. Whenever my condition would flare up, leaving me far too weak to eat, sometimes the only way she could coax food into my mouth at all was by being creative. Cottage cheese people. Raisin ants on peanut-buttered celery logs. Animal-shaped pancakes around syrup watering holes.

At the moment I didn't know whether to laugh or cry. A part of me felt a surge of love for this woman who had been so good to me, who had never done anything but care for me and protect me and guide me. Perhaps she'd dredged up this element of my youth simply as a fun way to say "welcome home."

But another part of me suspected a darker motive here. Deep inside, I couldn't help but feel she was also sending me a message, whether she realized it or not. She wanted me to know that despite having been allowed to go across the country and back, I was home, where I would stay from now on, still very much her little girl.

Unable to stop myself, I reached out and moved around the orange slice smile, turning it into a frown.

My mother returned to the kitchen at that moment, her face lighting up expectantly when she saw me sitting there at my place. "Well?"

"You made all my favorites…" I said, gesturing toward the food, unsure of how else to react.

"Including an old friend," she replied, grinning. "Remember how you always used to eat the mouth first, so she couldn't talk, and then you'd eat the ears so she couldn't hear?" Talking about the good old days, she poured me a glass of milk.

"Your father used to tease me that I was making a graven image," she continued, "but we both decided that faces created from food wouldn't exactly trouble the bishop. Good thing, because it got you to eat, which most days was not an easy task at all."

After setting it down in front of me, *Mamm* took a seat to my right and reached for her mending basket, which she'd placed on the floor nearby. She must have planned it all out, how I would sit there eating and she'd sit there mending, and together we could chat and laugh for an hour at least, gently reestablishing the bond that may have been strained because of my trip.

But then she noticed my expression and asked what was wrong. "You're not sick, are you, Ada? Feeling weak? Do you need to go lie down?"

Biting my lip I shook my head, not trusting myself to speak. So many emotions were warring inside of me at that moment that I feared I might run screaming from the room. Instead, I forced myself to put a hand on her arm, thanked her for going to so much trouble, and told her it was just a shame that I had already eaten.

"I had a huge sandwich in the club car at noon," I explained, adding that perhaps we could wrap up the plate and save it for my dinner.

A wave of hurt crossed her features, followed by something like resignation. She nodded, and so I rose, carrying my glass to the fridge and pouring the milk back into the carton. Afraid she might try to rope me into mending with her instead, as I washed my glass at the sink I talked about the tiny bathroom on the train and how I had been counting the minutes until I could get in the shower here at home. Grabbing plastic wrap from the cabinet, I covered the food, the little cottage cheese face staring up at me as I smothered it under the clear film.

"That's probably for the best," *Mamm* said. "After your shower you can lie down for a nice, long nap,"

I didn't reply. Opening the refrigerator door, I set the plate inside and stood there staring at it for a moment. Then, on impulse, I lifted one corner of the plastic to grab the raisin eyes, popped them into my mouth, chewed, and quickly swallowed. Now she couldn't see.

Just like my mother.

SEVEN

A half hour later I was showered, dressed, and in the buggy shed, harnessing Rikki to the carriage. Upon learning of my plans, *Mamm* had tried to stop me, insisting I needed my rest. I had politely but firmly informed her I wasn't tired and I had to talk to Levi Stolz to find out what was going on with the teaching position. After stewing on it for a bit, she must have run out to the barn and found my *daed*, because soon they both appeared in the doorway.

"Your father's going to drive you," *Mamm* announced, marching him inside.

I shook my head, clenching my jaw.

"Thanks, *Daed*, but I'm fine driving myself."

He hesitated, a lone man caught between two stubborn, determined women. Then he nodded, seeming to understand that the issue wasn't debatable as far as I was concerned. Stepping in to help with the straps, he told my mother he felt sure I'd be fine on my own.

Keeping my voice light, I said I would be happy to pick up *Mammi* while I was out. I didn't add that not only would that give me a chance to see Will—something I yearned for despite the pain I knew it would cause me—but a visit from me might also lead those gathered there to let me in on their big secret regarding Europe and this Anabaptist history matter.

"It's too much for you," *Mamm* said. "Your father can do it later."

I looked at *Daed*, wanting his answer, not hers.

"You've already lost two hours of work picking me up at the station," I told him. "The least I can do is help you out by getting *Mammi*."

Finishing with the last strap, he gave Rikki a firm pat on her haunches and stepped back, saying that sounded fine and he would appreciate it.

Moments later my horse and I were off. Rumbling up the drive toward the road, I glanced in the rearview mirror, not surprised to see them watching me go, deep concern clearly etched across both their faces.

The day grew hotter as I drove the buggy down the highway to the Stoltz farm. As much as I had been obsessing over this visit the last few days, I wasn't exactly looking forward to it. Once the rumor about the job had been confirmed, I had known there likely wasn't much I could do to change things. Mostly, I just wanted to know what had gone wrong, and why Levi had told me the job was mine when in reality it wasn't.

The heat and the gentle, rhythmic jolt of the wheels nearly put me to sleep, but I perked up by the time I reached their house. Sharon stood on the porch, holding her diaper-clad baby on her hip. I stopped the buggy.

"Come on in," she said. "I have a fan blowing in the living room. It's a bit cooler in there." Then she turned toward her oldest son and told him to run along and get his *daed*. Levi's blacksmith shop was on the other side of their barn. I couldn't imagine how hot it must be in there.

I followed Sharon into the kitchen, closing the door quickly to keep out the heat. We sat near the fan and chatted uncomfortably about my trip, the whirl of the battery-operated motor competing with our words. A couple of times we simply paused as the fan passed by, our faces turned toward it. It wasn't long until Levi stepped into the living room, mopping his forehead with his handkerchief. He sat in a straight-back chair, probably so he didn't dirty the couch. Sharon stood and handed him the baby, saying she'd get some lemonade.

I started to speak but Levi put up his hand. "I know why you're here, Ada," he said, as the baby grabbed at his fingers and smiled. "And before you say a word, I have to apologize for the way I handled this. It was all wrong. I should never have promised you the job. It was too soon." His hair was matted to his forehead over his kind brown eyes. "I hope you can forgive me."

I nodded. How could I not? "I was hoping it wasn't true," I said. "It is."

Sharon returned, handed each of us a tall cold glass, and then she took the baby and headed back into the kitchen. I appreciated that she didn't give me that long, sympathetic look I'd already received from so many others.

Levi drained his lemonade in one continuous gulp and then looked at me as I sipped mine. It was delicious—the perfect mix of sour and sweet.

Finally he said, "The other members were concerned about your health."

"My health is fine. It has been for months. As I told you before, I've never felt better. Who brought up my health?"

He blushed again. "A few of the members said someone mentioned it, out of concern."

"Leah?" I whispered.

"I'm not sure."

My face grew warmer. "Did it make any difference that she is the bishop's daughter?"

"Of course not. It did matter that she's a few years younger than you. The thinking is that you may be a little old to start teaching now."

"So age and maturity are considered disadvantages?" I leaned back against the couch.

He blushed again. "It helps if a teacher stays on a few years. Members thought that at twenty-four you might be marrying soon."

Now it was my turn to blush. In our schools girls usually stopped teaching once they got married, yes. But everyone on that board knew I'd never even been courted. "From what I hear, that's more of a concern for Leah than for me." My face grew even warmer and instantly I regretted my words. There was no reason for me to be snide.

Levi dropped his eyes and stared at the floor.

I took a deep breath. "Anyway. Thank you for your time and the lemonade."

He nodded and we both stood. I followed him into the kitchen with my glass. Sharon sat at the table, smiling at the baby and bouncing him on her knee. He grinned back at her. Levi stood behind Sharon and bent down over her shoulder toward the baby, causing him to chortle in delight.

"If I hear of another school that's hiring, I'll let you know," Levi said, stroking the little boy's cheek and then standing up straight again. I knew he had no idea of how much this job had meant to me.

Tears stung my eyes as I returned to my buggy, unhitched Rikki from the post, and started out for the road again.

Images of the usurper filled my mind as I clip-clopped slowly along the highway. Pretty and energetic and fun, Leah had always been a real go-getter. Three years younger than I, she wasn't nearly as interested in classes or reading or books as I had been. In fact, she'd never seemed to have much interest in learning at all. To my core I knew I had far more natural talent for teaching than she ever would.

On the other hand, she had always run circles around me when it came to playing volleyball or baseball or any of the other activities that usually sent me to the sidelines. And I had to admit she'd been a born leader, full of enthusiasm and bright ideas.

I had to see Leah Fisher, face-to-face, before going on to the Gundys'. Her parents' farm was only a few miles out of the way. Clicking my tongue and tugging on the reins, I steered Rikki in that direction now, turning from the busy highway onto an emptier side road.

When I finally arrived at the Fishers' house, I knocked and knocked on the door, but no one answered. I walked through the barnyard and peered into the stables. Their horses were there, but not a soul was in sight. That was probably for the best, I decided as I climbed back into the carriage. Had Leah been home, I might have said something I would later regret.

I was just looping the carriage around when two boys dashed across the drive in front of me.

"Do you know where the Fishers are?" I called out, and they stopped running to look up at me. I recognized them both, neighbors from another farm just up the road.

"At a family reunion. In Shippensburg," the taller one answered.

I thanked them for their information, realizing the Fishers must have hired a driver, which explained why the horses were here. Clearly, my speaking to Leah so soon wasn't meant to be.

The boys continued on toward the barn, so before driving off, I called out to them again. "Should you two be running around like this on the Fishers' property when they are not even home?" I asked, unable to keep my voice from taking on a very teacherlike tone.

"We're doing their chores for the day," one replied earnestly, holding out both hands, palms up.

Smiling, I gave them a wave as I urged Rikki forward.

With just a little zigzagging, I could take back roads all the way to the Gundys' place, avoiding the busy highway entirely. Riding along in the warm afternoon sunshine, I forced myself to breathe deeply, open my eyes, and take in the beauty of God's world surrounding me. I knew He had a plan for my life; I'd just always thought that plan included teaching. Now that that dream had been snatched from my grasp, I felt as if He had forgotten me. Sure, I was unremarkable to others, but I'd always felt special to Him. But now I wasn't so sure. Had God overlooked me? Was I invisible to Him too?

I chided myself. I was disappointed I didn't get the job, but how many times had *Mammi* told me that failure built character and patience? How many times had she told me that trials produced perseverance?

But that had always been about my health. This was about losing a teaching job. This was about losing what I'd joyfully thought, for the last few months, was God's plan for my life.

I gripped the reins tighter as I turned down the lane, realizing I always forgot how big the Gundys' farm was until I got there. By Lancaster County standards, it was huge, with nine greenhouses, two full-size homes, and numerous other outbuildings. Nursery stock—shrubs and trees—grew in the wide fields on every side. Beyond those were the large tracts dedicated to the growing of Christmas trees, rows and rows of blue spruce, Fraser fir, and Scotch pines, all in varying stages of growth.

The greenhouses lined the driveway, and as I drove past them now my eyes scanned each one, looking for signs of activity. All of the doors to the glass buildings were closed except the last, where inside a man was moving a ladder. My heart suddenly pounding at my throat, I pulled the buggy to a stop just outside.

Will Gundy stood at the base of the ladder, looking upward, the light streaming down through the glass ceiling, illuminating him. The sleeves of his blue shirt were rolled up over his biceps, his shirtfront unbuttoned all the way down in concession to the heat. Underneath, a white T-shirt clung to his muscular chest.

He turned toward me, his dark eyes growing bright. "Ada." He smiled and I shivered, even in the heat. "When did you get back?" Emerging from the greenhouse, he wiped his hands on a rag as he walked toward me. I noticed that his red beard was a little fuller than the last time I'd seen him. He reached the carriage and stopped, his arched brows perfectly framing his face and accenting his red hair.

"Just today."

"And you came straight here?"

I swallowed hard, reminding myself that his tone sounded pleased and hopeful to my ears only because I wished it so.

I shook my head. "I had some errands to run, and now I'm here to get *Mammi*."

"I see," he answered, taking a step back. "Well, this is perfect, actually. She and Alice both want to talk with you. So does the guest they have with them." He smiled, adding, "In fact, I think you're going to find what they have to say quite interesting."

I tilted my head, my mind swirling with curiosity. He clearly wasn't going to tell me any more than that, though, so I thanked him and said I would see him later. As I started Rikki moving again and we drew near the house, my heart raced even faster—both from having seen Will and from the impending encounter ahead.

How many times had *Mammi* said, "When God closes one door, He opens another"? Could there be an open door ahead of me? Pulling Rikki to a full stop and swinging myself down from the buggy, I was certainly eager to find out.

EIGHT

I tied my horse to the hitching post in the shade of a gigantic oak. Though Will's house was just a few years old, it fit in perfectly with the other buildings on the property. It was laid out in the classic farmhouse style, two stories high with a steeply-pitched roof and a broad front porch. The exterior was a stark white, as all of the homes in our local districts were, but still it felt colorful thanks to the flower beds and window boxes filled with blooms: red geraniums, purple impatiens, and blue lobelia. I took in the sight, relishing the beauty of it all. This was a lovely home.

A small white car was parked near the house, so I walked around it and headed up the walkway and onto the porch. But before I even reached the door, it swung open and in front of me stood Will's grandmother, Alice. Though the woman was in her late seventies, she seemed much younger than that, both in demeanor and appearance, except for her hair, that is. It was the same vivid white as her *kapp*—and had been for as long as I'd known her.

"Ada!" she cried, her face lighting up with delight. "I thought I heard a buggy. What perfect timing!"

My eyebrows raised. "Were you expecting me?"

"No, not at all," she replied, giving me a hug. She smelled of goat's milk soap and starch. "But we were just talking about you. To tell you the truth, we'd rather be talking *to* you."

I tried to see inside, over her shoulder, wondering what they had been saying—and whom they had been saying it to, for that matter.

"Come in, come in," Alice said, waving me forward, laugh lines crinkling around her eyes. "I cannot tell you how happy I am that you're here. Everyone else will be too."

"Everyone else?" I asked as she pulled me to the counter, thrust a pitcher of ice tea in my hands, and then grabbed a tray laden with a plate of brownies and three drinking glasses. As an afterthought, she grabbed another glass from the cabinet, added it to the others, and carried the whole thing on into the main room without any explanation.

I followed along behind her, spotting my grandmother as soon as I stepped through the doorway. She was sitting directly ahead on the couch, eyes sparkling, her cane propped against the cushion next to her. Moving forward, I set down the pitcher on the coffee table and then gave her a long hug, her leathery skin warm against my cheek.

"Welcome home, Ada!" she cried, holding on so tightly for so long that I truly felt welcome. "I missed you so."

"I missed you too, *Mammi*," I told her softly. "I can't wait to tell you all about my trip."

I pulled away, knowing we could save that discussion for later. For now, I wanted to know what was going on—and what it had to do with me.

"I thought you two had a guest," I said, glancing around the otherwise empty room.

"He'll be right back," *Mammi* replied, and from the sudden, rhythmic thud of the water pump, I realized that their guest was just up the hall, washing his hands in the bathroom.

Before I could get any advance information from either *Mammi* or Alice about who this person might be, a young man came walking back into the room, carefully drying his hands on a towel.

"That should be good enough, I think," he was saying as he did, but then he spotted me and stopped short.

"Oh. Hi."

"Hello," I replied, surprised to see that the guest in question was just a young man—about my same age, in fact—with a friendly face and light blond hair. Dressed casually in jeans and a button-down shirt, he was lanky, medium height, with cute, boyish features.

"Daniel Hart," he said, introducing himself.

"Ada Rupp," I replied, reaching out to shake his hand. He reached for mine as well but then jerked his hand back before we'd even touched.

"Sorry," he told me, setting down the towel and then holding both arms up, bent at the elbow, palms toward himself, looking like a veterinarian who had just scrubbed in to do a procedure on an animal.

"Daniel forgot his gloves," Alice said from behind me, as if that explained everything.

Turning, I looked from her to *Mammi* and then back to him again. All three were smiling widely, an excited gleam in their eyes.

"I don't know what's going on here," I said, shaking my head. "But I sure hope somebody let's me know soon."

Ten minutes later I was sitting on the couch, a glass of tea in my hand, still trying to make sense of the story that had essentially been coming at me from three different directions. Daniel had begun by explaining his odd reaction to my handshake, saying that he usually wore what were known as "archivist gloves" when he handled important documents, but that because he'd forgotten them today he'd had to settle for thoroughly scrubbing and washing instead. I was curious as to what sort of important documents he'd been planning to handle here, but before he could tell me Alice interrupted to share with me about Daniel's credentials as a scholar, which included a degree in Anabaptist history from Goshen College and another from the University of Zurich in Switzerland. He'd corrected her about that second one, saying that he hoped to get a master's at Zurich in the future but that he hadn't even officially enrolled yet.

At least *Mammi* seemed to recognize my desire for some concrete information, and she'd launched into an interesting tale, but then she ended up going down some long, confusing tangent, one that involved a power plant, an important waterfall, and a one-hundred-and-thirty-four-year-old property deed.

Daniel must have seen my confusion because he came and sat directly across from me, his gaze locked onto mine.

"Here's the bottom line," he said. "We need your help to save an important historic Anabaptist site from being destroyed."

I looked back at him, my eyes wide.

"The site is in Switzerland," Daniel continued, "a place where the

Anabaptists used to worship in secret. It's been left alone for centuries, but now its fate is in question. Thanks to the Swiss courts, a title dispute on the property, and a secret agreement made by your great-great-great grandfather more than a hundred years ago, this important site is about to be destroyed forever."

My mind swirled.

"The site is too important to be lost," Alice added. "But because of our ancestral ties, Ada, you and I can stop that from happening."

I looked from Alice to Daniel and back again.

"It's hard to explain. Why don't we begin where we were when you first came in," Daniel said, moving toward a pile of books and some cardboard tubes on a chair. "With a map. A very old map."

Alice and *Mammi* seemed content to remain settled on the couch, but I moved over to the dining table and sat as Daniel chose one of the tubes, pulled out a large, rolled-up map from inside, and spread it out onto the flat surface in front of me.

"This, as you may know, is the country of Switzerland, which is in Europe. Switzerland is divided into sections called 'cantons,' which I guess you could say are sort of like states. Of interest to us here today is the canton of Bern." Pointing to the cities of Bern and Zurich and the areas around it, he added, "Basically, this region is where the Anabaptist movement first started, back in the sixteenth century." Pausing for a moment, lost in thought, he said softly, "Of course, among scholars I might debate the stance of monogenesis versus polygenesis…." His voice trailed off, as if he were trying to decide how much detail he should go into. Finally, he shook his head and zeroed in on the map again.

"But I digress. Anyway, this is generally where the Anabaptists began, back in the fifteen hundreds. The early believers were persecuted, of course, and so starting in about 1526 a number of them left the cities to move into more rural areas."

As he traced their routes on the map with his finger, I couldn't help but feel a little irritated. Did he think I was ignorant, that I wouldn't already know this and much more? Somehow I had the feeling he wasn't even sure if I was aware that Switzerland was a country in Europe. Holding my tongue for now, I waited for him to continue.

"Many of them went to this region here, near the center of the country, which is known as the Emmental," he said, moving his finger in a loop from Bern to Lucern. "The Emmental has hills and valleys and forests and farms, so the Anabaptists were able to blend in a little better there. And the people of the Emmental were generally supportive, which helped too."

I nodded. So far, he still hadn't told me anything I didn't already know.

"Okay, I want to talk specifically about this spot right here," he said, pointing to the center of the Emmental region. "This is the municipality of Langnau, and not far from that is the village of Wasserdorf."

Leaning forward, he carefully rolled the map back up and put it away. Then he chose a different one and rolled it out.

"This shows both towns in a closer view." He pointed to various spots on the map where Mennonite congregations had been established. "They were able to live peaceably for a short while, but by 1536 persecution was happening here too. Some were sent to prison at Thun, brought to Bern and executed, and so on. Because of this the Anabaptists were forced to go underground, so to speak, gathering under bridges and in caves and ravines and such, where they could worship in secret. Now let's move in even closer to the village of Wasserdorf."

There was definitely a condescending tone to his voice, and as he switched to yet another map, I wondered how many we would have to go through until we had narrowed things down enough. Glancing over toward Alice and *Mammi*, I could see that they were both watching and listening, though *Mammi* had a bemused look on her face.

"All right. So you understand where we are. Wasserdorf is in the Emmental, which is in the canton of Bern, which is in Switzerland, which is in Europe. You with me so far?"

I was trying not to say something sarcastic when *Mammi* spoke from the couch.

"Daniel, I believe you'll find that Ada is a very intelligent young woman with a thorough knowledge of geography. She should be able to follow just about anything you need to explain to her with or without visual aids."

Daniel hesitated for a moment, as if trying to understand the meaning of her words. Then he must have caught on because he looked at me and blushed.

"I'm sorry, was I talking down to you? My friends say I do that to them all the time."

Hands still clasped in my lap, I simply smiled and accepted his apology, glad at least to know that he hadn't meant it as anything personal.

"Really, I am sorry. Let's fast-forward to the present, shall we?" Flashing me a boyish grin, he traded the map in his hand for what I hoped was the last one. After he spread it on the table, he sat, leaning forward on his elbows, and continued.

"This is a municipal map that shows part of Wasserdorf. Each area that's been outlined here indicates a separate piece of property. Thus, these little squares here average, oh, about half an acre a piece, give or take, most with single family homes on them."

Growing curious now, I wondered what that had to do with anything, but then he pointed to a different section of the map and I realized he was just trying to give me an idea of its scale.

"See this property here?" he asked, pointing to a far bigger shape near the upper right-hand corner. Wanting to make extra sure he still didn't think I was stupid, I quickly did the math in my head and decided that if the tiny lots near the bottom averaged half an acre each, this big section had to be about forty or fifty acres.

"Judging by your scale, then, I'm guessing this one's about…oh, let's see, point five times a hundred or so…um, around fifty acres?"

"Forty-nine, actually," he said. "But wow, good estimate."

Victorious, I glanced over at *Mammi*, expecting her to be smiling, but instead she gave me a stern look of warning. Immediately, I realized I had pushed it too far and now was acting in a way that was prideful.

Chagrined, I decided to stop posturing and just listen to what he had to say.

Pulling a pen from his pocket, Daniel surprised me by writing directly on this map, labeling the largest lot, the forty-nine-acre one, with the letter *S*. Along that lot's northern border sat a smaller lot, about five acres in size, which he marked with a *K*. He was about to return the pen to his pocket when, as an afterthought, he drew within the *K* section a strange little scribble that looked kind of like a waterfall.

"All across the Emmental," he told me, "are places where our Anabaptist ancestors lived and worshipped. Many of the sites have been preserved, including some of the spots where they gathered to worship in secret."

I nodded, looking again at the little drawing.

"Right here, on this five-acre lot, is a lovely waterfall with two natural caves that have been sort of carved out behind it. People in this region have always known that these caves were used by the Anabaptists for worship, starting back in the fifteen hundreds and possibly even as late as the early seventeen hundreds."

"Got it," I said, trying not to sound impatient.

"Recently I was contacted by the Wasserdorf Historical Society. They knew I was already doing research about Anabaptist historical sites in the Emmental, and they wanted to engage my services."

"Engage your services?"

"As a researcher, a scholar. They needed me to help them prove the historical significance of the caves here at this waterfall. This I could do, using old documents, letters, deeds, et cetera, whatever I could drum up that would help them substantiate the validity of the site."

"Why?" I asked, glancing again at Alice and *Mammi*. "Did they want to erect a monument or something?"

Daniel shook his head gravely and said, "No. They're trying to stop the township of Wasserdorf from installing a hydro power plant right here at the waterfall."

I sat back in my chair and looked at him.

"And that would be a bad thing?" I wanted to understand.

"Well, yes and no. Hydro power in and of itself is great. As I told Alice and Frannie, a hydro plant produces electricity by the use of falling water, so as far as pollution and by-products and all of that, it's an incredibly clean power source. Efficient too. Even a little plant like the one the village wants to put in here would supply energy for all three hundred homes in Wasserdorf."

"So what's the problem?"

"The problem is that they have chosen this specific waterfall. See, if a hydro plant really does go in here, then the historical value of the site will be completely destroyed. To put it in more local terms, it would be like tearing down the log cabins at Valley Forge and putting a power plant in their place." He hesitated and then corrected himself, saying, "Well, not exactly, because they're not planning to tear out these caves. I guess it would be more accurate to say it's like plopping down a power plant right in the middle of the battlefield at Gettysburg. The site would still be there, but for all intents and purposes it would be completely ruined. This waterfall and these caves in Wasserdorf are important, historically speaking, and should be preserved at all costs."

I nodded thoughtfully. I'd never been to Valley Forge or Gettysburg, but I had certainly read about them and seen photos, so I understood what he meant.

"We're not trying to get the township to scrap their plans altogether," he added. "The Swiss are very 'green,' you know, so the plant's been getting a lot of local support. All we're asking is that they relocate it to an optional site up the river that would work almost as well as this one."

"Sounds like a good compromise to me," I said.

Daniel grimaced, saying, "Yes, but plans are well under way to put the plant in right here, and the township isn't too happy about relocating to the alternate site unless they are absolutely forced to do so by the land and property commission. That's the government agency that arbitrates this sort of thing."

Looking down at the map, I was reminded that while, again, this was all very interesting, it was happening several thousand miles away. Leaning forward, I urged Daniel to get to the part that involved Alice and me. He pointed to the property he'd marked with a *K*, the one that had the waterfall on it.

"At issue here is the piece of land on which the waterfall is located. It has a complicated history of ownership. Originally, this property belonged to a man by the name of Kessler, which is why I put a *K* here. But then, back in the late eighteen hundreds, Kessler emigrated to America. Before he left he sold the property to his next-door neighbor, a man by the name of Sommers, who already owned this bigger property I've labeled with an *S*. When Sommers bought this land from Kessler, the two men drew up an agreement that limited Sommers' ability to sell the property to anyone else other than a Kessler in the future. I can explain it in better detail later, but why don't I cut to the chase?"

I nodded, suddenly glad that he'd taken his time getting me to this point.

"To save this important historic site and block the hydro plant, the Wasserdorf Historical Society has hired a lawyer who needs me to produce a descendant of Kessler. For an even better chance at winning this fight, we also need to bring with us a descendant of Sommers."

At that the hairs on my arm began to stand on end. Sommers. Thanks to Lexie's search for her birth family, one of the things that had come to light last spring was that we had an ancestor by that name who had lived in Switzerland.

I looked up at *Mammi*, who nodded and said, "That's right, Ada. He's talking about Abraham Sommers, my great-grandfather. I'm a direct descendant."

"And…" Alice added, eyes twinkling, "guess who's a direct descendant of Kessler?"

"You?" I replied, my mind racing.

"Exactly. Frannie and I always knew that our great-grandfathers were next-door neighbors over in Switzerland, and that their daughters had emigrated together with the same group of Mennonites when they came to the United States. In fact, that's how she and I became friends in the first place. When she moved here from Indiana, she specifically looked me up because of the connection our families had shared in the past."

"What neither woman knew," Daniel said, smiling broadly, "was that one day they would be able to save a very important place in history from being destroyed, just by coming back to Switzerland and satisfying some legal requirements of the land and property commission."

Alice clapped her hands and cried, "Can you believe it, Ada? For the sake of preserving our history, you and I get to go to Switzerland!"

NINE

My head spinning, I looked down at the map again and then up at *Mammi.*

"Is this Amielbach?" I gasped. "The place he's been talking about?"

Amielbach was a Swiss estate that had been owned by our ancestors and passed down through the generations to *Mammi.* She had sold most of it before I was born, retaining ownership of only one small parcel of land and a single cottage. As far as I knew, that cottage was the home of my birth mother, Giselle, who had lived there ever since she'd given me up for adoption and moved to Switzerland soon after I was born.

"Yes, dear," *Mammi* said, "Daniel has been talking about Amielbach."

"Is Giselle—"

"Giselle lives in a small cottage on the grounds there. If you look on the map, you can see exactly where. I spotted it earlier, before you got here."

Heart pounding, I looked back down at the map.

"Do you see a little square along the edge?" *Mammi* asked me. She was struggling to stand, probably so that she could come point it out. Instead, I picked up the map and brought it to her, sitting beside her on the couch.

Sure enough, there was a small square, indicating perhaps a quarter of an acre in size, that sat just inside the larger *S* property, not very far from the border of the *K* property. It was so small I hadn't even noticed it before.

Curious, Daniel came over to see what we were looking at. When he realized what it was, he went back to his papers and dug through them, pulling out a single sheet.

"Okay, here we go," he said, coming to stand by the couch. Looking through the paper from the other side, I could see that it was covered with words in boxes, and lots of arrows in between. "That property is owned by a Giselle Lantz, who bought it about twenty-five years ago. Now, Giselle is related to you people by..." His voice trailed off as he traced several arrows with his finger, and then he stopped short, looking at *Mammi*. "Oh! I'm sorry. Of course you would know this. She's your daughter."

He smiled sheepishly, pink splotches appearing on his cheeks.

"Yes," she said kindly. "When I sold the property, I made sure to retain that one small piece that held the cottage, and I signed the deed over to her."

"Isn't it exciting?" Alice added. "Once we're there, you'll probably get to meet your Aunt Giselle."

Looking at Alice's pointed expression and hearing her emphasis on the word "aunt," I realized she knew the truth, that Giselle was more than simply my aunt, she was also my birth mother.

During Lexie's life-changing visit last spring, I had learned that the woman who had been my *mamm* my entire life wasn't, in fact, my birth mother. Twenty-four years ago, Giselle had given birth to me and then given me to her sister Klara and Klara's husband, Alexander, through adoption. Thus, in one fell swoop, my birth aunt and her husband had become my parents, and my birth mother had become my aunt.

Since that time of discovery I'd continued to refer to her as "Aunt Giselle" out of respect for my parents, the sake of family privacy, and the knowledge that legally she was indeed my aunt. But, in my mind, I now thought of her simply as "Giselle."

Regardless of what I did or did not call her, more than anything I just wanted to see her. Face-to-face. In person. I wasn't sure what I wanted or why it mattered so much to me, but it was a dream that had been born last spring and grown steadily ever since. Now that it looked as if it might actually happen, I could hardly believe it. Turning to Daniel, I took a deep breath and then spoke.

"I'm in," I said firmly. "Just tell me what I need to know."

An hour later the four of us were still there in the living room going over this complicated property situation. While traveling with Alice to Switzerland and getting to meet my birth mother were both incredibly exciting prospects, I also knew that such a trip would drive a tremendous wedge between me and my mother, one that we might never be able to repair.

And yet given all of the changes in my life this past year, I knew in this moment that I had no choice but to press forward. In a sense, I felt as though I were stopped at a busy crossroads I'd never seen before. Either I could brave the traffic and drive my buggy to the other side, or turn around and backtrack to the only life I'd ever known. Given the choice, I was ready to take the risk.

Still, I needed to understand as much as I could about why Daniel needed us to go to Europe. Once *Mammi* and I were headed home and could speak privately, I would ask her how we should approach my parents about this. But whether *Mammi* ended up being the one to tell them or I did, either way I needed enough information so that I would be able to stand firm on the other reasons for the voyage.

And so around and around we had gone for the last hour, trying to sort everything out. *Mammi* and Alice had remained on the couch, though now Alice was doing some hand-stitching as she listened to us talk and added the occasional comment. Daniel and I were at the table, and he had cleared away the maps and books and replaced them with pen and paper. He seemed to be a visual person, so he'd tried to clarify more of the details for me by using various sketches and charts and doodles. But in the end, I thought it might be more helpful to grab a pen and some paper myself and simply write down the list of facts that made sense in an order that worked for me.

I understood about the family connections between *Mammi* and Alice and the two men who had been next-door neighbors in Switzerland in the eighteen hundreds. I also understood the conflict going on currently between the township that wanted to build a new hydro plant and the historical committee who wanted to preserve an important Anabaptist site. What I couldn't seem to grasp was how dragging two little old Amish ladies or their representatives halfway around the world could possibly solve that conflict. Trying again, Daniel laid it out for me as logically as he could, and so I started my list. I wrote:

Two pieces of land, one large and one small, sat directly beside each other.

In 1877, the owner of the smaller piece, Alice's ancestor Ulrich Kessler, sold it to the owner of the larger piece, Mammi's *ancestor Abraham Sommers.*

When they made that transaction, they also signed a legal agreement that would limit Abraham's options should he ever want to sell that piece of land to anyone else.

"Stop there," I said. "What sort of limits did he agree to?"

"We're not certain about all of them," Daniel said, "but so far we do know that the main restriction is similar to something we have here in America, known as what's called a 'first right of refusal.'"

"Which is?"

"A legality that works like this: If Sommers ever wants to sell the land, he has to offer it to Kessler or his descendants first. If they say they *do* want to buy it, then Sommers has no choice but to sell it to them—at whatever price was specified in the agreement."

"What if they don't want it?"

"Then Sommers is free to sell to whomever he wants, for whatever price he can get for it."

I sat back, thinking about that.

"Why would Sommers ever make such an agreement? It doesn't sound very fair. I wouldn't make a deal like that. If somebody chose to sell me their land, then that should be the end of it. I ought to be able to do with it as I please."

A strange noise came from *Mammi's* direction, and I looked over to see that she was sound asleep and lightly snoring. Alice looked as if she, too, might drift off at any moment, but for the time being, she was still with us, sewing away on a fabric potholder.

"This sort of agreement can be made for different reasons," Daniel told me, "but I believe in this case it was probably an act of kindness done by a man who could well afford it."

My eyes widened. At least that was good to know that great-great-great-grandpa Abraham had been a nice man.

To explain Abraham's kindness, Daniel recounted a little more Anabaptist history, describing how persecution in that region of Switzerland seemed to ebb and flow over the years. What a man was allowed to do freely at one time might get him arrested at another. And though executions stopped being enforced in the late fifteen hundreds, Anabaptists were still being mistreated and imprisoned three hundred years later. In fact, Daniel said, when Abraham Sommers was a young man, his own brother had become a Mennonite and ended up having to leave the country to stay out of prison.

Although there wasn't a large number of Mennonites left in the Emmental by the time Abraham moved there, there were still a few, including his own next-door neighbor, Ulrich Kessler.

"We know that a Mennonite was arrested for resisting the draft in 1875 and imprisoned at Thun. Once that happened, my guess is that Ulrich Kessler began to fear for his own sons, who were fast approaching the age of military service themselves. In 1877, Ulrich sold his land and moved his whole family to America. He probably didn't want to leave Wasserdorf and had hopes that the climate toward Anabaptists might soften in the future. I have a feeling that's why he wanted a first right of refusal on the property, so that if he or his children were ever able to return, they could buy back their family's homestead. Really, I doubt Abraham even needed the land. I think he just bought it so that Ulrich could afford to go and carve out a new life somewhere else."

"Is there a house there?" I asked. "Or just the waterfall?"

"There used to be a home when the Kesslers lived there. A small one. But once they were gone it fell to ruin and was eventually demolished. Now all that's left is the crumbling foundation."

I nodded, trying to picture it. Had I been in Ulrich Kessler's shoes, loving my homeland but knowing I needed to leave for the sake of religious freedom, I also might have gone to my wealthy neighbor and asked for such an arrangement. Fortunately for the Kesslers, Abraham Sommers had been willing to do as they had asked.

"Okay, I think I really get it now," I said to Daniel. "But how does what happened between those two men so long ago have anything to do with these ladies over here?" We looked toward the couch to see that now Alice had fallen asleep as well, the two of them both peacefully dozing away.

Sharing a smile, Daniel and I lowered our voices just a bit.

"As you probably know," he said, looking at his own notes for reference, "when Abraham died, his daughter Elsbeth inherited his home and property. Then when she died—"

"Wait, stop there. Elsbeth inherited just the big property, the one with the *S*?"

"No, both. She got *S* and *K*."

"Got it," I said, adding another line to my list. "So even with the agreement, it was okay for Abraham to bequeath that property to someone else, he just couldn't sell it?"

"Correct. But once it belonged to Elsbeth, she was under the same deed restrictions her father had been. If she wanted to sell the smaller property, the Kessler family still retained the first right of refusal."

"Makes sense."

"Okay. So when Elsbeth died, she left both properties to her daughter Sarah, and when Sarah died she left them to her daughter Frannie, your grandmother. Through all of those generations, no one ever tried to sell either property."

"Until my grandmother," I said softly, thinking again of how *Mammi* had sold the Swiss estate she'd inherited from her mother so that she could buy the farm we all still lived on now.

At the time *Mammi* had had great hopes that by doing so her two daughters could learn to live peaceably there together. Her hopes had been in vain, but at least *Mammi* had taken comfort in the fact that she'd been able to give her middle daughter somewhere to live, a place to start over and build a new life after giving up her children for adoption. And with a good amount of money left over even after buying our farm, *Mammi* had secured her future, helped our family, and blessed other members of our church community as well.

As for Giselle, none of us knew very much about her or her life. She'd kept her communications with us to a minimum, her answers always short and to the point, responding to emails Zed had sent her way on our behalf during the last few months.

My grandmother hadn't ever been sure Giselle still resided in the cottage until Zed tracked her down last spring. Now that I would be going over there, I would finally be able to learn more about her and fill many of the blanks in the picture I held in my head.

Of course, that all depended on if she would be willing to see me. I decided to pay a visit to Zed as soon as I could to have him send her another email. We could let her know I'd be coming her way and then see how she would choose to respond.

"Unfortunately, somewhere between Elsbeth and Frannie," Daniel was saying, interrupting my thoughts, "the old agreement between Sommers and Kessler was forgotten. When your grandmother was ready to sell her inheritance, however, it came to light. Do you know what a title search is?"

I shook my head, so he explained that whenever a property was sold, part of the process involved looking at the deed and checking to make sure there weren't complications or disputed issues or related contracts or other matters that could "murky the waters" of ownership. He said that most title searches resulted in a clearance, but for the occasional ones where a problem cropped up, the search was said to have come back "cloudy."

"When the title search was done for Frannie, she learned two things she hadn't been told before: First, that she held the deed to two separate properties rather than only one, and second, that the title search for the smaller of the two properties had come back cloudy. We realize now, of course, that the title didn't clear because of the old agreement between Sommers and Kessler. At that time, however, all anyone could say was that the deed had legal complications of some kind."

"So what did she do?"

Daniel shrugged. "She had a choice. She could either pay to have an expert track down the problem with the deed to try to straighten it out, or she could simply sell the larger of the properties and hang on to the smaller one. After discussing the matter with the buyer, who really didn't care whether he got those extra five acres or not, she decided to let it drop. The Realtor over there had told her some nightmare stories about title clearances, and she was afraid that she'd end up spending more on the clearance than the land was worth."

"So she retained ownership of the smaller property?"

"Yes. Her lawyer set up a fund to cover the ongoing taxes and insurance on it, but otherwise she hasn't had anything to do with it. The man who bought Amielbach, Herr Lauten, keeps an eye on the land. He makes sure it's kept clean and has it mowed occasionally."

"That's nice of him."

"He's a nice guy, for sure, but in this case he has a personal interest." Daniel grinned, and it struck me that he really was quite cute, especially when he smiled. "The waterfall is clearly visible from the main house on the estate. If you open the windows at night, you can even hear the falls as you drift off to sleep."

I closed my eyes, just picturing it. The image reminded me of *Heidi*, one of my favorite books as a child. Though Heidi's home with her grandfather wasn't nearly as grand as Amielbach, I was sure the beauty of the Swiss Alps from the window was the same.

"Herr Lauten has been in the process of turning Amielbach into an inn for the last year, so you can imagine how upset he is about the hydro plant," Daniel added. I opened my eyes, the pristine image of roaring falls and white-tipped mountain peaks shattered by the noise and sight of a power plant.

"So how can Alice and I help stop that plant from destroying the falls?" I asked, leaning forward.

"We had a hearing with the land and property commission, and they agreed to our petition to have the hydro plant relocated, but on one condition. Given the anticipated influx of visitors, they want the area to be developed as a legitimate historical site, with safety rails, directional signs, things like that. Even a small parking lot within a reasonable walking distance. Herr Lauten is perfectly willing to fund all of this."

"Okay…" I said, sure it was too good to be true.

"What they don't like is an absentee landowner an ocean away in possession of a murky title. Frannie is still willing to sell that land and Lauten is now eager to buy it, so if they could do that, the whole problem would be solved. The plant would be relocated upstream, and our important Anabaptist site would be preserved."

Pressing my hands to my temples, I tried to ward off the headache that was threatening there. "So if she wants to sell and he wants to buy but there's an old agreement standing in the way," I recounted slowly, "then why couldn't somebody do like you said earlier and pay to have an expert track down the problem with the deed and straighten it out?"

"They can, and they did. I'm that expert, Ada, and here's what it comes down to. The only way to settle this whole thing is for a Kessler descendant to buy the property from the current owner, a Sommers descendant. This would fulfill the old agreement and clear the title. Then as soon as that happens, she can turn around and sell it to Lauten, at which point the commission's stipulations will have been met."

Closing my eyes, I tried to understand, but one question loomed large in my mind.

"If any Sommers descendant will do, though, why do you need me at all? Why not just have Giselle represent the Sommers line? She's already living right there."

Daniel's brow furrowed.

"Herr Lauten tried that already. I don't know how well you know your aunt—"

"Not at all."

"Okay, well, me neither, but Herr Lauten says she's pretty stubborn. He tried repeatedly to convince her to represent Frannie in this matter, but she refused even to discuss it. All she would say was that she didn't want anything to do with her family's legal matters, including signing any papers on her mother's behalf. Period. No further discussion allowed."

As his words had sunk in, I stood, stretching my back. I heard laughter outside, so I went to the window and stood there for a long moment looking out. I'd thought I might see Will's children, but instead it was their cousin Rachael who lived next door, playing in the garden with her *mamm*. For some reason, I almost felt as much kinship with the Kessler line as I did with the Sommers'. Whether that was because of my feelings for Will or my own Anabaptist heritage and the debt I owed to their sacrifices, I wasn't sure. All I knew was that I was going to Europe to sell a piece of land and fulfill a promise made between two men more than a hundred and thirty years ago—and perhaps meet my birth mother in the bargain.

"There's just one more issue," Daniel said, and from the tone of his voice, I knew it was something important. I turned and looked at him, waiting.

"Well, two more, actually." He chuckled nervously. "First, I want to make sure you understand that this isn't a sure thing. Despite an exhaustive search, we still have not been able to come up with the original signed agreement between the two men. We have found enough information about what that agreement contained to present our case to the Swiss property courts—and having the two of you there could make all the difference in their decision—but I don't want to paint too rosy of a picture here. Unless by some miracle we find that missing agreement, we have no guarantees that this plan is going to work."

I thought about that for a moment and then nodded, saying that if Alice was willing to take that chance, then so was I.

"Thank you, Ada. Thank you very much. Herr Lauten still has great hopes of finding the agreement tucked away somewhere at Amielbach. But I think that's a long shot at best. I'd prefer to take a more pragmatic approach."

"Do you know how much involvement will be expected of us on a legal level?"

"Are you asking because of the Amish position about not taking people to court?"

I nodded.

"The dispute is between the Wasserdorf township and the historical society. You're needed to simply clarify the situation. Alice already talked with your bishop, and he's fine with your involvement."

"Okay, thanks," I said, moving back toward the table and sitting down. "What's the other thing? You said there were two issues."

He leaned forward, placing his elbows on his knees, and looked at me intently.

"I need you to understand that we don't have a lot of time. The commission has given us a limited period to solve this matter, and the clock is already ticking. But Alice is not willing to fly, for religious reasons, which means we'll have to go by boat. I can get us on a cargo ship that leaves New York City on the nineteenth—which is just as well, I suppose, because it'll probably take that long for your passport to come through—but even once we take off, the transatlantic crossing takes seven days. Then, once we're in Europe, getting from the port at Le Havre to the village of Wasserdorf will take us two more days. By the time we finally arrive at Amielbach, we will have only five days left to get that title cleared before our deadline is up."

"And if we can't make it happen by then?" I asked.

"Then the fight for the waterfall is over. We lose. Frannie loses her land to the Swiss government, Herr Lauten loses the ambience of his inn, and we all lose an important piece of our Anabaptist heritage."

That was a scary thought. Then again, I couldn't help but think of what I would lose if I *didn't* make this trip: all hope of ever meeting my birth mother.

TEN

Daniel left first, departing in his little white car. As I helped *Mammi* across Will's porch, his two-year old twins, Melanie and Matty, came running across the lawn.

"Ada!" Mel yelled. Their little *kapps* bounced around on their heads and their bare feet were dirty.

At the sight of the two children, *Mammi* and I paused, smiling. It wouldn't hurt to take a minute for a quick visit, so I helped *Mammi* sit down in a chair on the porch, in the shade. By the time I turned back around toward the children, however, I realized my mistake.

Not far behind the twins I spotted Leah Fisher, who was just jumping down from the fence and starting toward us. It appeared she hadn't joined her family for their reunion in Shippensburg after all. Instead, she had been here, out in the field with Will's children, more than likely playing a game of hide-and-seek among the rows of Christmas trees.

Behind Leah came Will's older daughter, Christy. She climbed down from the fence tentatively and then shuffled after her soon-to-be teacher. The preteen seemed short for her age and a little peaked, but at least she looked better than she had in the spring. Her hair was strawberry blond and her skin was fair, with a few freckles sprinkled across her nose.

"Ada," Leah called out, hurrying her pace. "Welcome home!"

Somehow her apron was still clean, even though she'd been out there running around with the children. A curly lock of chestnut hair had fallen free from the pins that secured her hair, and she swiped at it quickly with her hand. She was cute as a bug, there was no way around it.

"I hoped I'd see you soon," she added, reaching the lawn and scooping up Mat, who giggled. Mel ran ahead of them, up the stairs, and then flung herself at me. I lifted her and kissed the top of her bonnet. She smelled like soil and warm grass and the sweet sweat of a toddler. I hugged her tightly.

"How was your trip?" Leah was a little out of breath by the time she reached me.

"Good, except for what I lost while I was gone."

Mammi clucked her tongue at me, but I ignored her.

"Yes, I wanted to talk with you about that," Leah replied quickly, her cheeks coloring just a bit.

I cocked my head, waiting. I wasn't going to make this easy for her.

"When they offered me the job, I had no idea you wanted it. I felt horrible when I heard you thought it was yours." Her green eyes widened as she spoke. "I'm truly sorry."

I needed to forgive her, but the only way I could do that was by telling myself that this was all part of God's plan. If He had truly intended for me to get the job, then I would have. It was that simple.

"No matter," I finally answered. The issue was settled between us.

Then Will came through the kitchen door, and I realized I had much further to go before I would be able to forgive her for the theft of his heart as well.

Seeing her father, Mel squirmed in my arms. I lowered her to the porch, and she bolted toward him. He picked her up as if she weighed no more than a loaf of bread.

"There you are," Leah said to him, turning on her brightest smile as she stepped closer. He didn't seem to notice but was instead anxiously scanning the yard in front of him.

"Where's Christy?" He stepped to the railing.

We all looked out to find her, spotting her under the oak tree, her back toward us.

"I'll go get her," Leah said, putting Mat down and heading toward

Christy, the twins running after her like two little ducklings following their mother. Watching them all, my heart grew heavy.

"Is your daughter okay?" *Mammi* asked Will from her perch in the shade.

Moving closer to her, Will nodded and lowered his voice. "Christy had a rough go of it last spring in school, both from being sick and from the loss of her mother. I thought it might do some good for her to spend time with Leah before school started as she'll be her teacher this year."

Unaware of the pain his words caused me on several fronts, Will glanced my way, eyebrows raised, as if waiting for my approval. I couldn't help but picture it: Will confiding in Leah his concerns for his daughter and the two of them coming up with a plan to make this school year a better one for her. Unable to respond, I was relieved when *Mammi* spoke instead, saying something about how difficult it was for a child to lose her mother but especially so at such a tender age.

We fell silent after that, watching as Leah knelt down beside Christy and they quietly talked, the twins running in circles around them.

"Maybe I should go out there too," Will said, moving toward the steps.

Unable to bear the sight of such a scene, I began helping *Mammi* up, saying that we needed to be off. Will hesitated, one hand on the porch railing.

"About the passport," he said. "Bishop Fisher has given permission for the photos. Alice and I had ours taken at Miller's Drugstore in Lancaster. They give them to you right there."

I nodded, saying that I would go tomorrow myself, first thing.

"File at the post office, and make sure and tell them to rush it," he added. "You should get it in about two weeks."

Then he continued on down the steps and across the lawn toward his children and the woman who intended to be his wife. My stomach churning, I turned away, eyes blurry with tears as I helped *Mammi* move toward the buggy.

On the way home she and I were both exhausted, mentally and physically, and we didn't talk much. In fact, we shared only two brief exchanges the whole way there.

The first was when I asked how I could tell my parents. *Mammi* replied simply, "You're going on my behalf, Ada, I should be the one to do it."

In fact, she didn't even want me around for the argument we both knew would ensue. Thus we agreed that she would speak with them tomorrow morning while I was out arranging for my passport.

That was the extent of our exchange the rest of the way until we turned into the drive. As we did, I put a hand on *Mammi's* arm to gently shake her awake.

"I'm not sleeping, I was praying," she said, opening her eyes and sitting up straight.

I smiled sympathetically. "About tomorrow's conversation?"

"No, about Giselle."

As we drew to a stop near the *daadi haus, Mammi* suddenly turned to me, eyes filled with pain and regret.

"Promise me something, Ada," she said, her voice low and urgent.

I nodded. Of course. I would do anything for this woman I loved so much.

"Promise me that before you come home you'll talk to Giselle about God, about her soul. I don't expect her to become Plain again, but I need to know that she hasn't rejected Christ and that she's managed to make her peace with God."

I inhaled deeply, knowing the depth of the burden my grandmother had just laid at my feet. Yet on so many levels, how could I refuse? Meeting her eyes, I swallowed hard and spoke.

"I promise I'll try, *Mammi*," I said. "If she's willing to see me, I'll try."

The next morning after breakfast I told my parents I had some errands to run and had already hired a driver, a middle-aged woman that we sometimes used. I mentioned I'd be visiting the library but didn't bring up the passport. I felt guilty for not elaborating further, but as *Mammi* had said yesterday, it would probably be best if she talked to *Mamm* and *Daed* by herself. Just thinking of their conversation—and the fact I was going to have to face my mother upon my return—made me feel sick to my stomach.

Traffic was heavy, as usual, but eventually the driver was dropping me off in front of the Lancaster courthouse, saying she would run some errands of her own and return for me in two hours. As she drove away, I oriented myself and then began walking toward Miller's Drugstore down the block, not realizing until I got there that it wouldn't be open for another twenty minutes. I was just settling down on the front step to wait when I heard a voice call out my name. Looking up, I spotted Silas standing at the far curb, waving at me. After a minute, traffic slowed and he darted across the busy street.

"What are you up to, Ada?" he asked, coming toward me with a grin. His straw hat was off kilter, just a little, and he held a large, plastic box in his hands that was empty.

"Killing time until the drugstore opens. How about you?"

"Just made a delivery to the toy store down the street." Silas's father had several businesses, including a woodworking shop. "But I'm in no rush to get back. Let's grab some coffee."

We went to the café on the corner, the smell of coffee perking me up as I stepped through the door. Choosing a booth near the window, we sat and ordered coffee and biscuits. Though Silas was as chatty as he'd been on the train, something about his demeanor today seemed a little down in the dumps.

"I heard you're going to Switzerland," he said after our order came. "With Alice, right?"

My eyes widened. "How did you know that?"

"Leah told me. I saw her yesterday."

Leah! Of all people! I didn't understand why Alice had told her, especially this soon, but I could only imagine what might happen next. If word was already out, there was a good chance that *Mamm* or *Daed* would hear about it before *Mammi* even had a chance to talk to them herself. I couldn't imagine the sort of firestorm that could kick off. Swallowing hard, I prayed that God would keep the lips of our neighbors silent even as He gave *Mammi* the right words to say as soon as possible.

"She really does feel for you, considering she got the job you wanted," he said, pushing his glasses up on the bridge of his nose.

"What?"

"She hadn't realized the two of you were competing for the same job."

I nodded, knowing that was a complete and utter lie.

"She's sure you must despise her."

I tilted my head. It wasn't our way to despise people. "Over the teaching job?"

"And Will."

I tried to look perplexed, as if I had no idea what he was talking about.

"Come on, Ada, everyone knows Will was interested in you—"

"Silas," I chided. "No one knew any such thing."

He gave me a pathetic look and picked up his hat from the table. "Do you realize if you're all the way over in Europe that there's nothing to stop the two of them from courting? They could be married before you even get back."

"Weddings aren't till November, Silas. You know that."

"*Ya*, but Will's a widower. The bishop can make an exception."

Silas was right. I swallowed hard, trying not to picture it.

Across from me, he was obviously sick over Leah as well. I felt sorry for him, but I didn't want to talk about it anymore. Just hearing the mention of Will's name filled me with pain.

It was nearly noon by the time the driver dropped me off at home, plenty late enough for *Mammi* to have had her conversation with my parents. Stomach churning, I wondered what would happen now as I walked toward the side of the house with my stack of library books, listening intently for the sound of voices, perhaps even yelling. Instead, all was oddly silent. I moved quietly into the backyard, looking around, but saw neither of my parents. No *Mamm* at the clothesline, no *Daed* at the tool shed. Nobody anywhere.

Taking a deep breath, I veered off toward the *daadi haus*, deciding I would go straight to *Mammi* and find out from her how it had gone.

The moment I stepped inside, I knew that the answer was "not well."

She was in her chair, eyes red, a handkerchief clutched in her hand.

"Well?" I whispered.

She hugged herself tightly. "It's done." Her eyes filled with tears.

Trying not to cry myself, I crossed the room quickly and hugged her. "What did *Daed* say?"

"Not much, but he wasn't opposed."

"And *Mamm*?"

My grandmother looked away, saying, "She'll come around eventually."

I nodded. "Did she bring up Giselle? Is that part of it?"

"Of course it is. But there's so much more. It's hard enough being a parent, and harder still when you only have one child. Then that child grows up, and, well…" Her voice trailed off, but I knew what she saying. In more ways than one, my mother did not want to let me go.

But I was going anyway. In more ways than one.

When I left the *daadi haus*, I spotted *Mamm* standing out by the flower garden near the windmill, which was completely still. I couldn't help but move toward her. She didn't turn or acknowledge me as I approached.

"*Mamm,*" I said as I walked closer. She held her apron up to her face but lowered it as I stepped in front of her. Seeing that her eyes were red and puffy, a wave of compassion swept over me. "Talk to me," I said softly.

She took a deep breath. A horsefly buzzed by, and I brushed it away. The heat of the day was heavy.

"*Mamm*? What are you thinking?"

She looked at me then. "Honestly?"

I nodded.

She pursed her lips together and then said, "That I gave you a continent. Freely, and with love. I thought it would settle this thing inside of you. I gave you a *continent*, Ada, and how do you repay me? By asking for an ocean."

Her voice caught on the last word, bringing tears to my eyes as well.

"It's just a trip. I'll be back."

"What if you don't?"

"Don't?"

"Come back. What if you don't come back at all?" She shook her head. "You don't know Giselle the way I do, Ada. She'll wrap you around her finger as tight as a thread. What if she wants you to stay with her in Switzerland?"

That was ridiculous. Of course I would come back. "There's no reason I would stay," I said. "And why would she want me to anyway?"

"Oh, she'll come up with something, I'm sure."

"*Mamm*, I don't know if she wants me to come or if she'll even agree to see me once I'm there. I'll have Zed email her to let her know about the trip, but beyond that, there's a good chance I won't have much interaction with her. It's really up to her."

We were silent for a moment as my words hung there between us.

"What if you get sick?" she ventured. "What if your health takes a turn and you're in the middle of the ocean somewhere?"

"My health is good, *Mamm*. It's very, very good. You must see that. You must be able to look at me and know I'm not like I was. Not at all. Not anymore."

My words were so emphatic she didn't even reply. Again, we were quiet for a long moment.

"I wonder what Marta would say about this," she said finally.

"She'd probably be all for it," I answered. Considering that my taking this trip would save Aunt Marta from having to go herself, I had a feeling she'd be thrilled. "I thought I might go over there later to talk to Zed about emailing. I can speak with Aunt Marta too."

"Go this evening. I'll go with you." *Mamm* let go of her apron and brushed it straight. "Maybe she can talk some sense into you."

I bit my lip, hoping *Mammi* had made it clear to my mother that this trip was already a done deal. The wheels had been put into motion whether *Mamm* liked it or not.

Of course, it wouldn't help matters for me to remind her of that now. Instead, with a final pat on her arm, I said, "Maybe so."

Then I turned and walked away.

ELEVEN

Aunt Marta ended up talking sense into both of us as we sat in her tiny living room. Zed was in the even smaller dining room, at the computer, emailing Giselle. Ella was off babysitting for a neighbor, which I knew because she'd sent me a text earlier. Since the trip she'd been keeping me updated about her life regularly, no matter how trivial. I didn't mind, most of the time.

"Maybe Giselle has changed." Aunt Marta looked from my mother to me. "Or maybe she hasn't. I actually think it's a good thing you're going, Ada. Someone in our family needs to connect with her." She turned back to *Mamm*. "And honestly, Klara, why do you think Giselle would want Ada to stay? I think you're letting your fears get the best of you."

Of course I agreed but didn't say so now.

"Got one!" Zed called out from the dining room.

"From Giselle?" I was on my feet before I realized I shouldn't react so enthusiastically. Forcing myself to move far more slowly than I wanted to, I walked to the dining room.

"No. From Herr Lauten."

"Oh." I hadn't realized Zed had emailed him too.

"He says he just wants you and Alice to know how thankful he is you

100

are coming. Not only will you save an important historical site, but you'll also be saving his home as well. He said he's spent the last year renovating Amielbach with an eye toward turning it back into an inn."

"I thought it already was an inn," I said. "That's what Lexie told me, last spring."

"I thought so too," Zed said, growing quiet as he read the words on the screen. "Looks like a long time ago it used to be a boarding house, but that hasn't been the case for years. He says now that he's retired, he's decided to turn it into an inn and make it a lot fancier. Says he's been renovating for a whole year." Zed skimmed some more and then added, "Poor guy. Sounds like he's really been going all out, but with a hydro plant next door to destroy the peaceful setting and the beautiful view, an inn would be doomed before it ever opened."

"You hear that, Klara? In more ways than one, this is a good thing that Ada and Alice are doing. You should send Ada on her way with your blessing. This was meant to be."

Mamm never actually gave me her blessing, but she didn't give me the silent treatment anymore, nor did I find her crying into her apron. Our ship to Europe would be leaving in three weeks, so I tried to do everything I could to help with the chores around the place until then. It felt good to work without tiring easily, as I used to. Staying so busy also helped me to not think about why Giselle hadn't returned Zed's email.

Perhaps it was prideful of me, but during the next few days I tried to work extra hard, just so my parents could see how very healthy I had become. I knew it registered, because *Daed* commented one night at dinner.

"I was looking around for the other ones today," he said cryptically, reaching for the squash casserole. "Never found them, though."

Mamm and I looked at each other and then at him.

"The other what?" she asked.

"The other Adas." Glancing my way, he gave me a sly wink. "Considering that she does five times the work she used to, I figured the good Lord must have duplicated her somehow."

I laughed heartily at his joke, though *Mamm* merely smiled and clicked her tongue. Prideful or not, I thought it showed great restraint on my part not to turn to her and say, "I told you so."

The day after Lexie and James got home from their honeymoon, I called her to tell what was going on. By the time I finished, she was practically beside herself with excitement.

"What an adventure! Are you sure you won't take a camera and send me pictures?"

"No, but I could mail you some postcards of the scenery, if you'd like."

"How about the box with the image of Amielbach on top? I think you should take it with you. Maybe someone over there will know who carved it."

"That box is awfully old, Lexie," I said. "*Mammi* inherited it from her grandmother."

"Yeah, but it must have come from over there. If you're willing to give it a try, I'll stick it in the mail to you first thing tomorrow. We still have enough time that I won't even have to send it FedEx."

I knew how Lexie treasured that box, and I was a little nervous about being responsible for it. But she did have a good point. It must have come from over there, and so back to over there it would go. Maybe Herr Lauten, the nice man who owned Amielbach, would know something of its origins.

There was much to do before our trip, and in all of the excitement and business I let one thing catch me by surprise a few days later. I was out in the pasture, tending to a calf, when I heard it: the sound of a clanging bell in the distance.

I gasped, jerking my head up. This was the first day of school.

The bell I could hear was coming from the local school, not Willowcrest, which was a bit farther away. But the pain of its clanging hurt just the same, each ding and dong bringing to mind Leah Fisher's face, smiling as she welcomed her class full of students to a new year of school.

Five days before we sailed, I went to see Alice. We needed to discuss final plans, and I wanted to let her know that my passport had come in on time as expected.

Driving up the lane, I spotted Will halfway under his tractor, a toolbox at his feet. At the house I tended to Rikki and then hurried up the back steps to the kitchen door. Alice greeted me warmly, saying we had a few minutes of quiet before the twins woke up from their nap. We sat at Will's long table with cups of tea and talked. We covered everything, including the lack of any return email from Giselle.

"Don't take it personally," Alice said. "She doesn't seem to communicate well with anyone."

I couldn't help but be aware of the irony of the situation. By not cooperating with Herr Lauten's request to represent *Mammi* in this matter, Giselle was bringing more of the family—and more of the past—into her life, not less.

Alice reached for my hand and squeezed it. "I'm so thankful you're willing to make this trip. I'll be honest, Will and I are hoping we can make enough money from selling the property to update the greenhouses— new compressed air fans, rollup sidewalls, things like that." Glancing at me, she elaborated. "Better temperature controls could have a huge impact on productivity and thus profits. Goodness knows, we could do with some profits."

I hadn't realized that the Gundys' nursery was having financial issues, but I supposed it wasn't all that surprising. A lot of family businesses in our community had been hit hard by the economy and were, as the *Englisch* liked to say, land rich but cash poor.

"There's something else I want to talk with you about," Alice said. "How would you feel if we brought Christy with us?"

Her question caught me totally by surprise. Shifting my mind onto this new topic, I simply looked at her, speechless for a moment. Christy? If it were any other child, I'd say yes, of course, what a delightful idea. But not her, not Christy. At eleven, she was old enough, perhaps, but she was very troubled. Since her mother's death she'd become sullen and withdrawn, barely speaking to anyone anymore—except perhaps her father. I couldn't imagine how she'd bear being away from him for so long.

"This is what I'm thinking," Alice continued, her hand flat on the table. "Will is clearly overwhelmed here, and Christy is still struggling mightily with her mother's death. For those reasons alone I think it's a good idea."

A giggle erupted from the staircase, and my gaze darted across the room. Mat stood at the bottom. She giggled again when she realized I saw her. Mel was behind her, pushing against her sister. Together, the two came trotting toward us, reaching up for hugs from their grandmother and from me.

"Outside?" Mat asked, her eyes dark and beautiful.

"Sure," Alice told her. "You don't mind, do you, Ada?"

"Of course not."

The little girls ran toward the back door and had it open before we got there. Out they rushed, laughing now, their bare feet slapping against the wooden slats of the porch.

"They'll play on the lawn," Alice said, gesturing toward two Adirondack chairs that sat against the house. "We can watch from here."

Will was coming toward the yard now, a rake in his hand. The girls squealed in delight and took off running toward him.

"Where was I?" Alice asked as we settled into the chairs.

"Christy," I reminded her. "You were talking about Christy."

"Oh, yes." She turned toward me. "Bringing her with us would be a burden, I know, perhaps more so for you than for me. I'm looking forward to this trip, immensely, but caring for Will's girls these last months has nearly worn me out. I'm not as young as I used to be." Her blue eyes seemed faded somehow. "I believe I have enough energy to make the trip, but I'm afraid that adding Christy to the mix might be too much without a lot of assistance from you."

I nodded, realizing yet again how different Christy was than most young girls. Normally, bringing along someone of her age would be a huge help, not an extra burden. Whether because of her mother's death or her own physical condition I wasn't sure, but most of the time Christy seemed more like a nine-year-old than the eleven-year-old she really was.

"To be honest," Alice continued, "if she comes with us, I believe you'll end up bearing the brunt of the burden, acting as a nanny of sorts. Keeping an eye on her. Helping her with her lessons. That kind of thing."

"What about her missing so much school?"

Peering off, Alice shook her head. "Even when she's there, she's not really there, if you know what I mean. If you'd be willing to help with her lessons during the trip, that would be wonderful. I think she might even do better one-on-one than she has in the classroom."

Emotion rising up in my chest, I felt my mind move into prayer without even closing my eyes. *This is how You work, isn't it, Lord? This is You, opening yet another door.* I swallowed hard, trying not to weep with sudden gratitude for His grace. I realized that the loss of the teaching job at

Willowcrest had made this moment even sweeter still. God *did* want me teaching after all—not to thirty shining little faces, as I had thought, but just one. Just Christy, a very troubled, very special young woman who likely needed a friend as much as she needed a tutor or a nanny.

"What about her passport?" I asked, afraid now that she might not be able to come after all.

"She has it already. When you were out in Oregon and Will and I were first learning of the situation in Switzerland, we thought he and Christy and I would be the ones to make the trip. We applied for our passports and made some tentative travel plans, but we both soon realized it wasn't going to work. Will can't be gone that long from either the twins or the business. Christy was devastated when we told her she and her *daed* wouldn't be coming. But then once you agreed to go with me, an idea was planted in my mind. That idea began to grow, that maybe, if you were willing to serve as her nanny, so to speak, Christy could come along after all."

She looked at me, eyes shining, and repeated her original question. "So what do you think, Ada? Would you be willing to help out our family in this way?"

Reaching out, I put a hand on Alice's arm and gave her a squeeze, saying yes, that she had no idea how very much I wanted to do this.

"Thank you," she whispered, patting the top of my hand before I let go.

Out in the yard, Will had raked a pile of leaves together and was motioning for the girls to jump into it. They ran toward it and then abruptly stopped. He leaned the rake up against the tree trunk and showed them how, jumping dramatically into the leaves and then rolling around on the ground. Both girls jumped on top of him, squealing and giggling all the while.

I kept my eyes on the father and his daughters as I asked, "What does Will think of Christy joining us?"

"He's getting desperate about her, to tell you the truth. He thinks it's a wonderful idea, but he doesn't want to overburden you."

That was just like him—thoughtful and giving to the core, except for when it came to the one thing I wanted most from him, his heart.

Mel rolled onto the grass and picked up a large acorn, holding it daintily like a tea cup. She picked up another and handed it to her father. He took it from her gently and lifted it to his mouth, mimicking a sip as Mat plopped down into his lap.

"Ada?"

Startled, I turned my attention back to Alice.

"I was talking about Christy's medical problem."

"Sorry," I said. "The twins are just so cute. It's hard not to watch them." My eyes wandered again. The little girls were up and running now, toward the side of the house, with Will in pursuit. In a moment they were all out of view.

Alice laughed. "I know, I know. And thank goodness they are so cute— otherwise, sometimes, I don't know…" She sighed, shaking her head. "As for Christy, like I said, medication seems to be controlling her irregular heartbeat. But she's still frail. It's almost as if she thinks she can do less than she actually can."

I understood. Having grown up with a chronic medical condition, I didn't want Christy to be sidelined the way I had all those years, to have people hovering around her, always asking how she felt, never letting her go anywhere or do anything. I could help her with her studies *and* her attitude about her health, teaching her how to navigate this difficult time in her life.

"So this is really okay with you, Ada? You're certain you want to do this?" Alice's voice was soft.

"Oh, yes," I said. Sighing deeply, I didn't add that it wasn't just a *want* but a *need*. In some way, I needed Christy every bit as much as she needed me.

TWELVE

Early the next morning, I paid a visit to Leah to collect copies of Christy's books and find out about the curriculum that would be covered while we were away. I purposefully arrived a half hour before the children so I would not disrupt the lessons, but Leah wasn't in the school and the door to the building was locked. The early September morning was crisp and dry. I sat in a swing on the playground and twirled around a little, my shoes dragging over the dirt where the grass had worn away.

When I was younger, our family and the Gundys had belonged to the same church district. Amish families grew quickly, and because our districts were based as much on population as geography, they always had to split when they reached the maximum number of members. Such had happened a few years ago when our one district had become two. But as a child, I had not only worshipped with the Gundys but had gone to school with them as well.

The year I started kindergarten, Will Gundy had been in the seventh grade. His brother John was in the fifth grade, and his sister Hannah was just a year ahead of me. Ezra was a one-year-old, but I would see him often at church, or when their mother, Nancy, came to the school to help. I used to daydream about their family, wondering what it would be like to have three redheaded brothers and a big sister with auburn hair. They were all outgoing and confident. And kind to me. Soon I had a crush on Will, even though it was obvious that he and Lydia Miller were sweet on each other.

Lydia was beautiful, with blond, blond hair and blue eyes. She was always kind to me, too, sitting with me under the oak tree when the older kids played baseball or helping me with my letters by drawing them in the dirt with a stick. She didn't play sports, either. She knew I had a crush on Will but didn't seem to mind. In fact, when I would scurry ahead and take his hand after recess, Lydia would smile. I'm sure she just liked that Will was so kind and gentle with a little girl who always gazed up at him so adoringly.

At home I would play school with my dolls under the pine trees, drawing the letters of the alphabet in the dirt for them as Lydia had done for me. From my first day of school I told my parents and *Mammi* I would be a teacher someday. They smiled and said, "Good for you, Ada. That's a fine thing for a girl to do until she gets married." Because I couldn't imagine myself marrying anyone else but Will, I decided then that if he married Lydia, I would just teach forever.

Even when I was most ill, the dream of teaching did not fade. But then, when I was sick year after year, I began to question my plan to teach at all. How could I take care of thirty students when I was so unwell all the time? At age twenty, when the doctors finally diagnosed my blood disorder, I thought I'd never teach or marry. It wasn't until last spring that my dreams truly began to live again.

Breathing in the dry air, I turned toward the highway. Leah's buggy was almost at the school. I stood, holding onto the chain of the swing, until she'd fed and watered her horse and put him away.

She knew I was there, but it wasn't until she started toward the school that she acknowledged me with a quick hello.

"I wanted to get some of Christy's lessons for our trip," I explained.

I followed her into the schoolroom. Scraps of green and yellow paper were all over the floor. "We did an art project yesterday," she said. Construction-paper sunflowers were stapled above the chalkboard. "I told them to clean up, but—" she spread her arms out "—you can see how well that went over." She sighed.

I felt for her. She was new and trying, but looking around at the chaos, I was sure I would never be so disorganized. Her desk was stacked high with papers. Her face contorted a little, and then she asked me to give her a minute.

I walked around the room, picking up trash and looking at each sunflower. I found Christy's. It was perfect. Every petal in place. The stem centered exactly. Her name written in perfect penmanship in the bottom right-hand corner of the paper.

"Here are a few things," Leah said, approaching me. She handed me a math workbook, a grammar book, and a reading book. "I marked where we are in each."

I thanked her.

"Good luck," she said, stuffing her hands in the pockets of her apron.

I gave her a questioning look.

"It's just that I hope she responds better to you than she has me," Leah said. "I've tried and tried, but she's hard to engage. I asked the older teacher at the school down the road what I should do."

That caught me off guard—Leah Fisher asking anyone for help. "What did she say?"

"To give Christy time. She's been traumatized, and I need to be patient with her."

That sounded like good advice for her teacher, but as her nanny I was going to be in a completely different position. I was pretty sure I could win Christy's trust just as soon as we had a little time together. I said goodbye and slipped out before the first students arrived.

The day before we left on the trip, I went over to Will's to meet with my young charge. When I arrived, Christy was sitting under the oak tree, her skirt and apron perfectly arranged, a thick book open on her lap.

I hitched Rikki to the post and joined her.

"What are you reading?" I asked, though by the size of the volume I knew.

"*Martyrs Mirror*," she answered. Nearly every Amish home had a copy of the massive book, an account of our ancestors who perished for their faith. Christy sighed. "My *grossmammi* told me to read as much as I could."

"What do you think of it?" I kneeled beside her.

She began to yawn and covered her mouth. Then she said, none too quietly, which surprised me, "*Bo*-ring." Maybe Christy Gundy wasn't as shy as I thought, nor as compliant. Maybe that's what Leah had been alluding to.

"History is stupid," she added, quite an unusual statement for a person of our faith to make. From the day we were born, our history was practically drilled into us. It was a huge part of who we were as a people. I couldn't imagine, for example, that she found the story of Dirk Willems boring, the man who rescued his pursuer who had fallen through ice, only to then be arrested. I said as much, and she merely yawned in response.

"So many were martyred, Christy. They were hanged, drowned..."

She put her hands over her ears.

"...burned at the stake. It's in the book on your lap." It registered that she couldn't hear me, so I stopped talking but kept my face straight without a hint of frustration.

She removed her hands.

"You'll see," I said to her, "history won't be boring on this trip. Not the way I'm going to teach it. It will all be very much alive."

She didn't answer as she closed the book and placed it on the grass.

"What do you like to read?" I scooted to a sitting position beside her.

"I don't."

I couldn't imagine not liking to read and couldn't quite believe her. "What's your favorite book so far?" I prodded.

"My *mamm* read me the Little House books when I was young. I liked those."

I agreed. Those were wonderful stories, but she hadn't actually read them—they had been read to her. I decided to change the subject. "How are you feeling about the trip?"

"Fine."

"Have you been away from home before?"

She shook her head.

I remembered spending the night at Aunt Marta's when I was ten, when Ella was two. It was the first time I had ever spent the night away from home, and by midnight I'd worked myself into a full-fledged bout of insomnia. That was when Uncle Freddy was still around because he stayed with Ella while Aunt Marta drove me home. There would be no getting

Christy home in the middle of the night when we were in Europe. I told her my story and she rolled her eyes. I added that the next time I stayed at Aunt Marta's I was fine.

"I'm not worried about being away. I'll have my *grossmammi*," she said.

And me, I wanted to add but didn't. Christy stood and I followed her toward the house.

"What are you looking forward to the most?"

She shrugged.

"Have you ever been on a train?"

She hadn't. We stopped and sat on the steps to the porch, the heavy book balanced on her knees. Sitting there, I told her about my first train ride—my trip to Oregon—and what it was like. "And then, just think, we'll go on a ship. I'm really excited about that." I was aware I sounded as if I were speaking to a little kid. Suddenly I couldn't remember what it was like to be eleven.

"Are you worried about anything?" I ventured.

"*Grossmammi* said we'll be walking a lot. I'm a little worried about that."

"Because of your health?"

"No," Christy responded. "I take a pill every day for that. I just don't like to walk."

I took a deep breath to keep from laughing.

A buggy approached, and I lost Christy's attention. I followed her from the steps to the driveway, expecting to see Hannah or her husband, Jonas.

It was Will, his sorrel prancing along, and beside him on the bench of the spring wagon sat Leah Fisher. Her horse was tied to the surrey hook in the back.

"A wheel fell off my buggy," she explained as Will stopped his horse, and she climbed down. "Will came to my rescue."

Will nodded his head toward me. "Leah's going to call and see if she can reach one of her brothers or her father."

I stood and offered her my cell phone. She took it and said, "I just gave mine up. I'm joining the church, you know."

I didn't tell her I'd heard that. She must have dialed one of her brothers because someone picked up right away. From the one side of the conversation it seemed he would be on his way to collect her soon. She hung up, handed me the phone, and thanked me.

"Come on in to the house," Will said to all of us. "We'll have a snack."

I hesitated, sure Christy didn't want to spend any more time with me and knowing I didn't want to watch Leah spending time with Will. Leah was already leading Christy inside, so I decided I should check in with Alice and then go.

She was in the kitchen slicing apples, and Leah was settling onto a bench at the table, the twins clamoring to sit on either side of her. I wondered how much time she was spending at the house that made the little girls so taken with her.

"Hi, Ada," Mel said, and Matty nodded her head in agreement.

Christy handed her grandmother the book, and Alice set it on the desk near the counter. I told her my passport had arrived but that Zed still hadn't heard from Giselle. The carved box from Lexie hadn't arrived either, but I didn't mention that. We discussed a few last-minute things about the trip, and then I decided to head for home. It was becoming clear that Leah was right. It was going to be difficult to get to know Christy. I'd never known a child who was so distant.

As I drove the buggy, I thought about how comfortable Leah looked with Mel and Matty on either side of her, but Christy puzzled me. I knew how special it was to have one's teacher stop by. I'd had that happen many times during my growing-up years. But Christy didn't seem impressed. She was definitely hard to figure out. Then again, maybe she could see through Leah the way I did. Maybe Christy was a lot smarter than the average eleven-year-old.

When I turned down the lane to our house, I saw Aunt Marta's car parked near the pine trees. *Daed* met me as the lane curved toward the barn, and he said he would unhitch Rikki for me because Marta and her children were waiting in the house to tell me goodbye. When I walked in, Ella hurried toward me, wrapping her arms around my shoulders.

"I wish I were going with you," she chirped.

I wished she were too. For all her faults, she had been a fun and lively traveling companion, and during our trip west we had established certain rhythms and routines that had made our journey run much more smoothly. I hoped Alice and Christy and I could do the same.

Aunt Marta stepped toward me and gave me a hug too. Zed just smiled and waved as he flicked his bangs from his forehead. "I have an email for you," he said. "Giselle finally wrote back."

I snatched the message out of his hand.

> Sorry I took so long to respond. I've been busy. Not sure
> of my schedule during the time you're in Switzerland, but
> call when you arrive and I'll let you know if I'll be around.

She left a number, her cell I assumed, and that was all. I felt sick to my stomach as I folded the paper. Zed and Ella both looked at me with sympathy.

"May I read it?" *Mamm* asked.

I handed the piece of paper to her and watched her as she read it, her expression growing smug. No doubt she was feeling vindicated that her sister obviously would have preferred not to hear from me at all. Once she was finished, though, the smugness faded, and when she looked at me, she did so with compassion in her eyes.

"It's better than nothing," she offered, handing the note back to me. Considering the circumstances, all I could do was agree.

"Your package came today," *Daed* said, nodding toward the table.

I rose and quickly opened it. Lexie's box was inside. I ran my fingers over the carving of Amielbach—the turrets and balconies and surrounding trees, and then over to the waterfall. I'd begun to think Lexie had forgotten to send it. I knew she'd been busy with work and being newly married, and I was grateful she took the time to get it in the mail. It comforted me to bring my sister's box with me, and I decided I'd fill it with Christy's schoolwork to justify the room it would take up in my suitcase.

After I'd said goodbye to Marta, Ella, and Zed and they had left, *Mamm* put an arm around me. "I'm sorry about Giselle."

I leaned against her shoulder. "See? You were worried about nothing."

"*Ya*," she answered. "It looks that way." She sighed. "Giselle was so warm and caring when we were little. Then she made some bad decisions and became self-centered, thinking only about her own wants and not caring how her actions affected all of us. But I realized just now that I have no idea anymore who my sister is. Is she warm and caring again? Or did she stay selfish and self-centered? I actually do hope you'll be able to find out."

I shivered as my mother pulled away. This wasn't like going to Oregon.

It wasn't like taking the train across the country, knowing Lexie would meet me at the station and Sophie would take me back. No. This was a journey of uncertainty.

I was traveling to Switzerland as the nanny of a child who didn't even like me, looking to straighten out a property matter that was more than a hundred and thirty years old, and hoping to see a birth mother who didn't want to meet me.

For a moment, I questioned whether going was something I was meant to do at all.

THIRTEEN

We said our goodbyes the next day beside the van Will had rented to take us to the train station. The sun was high over the cornstalks, but the weather had turned cool during the night and the first hint of fall was in the air. *Mamm* stood with a shawl wrapped tightly around her shoulders. Her face was pale, but it seemed she was doing her best.

"Just come back to us, *ya?*" she whispered when she hugged me one last time.

"*Ya*, of course," I said in return. Of course.

She pulled away from me and reached into her apron pocket. "I put together a list of emergency phone numbers for you—Dr. Morton, Bishop Fisher, the Gundys, Marta, a few others…" she said, handing me a piece of paper. "Just in case."

"But I told you, I'm not taking my cell phone—"

"I know, Ada, but you never know what might come up. Better safe than sorry."

"You're right. Thank you." I slipped her list into the inside pocket of my purse, feeling appreciative of the gesture and smothered by it all at the same time.

Daed hugged me next, but he kept silent, probably to keep the tears in his eyes from spilling onto his cheeks. Alice had stepped from the van to hug *Mammi*, and the two friends clung to each other for a long moment. Then Alice let go and climbed back into the vehicle, returning to her place on the front bench seat next to Will.

I hugged my grandmother tightly, thanking her for making the trip possible. She squeezed me in return, saying, "Tell Giselle I love her. Tell her God loves her."

Unsure if I would get the chance to meet Giselle at all, I merely nodded and asked *Mammi* to keep us in prayer. I hadn't had the heart to show her Giselle's email. Instead, I'd simply said that she'd sent her phone number with instructions to call once we arrived.

I sat in the backseat of the van, next to Christy, and as we pulled out, I turned around to look through the rear window. My parents and grandmother were standing in a huddle in the driveway, watching me leave—once again. Far behind them towered the windmill, its blades slowly rotating in the breeze.

The last time I'd been driven to the Lancaster train station, it had been to set off on an exciting adventure with my cousins, one that would culminate in the sharing of my sister's special day. This trip, however, was far more complex than that, and my stomach was gripped with equal amounts of excitement and fear. All I could do was pray for peace and wisdom—and I hoped they would come soon. Right now my emotions were like our windmill during a storm, spinning wildly out of control.

At the station our driver stayed with the van while Will helped carry our bags to the check-in area. He planned to wait with us until our train was called, which was a good thing, given how sullen and withdrawn Christy had begun acting on the way. We settled in a row of chairs, with the little girl between Will and Alice, and me on Will's other side. Will and Christy talked for a while, but when she grew silent, eyes closed as she rested against Alice, he turned to me and spoke softly.

"Thank you," he said.

"For?"

"Going along. Helping Alice. Taking care of Christy. I'm afraid it's caused some division in your family. We never intended that."

I inhaled deeply. He must have heard about my mother's fears. Perhaps

Ella had told Ezra, who told Will. Or maybe *Mammi* had said something to Alice directly. I shook my head, wishing I could explain how hard *Mamm* was trying, how much I needed to do this, how desperately thrilled I was at the very thought of meeting my birth mother in person. But none of that seemed quite appropriate.

"It's not too bad," I murmured as I gave him a reassuring smile.

He shifted his leg, accidentally pressing his thigh against mine. Quickly, he sat up straighter and pulled it away. We remained silent for a couple of minutes, and then he spoke again. "I'll be praying about you seeing Giselle. I hope it will work out and that it will be a good thing."

I thanked him even as I felt my cheeks flushing with embarrassment. I wondered how much he knew about Giselle, about the fact that I had been conceived out of wedlock, the product of an adulterous relationship she'd had with an older man, one who had left his wife and child to run away and play house for a while with her. Since learning the facts of my life, I had struggled some with the shame of it all, but never more so than now, sitting next to this upstanding man from a perfect family, where the worst thing anyone had ever done was maybe fall asleep during church or tell a little white lie. He must think of me as damaged goods, with an ugly background to go with my very average face.

"I'll also be praying for safety for all of you," he said. Then he smiled, his brown eyes lighting up, and I felt that jolt I often got when I was with him. "I have to admit, I sure wish I were going too."

Before I could think of how to respond, he added, "Make certain Christy gets plenty of rest, will you?"

I nodded, telling him not to worry and that enough sleep was a requirement for me to keep up my health as well. I didn't know if Will was finished with instructions or not, but that was all he had a chance to tell me because it was time for our train. As the other passengers began moving toward the boarding area outside, we stood and gathered our things.

Will hugged his grandmother, and then he lifted his daughter and spun her around.

"Christy Gundy," he cried happily, "you are going to Europe! No one in this family has been there since 1877!"

She rolled her eyes, but once he set her back down and let her go she threw her arms around his waist and hugged him tightly. I could see in her closed eyes and scrunched forehead how very much she loved him. Just because she wasn't expressive with her words didn't mean the feelings weren't there, somewhere deep inside.

Then Christy followed Alice toward the door, a cloth bag over her shoulder and her coat in her other hand. After a quick goodbye to Will, I fell in behind. At the doorway I glanced back to see him still standing there. His face was solemn, but when he spotted me he grinned and waved. I smiled and waved in return before continuing on to the train.

We settled into our seats, with Christy and Alice side by side and me facing them. As we waited for the train to leave the station, Alice said when she was Christy's age she had ridden a train with her brother to visit their older sister in Maryland. Later, as a teenager, she had gone with another sister and her husband on a mission trip to Honduras.

Christy's eyes grew wide. "In Central America?"

"Yes. I was gone seven months."

Christy was clearly impressed. And so was I.

Alice leaned back against the seat. "As the youngest of fifteen children, I was always tagging along with someone." She turned her gaze out the window. "They have all passed away, though. Every single one of them except me."

The train lurched a little and Christy held on to her armrest. When we started moving, Alice clapped her hands together, her moment of sorrow behind her, and we all smiled.

"Oh, girls!" she exclaimed. "Our adventure begins!"

Adventure, indeed. As the train continued to pick up its pace, I felt as if my very soul was rising up inside of me, breaking free from something, surging with strength for whatever lay ahead. Thinking back to the last time I was on a train, I remembered the prayer I'd uttered that one morning, asking God to bless me with even greater adventures ahead. Now here I was traveling to Europe! I knew there was no way that any of this could have happened unless He'd made it so.

The scenery zipping by outside the window mesmerized Christy, and when she wasn't being lulled by it, she was staring at our fellow passengers. A businessman spoke nonstop on his cell phone as he worked away on his laptop. A woman dressed in a short skirt and high heels sat across the aisle from us, her head back against the seat and her eyes closed. Christy stared at the woman, soaking in the scene, until Alice gently patted her great-granddaughter's knee and shook her head. Christy stopped.

A woman with an infant and a little boy sat a couple of rows ahead of us. The little boy kept turning around to stare at Christy. The mother seemed too tired to care. I smiled at the little boy, and he shyly hid his head for just a minute but then grinned, his eyes twinkling.

Three hours later, when the train pulled into New York's Penn Station, I was practically bouncing in my seat with excitement. I'd always wanted to see New York. When others bemoaned the crime and worldliness, I defended it for the museums and the architecture and the people. I knew there would be no museums for me this time—and maybe never—but I was excited to see the city life just the same.

Once we'd collected our bags, we followed the signs to the main lobby, grateful that Daniel had told us to get suitcases that had wheels on them. Each of us rolling a bag behind, we moved quickly up the wide hallways, but everyone else seemed to be walking even faster, streaming around us as if we were rocks in a river. People were in such a hurry that they scarcely even noticed our unusual garb, which came as a welcome relief, especially compared to my trip out West.

When we reached the lobby, it was easy to spot the big schedule board hanging from the ceiling at its center. The three of us made our way to it and then stood directly underneath, as instructed, to wait for the man who was to meet us there. I didn't know what he looked like, just that his name was George Mast, and that he would be escorting us to our hotel and would likely take us to dinner as well. Daniel would be joining up with us at some point later this evening.

As we waited for the man to show up, I asked Alice what she knew about him, and she explained that George was Daniel's partner in their new business venture.

"What kind of business?"

"Why, their tour company, of course. Didn't we tell you about that?"

I shook my head and then listened as she explained further. She said that Daniel and George had been working for months putting together a new tour company, one that would serve the needs of Plain travelers—Amish, Mennonite, Brethren, and more. Their main focus was going to

Anabaptist heritage tours, primarily in Europe. In fact, that was how Daniel had first become involved with our property deed situation. He'd been in Langnau doing research on several potential tour stops when he was approached by the Wasserdorf Historical Society and asked to help with the hydro plant issue.

"I have the feeling that if we can wrap this legal stuff up in time that George and Daniel would like to practice a little of their tour-guiding on us afterward," she added.

I smiled, thinking that we'd probably make quite an interesting sight as we trouped around: three Amish women and two Mennonite men, with an age span between youngest and oldest of more than sixty years.

Holding tightly to Alice's hand as we continued to wait, Christy asked her great-grandmother how we were going to recognize the man if we'd never met him before. Though George was a Mennonite, he wasn't Old Order, so we didn't even know what he'd be wearing.

"We don't have to recognize him, dear," Alice replied brightly. "We're just going to wait right here until *he* finds *us*."

Christy looked to me as if for confirmation, so I winked and said, "We're much easier to spot than your average tourist, don't you think?"

She giggled and looked away.

Ten minutes later, we were still standing there, waiting, when Christy began to get antsy.

"I'm tired," she said.

"We all are," Alice answered.

"And hungry."

"We'll get dinner when we get to the hotel." Alice pulled a bag of peanuts from her purse and handed them over. Christy took them from her sullenly, but at least she complained no further.

Finally, a man with a beard and no mustache emerged from the crowd and came toward us, a broad smile on his face.

"Hello!" His voice rang with enthusiasm. "Mrs. Beiler? Miss Rupp? Miss Gundy?"

He was George, no doubt. A man of about fifty, he had gray hair and a round belly, and he was dressed Plainly in suspenders, a plaid shirt, and black trousers. He held a coat over one hand and a satchel in the other, and I realized that the reason he was late was probably because he'd just come from a train himself.

We all shook hands and then he helped with our bags, leading us through the throngs of people not upstairs to the exit but instead down a side hallway, to the subway. After handing us tokens and showing us how to move through the turnstiles, George explained that we would be getting on here and going down to the financial district, which was close to the harbor. We'd spend the night at a hotel there and then board the ship in the morning.

We reached the area beside the tracks and waited for the subway to come. Nearby stood a man whose bare arms, neck, and even part of his face were covered with tattoos. With him was a woman who had tattooed arms as well, along with piercings all over her ears and nose. I had to force myself not to stare, but then I noticed Alice was staring too, not to mention Christy. It was practically impossible not to.

After a little wait we heard a distant rumble followed by the startling appearance of a sleek silver subway train that screeched to a stop in front of us. After a moment its doors slid open with a whoosh.

"This is us," George said, moving us forward into the train. We all managed to make it on board with our bags intact, but just barely. We hadn't even been able to sit before the doors slid closed again and we were being propelled forward.

I glanced over at Alice, who was standing across from me, gripping a silver pole so tightly her knuckles were white. An orange plastic seat was open right behind her, so I caught her eye and motioned for her to take it. Once she did, Christy leapt forward and squeezed into the seat with her as well. That left me and George to wrangle all of our bags and make sure they didn't tip over and nick anyone in the shins, especially not the tattooed guy, who had pulled out a small knife and was using it to clean his fingernails.

At the next stop a woman in a very normal-looking business suit stepped aboard, but as soon as she settled across from me, I realized that the large purse she was carrying wasn't a purse at all. Instead, it had mesh windows on each end—and a little dog inside! I hoped Christy would notice it, but she was still focused on the couple with the piercings.

Fifteen minutes later, George announced that we were almost to our stop. The next time we came to a halt and the doors opened, the four of us were ready. As one, we got off, gripping our bags tightly and moving forward against the throng of people who were waiting to get on.

Leading the way through the crowd, George was clearly in his element, but I was worried for Alice, who seemed pale and shaken. Once the train had pulled away and the crowd of people had thinned out, I told George we needed a moment to regroup.

"Oh! Of course!" he said, glancing back at the three of us and realizing what was going on. Taking Alice by the arm, he led her over to a bench near the wall. It was filthy, but she gratefully plopped right down on it anyway, apologizing for the delay. Looking at her as she sat there resting, for a moment I was afraid she might not be up to the trip, physically speaking. But then I decided this was more about her being overwhelmed than being exhausted. To be honest, I had found my first-ever subway ride pretty overwhelming as well.

When Alice decided she was ready to continue, George led us to an elevator tucked in near the stairs, and though it was a tight squeeze, we all managed to fit inside. Once its doors opened again, we emerged at street level. We, who were used to a horizontal world, now found ourselves stepping out into a vertical one, an astonishing jumble of towering skyscrapers, flashing signs, and honking horns. This place was amazing—and about as different from our Lancaster County landscape as I could imagine.

"Now we'll walk to our hotel," George announced, taking the handle of Alice's bag and once again leading the way.

"Will Daniel be there?" Christy asked, falling in step behind him.

"Not until later. He's doing research right now at the New York City Historical Society. He'll probably stay till they close."

We continued walking, and after a few minutes Christy spoke again.

"How much farther is it?" she asked with a slight whine to her voice.

George said it was just a few blocks. But those blocks were long, and as we continued, Christy's steps seemed to grow shorter and shorter. I kept an eye on her, concerned for her health. Then I remembered her saying how much she hated to walk and realized she was just being lazy.

I felt a little nervous when George paused at a street corner, pulled a map from his pocket, and compared it with the signs overhead. But then, after craning his neck to look in several directions, he finally grinned and pointed off to our right. Sure enough, halfway up the block was a sign indicating *The Harbor Hotel*, though it was hard to imagine a harbor anywhere around here when all we could see were skyscrapers.

Alice and Christy and I were soon settled in our room, which was small but clean, with a large window, two medium-sized beds, and a tiny little bathroom. Alice still looked tired, so I insisted that she stretch out on the bed to relax. As she did, I went into the bathroom with my comb to tidy my hair. All the while Christy busied herself with flipping various light switches on and off before turning on the television and playing with the remote control. Just when I was starting to get a headache from the barrage of sound, Alice told her that was enough and made her turn it off.

In the quiet, I tried to remember what I'd heard about Christy's medical condition. I wasn't sure of the name, but it had something to do with her heart and was the same disorder that had caused her mother's death. Lydia had died because she hadn't even know she had the condition and had ignored numerous symptoms, including extremely high blood pressure during pregnancy. My aunt Marta had been Lydia's midwife, and despite Marta's many warnings on the subject, Lydia had never gone to her doctor to get checked out. Consequently, she'd ended up dying in childbirth. Christy, on the other hand, wouldn't share the same fate, simply because knowledge was power. Being fully aware of her condition meant Christy could safeguard her health in all of the ways that would prevent the same thing from ever happening to her.

Daniel still hadn't shown up by dinnertime, so when we met up with George in the lobby, he said we would have to eat without him. George took us to a little Italian restaurant down the street, and though I'd never had real Italian food before, I found it to be quite tasty. Christy was especially taken with an appetizer called "calamari," though once George explained it was fried squid, she seemed to lose her appetite for it a bit.

By the time the main course arrived, George was telling us all about the new tour company he and Daniel were establishing. He thanked us for being a part of their research voyage, but we didn't remind him that our main reason for coming on this trip had nothing to do with his tour company's research and everything to do with settling a property issue.

"I couldn't have done any of this without Daniel, of course," George continued, sticking a fork into his platter of spaghetti and turning it slowly in a circle. "That kid is brilliant. I can't believe the information he's dug up. When all is said and done, we're going to have some amazing tours, with a number of stops that are exclusively available only through us."

Christy was watching George with fascination as he finished spinning the fork and lifted it from the plate, revealing a perfect, spiraled ball of spaghetti wrapped around the tines. Pausing, he added, "The only problem with that boy is that he gets so caught up in his work that he forgets to eat or sleep. I'm sure that's what's keeping him now. Probably doesn't have a clue how late it's gotten."

"Who could forget to eat or sleep?" Christy replied as George slid the large bite into his mouth and began to chew. "He sounds weird." I remembered Christy hadn't met him the day I did at her home.

"He's not weird," Alice corrected. "Daniel is a very nice young man." Clearly, through all of their dealings, he'd managed to win her trust.

Considering that in the morning we'd be boarding a ship to sail across an ocean, I could only pray that that trust was well founded.

FOURTEEN

The next morning we rose well before dawn, dressed, and packed our bags. When we reached the lobby, George directed us toward a room with coffee and pastries, and then he darted back out to the lobby, his cell phone in his hand. Daniel was nowhere to be seen. A few minutes later George came back in just as we'd settled down at a table and told us to hurry, that the taxi had arrived to take us to the ship.

Alice caught up with George in the lobby. "What about Daniel?"

"I'm not sure," he muttered, shaking his head. "I hope he'll manage to meet up with us. That kid…"

"If he doesn't make it," she persisted, concern furrowing her brow, "would we leave without him?" Clearly, this was not an idea she was in favor of.

Obviously hearing the tone of her voice, George assured her he had no doubt Daniel would get there in time.

The streetlights were still on as we hurried through the revolving door and out into the cool morning air, wrestling with our luggage while also trying to keep a grip on our pastries. Out on the sidewalk, Christy held back a little as the driver loaded our bags into the trunk of the taxi. "Seven days is a long time on a ship," she said.

I agreed. "But it's going to be a lot of fun."

"You know," George told her, "not very many people in this world can say they sailed on a cargo vessel."

Christy smiled a little at that, even though George was appealing to her pride. Alice remained silent as we all climbed into the taxi.

The driver drove down the narrow streets, swerving back and forth between lanes. Horns honked. A man darted across the street in front of us.

The driver said he didn't take many people down to the commercial part of the harbor. "I make a lot of trips to the cruise ship docks, but not the cargo docks."

George explained that the simplicity of the cargo ships suited our lifestyle more. But I also suspected it was easier, in this case, to book a cargo ship than a cruise ship at such late notice.

The driver looked in the rearview mirror, directly at me, then nodded and said he could see that we were simple people. I blushed at his words and quickly looked out the window. In a few minutes, a sea of cargo containers appeared and I knew we were close.

"What's in all of those boxes?" Christy asked.

Glad that I had read up on all of this with my library books, I explained that it could be anything, really. "Whatever's shipped by sea—clothes, appliances, electronics, food…"

She wrinkled her nose. "Wouldn't food rot?"

"There are refrigerator containers. Even freezer containers." I pointed to some mammoth contraptions ahead of us. "See those big cranes? They lift the containers onto the ship. The men who work down here are called longshoremen."

"Can women load the ships?"

"Sure."

"Plain women?"

I smiled. "What do you think?"

Her nose was pressed to the window now. "It looks like fun."

It did. Already I could feel an excitement, a vibrancy in the air, and I suspected Christy felt it too. We stopped at a little hut where a security woman in a uniform came out and checked our passports and George's paperwork.

"I usually just check in sailors," she told us, smiling. "I've never had a van full of Amish people come through my checkpoint before."

"Three Amish and one Mennonite," George corrected, smiling in return.

She stepped back and waved us on through. "You folks have a nice trip."

As we continued on, containers stacked four high lined both sides of the street, in colors of blue, orange, gray, and green. It felt as if we were miniature people plopped down among a child's game of blocks.

Ahead of us loomed a giant ship with cargo stacked on it from bow to stern, and more was still being added. The white superstructure, with a smokestack rising above it, contrasted against the colorful containers. The name *Whitebird Trader* was painted on the side, toward the bow, just above the anchor.

We marveled at the enormity of the ship. I'd expected it to be big, but the size took my breath away. It would cover our cornfield and pasture combined back home, and its height was equivalent, I was sure, to a building of at least several stories.

Our driver pulled into a parking space close to the dock, one that was near the loading ramp but out of the way of all the activity around us. Still staring up at the massive vessel that would carry us across the sea, we climbed out of the van into the cold air.

"It smells *salty* here," Christy exclaimed.

Eyes wide, Alice and I both agreed. Inhaling deeply, I realized I could almost taste ocean water, brine, and seaweed just from the scent of the air.

As the men were unloading the trunk, a jet flew overhead, coming in pretty low. The driver, who had seemed to take a liking to me, nodded up to the sky.

"This trip only takes eight hours by plane, you know," he said with a wink.

I smiled in return. "Ah, but just think of all the things we'd never see."

"Yeah." He hoisted another bag out of the back. "Water. Lots of water."

He laughed at his own joke, grabbing another bag.

"George!"

We all turned toward the shout to see Daniel coming toward us. He wore a button-down shirt with a brown jacket, faded jeans, and had a pack on his back. His hair was just as yellow as I remembered, the color of lemons in the early morning sunshine. As he got closer, I could see that there was a bounce in his step and a wide grin on his face.

"Where have you been?" George asked, sounding less irritated than he had a right to, in my opinion.

"The usual," Daniel replied, laughing. "I lost track of time, so I just went ahead and spent the night at the Y. I called you this morning, but you didn't answer. I left you a voice mail."

George pulled out his phone. "Is that what that symbol's for?"

Daniel laughed again, and as the two men shook hands he told George that while they were at sea he was going to sit down and give him a lesson on how to use the satellite phone he'd bought for the trip.

Next, Daniel turned toward Alice, giving her a warm smile and handshake. She did not smile in return. Obviously recognizing the stiffness of her demeanor, he added, "I'm very sorry if my absence caused you any concern. If you knew me better, you'd know it was no big deal and that I would show up in the end. I always do somehow."

Though his statement seemed prideful to me, it seemed to have the desired effect on her. Immediately, her shoulders relaxed and her features softened.

"Yes, well, try not to let that happen when you start giving tours for real," she scolded him fondly. "Your customers would find such behavior quite unsettling."

Appropriately contrite, Daniel nodded and thanked her for her input. Behind him I couldn't miss the gratified sparkle in George's eyes. No doubt the man had said the same thing to his young partner before. Perhaps the words would carry far more weight having come from Alice now as well.

The matter settled, Daniel then turned to me, saying it was good to see me again. He shook my hand, his grip warm and strong and sinewy. After that he focused on Christy, exclaiming, "And this must be Miss Christy Gundy!"

She giggled shyly and let him give her a handshake as well.

"I'm Daniel Hart. It's a pleasure to meet you. I've been looking forward to it." He spoke with a flourish, both in his voice and gestures. "I was so excited to learn you'd be joining us."

"Pleased to meet you too," she replied, her voice sounding stronger. For the first time that I'd seen, Christy's eyes lit up. She stood taller. Suddenly she seemed like the eleven-year-old that she was, not the eight- or nine-year-old she usually seemed to be.

"Just think, Christy," Daniel continued, "soon you'll be returning to the very ground your ancestors were forced to leave behind more than a hundred and thirty years ago."

She nodded solemnly, hanging on his every word.

"I spent all of yesterday learning more about those ancestors. I found a record and their names in an actual ship log from when they arrived here in New York. The history of your family is fascinating."

Christy's eyes grew wide. Funny, she'd had no interest in her relatives or in history before.

Before he could elaborate, George took a step forward to interrupt.

"Daniel, you can save all of that for later, if you don't mind. Now that we're finally all together, I wanted to say a few words and then we can board the ship."

Behind him, our cab was just pulling out of its parking space. Before driving away, the man rolled down his window, gave us a wave, and called out a "Bon voyage!" Grinning, we all waved in return, and then we focused again on George, who had to speak loudly to be heard over the clamor all around.

George gave us an overview of our itinerary, the schedule for while we were on the ship, and the sites he hoped that we'd be able to see while we were in Europe, if we had time to do any touring once the property matter was settled. His little speech seemed forced, but I realized that this was something he wanted to do for the actual tours, and he was practicing it on us.

"If there's anything else you want to see or do, let me know," he concluded, looking from Alice to me. "Any questions?"

We shook our heads.

He turned toward Daniel. "Anything you want to add?"

"Perhaps a quick prayer," Daniel replied. Then he surprised me by reaching out and taking the hands of George and Christy, who were standing on either side of him. Startled, Alice set down the bag she'd been holding and took Christy's other hand and then mine as well. George and I reached out for each other, our grasp completing the circle.

"I know the Amish don't generally pray aloud," Daniel told us, "but if you'll indulge me just this once, I'd like to do this one my way."

We bowed our heads, and he offered a brief but lovely expression of thanks, petition, and worship. As he spoke, I could feel myself being calmed somewhere deep inside. Even the hand-holding, which had felt uncomfortable at first, began to seem right, as if it were bonding us, under God, this little band of travelers embarking on the journey of a lifetime. Daniel ended the prayer with the exact words I needed to hear, saying, "And as we travel, Father, please bless all of the loved ones we leave behind. Calm their spirits, soothe their concerns, and give them strength and patience until we return."

Thanks to my last trip, I was ready this time. When Daniel ended and gave his "amen," I was right there with him, calling it out loudly just as everyone had done at Lexie's wedding reception. Strangely, George did not do the same, which made it a chorus of two.

We all opened our eyes, and though Daniel gave me a smile, I could see that both Christy and Alice were more than a little startled by my outburst.

"I guess that's it, then," George said happily, looking to Daniel. "Is there anything else to say before we go?"

"Just..." Daniel said dramatically, turning to sweep his arm wide toward the gangplank, "'Welcome aboard!'"

We all cheered. Christy surprised me by leading the way, marching ahead with a quick step up the narrow, metal ramp. I let the others, including Daniel and George, go ahead of me so that I could bring up the rear more slowly. I planned to savor every moment of this journey, starting now.

Stepping onto the ramp, I thought of a man Silas had told me about named Jonathan Fisher. Though Plain, he had managed to travel broadly in his time. A native of Lancaster County, Fisher had visited Europe as a young man in the early nineteen hundreds and later sailed around the world during the 1930s. In the 1950s, when he was in his old age, he had even gone back to Europe again. Somehow, I felt a kinship with him, with his adventuresome spirit. I, too, knew the feeling that propelled such travel, especially since I'd taken the trip out West.

Halfway up the ramp I paused, taking in the scene in front of me. Fog swirled around the harbor. A horn blasted in the distance. I tried to imagine where all the ships in the harbor would go, but the idea of it was more than I could comprehend. The world was so wide, so vast. All those places. All those people. All those experiences. One could travel for a lifetime and still not manage to see everything.

"Come on, Ada!" Christy called from a distance. I looked up to see her and Alice standing down a ways, at the rail, beaming at me.

Giving them a wave, I twirled in a tight circle, my head tilted upward toward the startling blue sky. Then I continued on up the ramp, my heart full of gratefulness for this opportunity. This trip would most likely be my last, and I vowed to make as much of it as I possibly could.

At the top of the gangplank, as I stepped onto the deck, I thought I could feel a loosening of something, an unbinding of sorts. Nearby, a sailor was untying a knot, and as I watched him, I realized exactly what that feeling was: my mother's tight grip, slowly slipping away.

FIFTEEN

After checking us in, the steward led us to our cabins. On the way, he showed us the dining hall and the recreation room, explaining the schedules for both. When Christy asked him about the other passengers, he said that only one other person would be coming along. Otherwise, it was all crew—forty of them, to be exact.

When we reached our cabin, I was pleased to see that it had two rooms—a dayroom with a couch and small table, and a bedroom with two beds. Though the bedroom had no windows, there was a large port-hole in the dayroom. Looking through the thick glass to the outside, we could see several vessels, a tugboat, and a ferry, which I pointed out to Christy.

"We'll set sail in about an hour," the steward told us as he was leaving, "so be sure you're up on deck by then. It's always exciting to watch."

Once he was gone, Christy sat down at the table and said, matter-of-factly, that there didn't seem to be very much to do here.

"Sure there is," Alice told her. "We'll visit. Read. Walk on deck."

"And do schoolwork," I added.

Christy groaned.

"And we can check out the recreation room." I turned around on the couch to face her. "The steward said it's always open, and we're free to use it any time."

Moving into the bedroom, we unpacked our things quickly and then decided to explore the ship. The three of us put on our capes and off we went. First we checked out the recreation room more thoroughly, which had some exercise equipment, including a treadmill, a game table with padded chairs, and a shelf full of much-used board games. In the back was a large Ping-Pong table with plenty of room around it for play.

Next we headed up to the deck and watched as the huge, spiderlike machines continued to load containers onto the ship, and then the longshoremen secured them in place. Daniel joined us there, and he seemed happy to answer our many questions and explain the various sights to us.

"What's a satellite phone?" Christy asked him after a while, referring to the earlier exchange between Daniel and George. I was glad she asked, because I'd been wondering the same thing myself.

Daniel explained that it worked just like a regular cell phone except that it connected through satellites instead of land-based cell towers. "That makes it a lot cheaper for overseas use," he added. "I'm glad he got it, because once we reach Europe I'll have to keep my regular cell turned off. Can't afford to use it over there."

I was about to reply that I had left mine at home for the very same reason when Daniel's eyes widened slightly and he gestured behind us, toward the gangplank. Christy and I turned to see a young woman just coming on board. She had long, chestnut hair hanging loose around her shoulders and was wearing jeans and a sweatshirt. Around her neck was a camera, on her back a pack.

She was cute, with an air of confidence, and as the steward greeted her and led her off to check in, I realized something about her reminded me of Leah Fisher. Great. That was just what I needed, a constant reminder of the woman who had stolen my true love and my job. *At least Leah wasn't able to steal this trip from me,* I thought. Then again, as Silas had said, it was because of this very trip that Will was now home and available, free for the taking.

The sun was growing warmer, but a chill was rising up from the water, so I tucked my hands inside my cape as we continued to explore. Off to our right was Ellis Island and the Statue of Liberty. I pointed them out to Christy, adding that our family had come to America so long ago that neither structure had even been built yet.

Daniel seemed impressed that I knew that. "Your ancestors arrived when the port of immigration was at the Castle Clinton in Battery Park," he said. "I was doing some research on that too." He pointed to the New York City skyline. "That's where the ferry to Lady Liberty departs from, but it's hard to see it from here."

Christy stared at Daniel with admiring eyes as he continued to point out various landmarks along the shore. As they talked, Alice stood next to them with her hands shoved under her cape, the wind whipping the ties of her *kapp* to the side.

Eventually, she interrupted to ask Daniel if he had received any updates from Herr Lauten.

Daniel said he had. The man had invited all of us to stay at Amielbach even though he was a couple of weeks away from his grand opening of the inn. Unfortunately, the agreement still hadn't been located, but Lauten was optimistic that we would find it before the township's deadline.

Alice nodded, and looking at her I realized she didn't seem worried about the contract or the deadline at all. I wasn't sure if that was because she was being unrealistic or because she had faith the needed document would be found in time.

Soon the longshoremen began to leave the ship, and the sailors started untying the thick ropes that had been holding us to the dock. Once they were done, and a truck had rolled the gangplank away, we were finally adrift.

After that Daniel brought us to the other side to show us the tugboats that would be pushing us out of the harbor. We watched the crew attach steel cables from the tugs to the ships.

"How can they move us?" Christy asked. "They're so small."

"Oh, you'll see," he replied sagely.

The ship's horn blew, startling us all. Christy's hands flew to her ears even as she grinned. My heart warmed at the sight of how animated she'd become.

The ship began to move as the tugboats pulled, slowly at first and then picking up speed. The red bricks of the buildings on Ellis Island contrasted against the blue sky, as did the vibrant green of the Statue of

Liberty and the gold of her flame. She grew bigger and bigger as the ship moved across the bay. A helicopter whirred past overhead. Boats bobbed on the water on every side. Seagulls screeched as they soared. Grinning, I took it all in, my spirit soaring as well.

Daniel pulled out his camera, snapped some photos, and then he asked me to take a picture of him with Lady Liberty in the background. I complied, though I had to press the button several times before I finally got it right.

Taking the camera back from me, Daniel slid it into his pocket and then surprised and touched us all by raising his arms and declaring loudly: "Give me your tired, your poor, your huddled masses yearning to breathe free, the wretched refuse of your teeming shore. Send these, the homeless, tempest-tossed to me!"

Swallowing down the lump that had risen in my throat, I prayed suddenly that during this trip Christy would come to realize the value of the most important thing America had given to our ancestors and to us: the freedom to worship.

Far down the railing, I spotted the young *Englisch* woman standing by herself, her long hair blowing out behind. I decided to walk down to her and introduce myself, but just as I started that way, she began moving in the opposite direction. Thinking she planned to walk all the way around the ship, I decided to wait until the curve of the rail brought her back to us again. But when time passed and she never reappeared, I realized I'd been mistaken. No matter. Lunch was only an hour away. We could introduce ourselves then.

The vessel picked up speed, and as it did the wind began to whip against my face and *kapp*. Soon, Christy complained of being cold.

"Let's stay put until we're out of the harbor," Alice said, placing her arm around the girl. I stepped closer too, trying to create a shield. We stayed that way for quite a while, not talking much but simply gazing at the rays of the sun shimmering on the surface of the water. Speaking loudly so she could hear me over the wind, I reminded Christy that we were retracing, in reverse, the route that our ancestors had taken so long ago. She nodded but did not reply.

A little later, as the ship left the bay and moved into open water, Alice offered to take Christy back down to the cabin. Although I was reluctant to leave the deck, I said I would come along as well. Christy was primarily in my care, after all. Beyond that, I wasn't sure I should be alone with Daniel, unchaperoned, even if we were out on deck in full view of anyone who happened to look our way.

At lunch we finally met the other passenger, though she seemed a little wary as she joined our group and sat down. The cook had already placed on the table a pot of beef barley soup, a platter of meat and cheese, a basket of bread, and a plate of vegetables, and we'd said our silent grace. We introduced ourselves as we served up the food and began to eat, explaining where we were from. By her expression she seemed slightly amused by our clothing, but she didn't actually say anything about us being Plain.

In response, she said she was from California and her name was Morgan McAllister.

"Like the horses?" Christy blurted out. When we all laughed, she blushed and covered her mouth.

"Morgan horses," I explained, patting my young charge on the arm, "are common in Lancaster County."

"I see," Morgan replied, looking at Christy. "I thought you meant McAllister horses, which are common in California."

Her face was so serious that we all thought it was true. Then she smiled and told us she was kidding, that there was no such thing as a McAllister horse. We laughed again, Christy the hardest of all.

"I decided to take a year off and travel," Morgan went on, relaxing a bit. "But only by train or ship. Airplanes use up way too many carbon points."

Before any of us could respond to that, she asked why we were traveling by ship.

"It fits our simple lifestyle," George answered.

"Same reason then," she said, her tone matter-of-fact.

Alice and I exchanged glances, knowing it really wasn't the same at all.

There was a silence around the table for a minute, and then Morgan asked if any of us had heard an update on the weather.

George nodded, and from their ensuing conversation I realized he'd neglected to tell us that some very nasty storms were out there, including a tropical storm brewing south of Bermuda. "But I spoke to the captain just a while ago," he assured us, "and he said that we'd be avoiding the worst of it. We'll get some rain for a day or two, but the winds shouldn't be too bad. After that it should be clear sailing ahead."

At least a few rainy days would give Christy and me plenty of time to do her lessons. I planned on starting in the morning, establishing a regular schedule we would maintain for the seven days we'd be on the ship.

Later, after lunch, Alice and Christy both wanted a nap, but I was feeling far too restless to sleep. Instead, I went back up on deck, where I was startled to find the wind whipping my skirt around furiously. I pulled on the down coat I'd brought along just in case, though I did so more for modesty's sake than because of the cold. Cut on a narrow bias and made of stiff fabric, the coat held its shape well and would keep my legs from being exposed, at least above the knees.

Looking out at the horizon, I saw there was no longer any land in sight, and that made my heart race, both for the thrill and the threat of it. Gray clouds scudded across the horizon, swallowing the blue sky. Walking slowly along the deck, I breathed in the salty air. Crew members stared as I walked by, making me decidedly uncomfortable. I was used to being the subject of interest to tourists, of course, but there was something a little too familiar about the way these men were looking at me. As I came around to the front of the ship, I was relieved to see Daniel there, talking with one of the crew.

He was wearing a blue stocking cap, his face red from the stinging wind. When he spotted me, he grinned and waved, and then he asked if he could join me on my walk. Thinking again about the suitability of our being unchaperoned, I decided it probably wasn't an issue. Chaperoned or not, I felt far safer with him by my side than I had when walking alone. I told him that would be fine, and he fell into step beside me.

Despite the wind that tried to carry our words away, Daniel and I managed to chat as we walked—about the enormity of the ship, the choppy water, the coming storm. He asked me about myself, wanting to know where exactly in Lancaster County I lived, what my father did, and how many siblings I had. He was surprised when I said I was an only child, as not very many Plain people could say they had no siblings. Of course, I now had Lexie, but I didn't want to reveal my whole story to him. As far as he was concerned, the woman I was hoping to visit in Switzerland was my aunt, which was true. That she was also my birth mother was a matter far too private to share with someone I'd just met.

I asked Daniel about himself, and he said he'd grown up in Ohio on a small dairy farm. Besides tending the farm, both his mother and father had taught at the local high school, education being a big deal in his family. Travel was important to them too, Daniel said. He'd traveled a lot with his parents growing up, and on his own he'd been to Guatemala and Brazil on mission trips, and he'd spent the previous summer in Europe.

"It must be exciting, to travel so extensively," I said.

He nodded, adding that it was also a lot easier when that travel was done by air. By the tone of his voice, I realized he wished we were on a plane right now rather than on this ship. He could have been, if not for us. As Mennonites he and George were free to fly, whereas we Amish were expected to limit flights to emergency or special situations. An Amish person on an airplane wasn't completely unheard of, but it certainly wasn't encouraged, and in some districts it was totally forbidden.

"I like traveling this way," I said, thinking of the nice taxi driver who didn't get it either.

He smiled. "In comparison to?"

"Well, a buggy. Or train. Or automobile."

He laughed. "Basically everything but an airplane?"

I smiled back, and though I felt no great need to experience flight, I couldn't help but envy him his freedom, including that he could spend the night in Manhattan by himself. I asked him what the Y was, as I wasn't familiar with that term.

"It's like a hostel," he answered. "Bare accommodations—bathroom down the hall, lousy mattress—but it's cheap." He grimaced. "Poor George. I'm what you might call a very organized airhead. I can track down an obscure piece of history in no time—but then forget to sleep for three days."

I couldn't imagine that. I asked how he managed to survive schooling, and if he had compromised his health for the sake of his studies.

He laughed, saying he'd been known to miss a meal or two, not to mention that he'd seen more than his share of sunrises without benefit of having slept.

"I hope to go to the University of Zurich for my master's degree," he added. "I suppose I'll end up being just as bad there, especially if the library is open twenty-four hours." He started to go on but then hesitated, saying I probably wasn't very interested in hearing about his educational plans.

"Oh, no. I'm fascinated by the life of a scholar."

"Even though it's not an option for you?"

I must have bristled because he immediately apologized.

"Apology not necessary," I said, and then I explained that I hadn't stopped studying just because I'd graduated, and that I loved to learn. "If you go to school in Zurich, all your classes will be in German, right?"

"*Ya*," he said. "But it's not a problem. I speak fluent German, and I've been taught High German and Swiss German too." Glancing at me, he added, "I'm kind of hoping that by the end of this trip I will have picked up a little Pennsylvania Dutch as well."

Smiling, I glanced away. I didn't tell him that even though Pennsylvania Dutch was our first language, we tended to shift into English when with others, lest we seem rude or exclusionary.

"So is there a family in your future?" I teased, changing the subject.

He blushed. "God willing. A small family. I can't see being able to support too many children—but a wife and one child would make me very happy."

Now it was my turn to blush. I hadn't meant to be forward. There was no doubt about it. Daniel Hart was an easy person to talk with. I would have to take care not to let my tongue run away with me in the future, but I couldn't resist saying, "I hope you'll have more than one child."

"Why?"

"It's so lonely. I hated it."

"No way! I was an only child, and I loved it," he said. I wrinkled my nose, and he laughed. "Of course you would feel that way. Look at who I'm talking to. What's the average number of children for an Amish couple now, anyway? Seven? Eight?"

I shrugged. I had no idea, though that sounded about right. Amish or not, I couldn't imagine not wanting a house full of children. I couldn't imagine loving someone who did.

Suddenly, images of Will filled my mind. Showing the twins how to dive into the pile of leaves. Sipping tea from an acorn handed to him by Mel. Holding Mat in his lap. That was the world I wanted, the world I would never have. My good mood evaporated at the very thought.

At that moment, several fat raindrops landed on my face. Wiping them away, I looked around and realized that the sky had grown dark—as dark as dusk—and the waves of the sea had begun to churn wildly beneath us. More rain began to fall, giving me an excuse to tell Daniel goodbye for now and head back down to my cabin.

Once there, I entered quietly, glad to see that Alice and Christy were still asleep. Moving toward the couch, I sat and leaned my forehead against the porthole, watching through the glass as the driving rain, like sheets of metal, cut sharply into the water, much as the pain was cutting through my heart.

SIXTEEN

At dinner all anyone wanted to talk about was the storm. Rain had been pelting the ship for a couple of hours, and we could feel the waves rocking us to and fro. I took comfort in the fact that our vessel was a big one, as I hoped that meant it would weather the storm well overall. At least none of us was feeling seasick thus far.

Morgan joined us late again, arriving just after we'd said the prayer. Sliding into her seat, she apologized for the interruption and immediately began serving herself from the platters of food at the center.

Making conversation, Alice asked Morgan about her plans once we reached Europe. She replied that she would be taking the train from Le Havre, France, where the ship would be bringing us, to Basel, Switzerland, where her father lived.

"We're going to Switzerland too," Christy volunteered, though Alice shot her a look for interrupting.

Nonplussed, Morgan went on to say that her parents had divorced when she was in high school and her father worked for an international bank. He'd lived in Switzerland for the last three years, but this was her first time to visit him. She planned to stay two months.

"I'll be taking a lot of short trips to other locations from there," she added. "Obviously, there's a lot to see and learn. It'll be handy to have him as my home base, so to speak."

"Will your father be able to travel with you?" Alice asked.

Morgan shook her head. "Nah, he's not one for museums and historical sites anyway. He's all about business. I'm afraid my mother is too. She's the vice president of a land management firm. I've always been the odd one out."

"How so?" Alice probed.

Morgan passed the mashed potatoes to Christy. "Oh, I'm just not into all that corporate stuff. I took an economics class my freshman year of college and nearly flunked it. I've never been so bored in my life."

"But all of life is business," George said. "Running a household. Making a living. Planning for retirement. There's no way around it, you know."

"I get that." She passed the gravy. "But I didn't want it to be my main focus."

"So what did you major in?" Daniel held his fork in his hand but hadn't started eating yet.

"Art history."

"I imagine your parents were pleased about that," Daniel teased.

She smiled at that, just a little. "Thrilled. They flipped, said a degree like that was useless and that I'd never amount to anything." She frowned. "Of course, given that I've been out of college for two years now, they may have had a point."

"Why? What have you been doing since you graduated?" Daniel asked.

"Nothing much, really. Mostly just trying to figure things out." She shrugged. "I did some volunteer work. Helped my mom start a recycling program at her office. Took a few classes, for fun, at the Los Angeles County Museum of Art." She started to take a bite of her food, paused, and then added, "This trip was my mother's idea. She thinks there's something I have to get out of my system first and then I'll be ready to settle down."

Listening to her, I decided we had that in common. During my memorable morning in Montana on the train, I had realized there was something I needed to get out of my system too, and thus I'd resolved to embark on my *rumspringa* for real. Whether Morgan used that word to describe it or not, her longings didn't seem all that dissimilar to mine.

"When I get back to L.A., my mom thinks I'll be ready to find a real job. But I'll probably just try to get on somewhere as a barista or a waitress. Something to carry me over until I decide about graduate school."

I felt a pang of empathy for Morgan McAllister, and it struck me that she was nothing like Leah Fisher at all. While Leah was flirty and giddy and upbeat, Morgan was darker, more serious, and most of all kind of sad.

The next morning, after breakfast, Christy, Alice, and I strolled along the deck of the ship. A light mist hovered in the air, but at least it wasn't raining. Ahead, Morgan was huddled under a blanket on one of the deck chairs, reading a book. We stopped and said hello, and Alice asked what she was reading.

"*Jane Eyre*. Have you read it?" Morgan lifted the book so we could see the cover.

We both said we hadn't.

"You should." She smiled at Christy. "I first read it when I was about your age, and I try to read it again every few years. It's my favorite, an old-fashioned romance."

Christy perked up a little at that, which wasn't missed by Alice—or Morgan.

"Not to worry. It's actually quite, um, wholesome. I'd be happy to pass it on when I'm finished." Morgan looked from Alice to me.

"I'd like to read it," Christy said.

Alice merely pursed her lips, so Morgan suggested she take a look at it first herself so she could decide if it was suitable for her granddaughter. "I'll be done with it in a couple of days, and then you're welcome to borrow it."

The book wasn't as big as the *Martyrs Mirror*, but it was large. I wasn't sure Christy would stick with it even if she started it.

"Speaking of reading," I said. "It's time for our first lesson."

Christy grunted.

"We'll do long division first."

Christy groaned.

"And then history and then a writing assignment."

Christy sighed.

"Oh, lucky you," Morgan gushed with sincerity. "Well, maybe not as far as the math, but the history…"

I agreed with her and appreciated her being so positive—minus her math comment—in front of Christy. Studying history and geography was the closest I'd come to traveling, until this year.

Twenty minutes later, back downstairs in our cabin and well into our math lesson, I realized Christy had no idea how to do long division. "Didn't you study it at school?" I pressed. Her last teacher had had several years of experience, so I couldn't imagine how this had managed to slip through the cracks.

"I think so," Christy answered. "But I didn't get it then, either." She had probably been too distraught after her mother died to focus much on schoolwork. She'd no doubt missed a lot of days because of her heart problem as well. When I was child, some years my condition had kept me home for weeks at a time. The difference between me and Christy, though, was that I so loved learning that even when I had to miss class, I still kept up with the work.

Focusing on my young charge, I wrinkled my nose. I hadn't prepared myself to teach her long division. "Let's see." I did my best but soon realized the problem was that she didn't know her multiplication tables either, at least not well. She always came up with the answer eventually, but every time was a struggle. Encouraged by my assessment, I quickly made some flash cards from the paper I'd brought, explaining I would create a complete set in our spare time. If I could drill her enough to imbed these multiplication tables in her brain, I knew long division would be a piece of cake.

I was totally engrossed in the lesson and couldn't believe it when Christy said, "It's noon."

Surprised, I looked at the clock on the bedside table. She was right. How had three hours disappeared so quickly?

After lunch, Daniel, Christy, and I headed toward the rec room to play Ping-Pong. Daniel said he needed to forewarn us that he'd studied Ping-Pong in college and was quite good. That made me laugh. Was that the sort of thing I'd missed out on by not having a higher education?

"For a gym credit," he said in his own defense. "We also did bowling, horseshoes, and shuffleboard."

Daniel said that if we had another person, we could play teams, so along the way we drafted a reluctant Morgan to join us. First up were

Daniel and Christy against Morgan and me. Though Christy had never played Ping-Pong before, she mimicked the way Daniel held his paddle and was soon slamming the ball with a flourish. She also laughed and giggled a lot, showing a playful side I hadn't seen in her before.

She also grew far braver, at one point openly mimicking Daniel as she tucked her foot behind her and swung for the ball.

"Is that really how I look?" he cried.

"No, wait. I left something out," she said. Then she did it again, only this time as she swung she called out, "Give me your weak, your tired, your poor people!"

We all exploded in laughter, even Daniel. Soon our game was done, with Daniel and Christy the victors.

"How about we play Round the World this time?" Morgan proposed, explaining a game that sounded as though it would have us running around the table a bit. We played it for a while, and it did. Eventually I dropped out, saying I needed to take a break.

Christy pointed her paddle at Daniel. "You and me, how 'bout it? Two out of three?"

He agreed, so Morgan stepped back to stand and watch with me.

"Looks like someone has a crush going," she said softly from the corner of her mouth.

I nodded, a little surprised at Morgan's confiding tone. She'd seemed so distant before. Knowing she was right, I wondered if Alice should say something to Christy, or if that would be my responsibility.

"Harmless enough," Morgan added. "And what a nice guy for her to be crushing on, huh?"

I thought of my girlhood crush on Will and relaxed a little.

"She hasn't noticed whom Daniel *is* interested in, though."

My eyebrows raised, I turned toward her. "Pardon?"

"I have knack for this sort of thing. You don't see it, do you?" Her hazel eyes were serious.

I shook my head.

"You," she told me, crossing her arms, her paddle bumping against my side. "She's crushing on him and he's crushing on you."

"That's ridiculous," I said, but as I spoke, Daniel looked my way, a smile spreading across his face.

The next morning Christy, Alice, and I went up on deck for a walk and some fresh air. The storm had completely passed—or we had passed it, I wasn't sure which—and the sky was a startling blue again, nearly the same color as the sea. The ocean glistened in the sunlight.

We found Morgan by the railing and joined her. Gripping the metal bar, Alice tilted her face heavenward, the ribbons of her *kapp* trailing down her neck. "Doesn't the expansiveness of this make you think of the good Lord?" she said. "Except we know the ocean ends while He goes on forever." Her face glowed as she spoke, and her snow-white hair and bleached *kapp* both lit up under the rays of the sun.

I stole a glance at Morgan, wondering if she agreed with what Alice said, but she stared straight ahead, her face frozen and her eyes focused on the water.

Alice and Christy decided to keep walking, but I stayed behind next to Morgan and asked what she was going to do on our third day at sea. She answered she would finish her book and then start another. "I'm afraid that's what my backpack is full of—books." She lowered her voice. "I was thinking, if it's okay with Alice, that I could read *Jane Eyre* out loud to Christy. In the afternoons. Maybe if we read far enough to get her interested, she'll continue on her own."

I said I would check with Alice and then asked, "How did you know Christy didn't like to read?"

"Just a guess, based on her reluctance to do her lessons in general."

I hadn't realized it was so obvious. "*Danke*," I said.

"*Bitte*," she answered.

"You speak German?"

"Some," she answered. "I've studied it for years. I'm hoping to get to practice it, although in Switzerland they mostly speak Swiss German and that's different."

"Daniel speaks German—and some Swiss German." I turned my face toward the morning sun.

"He's quite the Renaissance man, isn't he?" She paused and then said, "I wouldn't have thought it at first."

I wasn't sure what a Renaissance man was and asked.

"Someone who knows a whole lot about a bunch of different things."

"Oh," I replied, thinking that probably wasn't a term I'd use for Daniel at all. He was certainly smart and well read, but I doubted he could shoe a horse or mend leather upholstery or grow asparagus or snare a rabbit or lots of other things. My *daed*, on the other hand, could do all of those and then some. No doubt so could Will Gundy.

Seeing the expression on my face, Morgan elaborated. "He's quite proficient in literature, history, languages, music, and art. Like I said, a Renaissance man."

"Ah," I replied, understanding. Though I didn't comment, I rather preferred my definition to hers.

Later, back in the cabin, Christy and I sat side by side at our little table, delving into our history lesson. I spread out a map I'd brought and showed her where Zurich was and told her about the beginning of the Anabaptists.

After a while Christy yawned and looked up at me with her big brown eyes. "Can we do math now?"

"In just a minute." I kept on with the history lesson. When I told her that some of the Anabaptists were drowned for their faith, and that from 1527 to 1535 more than five thousand were martyred, she began shaking her head, her hands pressed against her ears.

"I don't want to hear about that stuff!"

I was startled by her reaction. She'd heard all of this before, dozens of times, if not hundreds. Most recently, she must have read it that day when she was going through the *Martyrs Mirror*—and or at least seen the gruesome illustrations. I reached out and gently pulled her hands from her ears.

"This is your heritage, Christy. It's important. Part of the reason the Anabaptists formed such a tightly knit community is because they were persecuted." I explained that in many places they hid in caves so they could worship, adding, "Caves we'll get to visit. In person." Then, pointing at Langnau, I showed how the Mennonites migrated to the Emmental.

"But they were killed too," she said flatly.

"*Ya*, some of them were martyred."

"Please can we do math?"

I sat back in my chair, disconcerted. Stories of our ancestors were vitally important to us as a people, and this was the first time I'd ever met anyone of our faith who didn't want to hear more about them.

Taking a deep breath, I decided that perhaps the talk of dying was too much for her. I folded the map, suddenly picturing her mother in the casket, the infant boy who died at birth tucked beside her, dressed in a tiny white gown. I had to admit, Christy Gundy had gone through more than many adults had in a lifetime.

"*Ya*," I said, smiling. "Let's start with the multiplication table again." I pulled out the flash cards I'd made and soon we were working through the drills.

After lunch Alice leafed through *Jane Eyre* as Morgan described the main characters and then gave an overview of the story. Once she made clear it had been written more than a hundred years ago and was a classic, Alice agreed it was fine. Christy, who had been listening intently, looked pleased.

We were still in the dining room when Daniel came in, his laptop open in his hands. "I received an email from Herr Lauten," he said. I knew that the Internet service on board had been spotty and slow, the only signal coming from the ship's tower. Still, Daniel had persisted, and now it seemed he'd finally gotten through.

Alice and I both leaned forward in anticipation. "Did he find the agreement?" she asked.

He shook his head. "He's searched all through his office. Now he's going through other rooms. He did find yet another property journal, and he's hoping it might give him the information he needs. But so far nothing concrete."

Alice folded her hands together but didn't say anything.

Daniel turned toward me. "He also forwarded a message for you. From…" He sat down at the table. "Giselle."

I nodded, my heart racing. "My mother's sister."

Daniel looked back down at his computer and read the message. "She said she's leaving for Germany for an exhibit and she's not sure when she'll return."

"Exhibit?"

Daniel read it again. "That's what it says."

"Is she an artist?" Morgan asked.

"Not that I know of," I responded.

"Is she Amish?" Morgan leaned forward, her arms crossed on the table-top.

"No." I kept my answer short on purpose. There was no way of saying a little about Giselle without saying too much.

"She lives in the cottage, right? Below Amielbach," Daniel said.

Before I could answer, he went on to explain about the property to Morgan, saying that it was a gorgeous Swiss estate that had been passed down through generations of my family, all the way to my grandmother, who'd had to sell it to someone else outside the family back in the mid-eighties. I'm pretty sure Morgan's estimation of me changed in that moment. I was no longer Plain Ada. I was someone with a story, or at least, someone whose family had a story.

"So your aunt owns it now?" she asked.

I shook my head. "No, she owns her cottage, that's all. My grandmother gave Giselle that part when she moved to Switzerland. At that same time, my grandmother sold the remaining bulk of the estate to someone else, a Swiss lawyer by the name of Lauten."

"Well, he bought all of it except for the one piece," Daniel corrected. "That one very small, very important piece."

"I'm confused," Morgan said, shaking her head.

I exhaled slowly, wondering how best to explain.

"It's a long story," Alice interjected, "but the bottom line is that there was one tiny little piece of the estate, five acres, in fact, that had been deeded separately from the rest. We call it the Kessler Tract. Because of some complications with the deed, Ada's grandmother had no choice but to retain ownership of it, even though she was able to sell all the rest. Back then no one involved really cared all that much because that little tract seemed fairly worthless. But recently some new issues have been taking place, issues that have suddenly rendered the Kessler Tract valuable after all."

"That's why we're heading to Europe," I added, "so we can straighten out the deed issues and sell the last remaining piece to Herr Lauten."

Morgan seemed to be catching on, but despite the interested gleam in her eyes, I was far more concerned with Giselle's message.

Turning toward Daniel, I asked if she'd said anything else.

He read it again, out loud this time. "It says, 'Ada, et. al, sorry, but I'm leaving for Germany for an exhibit and I'm not sure when I'll return. Giselle.' Nope, that's it."

Standing, I excused myself from the group, even though I knew that might raise some eyebrows. I didn't care what Daniel or Morgan thought about my family or anything else.

Walking out on the deck alone, trying to catch my breath, I thought of Giselle and of Amielbach. With tears welling up in my eyes, my mind went to *Jane Eyre*. Morgan had said that the novel opened with Jane being told that she wasn't welcome anymore at the home of her extended family. Just as I clearly wasn't welcome at Amielbach.

SEVENTEEN

The next few days followed the same routine. Breakfast, time on the deck, studies, lunch. Recreation, a half hour of reading with Morgan, more time on the deck, dinner, board games, and bedtime. Morgan often joined us for Ping-Pong and, of course, meals and *Jane Eyre*, but the rest of the time she kept her distance. She almost always came to meals late, just after we'd said our silent prayer. Every once in a while, I'd see her talking to one of the crew or doing exercises on deck, but mostly she was by herself. She wore jeans and a sweatshirt day after day, and she didn't wear much makeup, if any. Whenever she wasn't interacting with us, she was reading.

Morgan spent a little bit of time with Daniel, but as far as I could tell always on the deck or in other public places. A few times I overheard them speaking in German, and they both sounded quite fluent. Daniel also spent time with Christy and me, asking for clarifications about Pennsylvania Dutch and helping me teach history lessons. Not surprisingly, Christy was willing to listen to Daniel say the same things she'd balked at when I presented them. Thanks to him, she would learn Anabaptist history after all.

The value of that history was driven home to me personally one afternoon when Christy and Alice were napping downstairs and Daniel, Morgan, and I were playing Monopoly in the rec room. Morgan owned both utilities, and it seemed that every time Daniel went around the board he landed on at least one of them. When that happened yet again, he marched his game piece to the Electric Company, rolled the dice to set the rent, and groaned when it came up double sixes. As he counted out the money to her, he grumbled that she should dump the stupid Electric Company and consider going solar like the Amish.

"Yeah, right," Morgan scoffed. "Like that would ever happen, the Amish going solar."

Daniel and I looked at each other and then back at her. "The Amish and Old Order Mennonites were some of the earliest users of solar energy," he told her, but she didn't seem to believe him.

"No offense," she said finally, glancing at me, "but the Amish are totally anachronistic. They drive horse and buggies, for goodness' sake. Why would they be interested in something as innovative as solar energy?"

It was a common misconception. For once, I didn't jump in with an explanation but sat back in my chair, smiling as I deferred to Daniel.

"It's not about the electricity itself," he told her. "It's all about being off the grid, about not being dependent. They do use propane and that sort of thing, but solar energy is even better because of its self-sufficiency." The two continued talking, but my mind wandered to hydro electricity and the impending plant near Amielbach. He finished his explanation, but before we started up again with the game, I asked Morgan what she knew about hydro power, particularly in Switzerland.

"Hydro power rocks."

Startled, we both looked at her, and I realized we hadn't told her the specifics of the conflict that was raging around the Kessler Tract and the proposed hydro plant there.

"It just really ties in with green living," Morgan added. "Doesn't something like half of Switzerland's electricity comes from hydro? Maybe more than half. I mean, that's sort of a given with all of the rivers originating in the Alps and everything. But I heard they have really been trying to create more small plants for individual villages."

Daniel leaned forward. "Sounds like what Wasserdorf wants to do."

"It's a great source of energy." Morgan's voice was full of excitement. "One of the best, really. It's absolutely pollution free."

"But not when it destroys a historical landmark." Daniel was beginning to sound defensive.

"Well, no. And the wildlife and habitat of an area has to be considered. But historically speaking, the Swiss are very careful about their planning."

Daniel snorted. "We'll see, won't we?" He picked up both dice and shook them angrily, even though it wasn't his roll.

I realized I'd waited a little too late to intervene and jumped into the conversation now to explain. "You need to know, Morgan, that we have a personal stake in this. Daniel and I have been dealing with a particular waterfall that the township of Wasserdorf wants to turn into a hydro plant."

Calming down just a bit, Daniel told her what we were up against.

"Wow," Morgan said. "That's quite the predicament. I get what you're saying though and totally agree. Sites like that have to be preserved. What's the value of history if it can't be seen and experienced? Especially if there's an alternative site for the plant somewhere else?"

Daniel and I nodded in unison. I was pleased to see that as someone who had no connection with the Anabaptists, Morgan shared our sentiment.

It was my turn, so I took the dice and rattled them in my hand.

"For now, forget the Amish and solar power," I warned my opponents as I tossed the dice onto the board. "This Amish girl may not drive a car, but she's about to land on Free Parking."

By our last full day at sea, Christy knew her multiplication tables forward and backward, and she could even do long division without crying. I counted both as major victories.

That afternoon up on the deck in the bright sunshine, Morgan got ready to read to us from *Jane Eyre*. We'd skipped it the day before because we'd had a Ping-Pong tournament. Alice and George had even joined us and, not surprisingly, Christy had won. Our time on the ship had seemed to revitalize her health. Perhaps this exact balance of rest, activity, and studies had been what her body needed to function at its best.

Morgan recapped the story for us first before she began reading, reminding us that Jane had been sent off to Lowood School by her mean aunt and was sad and lonely. One teacher there was kind to her, as was her only friend, Helen. A few times I noticed Christy was engrossed in the story, and I hoped she didn't identify with Jane. True, both were motherless, but Christy had more people loving her and committed to her than most children whose *mamms* were still alive. After a while, Christy leaned against my shoulder. It was the most affectionate she'd been with me yet. When Morgan read the part about Helen passing, though, Christy sat up straight.

"She *died*?"

Morgan nodded.

"Helen died?"

"Yes."

Christy turned toward me, an odd, nervous energy in her expression. "Could we play more Ping-Pong?"

I hesitated and then said, "Sure." Giving Morgan a knowing look as we rose to go, I hoped she didn't think Christy rude. I invited her to join us for our game, but she declined.

As we were leaving, Morgan moved over to the railing of the ship and leaned into the wind, her hair blowing out behind her.

The next morning, through the porthole in our cabin, we could see land far off in the distance. By the time we'd finished lunch, we were much closer to our destination, the French port city of Le Havre. We went out on deck and watched as the pilot, who would navigate the ship through the lock and into the harbor, arrived by motorboat. The captain of the ship invited Christy and me into the bridge to watch as the pilot maneuvered the ship into the narrow space. George came with us as well, and the three of us stood near the back, out of the way. Though I was fascinated by the vast array of high-tech equipment displayed throughout the room, Christy couldn't get over the most low-tech item in the whole place: tiny windows in the floor, one on the port side, one at starboard, which provided a bird's-eye view of the sides of the ship.

Noticing her fascination, the captain explained that even with all their many instruments and devices, it never hurt to take a peek and make sure they were getting it right as they docked.

George laughed and added, "I guess you could say that's the Plain part of the equation!"

After the ship had docked, the three of us thanked the captain and then joined the others out on the deck. Numerous containers covered the lowlands on either side of us. The day was gray and overcast, and the colorful orange, red, and blue boxes contrasted with the drab sky. Huge cargo ships, bigger even than the *Whitebird Trader*, lined the wharf. Ahead was a dry dock, where a military ship was being repaired. Beyond that was the city of Le Havre, rising up in a gentle slope from the sea. Europe was before us. My eyes stung, but not from cold or wind. In fact, it was surprisingly warm and there wasn't even a breeze. I was tearing up because a dream I didn't even know to dream was coming true. God had provided.

As we disembarked, making our way down the metal gangplank, my joy subsided a bit. If only Giselle would make it possible for me to meet her! That would truly make this dream complete.

Stepping onto solid ground for the first time in a week, it struck me that my legs still felt as though they were on the ship. Glancing at Christy and then at Morgan, I saw from their odd expressions and stances that they were feeling it too. We were talking about it when a sailor walked past and spoke.

"The question is, now that you got your sea legs, how do you give 'em back?" He just laughed and kept going, but I really wanted to know.

"How?" I called after him.

Looking over his shoulder, he told us that the only thing that would fix the problem was time. "Give it a few days, at the most, and you'll be right as rain."

As we'd be spending the night here in Le Havre and taking the train on to Switzerland in the morning, I hoped I might be better by then.

George had hired a van to take us to our hotel, and as we waited for it to arrive he offered Morgan a lift to the train station. She gladly accepted and after we got there she even let Daniel help her with her heavy backpack while the rest of us sat in the van and waited just outside. She was twice as glad we were still there when she realized she'd miscalculated the time, missing her train entirely. She bought a prepaid cell phone and was getting ready to call her father when we invited her to stay with us at our hotel and catch her train the next day.

Morgan propped her backpack up against her leg and looked from Christy to me to Alice, a serious expression on her face. "I don't want to intrude."

"We're not going to leave you on your own," Alice said. "Please come with us."

"Please come," I echoed, absolutely sincere.

After a moment she nodded her assent and gratitude, and then she climbed back into the van for the ride to our hotel.

Despite having spent the past week doing almost nothing while onboard the ship, every single one of us was extremely tired. After checking into the hotel, we spent a quiet afternoon and evening resting, strolling, chatting quietly in the lobby, and sharing dinner at a small bistro.

Our hotel room had two double beds, each with two comforters on it. By eight forty-five Alice and Christy were both exhausted and changing into their nightgowns. As Christy knelt beside her bed to say her prayers, Morgan turned her head away.

After the little girl had finished, Alice told me her stomach was upset and she wondered if I could check at the hotel desk for a roll of antacid tablets. Morgan said she'd go with me and off we went. As we walked down the hall, I addressed the subject of prayer, saying all Amish children were taught to pray from a very young age.

"I can't remember a time when I didn't pray," I added. "It teaches us to depend on God and to thank Him every day for all He provides."

Morgan glanced at me a little furtively, but she didn't respond.

Confused, my face grew warm. "Would you rather I didn't speak about our ways?" I asked.

"Oh, no. It's okay. I find it interesting…" Her voice trailed off.

After a moment I apologized. "As you've probably already realized, there's an inner teacher in me that occasionally runs amok. At least that what my cousin Zed calls her."

Morgan laughed. "Your inner teacher? I like that."

"Yes, well, you don't even want to know what happened the last time she came out," I said, surprising myself by bringing it up. Morgan pressed me for details, and I found myself telling her all about the couple in the restaurant on the train back from Oregon, and how the wife kept telling her husband all sorts of ridiculous stuff about that well-known time in every young Amish person's life known as their "ringalinga."

"Their what?"

"The word she was searching for was *rumspringa*, though now that I think about it, I kind of like ringalinga instead."

"It does have a nice ring to it. Or rather, a nice ringalinga." We both laughed. "So what did you do?"

We searched the shelves of toiletries by the front desk as I continued with the story. By the time I'd found a roll of antacids and paid for them, Morgan was nearly doubled over with laughter.

"So is this trip *your* ringalinga, Ada?"

"Sure is," I replied. Lowering my voice to a whisper, I added, "But as soon as I can get myself pregnant and land me husband, I'm outta here!"

Blushing furiously, I clamped my hand over my mouth, shocked by the audacity of my own joke. Morgan thought it was the funniest thing I'd said yet, and soon we both had our hands over our mouths, trying to contain the volume of our laughter.

By the time we got back to the room, we had managed to calm down, which was a good thing because Alice and Christy were both sound asleep in their bed. After changing into my nightgown, I got into the other bed, but Morgan surprised me by wrapping up in a comforter and settling down on the floor. I told her we could share, but she insisted she was fine where she was.

I thought she'd gone to sleep when she said softly, "Ada, may I ask you a question?"

"*Ya*."

"Would you leave if you could?"

"Leave?"

"Your church."

"Oh, I can. No one would stop me."

"You wouldn't be shunned?"

"No. Not unless I had joined the church first and then decided to leave."

"But Daniel said you wouldn't be treated the same by your family."

I didn't answer her for a moment. "That's true, to an extent. It wouldn't be the same. But I don't want to leave." Most of the time, anyway.

"Even though you can't go to college? Or fly in airplanes? Or have a professional job?"

At the moment, Morgan wasn't going to college. Or flying in an airplane. Or working as a professional. I quietly pointed this out.

She didn't seem amused. "But I can do all those things if I want to. No one's going to tell me I can't. And I already graduated from college."

"Our church has its reasons," I answered, resisting the urge to let my inner teacher come out yet again. "It works for us."

A moment later she said, "Why did your aunt move to Switzerland?"

Turning, I peered over at the other bed, just to make sure Christy was still asleep. Watching the steady rise and fall of her chest, I took a deep breath and tried to decide how to answer.

I could have said something vague, but I felt compelled to be more honest. Maybe it was that I knew she wasn't going to judge me. Maybe I wanted to shock her a little, to show her I was more than she thought. "She's actually my birth mother," I whispered after turning back around. "She moved to Switzerland once I was born."

Morgan's head popped up, her chestnut hair falling around her face. "You're kidding."

"Nope." Keeping my voice low, I told her about Lexie arriving last spring and how her search for her birth family led her to me. I told her about Giselle moving to Switzerland all those years ago and how Zed had tracked her down. By the end of the tale, Morgan was sitting on my bed.

"Do Daniel and George know all of this?"

I said they didn't. "But I wasn't lying when I told them she was my aunt—legally she is." I had to explain that twice, how *Mamm*, Giselle's sister, and *Daed* had adopted me.

"Why didn't you tell Daniel?" Morgan asked. "I think he would understand. He's geeky, that's for sure, but he seems pretty thoughtful. Besides, I think he really cares for you."

I blushed. He was, indeed, quite thoughtful, but after a whole week together on ship, I still wasn't sure how I felt about him.

"Ada?" She was smiling and up on her knees now.

I shook my head. "Why would he care for me?"

"Why *wouldn't* he care for you? You're sweet, clever, easy to be with—not to mention totally DDG."

"DDG?"

"Drop-dead gorgeous, girlfriend."

A sharp laugh burst from my throat. I quickly covered my mouth, and both of us looked over to make sure I hadn't woken Alice or Christy.

"Don't say that, Morgan," I scolded in a whisper. "It's not nice to lie. I know very well how…unattractive I am."

She stared at me for a long moment. "Unattractive."

"Yes." Did she have to rub it in?

"Are the Amish allowed to use mirrors, Ada?"

"Mirrors? Of course—"

"Then are you just stupid?"

First she agreed that I was unattractive, and now she was insulting my intelligence? Before I could figure out how to reply, she was gripping me by the wrists and forcing me to look her in the eyes.

"You…are…drop…dead…gorgeous," she said. "Maybe not in a fashion model way, but in like a…" She searched for the right word. "Like in a pure way. Angelic. When people look at you, they see a beautiful face, a woman who seems delicate on the outside but is really tough and strong and brave on the inside."

Her speech over, Morgan surprised me by releasing my wrists, sliding back down to the floor, and wrapping herself in her comforter again. I was still sitting there, speechless, when she spoke one more time.

"It's been a long time since a guy looked at me the way Daniel looks at you, Ada. If I were you, I wouldn't take that for granted."

Eighteen

The next morning, as we waited in the train station in Le Havre, we were amused by the reactions of the French people hurrying past us. Morgan, Christy, and I sat side by side on the wooden bench. People would turn their heads a second time to get a better view.

"I take it there aren't any Amish in Europe?" Morgan asked.

"No," Daniel answered. "There are Mennonite but not any Old Order. We're going to draw quite a bit of attention everywhere we go."

The next woman to pass us turned on her high heels and stared, stepping back toward us, her mouth wide open.

"What's the matter?" Morgan called out. "Haven't you ever seen an Amish girl on her ringalinga?"

The woman gasped and then hurried on as Morgan and I both burst out laughing. My friend had more of a sense of humor than I'd thought. I was going to miss her.

George smiled at the exchange, but Alice stared straight ahead, her face solemn. Our way was to simply ignore stares and go about our business. Something I hadn't done.

As we boarded the train, it worked out that Daniel, Morgan, Christy, and I shared four seats together. Alice went on with George in seats kitty-corner from us. She kept an eye on us though, glancing our way every few minutes. She wasn't as relaxed as she'd been the evening before.

The train pulled away from the station in the late morning, and office buildings and shops gave way to apartment buildings and houses, alleys, and narrow cobblestone streets. We left the city, and the French country-side rolled out on either side of us, dotted with Jersey cows.

Christy pointed to a stone house. It looked ancient. A moment later there were more, and then we were passing behind a village, catching a glimpse of the road down the middle of it between the houses. Except for the asphalt, the scene could have been from the 1870s when my relatives were leaving Switzerland. They probably took the train to Le Havre. Of course, the shipyard wouldn't have been as busy, but the harbor would have been there even way back then.

The train stopped at Gare St. Lazare, one of the Paris stations, where we boarded the Métro to Gare de l'Est to catch the train to Basel. Morgan said she would come back to Paris, maybe on her way home. She definitely wanted to go to some museums. I would have enjoyed a chance to go exploring there as well, but I knew Alice and the others had no desire to see Paris at all.

In eastern France Daniel said there was an Anabaptist farm close by that had been confiscated by the Swiss government in the early seventeen hundreds. The current owner was fascinated by the history of his property and hoped they would include it on the tour. Daniel had visited the site last summer, but he and George didn't want to take time to visit it now. They wanted to go on to Amielbach. Perhaps, they said, we could stop on the way back.

We were going to spend the night in Basel, so we all disembarked with Morgan, happy to stretch our legs and have the opportunity to eat somewhere other than on the train. It had been a long day and was well past dinnertime. Morgan called her father on the cell phone she'd purchased the day before and then said he would arrive shortly. He was coming straight from work, even though it was a Saturday. I said I'd wait with her while the others went to the bistro.

"He's always late," Morgan said.

"He's probably stuck in traffic," I said, having no idea what traffic was like on a weekend day in Basel, Switzerland. I thought of my own *daed,* who was never late and hardly ever stuck in traffic, except maybe in a line of buggies on the way to church.

"May I ask you a question?" Morgan turned toward me. "What would you miss the most if you left?"

"Besides my family? Mutual aid."

"Mutual what?"

"Helping each other. When a barn burns down, everyone comes together to rebuild it. If someone's sick, everyone pitches in with meals and to do chores. If someone dies, everyone else helps out."

"So it's like you're never really alone?"

I smiled. "*Ya*, you could say that. Or maybe that we're never isolated."

"You know what's really cool?"

I shook my head, hoping she wasn't going to bring up the subject of Daniel again.

"That you and Christy and Alice all get along so well."

I cocked my head. "What do you mean?"

"You make it look so normal hanging out with someone so much older—and younger—than you. You seem to really enjoy them."

"Is that unusual?"

"Are you kidding? Of course it's unusual."

Shrugging, I explained that our generations always spent a lot of time together." I thought of *Mammi*. Sure, in the last few years since the stroke her health hadn't been good, and before that she sometimes had sad spells, which I now understood. I told Morgan I spent as much time with her as with my mother, working alongside her in the vegetable and flowers gardens, doing the washing and mending, and cooking together. She had read to me when I was little and helped me with my homework all through school when I needed it.

"Wow." Morgan stretched her hand out on the bench. "I only saw my grandparents once or twice a year. I wish I had seen them more. I really loved my grandmother." Her eyes were moist. "She used to pray for me. Every day, she said." She sighed. "Everything I learned about God, I learned from her and from reading *Jane Eyre*."

I raised my eyebrows.

"It's true," Morgan said. "It's quite a spiritual story. Where did we stop? Right when Helen dies?"

We definitely had gotten to that part.

"Helen teaches Jane a lot about God. It affects the rest of her life. You'll have to read to the end."

I nodded. I'd like that.

Morgan sat up a little straighter and squared her feet on the tile floor. "I wish I could have gone on a trip like this with my grandmother. She wasn't always in a hurry. If I went on a trip like this with my mom, we'd kill each other." She grimaced.

We were silent for a moment, and then I felt compelled to expand on the conversation from the night before. "Why were you uncomfortable when we prayed?"

"Ouch," she said. "Was I that obvious?"

"*Ya.*" I smiled.

She took a deep breath. "Probably for a lot of reasons."

"Such as…"

She shrugged. "I don't see God really caring about how I feel, let alone what I need." She repositioned her backpack at her feet.

There was no way to say it politely, but I had a feeling that one reason she thought God didn't care was because her parents didn't seem to care— at least not like they should. I shuddered, grateful to the core that I had parents who *did* care, even if sometimes they showed it too much.

We were silent for a moment and then she asked, "Do you like being Christy's au pair?"

"Au what?"

"It's French. For nanny." She laughed. "It sounds better, don't you think?"

"Better?"

"Than babysitter or child care provider or nanny." She shrugged. "Do you like it?"

"Au pair," I repeated quietly and then answered, "Yes, very much. It's the next best thing to teaching."

Her eyes lit up. "Can you do that?"

"I'm hoping for a position back home."

"But you could only teach until you get married? Right?"

"Pretty much." I knew of teachers who taught after they wed, but they quit before they had children.

She glanced toward the exit of the station and then back toward me, meeting my gaze. "I don't get it," she said. "Why do you want someone else telling you what you can and can't do?"

"What do you mean?"

"All those rules. About how you can dress. What you can drive. What job you can have. You must have a superthick what-not-to-do manual."

"Actually, it's called the *Ordnung* and it's not written down. We just know it. It gives structure to our lives."

"But it doesn't give you any choices."

I had to think about that for a moment. Then I said, "It isn't about choices. It's about a way of behaving that helps us follow Christ's teaching. It helps us avoid vanity, pride, and envy. That sort of thing. And remember—it's not as though we're told a bunch of rules and have no choice but to follow them." My mind raced for an example. "That's like saying a husband and wife have no choice about dating other people. Of course they don't. They took a vow that bound them to each other, and certain rules go along with that. When we commit to the faith and join the Amish church, we take a vow and *willingly* agree to do the things that go along with that."

She nodded thoughtfully.

"Plus, our rules keep our priorities straight," I added.

"How so?"

"Take telephones—land lines. Back when Amish families first started having them installed in their homes almost a hundred years ago, there was a fear that the telephones would take the place of face-to-face visiting, so that was one reason it was decided they would be put in sheds and barns instead, plus phones weren't as invasive that way too. For us, direct contact between people is more important than convenience. From what I've seen of the rest of the world, that decision was a pretty good one."

"So people come first? Instead of things and careers and stuff like that?"

I shook my head. "Jesus comes first. Then others. Then yourself. All of our decisions come down to that. Christ taught us to live in community. He wants us to be His hands and feet."

She shifted her eyes to the floor and, again, I was afraid I'd offended her, but then she said, "That's really cool. Thanks for the explanation."

We were still waiting for her father when the others returned. Daniel handed me a sandwich and Alice handed one to Morgan.

As we were finishing our food, a man approached. He had broad shoulders and silver hair and was wearing a suit and tie.

"Morgan," he called out. "So sorry I'm late." He was about to give her a hug but then stopped suddenly, taking us all in, and broke into a grin instead. "I see you're still a bleeding heart, taking in strays."

Morgan looked flustered and embarrassed as she stood, reaching out to hug him quickly and then introducing all of us. We said our goodbyes, and she promised to try and visit the Emmental while we were still there. She'd traded cell phone numbers with George, and she also gave me her email address, just in case.

Then she followed her father toward the exit. I stood and watched her go, surprised when she turned and pulled something out of her backpack.

"Ada," she said. "I want you to have this."

She ran back toward me, and as she did I could see it was her copy of *Jane Eyre*.

"Even if Christy doesn't want to hear the rest of the story, you should read it."

I thanked her with a final hug, and as I turned, I almost bumped into Daniel, who had been standing just behind me. He and I joined the others in our group to take a bus to the hotel, but we ended up getting off at the wrong stop. By the time Daniel asked the driver for help and got us redirected, it was growing late. When we finally arrived at the hotel, we were all exhausted.

Alice and Christy were both looking pale, so Daniel and I managed to get their luggage to our room, and then I made sure Christy took her medicine and that she and Alice laid down. Once they were resting, I stepped out into the hall where George was talking on his cell phone. It sounded as if he was confirming our driver for the next day.

When he finished, I explained my worries about Christy's health and Alice's age, saying that I didn't think either one of them was really up to this right now. Even though Christy had seemed fine on the ship, she still had a heart condition we needed to be mindful of and overtiring her wasn't in her best interest or anyone else's. He assured me that today had been, by far, our longest and most difficult day.

"It gets much easier from here," he said. "Make sure and call your aunt in the morning. We'll be in Langnau by tomorrow afternoon."

As tired as I was, I tossed and turned most of the night, thinking about Giselle.

The next morning as we ate in the hotel restaurant, George handed me his cell phone. I stood and thanked him and then made my way out the front door. This wasn't a call that I wanted anyone to overhear. I'd tucked Zed's printout of the email from Giselle into the zipped compartment of my purse along with my passport. I pulled out the piece of paper now and shook it open, my hand trembling as I did. Then I dialed the number. It rang. One. Two. Three. Four. Five. I was sure she wasn't going to pick up. Six. Seven. Eight. I shifted my weight to my other foot. It should have gone into voice mail by now. Nine.

"*Hallo?*"

"Giselle?" My heart raced as I spoke.

She spoke rapidly in German, and I could only make out a few words.

"This is Ada," I said in English. "You told me to call." My knees began to shake, and I put a hand up against the building to steady myself.

"Oh, Ada." There was a long silence and then, "Didn't you get my message from Herr Lauten?"

"I did," I answered, my heart thumping against my chest. "But you'd told me to call..."

"I'm still in Frankfurt..." Her voice trailed off.

"When will you be back?" I asked, praying I could see her.

"Any chance you're coming to Germany?"

"No."

"Well, I'm sorry our paths won't cross, but do go visit Amielbach when you're in Langnau. The owner is turning it into a boutique hotel. He might even let you stay there."

She finally stopped speaking. I swallowed hard and then said, my voice cracking a little, "So we won't be seeing you?"

A defensive edge sliced through her voice. "No, I don't think so."

"Alice will be disappointed." I wasn't sure why I couldn't say I would be disappointed as well.

"Alice Beiler?" Her voice was softer now. "*Mamm's* good friend?"

"*Ya,*" I said. "Didn't Zed tell you in his emails? She's with me."

"He said you were traveling with friends. But I was thinking friends your age. Not someone I would know."

"Her great-granddaughter is with us too. Will Gundy's oldest girl."

"My goodness." Her voice was brighter now. "Alice was always so good to me." She paused for a moment, as if she were thinking things through. "Let me see what I can do on this end. Maybe I can head home to Switzerland after all and come back here to Germany in a couple of weeks to finish then. Should I call this number if I can make it happen?"

I knew George wouldn't mind. I told her yes and that I hoped I'd be seeing her soon.

"Don't count on it, but I'll do my best."

After hanging up I waited for a moment, still braced against the building, my insides feeling icy cold even though the morning was surprisingly warm for the first week of October. She wanted to see Alice. I took a deep breath. But she didn't want to see me.

The door to the restaurant opened and I anticipated everyone coming out, but it was only Alice.

"Ada, are you all right?"

I nodded but my face must have given my emotions away. "She's in Frankfurt. She might be able to see us."

"Might?"

I nodded again. I thought of Lexie traveling to Pennsylvania by herself. I squared my shoulders. Lexie had wanted the truth. I wanted to meet our birth mother. It was my right to want that. But it was also my birth mother's right to decide whether to make it happen or not.

Ironically, my deepest hurt in this moment was also my one glimmer of hope, that if she wanted to see Alice she would have to see me too. Perhaps that would be enough to get her home.

Alice didn't pry for any more information, and I didn't tell her that Giselle was far more interested in seeing her than me.

Alice's eyes glistened. "You've come all this way. You need to see her. Frannie needs you to see her. And I'd like very much to see her as well."

I was about to ask her what we would do if Giselle didn't show up when the door swung open again and the whole group emerged, led by George.

Daniel stopped when he saw my face. "Are you all right?"

I nodded, the motion of my head forming a great big lie.

NINETEEN

We rode the train east through the bucolic countryside of green fields and patches of forest, past creeks and rivers. We saw houses of timber and stucco, with low, sloping roofs, their windows framed by shutters and fronted by boxes overflowing with geraniums. On a roadway near where the train passed, an older man was sweeping the street with a push broom. The yards and villages were tidy. Even the graffiti in the train tunnels was colorful and orderly.

We were traveling along the Jura Bernese Mountains, a range that Daniel said was much smaller than the Alps but that formed rolling hills ideal for farming. When the train stopped in Biel, we disembarked. George had a van waiting for us there.

After we'd stowed our luggage, he gathered us into a circle much as he had done in the parking lot of the shipyard in New York City.

"I know we're all in a hurry to get on to Amielbach," he said, "but even if we drove straight there without any stops, we wouldn't make it before the end of the business day. Thus, Daniel and I would like to make a stop along the way, if you folks don't mind, at an important historical site. We're hoping you'll indulge us a bit, considering that we can't accomplish anything official on the title issue till tomorrow anyway."

Alice and I looked at each other and then back at George, who added, "It's good practice for us because it will definitely be on our tour. And I know you'll find it fascinating."

"Will it add significantly to our time?" I asked. I was torn, because while part of me wanted to see and experience as many things as possible while in Europe, I was also anxious to get to Amielbach. And I was worried about Alice, who still seemed pale and tired today despite a full night's sleep.

"Not at all," George assured us, "especially if that's the only stop we make." He looped his thumbs around his suspenders. "We'll be passing through several towns of historical significance along the way, but if we don't linger in any of those, we should arrive at Amielbach by early evening."

That didn't sound too bad, but I deferred to Alice, who hesitated only a moment before saying it would be fine.

"Excellent!" George cried, clapping his hands together then rubbing his palms up and down. "Then all aboard. Our next stop will be the site of the Anabaptist Bridge." I was trying to picture what it might look like when George added that the bridge itself had fallen down long ago, its remnants taken away.

Once we were in the van rumbling down the road, Daniel explained that the bridge was an old secret meeting place of our ancestors, people who had fled the area of Bern. They would gather in a ravine under the bridge, hiding from the Anabaptist hunters, as they worshipped together.

After driving for half an hour, much of it up a steep road, the van pulled into a small parking area and came to a stop. From there we hiked down a narrow and overgrown trail. Alice held my arm as we walked. When we reached the bottom and gathered around, Daniel explained that this was the only historical site in all of Europe that included "Anabaptist" in its name. Christy stood beside him as he spoke, looking up at him with her ever-admiring eyes. He was kind and attentive to her but seemingly oblivious of her crush. He treated her as he did everyone else—as someone eager to soak up what he had to teach them. I smiled, thinking that in the midst of all her adoration, at least she was taking in a history lesson as well.

Before we headed back up the path, George led us in the song, "I Sing with Exultation," creating for us a moment of worship that was incredibly touching on this Sunday afternoon in Europe. Though I was engaged intellectually, I hadn't expected to react emotionally, so I was surprised to find that by the end of the song my cheeks were damp with tears.

Once we were back in the van and on the highway, Alice and Christy dozed for a while. Dusk was falling as we traveled past forests and farms—including more than a few dairy farms. They reminded me of home, and I thought of *Daed* caring for our cows, hooking up the milkers, cleaning the barn, day after day after day.

In the fading light we came into a wide valley, and the driver told us that the village of Langnau was just ahead. Sure enough we could see the outline of low buildings against the mountains. Alice and Christy both stirred.

Daniel said that Langnau had a population of nine thousand and had several small industries, including agriculture—which wasn't surprising, he added, given that it also happened to be the sunniest spot in Switzerland. That made Christy smile. The buildings there were solid and rustic with sloped roofs and shutters painted yellow and green. Abundant flowers filled these window boxes too. We passed a chapel with an ornate tower, and I asked with skepticism if that was the local Mennonite church, doubting that the Mennonites would have such a fancy place of worship.

"No. The Mennonite church is outside of town," Daniel answered, "in the other direction."

As we drove slowly down the main street of Langnau, Daniel said the place had changed surprisingly little since the Kesslers and Sommers had lived in the area. A mural of wildflowers was painted on the building across the street. Beside it was a bakery, and carved on a slab above the door was the date 1869. Perhaps my great-great-great-grandmother had bought bread there. I'd grown up with bits and pieces of stories from *Mammi* about how her grandmother, Elsbeth, had come from Switzerland to Indiana and had a big family. She told me her grandmother always missed Switzerland, even though she knew God wanted her in Indiana.

It wasn't until Lexie had given me a copy of the letter that had been in the carved box that I learned anything about Elsbeth's father, Abraham Sommers. I still had hopes of learning more. And I knew Alice wanted more information on her family as well.

As we left the outskirts of Langnau, the driver said that his own hometown of Wasserdorf was next. In English, but with a heavy accent, he described having grown up there, saying that twenty years ago, when he was a boy, he hiked in the woods around Amielbach with his friends.

"Back then the owner used to rent out rooms, like a boarding house," he said. "All sorts of people stayed there—people who were down and out. Others who just needed a place to live for a short time."

"The current owner is turning it back into an inn," Daniel replied, "though something far more upscale this time around."

The man nodded and then asked if we had family in the area.

"Yes, Ada's aunt," Alice said quickly, saving me from having to answer. "She lives very near Amielbach."

"She is an American?" he asked.

After a brief hesitation, Alice replied, "Originally. But she's been here a long time. More than twenty years now."

The driver was silent for a moment, seemingly lost in thought. Then his face lit up, and he said, "The artiste? There is an American artiste living on the grounds of Amielbach."

Alice looked back at me. I shrugged. Perhaps Giselle was an artist, but I didn't know for sure.

The driver downshifted as the incline of the road increased.

"She does not dress like you people though, no?"

"No," Alice replied, surely wishing this man weren't quite so chatty.

"You three ladies are Amish, correct? We have had the occasional Amish tour groups before, but I don't know of any Amish who live around here. We have Mennonites, of course, but they do not dress like Mennonites from America."

George laughed. "Both Daniel and I are Mennonites from America—and we don't dress anything alike either."

The driver nodded toward the middle seat at Daniel. "He would fit in just fine around here. But you? Not so much." He was quiet for a moment and then said, "None of the other Plain tourists I drive around ever asked about Amielbach."

George smiled. "We like it that way—for the time being, at least. It'll be our own little discovery."

"How long has it been since you have seen your aunt?" the driver asked.

It took a moment for me to realize he was talking to me. "What? Oh, never. She moved here when I was just a baby."

He nodded and then said, "The wife of a friend bought one of her pieces."

"Does she paint?" I asked.

"No." He was searching for a word. "It is fabric."

"Quilting?" Alice offered.

The man chuckled. "No. It is hard for me to explain in English." He scratched the back of his head. "It is like a web. She does it with a big—" He took both hands off the steering wheel for a moment and made a box-like gesture.

"Loom." Daniel sounded pleased with himself.

"Ah," Alice interjected. "Weaving."

"That's it," the driver said. "It is very beautiful."

I didn't know any Amish women who had looms. Giselle must have learned to weave in Switzerland.

The road turned and the evergreen trees gave way to a meadow, but in a few minutes we were back in trees again. Dark and gnarled, the heavy branches hung over the road from both sides.

"This is creepy," Christy whispered.

We rounded a curve and then the trees ended as the village began. Wasserdorf was much smaller than Langnau but every bit as charming. We passed homes with sloped roofs, a stone church with a steeple, and then a clock tower surrounded by a handful of shops. There was less traffic here as well, and fewer side streets leading off and beckoning us to explore.

Just a mile or two beyond the little town center, Daniel got my attention and pointed out of the window, saying, "The Kessler property is up on the other side of that ridge, though I don't think the waterfall is visible from here."

Leaning toward the glass, I squinted, trying to see it better in the fading light.

"They want to build a retaining wall at the top of the falls and then put the hydro plant a few yards away from that."

"Is he talking about the waterfall that's on your box?" Christy asked.

"*Ya.*"

We rode in silence for a couple more minutes and then Daniel said, "Amielbach is just around this turn."

Then the massive building came into view, its turrets and balconies barely visible in the gathering darkness. Trees surrounded it on three sides—maples, oaks, birch—their leaves crimson and orange and gold.

"This is where your aunt lives?" Christy's voice was incredulous.

"Oh, no," I said. "She lives in a little cottage nearby."

The driver pulled into the circle at the front of the mansion, and Daniel and George helped him unload our bags. By the time we all reached the top of the steps, the door was swung open by a middle-aged man with a head so bald and shiny I wondered if he used some kind of polish.

"*Willkommen in Amielbach*," he said.

"*Danke schon*," Daniel replied on our behalf.

I thought this was the owner, Herr Lauten, but when they switched to English, it was clear that this man and Daniel had never met. He told us his name was Oskar and he was Herr Lauten's son.

"I came last week, from Zurich," he explained to all of us in perfect English. "I manage a restaurant there, but I took time off to help my father get this property matter settled. He is overwhelmed. He has hardly been sleeping. He has practically torn the place apart looking for that agreement."

Alice and I glanced at each other as Daniel said simply, "Is he home now? He's expecting us."

Oskar nodded. "Your coming here is all he has been talking about. I haven't known whether to dread your arrival or welcome it. But you are here—so, what can I do? Six days from now, the township will claim the property and the waterfall. Then my father's frantic hunt for what doesn't even exist will be over. Now he's convinced himself that the authorities will honor the agreement on your word alone." He shook his head. "I'm sorry you have come so far to witness this debacle." He motioned us inside.

Biting my lip, I shot a look at Alice. She stared straight ahead, her face completely serene.

Inside, the narrow entryway was lined with carved benches. Moving toward a light, we emerged at the end into a grand room with a sparkling chandelier and an open staircase with an intricately carved banister. Looking up, I saw that a railing surrounded the open second floor. According to Daniel, above that was a third floor, though we couldn't see it from here.

The oak floor was polished, the light from the chandelier glimmering off the beautiful honey-colored wood. On the far wall was a carving perhaps six feet wide that ran from the floor to the crown molding at the ceiling. I stepped closer to it, trying to make out the scene it depicted. There was a waterfall, clearly the one on the Kessler property, and a group of people standing on the rocky ground around it.

Oskar must have noticed my interest because he said, "Abraham Sommers."

I jumped. "Pardon?"

"He's the one who carved this. I've been told he was prolific and that his work can be found throughout the area."

I found my voice. "I have a box with me that has a carving in a similar style."

"Yes," he said. "Apparently he was fond of making those little boxes, usually with scenic images on the top. This large carving is different from much of his other work, especially in that it includes people. He rarely carved human figures, preferring scenes of nature and such instead."

"Ada's box has this house on it," Christy told him.

"Does it, now? Then it must be very special to you indeed."

He was interrupted by a voice speaking in Swiss German, I assumed, from down a long hallway. Excusing himself, Oskar stepped away from us and disappeared in the direction of the voice.

Once he was gone, we all just stood there, silently, each of us taking in the beauty of the vast room. Soon Oskar returned with Herr Lauten, who was older than I had expected. Slightly stooped with white hair and a deeply lined face, he walked with a cane, though there was a spring in his step.

"At last!" he cried, smiling broadly as he approached.

As Daniel introduced each of us, the man's smile grew wider and wider. "Well, well," he said. "Look at this. History has indeed come full circle. For the first time in a hundred and thirty-four years, we have here, standing in this very room, Sommerses and Kesslers."

"Except the names have changed along the way," Alice reminded him.

"And that is why you'll have to tell me which is which. Kessler?" he asked, and Alice raised her hand. A little uncertainly, Christy raised hers as well, looking up at her great-grandmother, who nodded in confirmation. "Sommers?" he added, turning to me, and I raised my hand.

"I'm sorry my grandmother wasn't strong enough to make the trip herself," I told him.

"Ah, but she has sent you in her place. Thank you for coming, and please be sure to pay my regards to her on your return."

I nodded, saying I would.

Herr Lauten looked at our little group from one end to the other and told us, "A few months ago, this moment would not have meant nearly as much to me as it does now. I have spent the last few weeks completely immersed in my search for the agreement, reading every old record and document and letter of Abraham Sommers I could find. I feel almost as if I have come to know the man. Now that I stand here looking at his descendent and the descendants of his friend and neighbor, I am very happy to meet all of you as well."

We all thanked him. There was something very likeable about this old man, and at that moment I was deeply glad we had come.

He handed his cane to Oskar and then took Alice's hand in one of his and mine in the other. "Just imagine," he said, his voice resonating with a melodic charm. "Your forefathers, neighbors for all those years, torn apart by persecution, and then separated by the wide, wide ocean. And then, finally, descendants from both lines return." He squeezed our hands. "And here I am, the man in the middle, eager to honor the legacies of both families."

Oskar cleared his throat. "Legacy or not, I am sorry he has brought you all here on this—how do you say it? A fool's errand?"

Neither Daniel or George seemed offended by Oskar's comment, and Alice looked as calm as ever.

The old man frowned at his son. "Nonsense, Oskar," he said. "We are going to find that agreement and clear the title. And if we cannot find the agreement, we will try our hardest—with these ladies' help—to get the title cleared anyway. We must have faith that their presence and statements will be sufficient."

"There are six days left, Father—correction, five, now that today is almost over. You would be more likely to sprout a tail than to make this happen now."

Herr Lauten seemed undeterred.

"Well then, 'tis a good thing to have God on our side," Alice said.

Herr Lauten barked out a laugh, clapping his hands. "You are right, my dear! He did manage to create the whole world in just six days, after all. If He can do that, then surely He ought to be able to pull this off in no time."

Twenty

Herr Lauten asked if we'd eaten, and when Daniel told him we had not, he invited us to get settled into our rooms and then meet him in the dining hall for a simple supper of soup and bread.

"We can strategize over the meal," he added, sounding energized by the very prospect. I, on the other hand, thought combining dinner with that kind of conversation sounded like a good way to end up with indigestion.

Oskar led the way to our rooms upstairs, opening the door to Alice and Christy's first. It had two four-poster beds with a cherrywood dresser. It was furnished simply but everything was clean and tidy. Next was my room. Daniel had carried up my suitcase, and after he set it beside the dresser, the men continued on down the hall so that Oskar could show them to theirs.

Left alone for the moment, I took in a deep breath and simply let myself soak in the quiet.

My room held a double bed with a white comforter, the headboard carved with little flowers. *Edelweiss,* I thought. I left my suitcase where it was and sat down on the bed, running my fingers over the carvings. Abraham Sommers had led a productive life.

The window was open and a breeze came through the room, ruffling the sheer curtains. I stood. It was completely dark outside now, but I could hear the waterfall. No wonder Herr Lauten didn't want a hydro plant next door.

I breathed in deeply. Elsbeth had grown up here. *Mammi* had owned the place but sadly had never seen it. For a minute I wished that when Giselle had come here from Lancaster County that *Mammi* had come along as well—and brought Lexie and me with her. The four of us could have lived here in this mansion, my sister and I growing up together with each other, our mother, and our grandmother. I could just picture such an idyllic childhood. Sliding in our socks on the slick wood floors of the great hall. Exploring the waterfall and its caves next door. Playing in the woods with the other children of the village. There were no Amish living here, of course, but we could have gone to church with the Mennonites and gone to school in the village. A beautiful dream.

I frowned, knowing that a dream was all it was. Even if we had come here with Giselle back then, *Mammi* could never have afforded to maintain a place of this size. She would have had to sell it, and the four of us would have been forced to share a tiny cottage.

Most importantly, had I been raised here by my birth mother, I would have been denied the love and care of my adoptive parents. I couldn't even imagine that. *Mamm* may have been a bit controlling from time to time, but she was a good *mamm* and my father was a good *daed*, and we had had a good life.

That life had been God's plan for me, and I was grateful for it. Still, I couldn't help but wonder what might have been.

The dining hall was extremely long and narrow, designed so that it almost felt that the room had been built around the table rather than vice versa. As we sat, I glanced at Alice, who was gazing appreciatively at the shining wood surface. I knew what she was thinking, that a table like this would be a real treasure in an Amish home—or at least one with such a large family as hers. A table like this at our house, on the other hand, would have looked ridiculous. More than that, it would have been a sad and constant reminder to my parents that they had never been able to conceive any children of their own to fill the places at that table.

Our simple supper of soup and bread ended up being a feast: thick potato goulash, crispy loaves of ciabatta bread, and a beautiful platter of fruits and cheeses. In response to our enthusiasm about the delicious food, Oskar said he'd been a chef before he'd gone into restaurant management. Obviously pleased by our reaction to the meal he had prepared, he seemed to warm up to us just a bit.

I felt bad for poor George, who had decided to skip dinner so he could get some sleep. We were all very tired, but the meal had been worth staying up for.

Over a delectable dessert of steaming apple strudel topped with vanilla cream, we finally got down to business. Thankfully, there wasn't a whole lot to cover. We started by going over the schedule for the next day and where we would need to be when. Our first official act as the descendants of Sommers and Kessler was to take place in the morning, when Daniel would be bringing us to meet with Betsy Holt, an attorney who specialized in property law. Depending on her recommendation, later in the day we might also need to attend one or two other meetings relevant to our case.

According to Daniel, because the written agreement had not yet been found, we were going to proceed for now on the assumption that it never would. By dotting every *i* and crossing every *t*, the hope was that our presence would be enough to sway a decision in our favor anyway.

In the meantime Herr Lauten would continue searching through the vast collection of old papers and documents that had already been here when he bought Amielbach. Here it had stayed, and I had the feeling he was the kind of man who never threw anything away. I supposed a lifetime of such a practice could actually come in handy to us now if it turned out he'd preserved the very papers we needed.

For the past three weeks, Herr Lauten said, volunteers from the historical society had been working at Amielbach, poring through every ancient scrap of paper they could find and scanning and sorting and organizing, but all to no avail. They had, however, found a set of business ledgers containing numerous entries by Abraham Sommers over the years. At this point, Herr Lauten felt our best hope was going to come from those. One of Sommers' entries mentioned the agreement he and Kessler had drawn up. Just as in the deed itself, however, there were no specifics about the requirements of that agreement beyond the main one, the first right of refusal.

"One other avenue I am desperate to pursue," Herr Lauten told us now, "is the letters."

"Letters?" Daniel asked, perking up considerably.

"Yes. In his ledgers Sommers frequently refers to letters he and Elsbeth wrote to each other once she moved to Indiana. She had emigrated to the U.S. along with several other Mennonite families, including the Kesslers, and we know she was fully aware of the agreement and its details because he listed her as one of the witnesses when it was signed. I am hoping the subject might have come up in some of these letters that went back and forth between father and daughter."

"You have them?" Daniel asked.

"Essentially," Herr Lauten said slowly. "I have seen them, an entire stack of letters that Elsbeth wrote to her father. The man kept everything, you know."

"Imagine that," Oskar said sarcastically.

Ignoring his son's comment, Herr Lauten continued. "I have not seen any letters Abraham wrote to his daughter, though that is not surprising. If anyone had kept those, it would have been Elsbeth herself, in America. There is no reason why they would have ended up back here."

Finished with his strudel, Daniel wiped his mouth with his napkin and placed that on the table beside his plate. "Let's get to it, then," he said eagerly. "If you have her letters to him, at least we have half a chance. I'll be happy to translate."

Herr Lauten's shoulders drooped as he said that he'd *seen* the letters but he didn't currently *have* the letters. "In other words, I know they exist and I know who has them. I just haven't been able to reach her to get them."

Looking suddenly at me, he added, "Actually, Ada, you might be able to help here. I understand that Giselle Lantz is your aunt. I gave them to her decades ago, when she first moved here, only knowing at the time she was somehow related to Frannie Lantz. Giselle was so reticent, and I thought sharing the letters with her might give us something to talk about. But doing so only made her distance herself even more from me. She's the one who has the letters. Do you know where she is right now?"

I was so startled by his question that for a moment I couldn't even speak. Putting a napkin to my mouth to buy some time as I recovered from my surprise, I was glad when Oskar jumped in and answered the question instead.

"She has that exhibit in Frankfurt, Father. Remember? She told you about it."

"Yes, I remember, Oskar, but I thought she would be finished and done by now. Does she not want to see her family?"

His question hurt, yes, but as it was the same question I'd been asking myself for several weeks now, hearing him also say it, out loud, made me feel oddly vindicated.

Frustration clearly evident on his face, Herr Lauten continued. "I just wish I had thought to ask her about the box before she left for Frankfurt." He looked up at his son. "Why don't you try calling her? I have a spare key to the cottage. Just ask her to tell you where the letters are and then you can run down and retrieve them."

Oskar shrugged. "I can call her. I'll send an email too, but you know how she is. She might not respond for days." Looking over at me, he added, "What kind of person doesn't answer their messages?"

Again, hurt yet vindicated.

"How about the letters Abraham wrote to Elsbeth?" Daniel asked, looking at me. "Have you ever heard anything about that from your family, Ada?"

I was about to say no when suddenly I sat up straight. "Yes! I have. In fact, I've seen one of the letters myself. Lexie gave me a copy. It was from Abraham to Elsbeth, and Lexie has the original." Thinking that through for a moment, I realized *Mammi* had given it to Lexie. Though I'd never heard *Mammi* refer to any letters, nor had I ever seen any others, there was certainly a chance that more than just that one had been saved and ended up in her care. I said as much now, looking from Daniel to Herr Lauten.

They wanted to contact *Mammi* immediately, though Alice reminded them that "immediate" in Amish terms wasn't exactly the swiftest of actions. A message left on the phone in the barn might not be answered for several days, and by then it would be too late.

We decided the best approach was to call Aunt Marta and enlist her help. She could run to *Mammi*'s and ask about the letters in person, and if *Mammi* really did have them, then Aunt Marta could drive into town and ship them to us via overnight delivery. I worried what such a shipment might cost, but Daniel assured me that it would be paid either by Herr Lauten or out of the budget of the historical committee.

Thus, while Alice and Christy helped Oskar clear the table, Herr Lauten led Daniel and me to his study, where I used his phone to call Aunt Marta. It was just two p.m. at home, and our hope was that if she moved quickly she could get the shipment off today. She sounded pleased to hear from us and didn't seem to mind our request for help. Fortunately, none of her patients were in labor at the moment, so she would be able to juggle around a few appointments and get right on it. If there were indeed letters at *Mammi*'s and if Aunt Marta was successful in sending them off in time, she would have Zed notify Herr Lauten via email.

Once the call was over, we said our goodnights, and I headed upstairs to my room. My body was tired but my brain was spinning, so once I was ready for bed I puttered around a bit first, going through my suitcase and organizing Christy's schoolwork. We wouldn't have time to do much more until the trip home.

Finally, I could feel myself winding down, so I climbed into bed and turned off the light. Pulling the downy comforter up to my chin and snuggling into the soft mattress, I felt as though I could sleep for a month. As I drifted off, I could hear the rush of the waterfall through the open window. It sounded like music, soothing my soul.

Twenty-One

Our visit with the lawyer the next morning lasted almost two hours. We spent most of that time going through papers, both the ones that Ms. Holt had already acquired and those that Alice and *Mammi* had rounded up from back home. The lawyer seemed disappointed, of course, when Daniel told her that the actual agreement hadn't yet been found—if indeed it still existed at all. But she seemed especially upset to learn that no one in either of our families had ever heard of the agreement or knew anything about it. At least she was relieved that we'd been able to provide ample documentation of our lineage and of *Mammi*'s inheritance, with numerous birth certificates, wills, deed transfers, and much more.

She did perk up a bit when Daniel showed her an entry in one of Abraham Sommers' business journals, dated May 22, 1877.

"This is the most direct reference to the agreement that we've been able to find," he told her. As she looked it over, he explained to Alice and me what it said. "Abraham documents the price he paid for the land and says that in conjunction with the deed transfer, the two men had also signed an agreement that would preserve the property for the potential return of Kessler or of his descendants."

I nodded, glad to know that at least we had that much.

"You saw this part here?" Ms. Holt asked Daniel, then she glanced over at Alice and me before looking back down at the paper and translating it into English for us. "Once the sale was completed, he says, 'The notary has filed the deed with the land register and has provided me with the appropriate transfer of ownership papers. I have retained the related agreement myself, preferring not to have its contents available publically, and have put it in a safe place, one that offers more privacy than the land registry office.'" Looking up at us, she added, "I guess that explains why the agreement hasn't turned up. Sounds like ol' Abe tucked it away somewhere a little too safe."

Alice and I looked at each other. Though I was feeling more defeated by the moment, her expression was still calmly, faithfully optimistic. I knew I would do well to follow her example.

We moved on from there, reviewing the rest of the documents. The ones I found the most interesting were those dated in the late 1870s that related to the small group of Mennonites who had emigrated together from this region of the Emmental to Indiana, including Elsbeth and her husband, Gerard Gingrich, and Ulrich Kessler and his family. The various marriage licenses, naturalization records, land patents, survey plots, and more provided an intriguing picture of how their story might have played out. I only wished there was some way to go back and get more details straight from those who had lived it. Perhaps the letters between Abraham and Elsbeth would end up giving us exactly that—providing we'd be able to find them, of course. At breakfast we'd learned that not only had there been no word yet from Marta as to whether she'd had any success at *Mammi*'s or not, but Oskar still hadn't heard back from Giselle, either.

Once we'd reviewed all of the documents and answered Betsy Holt's many questions, she sat back in her chair and explained to us what would happen next. She said that the registry handled this type of matter at the district level.

"That means our hearing will be here in Langnau," she said. "We're scheduled for Wednesday morning at ten."

My heart sank. That was just two days away! Even if we were somehow able to get all of the letters by then, that wouldn't give us enough time to go through them, at least not thoroughly. Daniel was obviously thinking the same thing, because he asked if the hearing could be postponed until Thursday.

Ms. Holt shook her head. "With such a complex case, I feel sure we won't be handed a ruling the day of the hearing. The more time the judge has to make his decision, the better. If the case is heard on Wednesday, that gives him until Friday to give us a ruling. The land commission's deadline is at four p.m. Friday afternoon, so it has to happen before then. We'll make sure the judge is aware of that, and as long as he can decide this case in time, we're good."

"But what about the letters?" Daniel pressed. "What if they contain new evidence that doesn't come to light until Thursday?"

She shrugged, saying if we found any new evidence that was extremely compelling, she could pass it along to the judge after the hearing but prior to his ruling.

She glanced at her watch and began closing up the files and gathering the papers. As she did she briefly explained the approach she planned to take with the court. A lot of what she said was way over my head, but from what I could tell, the biggest factor in our favor was the deed itself, which clearly stipulated a first right of refusal for Ulrich Kessler or his heirs. "As you know, Daniel, it's the associated language that's causing all the problems," she said, pointing to a paragraph on her copy of the deed.

"And Lex Koller?" Daniel asked as he tucked his own papers away. "Any help there?" I wasn't sure who Lex Koller was, but this was the first I had heard of anyone by that name. Her answer made no sense to me at all, so I decided to ask Daniel about him later.

As they wrapped things up, I glanced over at Alice, who had sat quietly through the entire meeting. At the moment she looked as if she might be just a few more complicated legal terms away from a sound sleep. I wasn't doing much better myself by that point, so I was glad we seemed to be finished. When we all stood, Daniel asked the lawyer if there was anything else official we needed to do before the hearing on Wednesday.

"Find me that agreement," she urged, smiling. "Or at least find those letters, and keep rounding up every other pertinent document you can locate. My hope is that we can paint such a complete picture of the situation that the judge will rule in our favor. Beyond that, I suppose you might, uh, pray." She said that last word with a glance at Alice and me, though I couldn't tell if she was being sarcastic or sincere. She was an odd woman, her manner brusque but her English so natural that I had a feeling she must be a native speaker. Either that, or at least she'd spent extensive time in the States.

"Herr Lauten said something about some meetings this afternoon that you might want us to attend?" Daniel asked.

Her face lit up, and she looked again at Alice and me.

"Oh, right! Not meetings, just a little PR. Thanks for reminding me," she said, and then she reached for her phone and started dialing a number. It sounded as though she was put on hold, after which she placed a hand over the receiver and asked Daniel if he could have us over at the waterfall around two or three today. "I have a buddy over at the *Wochen Zeitung* who is willing to do a cover story. Can't beat this photo op, huh?"

She gestured toward Alice and me, but before either of us could respond, she was talking into the phone. I looked over at Daniel in alarm, hoping she wasn't talking about what I thought she was talking about.

"Daniel—" I whispered, but he waved me off, listening intently to her conversation. I couldn't understand many of her words, but by the time she put the person on hold, she didn't seem happy.

"Figures," she said, looking at him. "Wouldn't you know, the township has surveyors over there on the property all week. We can't even get close to the falls. Can you think of an alternate setting, something that could still help us in swaying the greenies? I don't want to use the mansion at Amielbach. That could actually be counterproductive."

Glancing at us, Daniel shook his head slowly and told her that in no way would Alice or I be willing to pose for any photographs. She looked shocked, but even after he explained that it was against our religion, she just pursed her lips in irritation, shaking her head. "Without pictures, the article will end up getting buried somewhere in the middle, if they decide to run it at all."

Seeming ambivalent, Daniel looked at Alice and me and explained that one way to help our case was to sway public opinion. Right now, he said, most folks in Wasserdorf were siding with the hydro plant, thanks to some very well-placed newspaper ads and articles highlighting the ecological benefits of such a clean energy source.

"The thinking is that we can trump that big time," the lawyer continued, turning to appeal to me directly, "by showing how two poor Amish women came all this way—by cargo ship, no less—just to preserve this site that's so vitally significant to their heritage." She paused for a moment and then added, "The original vision was to get some shots of the two of you in your costumes there at the falls, looking off toward the caves where your ancestors hid. But even with the falls off-limits, I'm sure we can come up with something almost as effective." As an afterthought, she added, "Bear in mind, ladies, in a case as politically delicate as this one, a couple of quick photos could make the difference between winning and losing."

Her little speech finished, her words hung in the air for a long moment as I tried to think how to refuse without sounding as rude to her as she had just been to us. Before I could come up with anything, however, Alice spoke instead.

"Thank you, but no," she told the woman, her voice polite but firm. "Better to lose with integrity than to win with compromise."

I was glad once we were finally out of there and on the sidewalk, the sun warm on our shoulders, the fresh air a relief after the stifling atmosphere inside. George had offered to keep an eye on Christy during our appointment, taking her through the clusters of little shops that lined the streets of the town. We were to meet them in the ice cream parlor on the corner at noon. Even though we'd be early, we headed there now, ignoring the stares of passersby as we walked.

Glancing at Alice, I wanted to say something about the lawyer, in particular her comment about us in our "costumes." But her face looked as serene as always, and so I held my tongue, not wanting to sound petty or spiteful.

Instead, I asked Daniel my questions. I started with the one about the deed, saying I wanted to know what the lawyer had meant by the "associated language" in the document that was causing problems.

"Ugh, I practically know it by heart," he replied, not even pulling out his photocopy for reference. "'The Grantor hereby conveys this property deed free and clear of third-party claims and encumbrances with the exception of those stipulated in the agreement regarding first right of refusal for Ulrich Kessler or his heirs. See related agreement for complete list of stipulations.' It's that last sentence that's troubling us, because obviously there's more to the agreement than just the first right of refusal. Otherwise, why would the deed even mention that there were other stipulations?"

I nodded. No wonder they were concerned.

We passed the open door of a chocolate shop, and for a moment I was distracted by the incredible smells coming from inside. Seeing my hesitation, Daniel assured me that far better chocolate could be had at the ice cream parlor where we were going.

"This joint's for tourists. If you want the real thing, you need to get it at Eiscremezeit."

We kept going, and I asked my next question about the man he'd brought up, the one whose name I hadn't recognized.

"What man?"

"Lex, I think? Lex Carter?"

Daniel thought for a moment and then surprised me by laughing.

"Lex Koller?"

"Yes. Who is that?"

Still smiling, he said, "That's not a who; that's a what. Lex Koller is a law, also known as the *Bundesgesetz über den Erwerb von Grundstücken durch Personen im Ausland.*"

"Huh," I replied. "Guess I prefer Lex Koller."

He chuckled. "Anyway, Lex Koller is the federal law that deals with the acquisition of real estate by what's known as 'persons abroad.'"

"And that's us?"

"Yep." Glancing around, he lowered his voice and said, "In my opinion, the Swiss government wants to limit as much foreign-owned property as possible. They make it difficult to buy in here, with all sorts of requirements and stipulations, whatever it takes to discourage foreign ownership. My hope is that this attitude may actually work in our favor, because we can show the court that if they will clear the title, we will sell it back to a citizen of Switzerland."

"And did Ms. Holt agree?"

He shrugged. "She said it could work either for us or against us. It's kind of complicated, but the township of Wasserdorf could actually turn around and use Lex Koller to seize the property for the hydro plant, claiming that a past, unauthorized transfer of the land invalidated your grandmother's ownership entirely."

"I see."

When we reached the ice cream parlor, I decided I didn't want to talk about the subject any more. My brain was tired, and Alice was looking so bored her eyes had practically glazed over.

Daniel held the door for us, and as we stepped inside, I took a deep breath, inhaling not just chocolate but other delicious smells as well. Moving forward, I realized they were making waffle cones behind the counter, which accounted for at least one of the delectable scents enveloping us.

The place was fairly empty, though Daniel said that by late afternoon the line for ordering would be out the door. I wanted to get some ice cream, but as we hadn't even had lunch yet, I decided to settle for a piece of chocolate instead.

I moved toward the large case of assorted treats, eyeing them hungrily as I tried to make up my mind. Alice excused herself to find the restroom, and then Daniel said he needed to slip out for a minute as well. His watch had been running slower every day of this trip—risky business in so punctual a place as Switzerland—but he had spotted a little shop next door where he thought they might be able to sell him a battery. "We still have some time before the others get here," he said, glancing at his watch. Then he added, "Of course, how would I know? According to this, it's just about time for breakfast."

We both laughed, our eyes holding for a moment. I was thinking what a delightful friend this young man had turned out to be. But then I realized he wasn't looking back at me in quite the same way. Between the sparkle in his eye and the tilt of his head, it struck me that Morgan may have been correct, that maybe he really did like me as more than just a friend. I broke our gaze, looking away, and after a beat he said, "Okay, well, be back shortly."

Then he was gone.

Twenty-Two

Left alone, I put thoughts of Daniel out of my mind and focused on the confections in the display. I settled finally on a fat pretzel coated in white chocolate and drizzled with a ribbon of dark. It wasn't until I went to the register to pay that it struck me that I had no local currency. Apologizing to the cashier, who did not speak English, I tried to make her understand by showing her the contents of my wallet. Nodding, she gestured toward the bills, and I realized she was willing to take U.S. currency instead. I handed over a single bill, and then two, but she didn't seem satisfied until I had given her five. Even at that, all she dropped in my hand in return were two small silver coins. Too embarrassed to tell her I'd changed my mind, I carried my treat to a booth near the window and sat. Soon Alice appeared from the back and slid in across from me.

"Ooo, yummy. What did you get?"

"The world's most expensive pretzel," I replied, holding it up and peeling back the cellophane wrapping. "Would you like some?"

"Thank you, dear. No."

"Just as well," I said, breaking off a tiny piece of the chocolate and setting it on my tongue to melt. "I'd have to charge you a dollar per inch just to break even."

She chuckled, pulling a napkin from the holder and wiping at a smudge on the table. I offered to go get something for her too but she said no, that she had indigestion and didn't want to make it worse.

I took my first full bite, the surge of rich, chocolaty goodness filling my senses. It was worth every penny.

Alice asked where Daniel had gone, and after I explained, she and I sat in companionable silence for a while. She looked pale, but after the meeting we'd just endured, I had a feeling that I probably did too.

"How are you doing, Alice? Are you holding up okay?"

She nodded and then replied that she was just a little tired. "I didn't sleep very well last night," she added, "that's all."

I glanced at the clock. We still had a few minutes before Christy and George were due to arrive. I leaned forward and spoke, lowering my voice.

"How about Christy? Do you think she's doing all right?"

"Her health? Definitely. I haven't seen her so active and lively in a long time."

"How about...in other ways?"

Alice thought for a moment. "She seems to be opening up more. Don't you think?"

"Yes. That's true." Christy *was* more open, though I still felt there was somewhat of a wall between the two of us. I guess I had hoped that the girl would be more trusting of me by now. At least she seemed to come alive when Daniel was around.

"She's definitely doing better." Alice folded up the small napkin and set it aside. "They say the first year is the hardest—she and Lydia were so close, especially with Christy being her only child for so long."

That made sense. Lydia must have poured herself into her daughter. "Have you noticed how Christy reacts to talk of death?"

Alice shook her head.

"She didn't want to discuss the early Anabaptists having been killed. And in *Jane Eyre*, when Morgan reached the part about one of the characters dying, Christy became very agitated and didn't want to hear anymore."

"Oh, dear." Alice's white eyebrows furrowed.

"It's probably pretty typical, don't you think?"

Alice grimaced. "I suppose. I've tried to get her to talk about how she feels, some. I'll try again soon."

We were interrupted by an excited squeal from the doorway. The very girl we'd been speaking of had burst into the room, spotted us, and was dashing to our table. Eyes sparkling, she began to recount the adventure she'd just had. Behind her came a smiling George, looking not unlike a jolly, plaid-shirted Santa Claus. Apparently, when they had grown bored with shopping, he'd taken her to a local cheese factory. Christy had found the whole thing fascinating, especially the gift shop on the way out, where they sold tiny cheeses molded in the shapes of animals.

While she chatted on happily to Alice, George went over to the counter, probably to get some ice cream. The bell over the door jingled, and then Daniel was stepping inside. He spotted George and headed toward him. I could hear pieces of their conversation, and when I realized they were talking about the letters, I excused myself and joined the two men. George said he'd just checked in with Herr Lauten for an update, but we'd still received no word from Giselle. Aunt Marta, on the other hand, had sent us a brief message via email—or rather, Z-mail, as I was starting to think of it thanks to the role Zed played—that said something like "Problems on this end, but we're working on it. Will keep you posted." I had a feeling that meant that *Mammi* indeed had some letters in her possession but was having trouble locating them. I wasn't surprised, as the pack rat gene seemed to have passed all the way down from Abraham Sommers to *Mammi*, and the attic over the *daadi haus* was so full of old trunks and boxes that I knew it could take days to get through them all. I hoped Aunt Marta wasn't just conducting the search herself but had enlisted a whole army of helpers. The community knew what we were doing here, and I had no doubt they would jump in at a moment's notice, as they always did when one of us was in trouble or had a need.

"Until we have the letters, there's not much more we can do back at the house," Daniel said. "Guess we can go ahead and make that stop after all."

"Sounds good to me," George replied. His ice cream was ready, and as he reached across the counter to take the loaded waffle cone from the young woman, I looked at Daniel inquisitively.

"We thought you folks might want to see the oldest Mennonite church in Switzerland, which is right here in Langnau."

"It's one of the highlights that will be on our tour," George added before taking a big lick of his ice cream.

I wasn't sure how to respond. While I would enjoy seeing the church some other time, right now I wanted to get back to Amielbach as soon as possible. "I was hoping we could explore the Kessler property today," I explained. "I'd love to see the waterfall up close and take a peek at the caves behind it." I also wanted to get a look at the nearby cottage where my birth mother lived.

Daniel shrugged. "You heard what the lawyer said, Ada. The township currently has the place all tied up with surveyors." Seeing the disappointment in my face, he added, "We can do that tomorrow, or as soon as they are finished. For now, why don't we grab a quick lunch here in town and then head over to the church?"

I glanced over at Alice and Christy, both of whom would likely vote for seeing the church. Nodding, I agreed to his plan, thinking I could always get a look at Giselle's cottage later, once we got back.

The church was two stories tall with a covered entrance. Green shutters framed every window, and both the building and the grounds were well kept. George requested an English-speaking guide, which meant we ended up getting our own private tour. Deferring to the volunteer's expertise, he moved to stand beside Daniel as we gathered together outside the front entrance of the church and she began her spiel. Speaking in stiff-but-articulate English, she said the building had been constructed in the late eighteen hundreds but that the original congregation had first formed here long before that, in 1530, to be exact.

As she moved toward the double doors and propped them open, she added, "That was just seven years after the first of the martyrs had been drowned in the Limmat River in Zurich."

Alice and I both glanced at Christy, but fortunately she was distracted with a small ladybug that had landed on her sleeve and didn't seem to have heard.

We entered the building through the double doors and then walked down a long hall to a room where the old records and registries were kept. Shelves of books lined the wall at the far end. "We have quite the compilation of resources," the woman said. "Copies of documents from Bern along with our own member records."

Daniel nodded in agreement, whispering to me that he'd visited here last summer and found lots of helpful information.

We passed various classrooms as we circled around the building and finally ended up in the sanctuary. The pews were clean and polished, and I ran my hand along the back of one as the guide explained that the pastor preached in Swiss German, although some of the hymns were in High German. She went on to say that in 1947 the church officially joined the state church of the canton of Bern so they wouldn't have to pay taxes. Daniel met my eyes. It seemed we both caught the irony of the decision, and I was sure Alice and George did too. The early Anabaptists had suffered greatly to separate themselves from the state. Now, it seemed, this church had willingly joined back up for financial reasons. None of us said a word, but my heart felt heavy just thinking about it.

As the guide continued on with the history of the church, Alice moved toward a back pew and sat. She was pale and tired looking, and I wondered if the tour had been too much for her after our long morning at the lawyer's office. I walked over to her, but just as I got there she stood and whispered that she needed some fresh air. She began moving toward the door, so I went with her and Christy followed as well.

Outside, the three of us sat on a bench near the building's entrance, the afternoon sun warm on our faces. At first I thought Alice was reaching for something because her movement was so graceful, but by the time she hit the cobblestones, I realized she had fallen.

"Go get help!" I commanded Christy, kneeling beside Alice. She was unconscious. I put my fingertips to the side of her throat, searching for a pulse.

"Christy?" I turned toward the child. She was frozen to the bench. "Go!" I urged, but she didn't move.

Once I found her pulse, I sprang to my feet, calling for help as I ran, pushing through the door and running toward the sanctuary. "Alice fell!" I shouted.

Daniel tore past me and out the door, reaching Alice first. Then came George. The guide stopped a few feet away, saw what was happening, and ran back inside, I hoped to call for an ambulance.

Through it all, Christy remained frozen on the bench, her hands tightly gripping the edge.

Daniel and I knelt down on each side of Alice, who was still unconscious.

"Alice," I said, gently shaking her by the shoulder. "Can you hear me?"

Her legs moved a little and then her hand. I reached for it. She opened her eyes.

"What happened?" She turned her head toward me.

"You fainted."

"Oh, dear." She tried to push up on her elbow, but Daniel told her to stay still.

"Where's Christy?" she rasped.

"Right here, on the bench," I said. Turning, I motioned for Christy to come to her great-grandmother, but she shook her head and wouldn't even look at us.

Alice insisted on sitting up, but when she did her face grew ashen and she held her arm in a funny way.

"Put your head back down," George said, rolling his jacket and putting it under her neck as Daniel and I helped lower her again.

The tour guide returned. "I called for a *Krankenwagon*. It's on its way."

"Did you hear that, Alice?" Daniel said, patting her good hand. "The ambulance is coming."

"Oh, please. I don't need that. I bruised my arm, that's all."

"Just lie quietly," I said, hoping she was just tired from traveling but afraid it was something more.

Christy stayed statue still on the bench as the rest of us tried to make Alice more comfortable. I thought of the last time an ambulance had come for someone Christy loved. It was the middle of the night. Had she been awake and downstairs? Looking out her bedroom window?

The guide went back into the church and returned with a blanket.

The Swiss equivalent of EMTs arrived, examined Alice, and then readied her for transport to the hospital. Daniel rode in the ambulance with her so he could communicate with the paramedics, although it seemed that they all spoke at least some English. George was trying to figure out the fastest way to get the rest of us to the hospital when the tour guide offered to drive us over in her car.

On the way I sat with Christy in the tiny back seat and tried to comfort her. But she was acting as stoic as an old woman, looking straight ahead and telling me she was fine. Closing my eyes, all I could do was pray for her and for Alice, begging God to let them both be all right.

TWENTY-THREE

By mid afternoon, the doctor joined us in the waiting room. "There are two things of concern," he said in near-perfect English. "First, she has broken her arm. It's a clean break but still very painful. We will cast it. But the more serious issue is that she has congestive heart failure."

"Failure?" I gasped, glancing toward Christy and lowering my voice. "Alice's heart is going to fail?" I was glad to see that the girl was on the other side of the room, watching TV.

"It is a chronic, long-term condition. The heart can no longer pump enough blood to the rest of the body, which in Alice's case has caused congestion to build up in her lungs. We are working on reducing her fluid levels. They need to come down before she can travel home."

"How long will that take?" I asked.

He hesitated. "It is difficult to say. A few days. Maybe longer."

I looked at Daniel and then back at the doctor, processing that.

"I'm sorry doctor, but by home, do you mean the place we're staying while we're here? Or are you talking about her home in America?"

The doctor looked confused, so Daniel explained that we were staying locally for a week, at which point we'd be taking a cargo ship back to the States, where we lived.

"Oh," the doctor replied, looking surprised I had even asked. "I am sorry, but right now it is unsafe for her to fly, much less get on a ship. You must alter the plans for your return entirely. We will stabilize her and reduce her fluid levels, but once she is released she will need to stay somewhere locally for another day or two, just to be safe. After that, you can see about getting her back to the U.S.—but via airplane and absolutely not on a cargo ship."

Ignoring the disdain in his voice at the last two words, I said I understood and we would take care of it. More than anything, I needed to talk to Will as soon as possible.

Daniel asked if Alice should be transferred to a larger hospital, maybe in Bern.

"That's up to you, but we're well equipped to deal with this. It's quite common, especially in elderly patients. We can stabilize her so she can get home. Then her own doctor can take over any long-term care."

"When can we see her?" My eyes were on Christy as I asked.

"In an hour or so, but for only a short time."

After the doctor left, George, Daniel, and I spoke softly. I said I would leave a message for Will, and George said he would rent a car. That way, he could get us back and forth to the hospital as needed. Oskar had given us a lift into Langnau that morning, but we couldn't expect him to keep shuttling us around. At least a rental would be cheaper and more convenient than hiring a van and driver every time.

Daniel asked how we were handling the hospital expenses, and I told him about the conversation George and I had had with the admissions office when we first arrived. With George's help as translator—which had left a lot to be desired, compared to how Daniel would have handled it—I had tried to explain to the woman there that the Amish usually paid for their medical expenses in cash, but that when the cost was catastrophic, we used a faith-based type of community insurance that would cover expenses above and beyond what we could handle. The woman had never heard of such a thing, but she'd admitted Alice anyway, telling us to round up the necessary documentation and get it back to her as soon as possible. Obviously, Will was going to have to find out how Church Aid worked when the patient was in another country and then fax over whatever paperwork he could.

"What are you going to tell Christy?" Daniel whispered.

"I don't know," I said. "I think I'll just tell her about the broken arm and say that Alice will be in the hospital for a while." Figuring out what a child needed was a lot harder than I thought it would be. I hoped Will would have some ideas for me.

I opened my purse and pulled the folded piece of paper with emergency numbers on it, including the one for the Gundy farm. I felt grateful that *Mamm* had compiled the list and insisted I take it.

Because Christy and I wouldn't be able to see Alice for at least an hour, I'd go ahead and call Will. It was 3:30 p.m. here, which meant it was 9:30 in the morning back home.

"I can call the main office of the nursery. They'll know where he is," I said, adding I would get some change and find a pay phone.

"No, use my satellite phone," George told me, handing it over. "If you have to leave a message for him to call back, just give that number." He grabbed a pen from his pocket and wrote it out at the bottom of my phone list. "I can always use the phone at the front desk to make the car arrangements."

"Thank you. I'll be right back, then." Moving down the hall so I could speak privately, I found a quiet alcove beside a water fountain and dialed the Gundys' farm. I'd expected someone to pick up, but instead it went to a machine, so I left a brief message for Will saying Alice was going to be all right but that she was in the hospital in Langnau, and I needed him to call me as soon as he received this message. I read out the number for George's phone and then hung up.

George arranged for the car, which he and Daniel would pick up at a hotel a few blocks away. Once they headed out to do that, I asked Christy if she'd like to go to the hospital cafeteria for a snack. She shrugged, not seeming to care one way or another.

Once we were seated at a table and sharing a bag of chips between us, I told her what the doctor had said, leaving out the part about Alice's heart, thinking Christy might confuse it with her own heart condition and the death of her mother.

"We can go in and see her in a little while," I said.

Christy shrugged.

"She's worried about you," I added. "Remember at the church when she asked where you were?"

Christy shrugged again. I reached across the table and tucked a lock of hair back under her *kapp*.

"I don't want to see her."

"But that would help her by easing her mind that you're all right. You do want to help your great-grandmother, don't you?"

"I guess," she said reluctantly, reaching for the last chip and popping it into her mouth.

Will returned my call a little while later, soon after Christy and I had gone back to the waiting room. I took a deep breath as I answered, but my hands were shaking as I said hello.

"Ada," Will said, his voice sounding far away. "I got your message."

My heart pounding, I stood and walked away from Christy so I could speak more freely. Sounding far calmer than I felt, I gave him the details of what had happened to Alice and what the doctor had told us. I also explained about the insurance issues and read off the fax number the admissions woman had given me. Then, finally, still trying to keep a handle on my emotions, I told him I was worried about Christy too, and I explained her reaction to Alice's collapse.

"Let me speak to her."

I walked back into the waiting room and handed her the phone, leading her away from the TV. She mostly nodded and said yes or no. After a little while she handed the phone back.

"It's Ada again."

Will told me he thought she'd be all right. "She's frightened, that's all." Then he said he would buy a plane ticket and leave as soon as possible.

"You're coming here?" I choked.

"Of course. I'll call this number as soon as I know when. Tell my grandmother. I already told Christy I would see her soon and that she needed to stay strong and be of help to you."

Will said he'd try to fly into Bern instead of Zurich because it was closer. "Maybe Giselle could pick me up."

"She's not here." I explained to him about her exhibit and how it didn't sound as though we'd be seeing her at all.

"Call her again," he said firmly. "Tell her what's going on. She's family. She should be there to help you, Ada."

I shivered a little at the sound of my name.

After we hung up, I cried just a bit, out in the hall away from Christy, mostly from relief that Will was coming to help. Then I thought about what he said and pulled out Giselle's number. I stared at it a moment, not sure of what to do. What if I asked her to come and she said no?

Just then a nurse motioned to me and said we could see Mrs. Beiler now. I put the phone in the pocket of my apron and called to Christy, and then we went into Alice's room together. There were two vinyl chairs, one on each side of the room, and Alice was propped up in the bed, her broken arm in a sling, with an IV tube going into her good arm. She wore a hospital gown and no *kapp*, her straight white hair hanging down in a single braid instead of tucked up in a bun the way it usually was. Lying there, she looked so vulnerable—not to mention almost naked without her *kapp*—and I was shocked that in the span of a few hours she went from seeming so healthy to being so frail. But the fact was she hadn't actually been in good health. I'd just thought so.

"Come here," she said to Christy.

The girl obliged, even though she seemed uncomfortable. She approached the side of the bed.

They didn't say anything for a moment. Then Christy stepped closer and Alice reached out with her good arm. "See, I'm fine," she said. "I do have a break—all these years I've never had a broken bone, and then I end up with one in a foreign country. Isn't that something?"

Christy shrugged, offering up a small smile.

"Once the swelling goes down a little, I'll be getting a cast. Do you want to be the first to sign it?"

Christy smiled a little more, but she didn't say anything, so I told Alice Will was coming.

"Why ever for?" Alice sat up a little straighter. "And leave the twins? And the business? He shouldn't do that."

I hadn't thought that someone else could come—Benjamin, Will's dad, or his mother, Nancy. It was harder for me to imagine them navigating the trip. Will would do much better.

"It was his idea to come."

"I'm sure it was." I could tell she was in pain by the edge to her voice. She was probably thinking about both the loss of work and the cost of Will traveling. "I'll be fine. They'll put a cast on my arm…"

I wasn't sure if she wasn't talking about her congestive heart failure because of Christy or because she didn't comprehend the condition.

"The doctor said you'll be in the hospital for several days, maybe longer." My voice was calm and gentle. "And then once you are out, after resting a couple more days, you will need to be flown home, not go by ship."

Alice closed her eyes. "We'll see."

We were all silent for a moment. I wondered at Alice's denial, while Christy picked at the cotton blanket.

The nurse shooed us out then, and I left Christy in front of the TV again. Stepping back out into the hall, I thought of *Mammi* and of how much she wanted me to see Giselle.

I leaned against the wall, touching the phone through the pocket of my apron. No matter how much my birth mother might not want to see me, we still needed her here regardless of how it turned out. I had to try, for Alice's and *Mammi*'s sakes, if not my own.

I took the paper from my purse again and dialed slowly, expecting the call to go into her voice mail. It didn't. Giselle picked up on the second ring.

"Ada." She must have recognized the number. "I've been meaning to call you. It turns out I can't—"

"Alice is in the hospital in Langnau," I interrupted. "We need you to come."

"Pardon?"

I repeated myself, verbatim, adding, "She collapsed. Besides breaking her arm, the doctor said she has congestive heart failure."

There was a long pause. Then she said, "I'll leave within the hour."

I thanked her and hung up, realizing I had no idea how far away Frankfurt was or when she'd arrive. I slipped the phone into my pocket, and only then did it occur to me that I hadn't thought to ask her about the letters. Somehow, at the moment they seemed like the least important thing going on here.

Christy stood in the doorway of the waiting room, watching me. "Is your aunt coming?"

"*Ya*," I answered.

"What's wrong?" Christy stepped closer to me. "Besides that my *gross-mammi* is sick."

I sighed. She would find out sooner or later anyway. "Giselle is my aunt," I said. "But she's also my birth mother. I was adopted by *Mamm* and *Daed*."

"Oh," was all Christy said. But when we went back into the waiting room she sat next to me on the couch. "Did you bring the book?" she asked.

"Which book?" I thought she was referring to her schoolwork.

"*Jane Eyre*."

"It's in my purse."

"Would you read it to me?" She scooted a little closer.

I pulled it from my bag and we settled in, the weight of her shoulder warm against my side, the scent of her hair sweet and calming to my soul.

I opened the novel, but before I found our place, Christy said, "Ada?" Her voice was soft and pained.

"What is it?" I put my arm around her and drew her closer.

"Did I make *Grossmammi* sick?"

"What? What are you talking about?"

"I was really mean to her this morning in our room, when she told me where we were going and I thought I'd have to sit in some dumb lawyer's office all day. Then, of course, there was that whole shopping thing, at breakfast."

"What shopping thing?"

She thought for a moment and said, "Oh, right. You'd left the table by then."

She squirmed a bit, so I tried to look into her eyes as I asked what had happened.

Her face contorted with shame, she explained. "I was complaining about having to go to the meeting and George offered to take me shopping instead. I didn't even ask her if it was okay. I just looked at her and said, 'You can do whatever you want, *Grossmammi*, but I'm going shopping with George.' Everybody laughed, but she and I both knew I was being disrespectful. It was wrong of me to talk to her like that, especially in front of the others. I never apologized, not even later at the ice cream parlor when she was being so nice to me." By the end of her confession, her chin was quivering.

I was at a loss for words but tried to do the best I could, assuring her that what had happened to Alice had absolutely nothing whatsoever to do with her.

"But she was fine until she fell. Maybe she was overtired because of me. *Daed* says that she's old and we need to be cooperative—"

"Christy," I interrupted. I realized I had to tell her about Alice's heart condition because it would hurt her more not to know. So I did, adding, "It's what older people get. It's very different from the condition you have and what your mother had."

She buried her head against my arm, sobs racking her body.

"Sweetie, you are not to blame one bit," I said, bending my head toward her. At that moment I wondered if guilt was one of the biggest weights she'd been carrying all these months. "You don't think you're to blame for your mother, do you?" My voice was soft and gentle.

Her head bounced against my arm, and a muffled, "*Ya*," escaped her.

"Oh, Christy." I lifted her chin with my hand and gazed into her red-rimmed eyes. "Your mother's death had absolutely nothing to do with you. There's nothing you could have done that would have made it your fault."

She sobbed again.

"Nobody knew she was ill, not even the doctors. It's the absolute truth, Christy Gundy," I said. "You must believe me."

She nodded her head, just a little, but I wasn't sure she was convinced. I wrapped my arms around her and hugged her tight. She gripped me back even more tightly, as if she were drowning and I was her only lifeline.

TWENTY-FOUR

We headed back to Amielbach once hospital visiting hours were over. Will had called to say he had a ticket and would arrive in Bern tomorrow evening. I was amazed—and relieved—that he was able to make all of his plans so quickly. He also had some very good news. Thanks to the Ella-to-Ezra lifeline, he'd gotten wind of the hunt for the letters over at *Mammi*'s, and he'd just hung up with a very excited Aunt Marta, who said that they had found them. The plan was for him to bring them over on the plane when he came, which at this point would get them here even more quickly than a rush delivery.

On the drive Christy seemed to be more at ease with me than she'd been the entire trip. She and I sat together in the backseat as George carefully maneuvered the car around the curves. When he let us out at the bottom of the steps to Amielbach, Christy surprised me by reaching for my hand.

As we pushed through the front doors, I was thankful that we'd all had a bowl of soup at the hospital for dinner. That was one less thing we would have to worry about now. Daniel told Christy he'd seen a stack of games last night in the dining hall. "Want to play Scrabble?" he asked.

She shook her head.

"We could ask if there's a Ping-Pong table hidden away somewhere." He nudged her in his teasing manner, but she didn't smile.

She led the way down the long entryway, with me following closely behind her.

"Herr Lauten said something about a ballroom on the third floor." Daniel stepped quickly to catch up with us. "Maybe some rollerblades are around. That would be a lot of fun."

I wanted to see it, but not tonight. I just wanted to go to bed, and I could tell that Christy did too.

Oskar was behind the desk when we entered the grand room. "There you are," he said. "How's Alice?"

Before I could answer, Herr Lauten stepped into the room from the hallway. "Here you are, at last!" He hurried toward us, his cane tapping against the floor. "How was Alice when you left? And how are all of you?"

"She's resting comfortably," I said. "Her pain seems to have subsided." I added that the only new information we had was that Christy's father would arrive the following evening.

"Splendid!" Herr Lauten exclaimed, turning his attention toward Oskar. "We'll need to set up another room."

"Or not. Maybe just change the sheets. I had a call from Giselle." Oskar had a key in his hand and looked straight at me. "She asked me to get her cottage ready. She wants you and Christy to stay there. I stocked the fridge and made up the futon in her office."

I took a deep breath. I didn't want to move down to the cottage, not tonight.

Looking at Oskar, Daniel said, "Did you ask her about the letters?"

He shrugged, saying he did but she acted as though she didn't even know what he was talking about. "She was in a hurry," he added. "We can explain better once she gets here." Looking at me, he asked if we needed help with our luggage.

"I've got it," Daniel assured him.

"Wait, though," I said, even as Christy stood yawning beside me. "I'm not sure about this."

"Giselle was pretty clear it was what she wanted," Oskar said.

I couldn't imagine why. But if so it would be a goodwill gesture on my part to comply. After our strained phone conversations, I wanted to do whatever I could to encourage a connection. Oskar handed me the key, and Daniel took off toward the staircase with me following. Christy trailed behind us up the stairs and then took her time getting packed. I finally went in and finished up for her, accidently knocking Alice's silver hairbrush to the floor. As I picked it up, Christy stopped what she was doing and turned toward me. I noted tears in her eyes, and then I realized mine were brimming too. I placed the brush back on the dresser and said a silent prayer for both of us—and for Alice too.

When we went back down, Oskar met us at the bottom of the stairs with a flashlight. "Follow the walkway around the side and then veer off on the path to the right," he said. "Follow it down the hill about one hundred meters. You'll come to a shed and then Giselle's cottage."

Daniel carried both of our suitcases down the steps and then led the way around the building. Christy held the flashlight, shining the beam over the brick path. Moss lined the sides of the walkway. Tall trees grew here and there, but the grounds, covered with ferns and low shrubs, were more like a park than a forest. The path turned downward gently and then evened out. We were too tired to speak as we walked, and the only noise was the roar of the waterfall in the distance.

Ahead was the outbuilding with a light. By the time we reached the back of it, I was squinting to see the cottage. I heard a rustling in the trees and then the call of some animal. Christy yelped, but Daniel just chuckled and said it was an owl.

"The owls in Lancaster County do not sound like that," she protested.

Daniel didn't miss a beat, replying, "Guess that's because the owls here speak Swiss German."

We were so tired that it took a few seconds before either Christy or I laughed.

"There it is," I said, pointing ahead at another building. It was a quaint structure with a sloped roof. A moment later I was trying to find the keyhole in the weathered door. At first the key wouldn't turn, but I jiggled it around a bit and that did the trick. I pushed, and the door swung open.

The cottage was warm and a light was on. Christy and Daniel followed me inside. He left our suitcases in the hall, and we stepped into a small kitchen with tiny, stainless steel appliances and a window seat tucked into a corner past the small refrigerator. The seat there was more than inviting with its plush cushion and pillows. We came back out of the kitchen and moved on into the living room. The contrast between the charming antiquity of the cottage and the stark modernity of the decor was startling. Every piece of furniture was new. A white couch and chair were arranged around a low glass table. The lamps were silver with white plastic shades. Off to the side was a small table with two black, sleek chairs.

"The room we're to sleep in must be down the hall," I said. We back-tracked. Sure enough, the door to the first room was open and a futon bed was made up inside.

"Here's the bathroom," Christy said. I stepped out into the hall. She was at the end of it now. "And another room." She opened the door. "It's a bedroom," she said.

Most likely Giselle's. "Close the door," I said. "We don't want to snoop."

She obeyed and came back toward me. We both thanked Daniel, and then I tried to give him the flashlight to take with him, but he refused. "You might need it," he said.

I didn't plan to go anywhere until morning, but I kept it just the same.

"Lock the door," he said as he left, which I did.

I asked Christy if she wanted a snack before bed, and we went to the kitchen to see what Oskar had left for us. We found alpine cheese and yogurt in the refrigerator, apples in a basket on the counter, and hearty rolls in the bread box. There was also muesli for breakfast and a carton of milk. We each had a single slice of the cheese, and then, while she put on her pajamas, I brushed my teeth and washed my face.

Once she was ready for bed, we both knelt and prayed silently. My mind somersaulted from Alice to Giselle, and then from Will to Christy in such a tumble that I was sure my prayers were hardly coherent. I was thankful God knew what was in my heart.

I tucked Christy in and then climbed in beside her. She fell asleep right away, and I tried but only tossed and turned, wondering how Alice was, wondering what time Giselle would arrive, wondering when Will would be leaving for the airport. Finally I got out of bed and pulled from my suit-case the tour book of Switzerland I'd checked out from the library, want-ing to check the distance between Frankfurt and Langnau.

I grabbed the extra blanket off the end of the bed and tiptoed out of the room, deciding to settle on the window seat in the kitchen. I opened the guidebook to the map of Europe in the back and found Germany. From the map, it looked as if it would take four or five hours for her to drive from Frankfurt to Langnau, but I couldn't be sure. For all I knew she was taking the train, though whether that would make it a shorter or longer trip, I wasn't sure.

I looked through more of the book, absently flipping the pages and studying the photos. When I could feel my eyes growing heavy, I closed them without even turning off the light. It felt as if the temperature was dropping, and I wondered if perhaps frost was falling. I hoped Giselle would arrive soon.

Those were my last thoughts until I awoke to a woman with short red hair, streaked with gold, staring at me. "Ada?"

I recognized her face. She looked like Lexie—though older, of course.

I blinked, keeping the blanket around my shoulders, my gaze locked on Giselle. Her brown eyes seemed tired, and after a moment she flinched and glanced away. I started to stand, but she held out her hand and said, "Don't get up. We can talk in the morning." She was speaking in English, as she had when we spoke on the phone.

She turned away from me and walked through the kitchen. She was wearing skinny jeans, and the heels of her fashionable boots clicked across the hardwood floors.

My heart raced. She seemed both familiar and foreign, all at once.

"Wake me in the morning if you're up before I am," she called out over her shoulder.

Before I could answer the light went off and her footsteps were in the hall and then gone. I sat that way for quite a while. Then, with the blanket still wrapped around me, I headed back toward the office and climbed into bed beside Christy.

The next morning, Tuesday, my young charge was up and dressed and sitting on the edge of the bed when I awoke. Light was streaming through the window, and someone was knocking on the front door of the cottage.

"They have been knocking for a while," she said. "I didn't know if I should answer it not."

I groaned. Giselle must have been sleeping too soundly to have heard it. "Go ahead and get it. It's probably Daniel or George."

Christy came back a minute later. "It was Daniel. He and George are heading to town, and they wanted to know if we'd like a ride to the hospital."

"What did you tell him?"

"I said you weren't dressed yet, but he said they had an appointment and couldn't wait."

An appointment? For a moment, I wondered if there'd been a new development in our property case, but then I remembered George saying he had errands in town.

"It's just as well," I told her. "Why don't you have a bowl of cereal while I get myself together. Then we should see about heading down to the hospital. Giselle can take us."

Christy nodded and started to go, but then she turned back, adding, "Oh, yeah. He also said don't forget to ask her for the letters as soon as she gets up. If we go anywhere, we're supposed to leave them up at the main house with Herr Lauten so Daniel can start reading through them as soon as he gets back."

I crawled out of bed and took a couple of minutes in the bathroom, brushing my hair and teeth. Then I knocked gently on Giselle's door, but she didn't answer. I turned the knob. She was in bed with a blanket pulled over her head.

I cleared my throat. She stirred. "Good morning," I said.

Her head popped out from under her pillow. "What time is it?" Makeup was smeared under her eyes.

"Eight thirty. The people we're traveling with have gone off in the rental car. Could you give us a ride to the hospital?"

She yawned and then flopped onto her stomach. "Give me a few."

Once I was fully dressed and ready for the day, I joined Christy in the kitchen. We heard Giselle turn on the shower in the bathroom. After we washed our dishes, I suggested we look around the outside of the cottage while we waited for her.

My heart raced at the thought of interacting with Giselle in the car. Our brief meeting last night hadn't left me any more hopeful than our phone conversations had.

Christy and I put on our capes and slipped through the front door. A chill hung in the morning air, but it was another clear and bright day in our seemingly endless string of beautiful autumn weather.

Flower beds surrounded the little cottage. It hadn't frosted last night after all. The blooms were fading but were not dead yet—cosmos and dahlias, geraniums and lobelia, impatiens and snapdragons—all the same flowers we had at home.

Christy climbed to a little rise to the right of the cottage. "I can see the waterfall from here!" she called out.

I joined her. A wide creek divided the two properties. The falls themselves were high, the water spilling over them powerful. No doubt the site would make a great place for a hydro plant.

The door to the cottage opened and Giselle came out. She wore a different pair of skinny jeans, a darker shade of denim this time, a black jacket, and boots. Her hair was still damp and wavy around her face. She slid a pair of sunglasses over her eyes as she walked toward us.

I tried to think of something to say, but she looked right past me and zeroed in on Christy. "So you're Alice's great-granddaughter?"

Christy nodded, shyly.

Giselle stepped closer to her. "I knew your *grossmammi*, years ago." She seemed happy to see Christy, and the thought entered my head that perhaps she was the reason Giselle had asked us to stay at her cottage. "And you are Will's oldest daughter?"

Christy smiled and said yes.

"Well, doesn't that beat all. He used to be nothing more than a little squirt."

Christy chuckled. I doubted anyone had called Will "little" in her lifetime, much less "squirt."

Then Giselle looked at me, her smile fading into a vacant stare. "Shall we go see Alice?"

Twenty-Five

Giselle drove a black compact car and took the turns down to the village at a speed I thought was much too fast. I glanced at Christy in the backseat several times to make sure she was all right. Her eyes were big but she didn't seem frightened. Giselle wanted to know the details of Alice falling and what the doctor had said. Because Christy was with us, I gave her the short version and then said Will was flying in tonight.

"Really?" she said. "I can't imagine little Will all grown-up."

"He's not so little anymore," Christy chirped.

Giselle smiled and glanced into the rearview mirror. "He was younger than you the last time I saw him."

I quickly did the math. Will would have been around eight years old when she left.

Again, she glanced in the rearview mirror toward Christy. "I'm surprised your *mamm* let you travel all the way to Switzerland at such a young age."

I glanced quickly at Christy. Her face was frozen. I intervened, explaining that Christy's mother had passed away last winter. Giselle clearly felt bad. "I'm so sorry," she said to Christy. "You poor thing. And your poor *daed.*"

Again the silence was heavy. I wanted Giselle to ask about *Mammi*. And about my parents and Aunt Marta and even Ella and Zed. I wanted her to ask about Lexie. Mostly I wanted her to ask about me. But she didn't. There was an awkward silence, and I was at a loss as to how to fill it. I had no idea what questions she would be all right with my asking her. Finally, I inquired about her trip to Germany.

"It was fine."

"You were at some sort of exhibit?"

"Yes."

"You're an artist," I said, more a statement than a question. When she didn't reply, I asked, "Did the exhibit go well for you?"

"Sold a few pieces, yeah."

"Is that what is done at an exhibit? The artists sell their work?"

Giselle didn't answer. As she steered out of a curve, just past a clearing in the trees, there was a light brown cow with a bell around her neck smack-dab in the middle of the narrow road. I gasped, but before I could speak Giselle had deftly maneuvered around the beast. The cowbell clanged faintly as we sped away.

Then she said, "Yes, I do sell my work, among other things. I was supposed to talk about it, too, with slides and everything, but I had to reschedule. I'll go back to do that in a couple of weeks."

I imagined my birth mother in a classroom, the attendees hanging on her every word. I smiled, sitting up straighter. "Sort of like teaching?" I asked eagerly, thrilled at the thought I'd inherited my gift from her.

"I guess."

"Ada's been teaching me on this trip," Christy interjected. "She's really good at it, way better than any teacher I've ever had in school."

Before I could respond, Giselle said, "I'm not. I hate all that stuff. But it's a necessary part of what I do. Gotta play the game, you know."

I slumped back against the seat, disappointed my teaching gene didn't come from her after all. Deflated, I stared out the window at the passing fields until I mustered the drive to find a new topic of conversation. "Did you drive or take the train?"

"Drove," she answered brusquely.

She was silent after that, and I gave up, just too weary to keep trying.

Giselle took the corners in Langnau fast too, and in no time she was zipping her little car into the hospital parking lot and then stopping it abruptly in a space near the entrance.

She grabbed her purse and had slammed her door before I had a chance to step from the car. It took another moment for Christy to climb out of the backseat, and by the time she did, Giselle was already at the entrance of the hospital. "Hurry!" she called out to us.

"She's odd," Christy whispered as she walked beside me.

"Shh."

Giselle was at the receptionist's desk by the time we caught up with her. I said what room Alice was in before the young woman found the information. This time I led the way.

Alice was sitting up in bed, reading a Bible she held with one hand, her other arm now in a cast. Her *kapp* was back on her head, over a tidy bun, and she looked more like herself again.

"Oh, Giselle," she said, putting down the book.

Giselle stepped forward and fell into Alice's open arm. Christy and I stopped at the foot of the bed, watching. It was obvious immediately that Alice was crying, but it wasn't until Giselle stepped away that I saw she had tears streaming down her face too. She snatched two tissues from the box on the table, handed one to Alice, and then quickly began wiping her face, including the mascara that had smeared under her eyes.

Alice reached for Giselle's hand and pulled her close again. "Frannie said to tell you how much she loves you and misses you."

Giselle nodded. "I know. I miss her letters, even if it usually took me forever to reply."

"It's hard for her to write now," Alice said.

"I understand. But I still miss them."

The thought of *Mammi* writing Giselle left me cold. Partly because my grandmother had a secret I knew nothing about, and partly because I wondered if she'd written about me all those years ago. Did she write about when I learned to walk? When I lost my first tooth? When I started school? If so, had Giselle even cared? Had she written *Mammi* back with questions about me?

Alice turned her attention to Christy then and called the girl to her, asking how she was doing and what she thought of her *daed* flying on an airplane all this way. As Christy sat in the chair beside Alice, Giselle said she needed a cup of coffee and would be right back. Without asking me if I'd like some as well, she was gone.

Alice picked up the Bible again. "The chaplain found a High German translation for me," she said. "Listen to what I was reading."

She read Psalm 139 aloud, and though my mind was full with other things, I forced myself to concentrate on the words. Her voice rose slightly as she came to verses nine and ten, which promised that even when we went "to the far side of the sea," God would still be with us.

Alice paused and looked at both of us. "Isn't that fitting, girls? That's the three of us, right now, on the far side of the sea. And yet God is still with us."

She read until we were interrupted by the telephone. I answered it and was surprised to hear Daniel on the other end of the line. He said he was calling because he and George had just returned from their appointment at the cheese factory and wanted to know where the letters were I was supposed to have gotten from Giselle and left with Herr Lauten.

My cheeks flushing with heat, I realized I had forgotten all about them. The situation between Giselle and me was so emotionally overcharged that it shouldn't have been surprising. Still, he didn't understand any of that, so I didn't begrudge the fact that he sounded a little irritated with me.

"We were so eager to get down here to the hospital that I forgot to ask her," I said. "She's off getting a cup of coffee right now, but she should be back soon and then I can bring them up."

"Bring what up?" Giselle said from behind me, and I realized she had returned and was listening.

Telling Daniel to hold on for a moment, I pulled the phone from my ear and explained our request to her. As I did, a look of confusion swept over her face.

"They were in a carved box," I continued, "Elsbeth's letters to Abraham. Herr Lauten said he gave them to you when you first came here. Do you remember?"

Giselle shook her head as her face reddened. "That was twenty-five years ago," she said lamely, but I could tell from her expression and her voice that this was about more than the simple passage of time.

Alice put a hand on my arm. "Be patient. It may come to her eventually."

Glancing from Alice back to Giselle, I realized if Herr Lauten had given the box to Giselle just as she was moving in, that would have been when she was already distraught, depressed, frightened, and more. A box of old letters was probably the last thing on earth she felt like dealing with then. No wonder she looked so upset now.

Returning the phone to my ear, I told Daniel Giselle wasn't sure at the moment what she'd done with them, but that we'd get back to him if she managed to remember.

"You're kidding, right? Ada, you do understand the importance of these letters, don't you?"

His tone was so condescending that I was reminded of the day he and I had first met and he'd spoken down to me as if I were a child—a small, ignorant child. I hadn't liked it then and I certainly didn't like it now, so I managed to get him off of the phone quickly, before I said something I'd regret.

As I placed the receiver in its cradle, Oskar stepped into the room with a bouquet of flowers for Alice. "When Dad found out I was headed into town, he asked me to come by with these and a get-well greeting for you."

She thanked him sweetly, and I took the flowers and set the vase on the table while Oskar visited. After a couple of minutes he said he needed to be on his way. "Does anyone need a ride up to Amielbach?"

Christy was already bored and antsy, and Giselle's response to Daniel's demands had left me feeling unsettled. I told Oskar that Christy and I would ride along.

On the way out the door, he turned and told Giselle he was working on adding her pieces to the gift shop and asked if she wanted to help. She declined, saying she planned to spend the day with Alice. She seemed relieved to see us leaving.

I would have liked to have been able to overhear what was said once Giselle and Alice were alone, but knew if I was around, Giselle probably wouldn't be forthcoming anyway.

Once back at Amielbach, Daniel apologized to me for having been snippy over the phone. He, Christy, and I were all standing at the bottom of the staircase, and for a moment I considered telling him Giselle was my birth mother in an attempt to explain the swirling emotions he might have sensed, but then I decided against it. The time didn't seem right for such a complex disclosure. Instead, I graciously accepted his apology.

"I know you want to get a better look at the waterfalls," Daniel said. "Because the surveyors are still over there today, how about if we go up to the third-floor ballroom? The view is spectacular from there."

"Let's go see it." Christy was intrigued.

I followed her and Daniel up the open staircase, trailing one hand along the carved banister, to the second floor and down the hall, past closed bedroom doors. Christy stepped aside and let Daniel open the door to the third-floor staircase, but then she stepped right behind him, assuring I was last.

The staircase was dark and steep, its banister smooth and polished under my hand. We came to a landing with a large window that cast the morning sun across the oak floor. Straight ahead of us was a carved door featuring an elaborate scene of goats climbing up an alpine trail. A shepherdess followed the goats, staff in hand. Christy asked who the girl was. I said I had no idea, but maybe it was Elsbeth. Oskar had said except for the piece in the great room downstairs, Abraham rarely included figures in his carvings, so I assumed this girl had to be someone special.

Daniel opened the door. Before us was a grand ballroom with an oak floor and windows that surrounded the entire room.

"Maybe we should take off our shoes," I said. The floor hadn't been polished recently, but it was still in good shape. The others agreed and Daniel took his off and then slid across the floor in his socks. Christy followed with me close behind, giggling. We stopped in the middle. I tried to imagine Elsbeth as a little girl in the room. Did she dance with her father? Or maybe her dolls? Did she have friends come over to play?

Across the floor, between two windows, was a panel carving of a rugged mountain peak. Below it was a meadow and then a village, with a church steeple in the middle. I wasn't sure what the scene was depicting, really, though it obviously wasn't Langnau. The mountain was too steep and high.

We headed toward the windows facing the waterfall. There was a gazebo in the backyard I hadn't seen before and a trellis with vines covering it. Beyond was the Kessler property. From the higher view, it was obvious the land was rocky. The waterfall was also more formidable from this angle. There was no building, but a rock foundation indicated where a house used to be. Beyond the hillside of pines, we could see the Bernese

Alps. My eyes fell back on the waterfall. The cave wasn't obvious from the rise by Giselle's cottage, but it was from here. I asked Daniel how far back in the hillside it went.

"Quite a way. It's big enough to hold forty people or so."

"Isn't the roar of the waterfall loud in the cave?" I was wondering how they would have been able to hold meetings in there.

"Surprisingly not," Daniel said. "Especially once you're in it several yards."

"When will we see it?" I asked.

"Soon as those surveyors are finished and out of the way."

"How do you get over there?" There was no sign of a bridge anywhere on the creek.

"See that tree?" He pointed to a lone pine near the right bank. "Across from it is a grouping of stones in the water that make a fairly safe crossing."

I fixed my eyes on the tree and then over to the creek, just in case I had time to go exploring later. I had no idea when that would be, not with me being solely responsible for Christy now. Maybe after Will arrived I could sneak away to look around.

We stayed up in the ballroom far longer than I had intended. Christy and I were having so much fun with the slippery floor that eventually Daniel sat down in the corner and took a book out of his backpack. He seemed content to sit and read while Christy and I slid over the hardwood surface from window to window and side to side. She seemed to forget about her worries and simply enjoyed herself, laughing and giggling as she and I raced. By the time we stopped, her face was red and she was tired.

"It would be fun if the twins were here," she said, pulling her shoes back on her feet. I smiled at the thought of Matty and Mel playing in the ballroom. It would be fun, lots of fun. I think Christy and I were both missing them.

When we reached the main floor again, the gift shop door was open, so I slipped inside. Obviously someone had been working in the room, but no one was around right now. Music boxes, cowbells, linens, and chocolates were sitting on the glass case. Behind it was a table, and spread over it were three wall hangings that had to be Giselle's. I stepped closer. This was the first time I'd seen her work. One was a garden of dahlias—orange and purple with a single yellow bloom rising above the rest and then two pink blossoms floating away. The next one was of a huge silver star on a black background with two tiny stars far above it in the right-hand corner. And the third one was of a fire with the face of a woman in the flames. Above the fire a white bird flew, its belly pink from the heat with a small empty hole, with the sky showing through, in the middle.

"What strange artwork," Daniel said. He and Christy had joined me without my hearing them approach.

I couldn't take my eyes off the weavings. They were stunning, but more than that they captured a feeling. A feeling I knew I had, deep inside. Swallowing hard, I realized that Giselle had shown exactly what I had felt before I left Lancaster County. A restlessness. A deep longing. A missing piece of myself.

Incredible.

I expected Daniel to say more, but he didn't. In fact, he was already over on the other side of the room, looking at a shelf of books, Giselle's incredible weavings already gone from his mind.

Twenty-Six

I was still in a bit of a daze as we headed up the entryway, through the front door, and down the steps. There was more to Giselle than her short hair and skinny jeans. There was something in her soul I longed to know. Something Daniel obviously didn't see.

The sound of a car door slamming interrupted my thoughts. Daniel and Christy were ahead of me, walking toward the parking lot. I expected that George had gone somewhere and just returned, but there was only one car and it wasn't the rental. It was a sleek, silver car. A woman stood beside it. At the open trunk of the car was Oskar, wrestling a bag to the ground. He turned toward us. "You have a visitor," he called out.

The woman's hair was wrapped in a knot on her head, and when she turned toward us, I realized it was Morgan.

"Hello!" she called out to us.

I rushed toward her.

She hugged me tightly and then greeted Daniel. He stepped forward and gave her a quick hug. She greeted Christy next.

"Why are you here?" Christy asked, grinning.

Morgan answered that George had called her the night before and told her about Alice.

"So this morning, I thought, *Why not?* and decided to come see all of you. My dad's on a business trip to Geneva for a few days anyway. He let me take his car." Looking around at each of us, her enthusiasm seemed to lag for a moment, her expression growing uncertain. "Is it okay that I'm here? Are you happy to see me?"

"Of course to both questions." I laughed and gave her another hug.

She grabbed a bag out of the passenger seat and then we followed George toward Amielbach. "All I've been doing is surfing the Internet and watching German TV. I thought I could at least make myself useful if I came here."

We checked with Oskar, who said Morgan could stay in the room I'd had. I wanted to invite her to stay at the cottage with us, but it wasn't my place to do so. That would have been up to Giselle, and she wasn't here.

First we showed Morgan around the main floor of Amielbach, stopping in front of the wall-sized carving. She examined it for a long time and I took a closer look too, counting the number of people in the carving. There were eleven, from an infant to an old man, plus several animals—a couple of cows, some goats, and a dog. The waterfall was in the far distance, but the mountains beyond the waterfall looked closer than they did in real life.

She pointed at the rugged mountain peak topped with snow that towered over the people in the carving. "I didn't realize the Alps were so close," she said.

"The range that is close is the Bernese Alps," Daniel answered. "But that peak isn't one of them. The carving definitely has an odd perspective."

Our next stop was the gift shop. Morgan was as taken with Giselle's weavings as she'd been with Abraham's carving.

"Ada, do you have any talents in this area? Any artistic aspirations?"

I shook my head and explained that Plain people believed artistic endeavors led to pride.

"Too bad," she said, her eyes still on Giselle's weavings. "Because you must have the genetics inside you somewhere."

We stopped back by her car on the way to the cottage. "You're going to be so proud of me," she said as she pulled a bag out of the backseat. "Remember what you told me about mutual aid? Well, I brought food. Pasta, bread, and salad."

My eyes teared up. *Food.* That was one less thing I would have to figure out. When Morgan saw those tears, she welled up too. From the expression on her face, I gathered she was coming to understand that mutual aid was as much a blessing to the giver as it was the receiver.

After lunch Daniel went back to Amielbach to keep going through Abraham Sommers' property journals, and Morgan, Christy, and I decided to visit Alice. Morgan was happy to drive us, and when we were nearly to Alice's room we heard a burst of laughter. When we entered, Giselle was standing at the end of the bed, waving her arms around.

Alice was trying not to laugh. When she saw us, she pointed at Giselle with her good hand and said, "We were remembering when Will was little and tipped over a bee hive. Giselle was helping that week…we were canning, weren't we?"

Giselle nodded. "I've never seen anything like it." She wiped her eyes. "Will was running willy-nilly across the field, a swarm of bees behind him."

"What happened?" Christy was concerned.

"He jumped the fence and headed straight for the pigpen. Dove right into the mud. I was afraid I was going to have to go in after him, but he rolled around, totally covering himself except for his eyes. I don't know if it was the mud or the stench, but something worked."

Alice chimed in. "Giselle, Nancy, and I stood at the fence and watched him until the bees left."

"Then we fished him out," Giselle added.

I tilted my head, trying to absorb the story and the thought of Giselle staying with the Gundys, helping Nancy with the kids, canning with Alice. As hard as I tried, looking at the woman in front of me, I couldn't quite get there.

I introduced Morgan to Giselle before she could start in on another story, and Morgan told her how much she liked her artwork. Giselle was obviously pleased with the praise. Morgan asked how long she'd been weaving, and Giselle answered for more than twenty years. Their conversation moved into a discussion of local galleries, and as they chatted a little longer I stood back, taking the two of them in, wondering why I seemed to be the only person not able to have a normal conversation with my birth mother.

Eventually, Giselle said she had an order she needed to work on. After she left, Alice said that Giselle's memories had worn her out, even though she'd had a morning nap. Soon she was asleep, and Morgan, Christy, and I went out to the waiting room. Morgan asked if Giselle had told me anything about when I was a baby. I pursed my lips and shook my head.

Because I didn't want Christy watching more TV, I pulled *Jane Eyre* out of my purse and began to read it aloud.

Two hours later, after Alice had awakened and we were back in the room with her, the phone rang. It was Daniel, who was calling to say that George was planning to pick Will up at the Bern airport unless we wanted to.

"I can drive," Morgan said when I relayed the conversation to her. "I have my dad's GPS."

"I want to go too," Christy said.

"Of course," I said. I relayed their answers to Daniel, who said he'd like to tag along if that was okay. He said George had offered to come down and sit with Alice while we were gone. He'd much rather do that than drive in the dark on roads he wasn't familiar with.

We ate dinner at the hospital, stopped by Amielbach for Daniel, and then left for Bern. An hour later we were on the outskirts of the city. George had told Will he'd pick him up at the arrivals around nine thirty.

Daniel sat up front and helped Morgan navigate her way by the instructions of the GPS. He pointed out that the airport was west of the city, and we were bypassing the old part of town. When we approached the arrivals, Morgan said to Christy, whose face was pressed up to the window, "Keep an eye out for your dad."

Pedestrians rushed across the street and taxis lined the roadway in front of us. Morgan slowed. The car ahead of us pulled to the curb.

"He'll definitely be easy to recognize," Daniel said.

"There he is!" Christy reached for the door handle, but I told her to wait. I didn't see him. But then there he was, coming toward us with a wide smile on his face, his black hat firmly on his head, the only Plain man anywhere in sight. He must have spotted Christy through the window.

Morgan came to a complete stop and Christy bolted from the car. As Will rushed forward, swooping his daughter up into a hug, my pulse surged at the sight of him.

"Look at that," Morgan said, her head tilted so she could see out the window. "What a perfect picture they make."

Daniel and I climbed out of the car, and the two men shook hands. Will then gave me a warm pat on the shoulder. All he carried was a single bag and the box from *Mammi* under his arm. The trunk popped up—obviously Morgan had anticipated our need—and Will stashed the bag in the trunk and then ceremoniously handed the box to me. I took it from him, running a hand over the design that had been carved into the lid. It was of a farmhouse and a barn, nestled among wheat fields, with sloping hills in the background.

Daniel offered Will the front seat, but he said he'd sit in the back with Christy. Cradling the box to my chest, I hurried around to the other side and climbed in behind Morgan. Christy settled into the middle and then Will began trying to squeeze himself into the space next to her.

"Not exactly the same as American cars, eh?" Daniel teased, watching the struggle Will was going through. Christy chuckled but her father just grunted.

Once he managed to get his long legs all the way in and close the door, I took a moment to introduce him to Morgan.

"Oh!" he exclaimed, reaching up between the seats to shake her hand. "Here I was expecting a middle-aged Mennonite man to be sitting at the wheel, and instead it's a young American woman."

We all laughed.

"Sorry to disappoint you," Morgan replied as she put on her blinker to pull out from the curb. "Next time I'll wear a plaid shirt and strap on a beard." We all laughed at the thought.

Soon we were off. While Morgan navigated the busy streets of Bern and Will asked Christy about the trip, I turned my attention back to the box in my lap. Again running my fingers over the wood, I asked Will if he knew where this scene was from.

"According to Frannie, that's Elsbeth's family farm in Indiana."

"Indiana? But wasn't it carved by Abraham here in Switzerland?"

I knew Daniel was listening, and no doubt his imagination was spinning. "Did Abraham come to America after all?" he asked.

Morgan chimed in. "How else would he have known what to carve unless he saw the place himself? It's not as though they would have sent him a photo."

"I don't know if he traveled to Indiana or not," Will said. "Frannie didn't elaborate. She did say he sent the box from Switzerland, though. That I remember."

None of us could fault Will for not asking more questions. Clearly, his mind had been on other things.

"May I see it?" Daniel asked, eyeing the box eagerly.

As I passed it up to him, Will told him, "Frannie asked me to apologize on her behalf. She's embarrassed that she didn't remember the box of letters earlier when you came to Lancaster County. But she said she hadn't looked through them or even really thought about them for many years."

"It's not surprising she wouldn't have thought of it, then," I commented, feeling bad that *Mammi* was embarrassed.

"I just hope they'll prove to be of some use," Daniel said as he carefully lifted the lid and looked inside.

Will shrugged, glancing at me. "To be honest, I looked through the letters on the flight over, but the ink has faded and I could only make out a few words."

"Thanks for trying, at least," I responded, hoping Daniel would be able to do better.

Bored with our talk of letters and boxes, Christy asked her father who was caring for Mat and Mel while he was gone.

"Aunt Hannah mostly, during the days," Will replied, referring to his sister, "though others will be taking turns each night."

"Like who?" Christy pressed.

"Well, Leah Fisher came over and stayed with them last night. Tonight I think it's your grandmother, and then Sally after that. If this ends up taking longer than we thought, there's also Ezra, Ella, maybe Leah again…"

As he went on, I couldn't help but think that it sounded as though Leah Fisher had an active role in his life. Closing my eyes, I could almost imagine how the whole thing had played out. I thought of Will leaving a message for her, asking for her help. I imagined how pleased she would have been to spend the night at his house. Of course, he wasn't there when she did, but still I bristled.

Last night, once the twins were asleep, had she gone into his bedroom, perhaps even slept in his bed? This morning, had she stood at his stove cooking for his children and told herself it was only a matter of time until it was her stove, her children?

Stop it, I scolded myself silently, opening my eyes. How Leah and Will conducted themselves both before and after their engagement was their business, not mine.

I realized Christy was telling Will all about Amielbach and Giselle's cottage. Then she told him about the ship and the train. As she talked, I reprimanded myself again for even caring about someone else's relationship. It really wasn't my business. I needed to be happy for them, not always sulking about what obviously wasn't meant to be for me. After a while Christy stopped talking and soon fell fast asleep, curled tightly against her *daed*.

"She hasn't been this talkative in months," Will said to me in a soft voice.

"She's done better than I thought she would with Alice ill," I said. I didn't add that Christy finally seemed to accept me once she really needed me. It would be interesting to see how she responded to me now that Will was here. Later, I would have to tell him about our conversation regarding Lydia—or at least give him the gist of it so he could understand the feelings of guilt his daughter had been carrying.

Other than the soft music playing on the radio, we rode in silence. Daniel had put on a pair of white gloves and was reading the letters with the help of a flashlight, but he wasn't saying anything. His yellow hair was bright even in the darkness.

"How is Giselle?" Will asked, his voice low.

"Good," I said. "She was with Alice for the first part of the day."

"I'll stay at the hospital tonight."

"That's too much, Will," I said. "You'll be tired after your trip."

"I slept on the plane. I'll be all right."

I told him Christy and I had spent last night at Giselle's. "They're expecting you at Amielbach."

He said he'd figure it out in the morning and thanked me, again, for taking care of Christy. He pulled her closer. "I'm hoping we'll all be back together soon, and the twins won't be much out of sorts with me being gone."

After that neither one of us spoke. Will leaned his head back and closed his eyes. Morgan maneuvered the car around a curve, and Will and Christy scooted toward me a little. His hand, which was on Christy's arm, brushed against my shoulder. I shivered. As Morgan came out of the curve, Will and Christy scooted the other way.

"How are you doing back there?" Morgan's voice was low and soothing.

"*Gut.* I mean good," I answered.

Then I must have fallen asleep too, because I startled when we came to a stop. We were in the hospital parking lot, directly beside Giselle's car.

"I'll stay out here with Christy," Morgan offered as Will opened his door. Still buried in the letters, Daniel mumbled something and I realized he'd be staying in the car as well—in fact, he was so fully focused on the task that I wasn't even sure if he realized we'd arrived.

Will thanked Morgan and kissed Christy goodnight. She stirred, and he told her he'd see her in the morning. Her eyes flickered and she muttered something to him, but in a split second she was fully asleep again.

I led the way through the front doors of the hospital and down the hall to Alice's room.

When we stepped inside and Will saw Giselle, he stopped.

She stepped toward him. "Little Will Gundy," she said and then broke into a grin.

"Giselle Lantz," he answered. And then he hugged her. My heart ached at the sight of them, the two people who yanked at my heartstrings the most, embracing each other.

Giselle motioned for him to step closer to the bed. "I spelled George about an hour ago, but he said Alice wanted to be woken up when you arrived."

As he leaned toward his grandmother, she opened her eyes. "Will," she whispered.

He bent down and kissed her cheek, and she wrapped her good arm around his neck. When he pulled away, she swiped at her eyes. "I'm so thankful you're here." Her voice was barely audible.

Will told Giselle he would stay the night and she could go on home. As she bent to kiss Alice goodnight, I again felt a twinge of jealousy, wishing Giselle would be as warm with me as she was with Will and Alice.

"Did you bring the letters from Frannie?" Alice asked as she sat up a little in bed.

"Daniel has them in the car," Will said. "He'll give them to Herr Lauten."

Alice looked at me. "Anything so far?"

"The ink is pretty faint. Daniel's out there skimming them with a flashlight. As far as I know, he hasn't found anything yet."

"That doesn't matter now," Will said to Alice, his eyes tender. "All that matters is getting you home. Enough of this wild goose chase, *ya*? God will take care of us, one way or the other."

TWENTY-SEVEN

Giselle was fine with Morgan spending the night, as long as she didn't mind sleeping on the sofa. I was just flattered to know that though Morgan could have stayed at Amielbach, she chose to stay with us instead. While I got Christy settled, I could hear the other two women talking in the living room. After a minute or two their voices grew louder and then drifted down the hallway.

Christy and I kneeled beside the futon and said our prayers. I don't know what Christy prayed about, but I prayed that Alice would recover, that God would direct the course of the hearing tomorrow, and that Daniel and Herr Lauten would figure out where the agreement was. Mostly, I prayed I would get over Will, both completely and immediately. I didn't want to suffer through the pain of my longings. I also thanked God that Morgan had joined us and asked that she would see evidence of Him working in her life.

Images of Mel and Mat filled my mind, and I prayed they would do all right while their *daed* was gone. They were the ages now Lexie was when she'd been given up for adoption. My heart stopped cold. I couldn't imagine what Giselle felt back then when she agreed to relinquish Lexie. How could she bear it? How could she bear to see me now, for that matter, the one she had given up to her sister at birth? As I said "Amen," I was overcome with sudden sympathy for my birth mother.

After tucking Christy in and pulling the office door closed, I stood in the hallway, listening for voices to figure out where Morgan and Giselle had gone. Giselle's bedroom door was open and I peeked inside, but no one was in there. The room had a single bed with a traditional Amish quilt—small blocks of green, burgundy, purple, and blue squares on a black background. She had several candles around the room—on the bureau and bedside table and in two holders on the wall, but none of them had been lit. A shelf of books was on the far wall, and on top of it were skeins of thread. In the corner was a small antique spinning wheel. The room felt as if someone actually lived in it, unlike the stark living room and kitchen. There were two doors in the room, closets I assumed, but one was cracked open a little. I could hear a soft murmur, voices I was sure.

I paused for a moment, jealous that not only had Giselle picked up her relationships from twenty-four years ago with both Alice and Will, but that she was willing to have one with Morgan too. But not with me.

I felt I would be intruding to step through the door into the other room. I hadn't been invited. But if I was going to have any connection with Giselle at all, it had to be my doing. I didn't see that she was going to put forth the effort. It wasn't something she needed or wanted.

I forged ahead, stepping quickly through her bedroom. Rapping my knuckles on the door, I said, "Knock, knock," as I slowly pushed it open.

"Come on in," Giselle answered.

She and Morgan were standing beside a large loom.

"I asked Giselle to show me her studio," Morgan said.

I stepped further into the room. It was about the same size as the bedroom but far more cluttered. Shelves filled with thread and yarn lined one wall. Pieces of paper covered a long table. At the far end of the room were six wall hangings, five of them incomplete. The completed one was of the back of an Amish woman with three little girls huddled around her. Only one of the child's faces could be seen, and she wore a sad expression. The unfinished weavings were of stars and flowers, similar to the ones in the gift shop.

"She's working on a commissioned piece," Morgan said. "For the gallery owner where her exhibit is."

I stepped closer to the loom. It was only a third of the way done, but clearly Amielbach and the waterfall were in the weaving. It was in black and white, except for red flowers in the window boxes.

"The woman likes the idea of the traditional tapestries with a modern twist, so I'm doing an estate scene with a limited color scheme."

I knew nothing about art, but I didn't really like what I saw. It was too stark and sterile. Especially considering how vibrant the scene was in real life.

Morgan began asking her questions about the process she went through to execute her ideas. I excused myself after a couple of minutes and went back to check on Christy. She was sound asleep. I pulled *Jane Eyre* from my purse and an extra blanket from the end of the bed and went out to the living room to read until Morgan was ready to go to bed. After a few pages, I leaned my head back, feeling more restless than I had before I left Lancaster County. Seeing Giselle had resolved nothing except answering my question as to what she looked like. I closed my eyes, but the anxiety inside of me only grew more acute. The sound of my name startled me and my eyes flew open.

Giselle stood in the middle of the room. "Ada," she said again.

I sat up straight. I could hear water in the bathroom and surmised Morgan was taking a shower.

Giselle stepped a little closer. "It feels so odd to say your name."

"Why?"

She shrugged. "I named Alexandra—or Lexie, as she's called now."

"But you didn't have anything to do with naming me?"

She shook her head. "Klara did, as she should have." She looked past me, toward the window.

I wanted her to sit down and keep talking but she continued to stand. "What was that like for you back then?" I finally managed to say.

Her eyes jumped and she focused on me again as her eyebrows rose. "Honestly?"

I nodded.

"I can't remember. I haven't thought about all of that in years." She paused and then looked at me intently. "Do you know that you're the perfect picture of a Plain woman?" She didn't sound as if she was paying me a compliment, and I wondered if her use of the word "Plain" had a double meaning. "And I can see by the way you dote on Christy that you'll be a good mother." She sighed. "In fact, what's surprising is that you're not married yet. How long ago did you join the church? Six or seven years?"

"I haven't yet."

"Really?" Her dark eyes brightened. "Why ever not?"

"I had some health issues..."

"But you will, right?" she said, running her hand through her short hair.

"Probably."

She tilted her head to the side. I felt as if she were seeing something she hadn't seen before. "All these years I imagined you belonging to the church and married, with a brood of children already."

Heat rose on my face at her comment. "Lexie just got married," I offered, hoping to change the subject.

"Zed sent me an email about it," she said. "It sounds as though it was quite the trip to Oregon."

I wondered what else Zed had told her. I couldn't imagine him sharing too many details. I couldn't tell if she was happy that Lexie and I knew each other now, but instead of asking her, I said it was a blessing to me to get to know my sister after all these years.

She sighed. "I wasn't surprised that Klara never told you that you were adopted or that you had a sister. I thought maybe someone else would—maybe Alexander—but I suppose the fact no one did shows how much control Klara still has."

There was an awkward pause, and then I said, "She's better than she used to be."

Giselle wrinkled her nose. Then she said, "What do you want from me?"

Her question caught me off guard.

"You're not after my side of the story? Or an apology?" Her voice was harsh.

"No," I said, my heart sinking. Of course I didn't want an apology—it's not as though she could have kept me. And I'd had a good life. Any speculation of what my life might have been like, whether here or back home, was foolishness on my part. And I didn't need her side of the story. Just an acknowledgement that she cared about me would be nice. My expression must have given my emotions away.

"There's a lot I don't remember," she said. "I remember Alexandra as a baby and toddler, but that's about all. Everything else is a blur."

Desperate for anything she could tell me, I asked about Lexie, about what she was like as a baby. Giselle gave me an exasperated look.

I pushed ahead anyway. "You know, was she colicky, did she sleep well, when did she first smile, first talk, first walk? Can you at least tell me something about back then?"

Eyes filling with tears, Giselle shook her head. "Actually, I can't." Swiping at her cheeks, she turned quickly away and walked out of the room. I sat there, waiting for her to return, but she didn't. When Morgan finally came out of the bathroom, I gave up hope. Gathering the novel and blanket, I said goodnight to my friend, made sure she had everything she needed, and then retreated back to the office to slide into bed.

Mammi wanted me to speak to Giselle about spiritual things, but how could I do that when she hardly wanted to speak with me at all?

I woke before dawn, and when I couldn't get back to sleep I picked up Lexie's box and decided to carry it out to the window seat so I could go through Christy's schoolwork there. We hadn't done any lessons since we'd arrived in Switzerland and most likely wouldn't get to any more because the trip was coming to an end much sooner than we had anticipated. I'd decided to make a record of the lessons we had managed to cover so Leah would know where Christy stood once she returned to school.

A few minutes later, Giselle wandered into the room, yawning, and cinching up her bathrobe.

"Good morning," I said.

Startled, she jumped and then said, "Oh, it's you." She filled the kettle with water and then put it on the stove. "Would you like some tea?"

I said I would, and when she looked at me again she saw the box. "Oh, good. You found Elsbeth's letters after all. Where were they?"

"Oh, this isn't the box you had," I answered. "This is Lexie's. *Mammi* sent it with her when she went to Oregon all those years ago."

Giselle stepped forward and I handed it to her. "It looks a lot like the one I had here, though I think the carving was of something else." She set the box down on the table.

"Do you remember anything about the letters that were inside, about what they said?"

She shrugged. "I never read them. Herr Lauten kept pushing them on me, trying to get me interested. He wove this fascinating tale about how Elsbeth Sommers was a governess who fell in love with the father of her charges, but the man happened to be Mennonite, which forced them to have to go to America in search of religious freedom, blah, blah, blah. He thought I would care. He didn't have a clue."

Her words were harsh, but I reminded myself that at the time she'd been depressed, alone, and far from the only home she'd ever known. She'd lost whom she thought was her true love and left her two children behind to be raised by others. I could well understand how a box of old letters about Mennonites and religious persecution were the last thing on her mind. No wonder she'd misplaced them.

The water came to a boil, and as she made the tea, I decided to tell her about Lexie's box instead. Trying to use a pleasant, nonthreatening tone, I described how Lexie's adoptive father had hidden the box for many years but had finally told her about it on his deathbed just last winter.

Shifting from the window seat to the table to have my tea, I described how Lexie had retrieved the box from where her father had hidden it and inside had found a letter from Abraham Sommers to his daughter Elsbeth and two locks of hair.

"Lexie thought the hair belonged to you and her, but it turned out to be you and me. The second lock was mine, not hers. Marta had clipped it off right after I was born. She tried to cut—"

"Alexandra's too," Giselle interrupted nodding. "But Alexandra wouldn't let her." She stared down at the box. "I do remember that. She wasn't having any of it."

My hands began to shake, so I set down my mug. "We used the hair for a DNA test. That's how we found out we were full sisters."

Giselle leaned against the table, picked up the box again, and cradled it in her hands. Her expression was so distant, I wasn't even sure she was listening anymore.

"This carving," she said finally. "It's Amielbach. That's why *Mamm* gave it to Alexandra. She wanted her to know where I was."

I nodded, aware that no one had thought to give me any clues to my origins. "I'm assuming Abraham Sommers carved it? That's why Lexie sent it with me. She hoped the craftsman could be identified."

Giselle nodded, setting the box back down on the table. "Oh, that's his work all right. No question."

"I thought so."

Without saying anything more, Giselle busied herself at the sink, pouring out the tea she'd only half finished and washing the mug. As she worked, all I could think of was this: She remembered the day I was born after all.

Twenty-Eight

After I finished my tea, I dressed and then walked up to Amielbach, leaving a note for Christy and Morgan in case they woke up before I returned. I wanted to check in with Daniel about the letters and go over the schedule for the rest of the day, including the hearing in Langnau. I expected he would be up already, and I was right. He was coming down the staircase, the box and a dictionary in his arms.

"Hi," he called out. "I was just going to check in with Herr Lauten. He said he'd be in his library by seven."

The library was at the end of the dark hallway that veered off from the great room to the right of the floor-to-ceiling carving. As we walked, Daniel explained that he'd finished going through all of the letters last night, to no avail. While the letters had painted a fascinating picture of the past, he'd seen one mention of the Kessler family but otherwise nothing whatsoever that might help us straighten out the property issue or find the missing agreement. My heart sank, but I had to trust that God knew what He was doing.

Daniel knocked on the door and from faraway a voice called out, "*Hereinkommen!*"

I followed Daniel through the doorway. The room was lined with shelves that were stuffed with books, and woven carpets covered the hard-wood floor. High windows were above the shelves, letting in streams of sunlight. The ceiling was divided in sections, like boxes, with wood molding separating each.

Herr Lauten was at the back of the room, behind a desk, struggling to stand to greet us, leaning against his cane.

"Don't get up," I called out to him, hurrying across the room. I greeted him, expecting Daniel to be right behind me. He wasn't.

He was at the tallest bookcase, gawking. "Where did you get all of these? They're ancient."

Herr Lauten settled back down his chair. "Most of them belonged to the father-in-law of Abraham Sommers. The rest are mine."

"What did his father-in-law do?"

"Franz Amiel? He was a scholar. He was from Germany and inherited a large sum of money. He retreated here, built Amielbach, married a local woman, and had a daughter, Tresa, who married Abraham." Herr Lauten motioned to the vast collection of books. "My grandfather was illiterate, but thankfully he valued the books and cared for them. You're welcome to browse around in here later."

Daniel thanked him and joined us. We both sat down in chairs facing Herr Lauten.

Without missing a beat, he continued with what he'd been saying about Abraham. "Tresa died when Elsbeth was a young girl, leaving Abraham the property."

Herr Lauten was struggling to stand again, and I quickly jumped up to help him, holding on to his elbow as the old man tottered. "I just want to grab the journals." He pointed to two volumes on a table beyond his desk. Daniel retrieved them, and after I helped Herr Lauten back down, he handed them over.

"As I told you two before, Abraham kept several business ledgers through the years, but the last two were more like journals." Lifting one of the books, he added, "This is the first of those. I tried to give it to Giselle and am now so thankful she didn't want it. I regret giving her the letters. If I hadn't, we'd still have them now." He held up the second book. "Then I found this second journal. It's the one that has some information I think may prove useful." Herr Lauten handed it to me. "He's your ancestor, Miss Rupp. Technically it belongs to you," he said. Then, looking at Daniel he added, "Plus I'd like a second set of eyes to read it. To see if I've missed anything."

I opened the book, its leather cover worn with age. On the first page was the date, April 4, 1894. That would have been seventeen years after Elsbeth had left Switzerland. Under that was a list of numbers and a few lines written in old-fashioned script. From what I could tell, it was in regular German and not Swiss German, which I figured might be more of a spoken language. I could make out some of the words, such as *Holz*, which was "wood," and *Werk*, which was "work." But the ink was faint and the handwriting hard to read, so it wasn't easy to decipher. I turned the page to see a similar entry. I flipped ahead a little and made out the year 1895.

Daniel was peering over my shoulder. "He's written that he hired someone to help him manage the property." Daniel looked at Herr Lauten. "Your grandfather, Caspar Lauten."

The old man nodded, saying that when Caspar Lauten first came to Amielbach to serve as the property manager, that was the beginning of the Lauten family's connection to the estate.

"I'm afraid you'll have to translate this too," I said to Daniel.

"It'll be my pleasure."

I knew it would, and I was very thankful for his knowledge.

Next Daniel opened the carved box and took out the letters for Herr Lauten. "I skimmed these last night," he said. "You should look too, but I couldn't find anything about the missing agreement. In the very last letter, Abraham wrote that he had some important information for Elsbeth and he would send it soon."

"Important information?" Herr Lauten and I asked in unison.

"Yes, that's what he said. But then that's it. So we have no way of knowing what that information could have been."

"Oh, dear," Herr Lauten said. "That doesn't sound very promising does it? Is there anything else that might help us?"

"The only mention of the Kesslers is when he asked Elsbeth if she still kept in touch with Marie," Daniel explained. Glancing at me, he explained that Marie was Ulrich Kessler's youngest child and only daughter, and that she and Elsbeth had been friends. "Abraham knew Marie's brothers and father had all died, but he assumed she was still alive."

"But he didn't say why he wanted to know? Nothing about the agreement?"

"Nothing at all."

Herr Lauten asked Daniel if he could tell us what else he'd learned from reading the letters, relevant to the agreement or not.

Taking a deep breath, Daniel said he'd be happy to, though it probably wouldn't be of much use to our search.

"Just a summary, then,"

"Mostly, they showed how upset Abraham was that Elsbeth had left. He wrote to her, over and over, saying that family was what was most important in life. He said he'd imagined her marrying and living at Amielbach and raising her children, with him nearby, perhaps living in the cottage."

I glanced at Herr Lauten, who was listening intently.

"Letter after letter, he begged her to return. Every time she had another child, he asked her to come back and said he would welcome her husband too. He pointed out there was no danger for her sons. Things had changed here, and the Mennonites weren't being persecuted anymore. The more time went on, the more he begged her to return."

Herr Lauten folded his hands together. "Well, as a father, I certainly sympathize with him wanting his only child to come home."

Daniel scoffed. "But he sounded so desperate. So controlling. The whole time I was reading them, I kept thinking, 'Just let her live her life.'"

I thought of my own parents and swallowed hard, having a difficult time imagining what that would be like.

"Toward the end of the letters," Daniel said, "he does contemplate going to Indiana to visit her. There's a lot about that in the last letter. But then his letters end, so I don't know if he ever actually made that trip or not."

"What's the date on the last letter, the one where he discusses his plans to come?" Herr Lauten asked.

"May 1898."

"Then I can tell you what happened," Herr Lauten said. "I think he never went to America at all. I believe he died before he could get there." Pointing at the journal in my hands, Herr Lauten told me to turn to the back and read the final inscription.

"It looks like it's in a different handwriting," I said, reading out it loud and then running my fingers across the words:

Abraham Sommers, 1814 to 1898

"That answers it, then," Daniel said. "The poor old guy pined for his daughter for all those years, finally decided to go see her, and then died before he could get the chance."

"Sad," Herr Lauten said, and I nodded in agreement.

Very sad indeed.

Feeling far more somber than we had when we first came in, Daniel and I wrapped things up in the library, and then he, Herr Lauten, and I walked back down the long, dark hallway to the great room. It was time to head to the courthouse.

Soon we were off, rumbling down the road with Oskar at the wheel, each of us lost in our thoughts. As I looked out the window at the beautiful Swiss countryside flying past, I could feel myself growing more hopeless by the mile. Without that agreement, we really didn't stand a chance in court. Closing my eyes, I did the only thing left to do.

I prayed for a miracle.

TWENTY-NINE

Even with picking Will up at the hospital, we managed to reach the courthouse in plenty of time. Betsy Holt met us in the lobby, greeting us with handshakes and a solemn expression. Daniel introduced her to Will, explaining that he would be standing in for Alice. She shook his hand gravely and expressed her best wishes for his grandmother's speedy recovery.

My head was still swimming with all I had learned back at the house, so I was glad when she said it would be a little while before we were called in. She led us down a quiet hallway and gestured toward a door on the right, saying we'd be presenting our case to the judge in there.

A long, upholstered bench sat against the wall beside the door, and the five of us settled down on it to wait: the lawyer, Herr Lauten, Daniel, Will, and me—in that order. I was glad to be on the end, where I could quietly collect my thoughts. Daniel and Herr Lauten were asking Ms. Holt some final questions. A retired attorney himself, Herr Lauten seemed to know the woman already and obviously had great respect for her skills. At one point I heard her refer to her schooling at "Rutgers," and then Daniel asked if she meant Rutgers Law School in New Jersey. Nodding, she explained that her mother was an American who had moved to the States after divorcing her Swiss father. Ms. Holt not only had dual citizenship but also dual law degrees, one from Rutgers and one from the University of Geneva School of Law. I realized that her family situation sounded much like Morgan's.

With just a few minutes left, the woman began addressing all four of us, saying that at least we'd landed a good judge with a keen legal mind, especially with regard to contract law. Though she was obviously trying to give us a pep talk, I could tell by the look on her face that she was still feeling pretty skeptical about the outcome. Our best bet, she said, was that single entry from one of Abraham's journals, the one where he mentioned the purchase of the land and the agreement, saying how he'd hidden it in a safe place.

The door beside us opened, and then a man in a uniform was waving us in. We all rose, and as we filed through the doorway, the lawyer turned to me and Will and whispered, "Just relax. There's nothing to be nervous about or intimidated by."

Once she'd turned back around and continued toward the front of the room, Will gave me a look of something not unlike amusement. I was less amused, as the possibility of being nervous hadn't even dawned on me until now. The more I thought about it, the more my legs began to feel a little shaky.

The courtroom was good sized, as large as an Amish living room back home, but not exactly cavernous, as I'd expected. Bright and sunny with tall windows along one side, the back of the room held three short rows of seats, and Ms. Holt directed us to sit in the first row. Moving forward, she set her briefcase on a table in front of us.

At the other end of the room, facing us, was a large, curved desk, with seating for five. The center seat was elevated, and I assumed that was where our judge would sit. The room also held two podiums at the center and desks along each side, though all were empty.

Once the judge entered and the proceedings began, I found my nervousness fading the longer I sat there. Standing at one of the podiums, Ms. Holt presented our case well, I thought, though her Swiss German made it difficult to follow completely, even with Daniel quietly translating most of what she was saying for Will and me. I was a little uncomfortable with how heavily she stressed what had happened to Alice yesterday. I supposed she was trying to play on the judge's sympathies, but her description of the "poor old Amish woman" who had come all this way "risking her very life for this cause" seemed a bit heavy-handed and was not altogether true. Though Alice had indeed risked her life by coming here, we hadn't known that at the time. It wasn't as though she'd boarded the ship unsure if she'd ever return home.

When the lawyer got to the part where she would tell about the page from Abraham Sommers' business journal, she gave the actual journal over to the judge and then returned to the podium to read the relevant passage in German from a photocopy, out loud, giving the date of entry as May 22, 1877. As she read Abraham's own words, I understood a good portion, but thankfully Daniel whispered a rough translation, saying:

> I want it documented for the Lauten family, the Kessler family, and my own descendants that I have bought the property adjacent to Amielbach from a man named Ulrich Kessler for the price of 80,000 Swiss francs. In conjunction with the deed transfer, Ulrich and I have also signed an agreement intended to help preserve this property for the potential return of him or of his descendants. Primarily, our agreement stipulates that I may not freely sell this property elsewhere unless I first offer it to Ulrich or his oldest living descendant for purchase. The notary has filed the deed with the land register of the Canton of Bern and has provided me with the appropriate transfer of ownership papers. I have retained the related agreement myself, preferring not to have its contents available publically, and have put it in a safe place, one that offers more privacy than the land registry office.

The judge gave back the actual journal, trading the lawyer for her photocopy. She handed the original back to Daniel and then went on to present, item by item, many of the other documents we had reviewed in her office. She finished up by reading several excerpts Daniel had given her from Abraham's letters. Obviously, Ms. Holt was trying to paint a picture of a kind and generous old man, one who had lost his daughter—the only light of his life—to emigration, thanks to the persecution of the Mennonites.

"Let this persecution end now," she finished, speaking strongly and dramatically. "Let these good and decent people bring history full circle. As demonstrated by the documentation entered here today, I present to you a direct descendant of Abraham Sommers," she turned and gestured toward me, "and a direct descendant of Ulrich Kessler." She gestured to Will and then turned back to the judge. "Your Honor, it is our desire that the paperwork we have been able to provide the court, along with the presence and cooperation and petition of these two people here, will clearly convey the appropriateness of your decision to clear this title once and for all, fulfilling the agreement first struck more than one hundred and thirty years ago between their ancestors. Thank you."

By the time she sat, Daniel looked as though he wanted to applaud.

The judge then asked a lot of questions, and at one point he spoke both to me and to Will in English, clarifying some of the facts of our family history. He also questioned Daniel and Herr Lauten about other miscellaneous details. When it seemed as if things were wrapping up, Ms. Holt reminded the judge of our need for an answer by this Friday at three p.m. at the latest, thanks to the time limit imposed by the land and property commission. Though he seemed a little irritated to be given a deadline, he said he would take that into consideration.

Before ending the session, he and the lawyer had one last exchange, but neither Daniel nor Herr Lauten translated for us until they were finished and we were dismissed.

Moving out of the room and into the hallway, I asked Daniel what he'd said there at the end. His brow furrowed, Daniel replied, "That as much as he appreciated the families' efforts in coming here and the presentation of such a clear and ample paper trail tracing the heritage and related events, he was not optimistic about being able to give a ruling in our favor unless we could provide the one piece of paper that would make all the difference: the agreement itself."

Once outside, we parted ways with the lawyer, who urged us to keep looking and promised to give us a call as soon as we got our ruling. After that we all trudged to the parking lot, where both Oskar and George were waiting for us. A very exhausted-looking Herr Lauten climbed in with Oskar for a ride back to Amielbach, and the rest of us got in with George, who drove us to the hospital.

There, we all went inside and found Christy and Morgan in the room with Alice. They wanted to hear everything about our morning in court, so we recounted the main points, ending with the bad news that our prospects did not look good.

We all brainstormed for a while, the words from Abraham's journal ringing in our ears, that he had put the agreement "in a safe place." What sort of place would he have considered safe? That was the question of the hour.

Eventually, Will seemed to grow tired of the entire matter, saying we had tried our best and now it was up to the courts.

"God's will be done," he added, "whether His matches ours or not."

The matter at an end for now, he moved closer to Alice and asked if the doctor had made rounds yet for the day. She said that he had, and that he'd told her that although she was doing a bit better, she still wasn't well enough yet to be discharged or travel home.

"He said it could take a few more days for the fluid to decrease enough for that," Morgan added.

Will's expression was grim, but Daniel actually seemed pleased.

"I'm hungry," Christy announced to no one in particular, but I realized as she said it that I was hungry as well.

Will wanted to stay with Alice, but the rest of us trooped off to the cafeteria for something to eat. On the way we fell back into brainstorming mode about where the agreement could be, and then a suggestion from Daniel opened up a whole new realm of possibilities.

"Abraham said he'd put the agreement in a safe place, one that would offer 'more privacy than the land registry office.' What if the safe place was some other kind of office? Somewhere that a document could be legally filed but then wouldn't be so easily accessed by the public?"

"You mean instead of the land registry office he filed it with the property tax office or something like that?" Morgan asked.

"Well, think about it," he said. "Government offices, private libraries, archive centers, church historical preserves—there are all sorts of places a man might consider safe but also somewhat private for storing an important document he would want to preserve for future generations."

We tossed around that line of thought as we got our food, chose a large corner table, and ate together. On a paper napkin, Daniel wrote out a list of every possible entity we could think of where a man of that era could have stored an important document. He crossed some of them back out, narrowing things down, and finally we had a short list of possibilities. Then he grabbed another napkin and mapped out the most efficient route we could take to explore them all.

Given that we had both George's rental and Morgan's car for transportation, I thought we should divide and conquer. But I was outvoted by everyone else, who wanted to stick together, especially because we all needed Daniel to lead the way. Thus, while George got on the phone to arrange for a van and driver, and Daniel consulted a map for our exact route, Christy and Morgan and I headed back to Alice's room to bring Will a sandwich and tell them where we were going.

I thought Christy might want to stay there with her *daed*, but she was eager to tag along on our treasure hunt. With a smile and a hug, Will urged her to do so, saying he wanted her to get the very most out of the time we had left here, especially if we were heading off to visit more of the sites we'd been wanting to see anyway. As we left, I found myself wishing that Will were coming too.

The van was a lot roomier than either of the cars had been. Daniel and Morgan sat in the middle seat with Christy and me in the back and George up front with the driver. Daniel pulled out one of Abraham's journals, saying he wanted to go through it again to look for clues in light of this new theory. As he did, Morgan clapped her hands in delight, saying, "I *love* this sort of thing."

"The first entries are all business..." he said, paging through them quickly.

"Can I give it a try?" Morgan asked, reaching for the journal.

"Wait," Daniel said, pulling a pair of white cotton gloves out of his backpack. "Wear these."

"You are such the geek," she teased, taking them.

Christy gave me a funny look and chuckled. I remembered she'd been asleep when Daniel had worn gloves the night before to read the letters.

He turned around and waved another pair in her face. "All serious archivists carry these with them." He grinned, happy as could be.

Christy asked if he had any more, and he ducked his head down and then popped back up with a third pair. She slipped them on her hands.

Morgan flipped through the first pages of the journal and then said, "I'll start here, where the narrative begins."

"When he hires Caspar Lauten?" Daniel interjected.

She nodded. "Yep, right there, at the *Cas-par*," she said, drawing out the name so that it sounded like "at the Casbah." Then she laughed, and I marveled at how much more comfortable she seemed with all of us.

"Okay," she continued. "The next one is December 2, 1895." She quit speaking as she read and then lifted her head. "The gist of it is that he's worried about the finances of maintaining the property. He feels he made a mistake in hiring the young man to help, but he knows he can't do it alone. He writes that Caspar came across some of his old carvings and encouraged him to sell them and make some more. He's sure he could generate some income that way, but he feels too old to take up carving again." She read a little more. "This is a couple of months later. It's about Elsbeth." Morgan looked up with a questioning look on her face.

"That's his daughter," I explained. "My grandmother's grandmother."

"Got it." Morgan pointed a white gloved finger at the page. "Anyway, he writes that every day he mourns for Elsbeth, even though it's been eighteen years since she left. He thinks of her children—all twelve of them— and if she'd stayed how fulfilling his life would have been. He feels as if God, by leading Elsbeth away, paid him back for his..." She paused and then sounded out, "*Überschreitung*?" She glanced at Daniel. "What's the translation on that? Do you know?"

"Transgression," he said. "Sin."

Morgan glanced back down. "'By taking you away from me, God has paid me back for my sin.' Huh?" She didn't say anything for a moment but then glanced back at me. "What sin is he talking about? What'd he do that was so awful?"

I shook my head, as this was the first I'd heard of it. I looked to Daniel, but he just shrugged and said, "I didn't run across anything like that in the letters. He never mentioned any big sin."

As we continued along the road, I thought about that. I'd been picturing Abraham Sommers as a kind and good and generous man. Obviously, if he had some big unconfessed sin, some dark and mysterious *Überschreitung* as he called it, then the picture was a little more complicated than I had previously imagined.

I only hoped that his big sin had nothing to do with the agreement we were trying so desperately to find.

THIRTY

W e rode along in silence for several minutes. Christy seemed enthralled with the archivist gloves on her hands and kept flicking her fingers around and up and down. Daniel had his nose buried in his dictionary, probably double- and triple-checking the word *Überschreitung* to make sure he wasn't missing anything. Morgan was leaning forward over the journal, reading intently.

Finally she said, "Abraham sounds kind of bitter. Though I guess more with himself than anyone else." She read some more. "Caspar seems to be helping though. It's Caspar's idea to rent out rooms during the summer to attract people from Zurich, Bern, and Lucerne. And Abraham starts carving again. He writes it isn't as good as when he was younger but it has its own style. He received a commission to carve a bench for an official from Zurich. He's hoping it will lead to more government work." She was silent again and then said, "And he's started going to church with Caspar. Not to the Mennonite group—" She looked up again. "But to the chapel in the village. He says it's good to be hearing the Word, regardless of who reads it." Morgan's voice changed. "So what's his story? Abraham was Mennonite?"

"I don't think so." I'd never heard anything from *Mammi* to indicate that. "Amish?"

"Probably not with a place like Amielbach. It was his daughter who was Plain," I said.

"And there were no Amish left in Europe by Abraham's time anyway," Daniel said. "No, Abraham was affiliated with the Reformed Church, at least at the time of his death. I'm not sure if that was the case throughout his life, although online I found his birth recorded in the Swiss Reform Church registry in Frutigen."

Morgan turned back around. "I'll read one more and then it's Daniel's turn." She was silent for a couple of minutes and then said, "He says he sold one of his old carvings to a priest in Zurich who had seen the bench he did earlier at the university."

"Ah, the University of Zurich. They have a variety of archives," Daniel said, happily adding it to our list. "Wouldn't it be wonderful if we could find the agreement *and* the carving there?"

I agreed but knew the chances were highly unlikely.

"I'm getting carsick," Morgan said. "Translation and riding in a van don't mix." She handed the book to Daniel.

While he read, I focused on the landscape straight ahead of us. The Alps rose up like giants, even at a distance—stone faced and capped with snow. Rugged and jagged. Breathtakingly beautiful.

Morgan groaned after a while. "Daniel, you're supposed to translate each entry—not read the entire thing to yourself."

He didn't look up as he spoke. "There's a lot of stuff in between entries. The price of wood. Taxes. That sort of thing." He made various notations on our napkin list and then put it aside and began to translate some more. "This one is dated August 13, 1896. It was a good summer. They rented five of the rooms and took in some income. He says he's had a letter from Elsbeth and he worried about her health with so many children to take care of, plus the farm and her husband, Gerard. He asked her to send a couple of her sons to stay with him and mailed the letter that morning." Daniel's head popped up. "I saw the actual letter last night. This is so fascinating."

I hoped more puzzle pieces would come together soon. "Did Elsbeth send her sons over here?" I asked.

He shook his head. "She wrote that none of them wanted to come. She asked Abraham to come to America to visit them though." Daniel's head popped up again. "That fits in with his letters too."

His head was back down over the journal. "He also says he attended church regularly through the summer and planned to meet with the priest soon."

"Maybe he wanted to talk to the priest about what he did to deserve God's wrath," Morgan offered.

Christy yawned. I could only imagine how bored she was with the translation of the journal.

Morgan poked Daniel. "Hey, schoolboy," she taunted. "What else have you got?"

Daniel closed the first journal. "Lots more info about his finances through 1897." He put the first journal in a resealable baggie he pulled from his backpack and then opened the second one.

The Alps were back in sight, and much closer. I watched them until Daniel started translating again.

"He's been doing more carvings. Boxes. Headboards. More benches. He mailed a couple of his boxes to Elsbeth, including a very special one."

"What's the story on that?"

Daniel shook his head. "Dunno. That's all he wrote about it." He read some more and then said, "Things are turning around. He almost has enough money saved for his trip to the United States. He's thinking about the Kessler family and hopes to be able to visit Marie too. He's packed the paperwork she needed."

I groaned. "What if he planned to take the agreement with him? It could have ended up in any number of odd places."

"Or not," Daniel countered, jumping right back into the translation. "He's made arrangements with Caspar to stay on the property and has drawn up papers so that when he dies Caspar can continue managing the place for Elsbeth until one of her children or grandchildren returns. Caspar is to pay the taxes and maintain the buildings and grounds. But then Abraham's health worsens and he's not sure if he will be able to make the trip."

Daniel explained that the next several entries were full of financial information about the estate, and it looked as if Abraham was trying to get everything in order. "The last entry was written on May 4, 1898. Abraham says he poured out his heart to Elsbeth in a letter and finally confessed to her his great sin, his *Überschreitung*."

"Do we have that letter?" I asked.

He shook his head, reminding me that the last letter we had was the one where Abraham said that he had some "important information" for Elsbeth and he would send it soon. "That information must have had to do with his big sin, whatever it was."

"What else does it say?" Morgan prodded.

Daniel skimmed for a moment and then continued. "After talking about the letter where he pours out his heart, he writes that he's too tired to write much more, but he's told the truth and he hopes it will set him free. He says, 'Just like the Israelites, I did not inquire of God. I am proud of her for doing what I haven't and pray her children and grandchildren will follow her good example.' That's it," Daniel said. "Then he died."

I wondered what sin Abraham Sommers had confessed and what Elsbeth had done with the letter after she'd read it. If the letter didn't exist—or couldn't be found—we'd never know his secret.

I thought of my own father and how sad he would be if I never returned from my trip across the sea. Elsbeth was younger than I when she left. Where did she find the strength to leave her home, a place like Amielbach, no less, and her father, who obviously cared deeply for her, to go all the way to America? Worse, how could her father abide seeing her go—especially knowing she would most likely never come home in his lifetime?

I mulled these things over as we rode on in silence. Christy leaned against my shoulder and fell asleep, but when we reached the outskirts of Zurich, I woke her up, not wanting her to miss anything.

Daniel pointed out the two towers of the Grossmünster Church, which would be our first stop. The buildings around us had steep, pointy roofs and lots of small windows, their architecture very medieval looking. We bumped onto the bridge crossing the Limmat River, and I thought of the old prison tower that used to stand in the water. Early Anabaptists had been imprisoned and martyred there.

A few minutes later the driver parked the van across the street from the church parsonage. We all exited from the vehicle, walked around to the front of the church, and approached a large bronze door that consisted of molded panels depicting scenes from the Bible. As Morgan snapped photos, the door opened and a man stepped through it, greeting George and then Daniel. He was middle-aged, with gray hair, a mustache, and wire glasses. The three men spoke for a moment and then Daniel excused himself, saying he was off to look for the agreement.

George introduced the man as our tour guide. After welcoming us, the fellow began by saying that the original building on the site had been erected in the ninth century and founded by Charlemagne, although not much of it remained except for the crypt. The bulk of the existing structure had been built in the late eleventh and early twelfth centuries, although the towers had been added later.

As we toured the church, the guide explained that officials of the Reformed Church in Zurich had recently begun addressing the dark side of their history, the past persecution and execution of Anabaptists. "What started out as a movement of renewal turned into a story of separation and death," the guide said. He looked at us sincerely. "For that we are truly sorry."

Daniel had told me the Swiss government had been making a concerted effort lately to demonstrate their regret and take steps toward reconciliation with Anabaptist groups. George, Christy, and I nodded solemnly at the guide's apology. Though we as a people had long ago forgiven the matter, I felt touched and, in an odd sense, healed by his words.

Next we passed by stained-glass windows, through the nave, and then down the stone staircase to the crypt. Christy needed the restroom, and when she saw a sign at the top of the staircase, she pointed to it and we ventured down the hallway together. On our way back to find our group, she stepped into a little alcove. A table and a chair were there, and above the setting was a carving. I stepped closer. It was an empty cross towering above a village with a mountain peak rising behind it.

We hurried to find the others back in the nave and asked the tour guide about the carving. He couldn't recall it, so he led the rest of us back down the hall to take a look.

"Oh, that one," he said. "We don't know who carved it. But isn't it something?"

Morgan took a photo of it, and then George stepped closer and examined it. Both shrugged their shoulders. "It's hard to tell," George said, "but it might be Abraham's work."

"It could be the one we just read about. The one he sold to a priest," I said.

Morgan explained our line of thinking to the tour guide, and he said he would surely be interested in knowing more about Abraham Sommers in case the work belonged to him.

"Someone needs to inventory Abraham Sommers' work," Morgan said to me as we continued on with the rest of the tour. "A small carving like that one could be worth five hundred bucks, maybe more. And that giant, wall-sized one at Amielbach? I'm just guessing, but I'd say it could bring... oh, I don't know, probably well over ten thousand dollars."

I gasped at the very thought.

"We would never sell them," I said, realizing even as I said it that it wasn't up to me. It was up to Herr Lauten. Someday, it would be up to Oskar.

"Oh, I know. No one would want them sold," Morgan said. "But it would still be good to know what they are worth. And one like this, in a public place, should definitely be labeled. People need to know."

As we finished the tour, I kept my eyes out for other carvings that could be Abraham's but saw none. Daniel joined us just as we finished, and it sounded as though he'd had no luck in his search for the agreement.

On a regular day, we would have enjoyed visiting the other sites within the old-walled city of Zurich, but for now we needed to keep moving. Our next stop was the University of Zurich. Daniel had thought of several places we could look for the document. As long as we were already there, he also hoped to accomplish a personal errand regarding his future enrollment. Either way, given the time I had a feeling this would be our last stop for the day. If it didn't pan out, we would have to visit the other places on Daniel's list tomorrow.

The driver turned onto the campus and parked. We all climbed out and followed Daniel across the tree-lined grounds. The leaves were turning, although they weren't as glorious as the colors back home in Lancaster County. The day was sunny, but the air was growing cooler.

Daniel turned around, a smile on his face. "Just think of the learning that's gone on here through the centuries."

I couldn't help smiling with him. I'd read that several early Anabaptists studied at this university and other places in Europe too, including Italy.

Unfortunately, none of the places he'd had in mind for the agreement panned out. In the end we headed toward the admissions office, glad at least that our visit wouldn't be a total wash. On the way Daniel stopped walking and pointed to a bench.

"Ada, look."

The back of the bench was carved. I stopped in front of it. It was the same style as the boxes.

"That's a carving of the church where we just were," Christy said. She was right.

Morgan took a photo of it. Then Daniel posed by it, and she took another. As she moved in to get some close-ups of the gleaming wood, Daniel came and stood by me.

"You have quite a history, Ada," he said softly as the others laughed and chatted nearby. "If we could only figure all of it out. That's the challenge."

Suddenly, I felt the pressure of Daniel's hand at my waist, and I realized he had put his arm around me and was pulling me closer to him. I froze, afraid he might even try to steal a kiss if he though no one was looking. He must have sensed my discomfort because he just chuckled before releasing me and stepping away.

I stood there, stunned, until I caught Morgan smiling at me. Cheeks burning with heat, I reached up and pretended to adjust my *kapp*, wondering if Christy had seen us as well.

Perhaps it was best that Will hadn't come with us after all.

THIRTY-ONE

The rest of us waited in the lobby of the admissions building while Daniel talked with the woman at the desk. He returned with a stack of brochures. "At least this part of the stop was fruitful." He grinned. "This master's program is looking better and better."

I could see him in a few years, living in Zurich, married with one child. Conducting tours and still doing research. Always learning. Always seeking. As if he could read my thoughts, he stepped close to me. "Can you imagine living here? Going to school here? Wouldn't it be wonderful?"

"For you, yes," I said, laughing. "But not for me. Remember, I have an eighth grade education."

"You could get your GED. That would qualify you for college. And who knows after that? You love learning so much. Maybe you'd like to get your master's too. You're certainly smart enough."

I gave him a funny look and then glanced behind me, hoping no one else was listening. Morgan was taking photos of the buildings. Christy was a few steps away, but I couldn't tell if she'd heard him or not.

I met his eyes. "And who would I hang out with if I went to school here?"

"Me, of course," he said.

"You and your wife?" I asked, turning up my nose a little. "And your one child?"

He looked hurt. "You can be so dense."

My heart fluttered. What was he saying?

"Walk with me." He increased his pace, and I matched him stride for stride. "Ada," he continued, his voice low and firm. "I would like to court you."

"Pardon?"

"Court you. In the proper sense. Get to know you with the intention of moving toward marriage."

"Daniel—" The word came out as a gasp. "You hardly know me."

"But I do," he said. "I've been watching you closely. In a sense, I feel as if I know you better than any woman I've ever met."

I could understand what he meant. Honestly, in a short time, I felt I knew him pretty well too.

"I can't move to Lancaster County," he continued, "but you could move here. It would be the only way for us to spend enough time together to know if this is what's right for us."

"I would have to leave my family. Everything I know."

"But you haven't been baptized yet. You wouldn't be shunned."

Did he have any idea what he was asking of me?

I was quiet for a long moment as we continued to walk. I wondered if he could be the answer to my prayers. Maybe I didn't have to grow old alone after all.

I heard footsteps from behind and turned. Christy was running toward us.

"Think about it," he whispered.

Christy grabbed my hand and swung it back and forth, and then the three of us stopped, waiting for George and Morgan to catch up. I stole a look at Daniel. He was watching me, smiling. Blushing again, I returned his smile.

Once we were all together, we walked as a group toward the parking lot, Morgan commenting along the way that we had "struck out again."

That led to everyone else bemoaning the probable loss of the waterfall and those ever-important caves behind it. As they talked, I could feel myself growing even more disheartened, afraid this entire trip had been for naught. Finally, Morgan admitted that, while the treasure hunt was great fun, she still didn't quite understand the historical significance behind our efforts. "Why are those caves so important to you guys?"

Taking a deep breath, Daniel began to explain. "For many years, being Anabaptist was against Swiss law and at times even punishable by death. Those who persisted in their beliefs had no choice but to gather in secret. One of the places where they did so was in the caves behind that waterfall. Each time they worshipped together there, they were risking their freedom and, in some cases, their lives. But they did it anyway. If the Anabaptist hunters had found them, the group members would have all been arrested and perhaps even executed."

"Why take that risk?" Morgan's face was troubled.

"Because we're commanded to worship together," Daniel said simply.

"Those caves are a symbol of our faith," I added. "A reminder of those who were willing to die for their beliefs. Our beliefs."

Morgan shook her head as we all reached the van, saying, "I still don't get it."

"It's all about what you'd be willing to give your life for," Daniel said as we climbed inside. I don't know if she heard him or not, but she didn't answer.

I thought about his words as the driver navigated his way out of the city. *It's all about what you'd be willing to give your life for.*

Glancing at Christy, I thought of Lydia, who had risked her life to have children, whether she'd known it at the time or not. Lydia had survived giving birth to Christy and later to Mel and Matty. But the pregnancy after that had ended up killing her and the baby, thanks to the heart defect Lydia hadn't even known she had.

I shifted in my seat, trying to get more comfortable. In a way, I realized, every woman risked her life when bringing a child into the world. Labor and delivery were serious business, and not for the faint of heart. Yet down through the centuries women took that risk, willing to trade life for life.

Even Giselle, a small voice said inside of me.

Giselle? Perhaps it was true. She hadn't planned to conceive me, but once she did, she'd willingly carried me to the end—even though she knew once I was born that she would be giving me up. Taking a deep breath, I decided to try to change my attitude. Now that we'd met, it seemed as though it didn't matter to Giselle whether I existed or not. But perhaps I could take comfort in the thought that, at least, years ago she had risked death simply to give me life.

We stopped to buy bread and cheese for a snack halfway back to Amielbach, and afterward Morgan climbed in the back of the van with Christy, leaving me to sit by Daniel. He opened up his packet from the university and was studying it. I asked if I could look at something he wasn't, and he handed me a brochure on the history of the university. There were photos of the stately buildings and drawingsof men from long ago. In a minute, Daniel was looking at the brochure too.

"What would your parents think of you going to school here?" I handed the brochure back to him.

"They would be thrilled," he said. "It would be a dream come true."

"But what if you stay and never live near them again?"

Daniel shrugged. "They would come visit. We'd email. Talk. I'd visit them." He looked at me sheepishly. "They want me to be independent. That's how they raised me." We rode on in silence for a few minutes and then he said, his voice low, "How about your parents? What if you decided to stay here?"

"It would be hard for them," I answered, not being completely honest about just how difficult it would be. And there was the matter of my church. I hadn't joined yet, but I'd always intended to. I knew I would have a relationship with God no matter what church I belonged to, but for me my faith and my community were woven together. I couldn't quite fathom leaving the community part behind.

But I definitely felt a draw to Daniel's future life. Studies. Traveling around Europe. Researching. Teaching travelers what he'd learned. There was a strong appeal to it, especially considering that I could never have anything of the sort back home. Now that Leah had stolen my teaching job, I didn't even have that. "Have you thought of gearing any of your tours toward kids?" I asked.

Daniel turned toward me. "What age group?"

"Not Plain kids...well, Mennonite, maybe, but teenagers." I told him about the tours of children that came through Lancaster County, oftentimes eighth grade classes from *Englisch* schools. "What if you did something like that? Do you think the schools would be interested in a European trip?"

"Maybe not for middle schoolers, but they might for high school kids. A graduation trip, that sort of thing. They'd have to be pretty wealthy…"

"Or the kids would have to earn the money," Morgan chimed in. "There are plenty of fund-raisers for that sort of thing."

I could imagine Amielbach filled with teenagers. That would have made Abraham Sommers very happy.

Daniel was staring at me with an impish smile on his face. "Ada Rupp," he said, "I think you've just created the perfect job for yourself. That would make our plan that much easier."

"How so?" I wrapped my finger around one of the ties to my *kapp*.

"It would give you the perfect reason to stay in Switzerland. Authentic tour guide. Who would be better than you dressed in your cape and apron, talking about your ancestor Abraham Sommers, the history of Amielbach, your own family's journey to America and back to Switzerland. And you're a born teacher." He grinned broadly.

I blushed. "Daniel…" I whispered. Surely he was joking. Such a thing would turn my clothing into a costume. My teaching into living history. My modesty into pride.

"It's brilliant, isn't it?" His voice was louder now.

I hesitated, not sure I could correct him without unleashing my inner teacher. I didn't want to embarrass him in front of the others, but he needed to understand that I could never serve as some caricature of an Amish woman. Later, when we were alone, I would explain the fallacy of his reasoning in full. For now, I held my tongue.

"You could live with Giselle at first," he continued, his voice low again, "and I could stay at Amielbach until I start my studies. We should know within a year if we have a future together."

He made it sound so doable. I glanced toward the backseat. Christy's head was leaning toward the window and her eyes were closed. Morgan was looking out her side of the van, seemingly intent on the countryside.

"I really would like to get to know you better," he said. "I really do want to court you."

I nodded but didn't speak. Just last night I was still pining away for Will Gundy, and now I was sitting here with Daniel, listening to him say he wanted to court me. Maybe Daniel *was* the one who would heal my broken heart and make me forget how I'd ever felt about Will. I just didn't know how I could know for sure.

Overwhelmed with exhaustion, I told Daniel I would think it over and pray about it, and let him know.

Then I closed my eyes and slept the rest of the way to Langnau.

It was early evening by the time we arrived back at the hospital. After visiting with Alice for a while, some of us were getting hungry for dinner. Morgan offered to take us on a grocery run, so George said he would stay there with Will for now and give him a ride up to Amielbach for the night later.

We were just about to go when the telephone beside Alice's bed rang. Will was closest to it, so he answered.

"Hello," he said tentatively, but then he smiled. "Oh, hi there, Leah. I see you tracked us down."

Inwardly, I groaned.

"Let's go," Daniel said to Morgan. Christy gave her *daed* a quick hug and then kissed her *grossmammi*. I told Alice I would see her later, and she waved to me. Will was listening intently to Leah as we left the room.

While Morgan, Christy, and I shopped for groceries, Daniel found a pay phone and called Herr Lauten. Once we were all back in the car and on the road again, I asked Daniel how the conversation had gone, certain that the old man must be feeling as disheartened as we were about the fact that our search today had been fruitless.

"Actually," Daniel said with a smile, "Herr Lauten had a good idea about the letters he gave to Giselle. As you know, she can't remember what she did with them. We've all been assuming she just threw them away, but if not, there is a logical place where she might have stashed them. For all we know, they're still there."

"Where?"

"In the shed near her cottage. He lets her use part of it for storage."

"Wouldn't it be locked?" I asked. "What if she's not home to give us the key?"

"She isn't home, but he said we can use his key instead."

When we reached Amielbach, Morgan and Christy headed down to the cottage to start dinner, while Daniel and I went up the steps to the main house to find Herr Lauten. We arrived at the door just as he was coming out, one hand on his cane, the other gripping a small metal key.

He greeted us eagerly and began moving toward the steps. Watching him, I realized he intended to go down to the shed with us. I wanted to tell him not to bother, that Daniel and I could take care of it, but I could tell by the determined gleam in the man's eye that he wanted to come along no matter how precarious for him the walk might be.

Standing close, hands at the ready to catch him if he fell, I held my breath as he made his way downward, one step at a time. Daniel, apparently oblivious to the whole situation, waited at the bottom, talking about the journals of Abraham's we had read in the car. He asked Herr Lauten about one particular entry, wondering if he knew what Abraham's big sin—his *Überschreitung*—had been. Herr Lauten said no, that he'd been hoping one of us might know.

We finally reached the bottom steps and moved onto the pathway. As we walked slowly along the uneven ground, I asked Herr Lauten if he was sure we wouldn't be violating Giselle's privacy by going through her things in the shed.

"Nah," he said, dismissing the thought with a wave of his hand. "She and I share the space. I haven't been in there in a long time, but she's never minded me going in before."

I wondered if she would feel the same way about *me* specifically. Of all the people in the world, I was probably the last one she'd want rooting through her stuff.

"Where is she now?" I asked.

"Out shopping with Oskar," Herr Lauten replied. "They went into Bern this afternoon to find some special hardware to hang her weavings in the gift shop."

"Oh." That surprised me. For all her aloofness with me, here she was interacting with yet another person.

Daniel walked ahead of us, and soon he was waiting by the shed. When we caught up to him, he stepped aside so that Herr Lauten could unlock the door. As it swung open, my nostrils were greeted with the smell of dust and must.

We stepped inside. Looking around, I spotted a collection of old furniture against one wall—a bed and dresser, a camelback couch, a table with rickety chairs, and a bookcase. Shelves lined the other walls and were filled with large plastic boxes. By my rough count, there were almost a dozen of them.

Herr Lauten clucked his tongue. "Giselle's added more things since the last time I was down here. Isn't she organized?" He lifted his cane. "Just look at this."

We scanned the pile of furniture and then the shelves, looking between each plastic container, but there was no sign of the box. I peered through the plastic walls of one of the containers, but I saw nothing inside that resembled an old wooden box or a pile of letters.

Daniel started to pull off the lid.

"I don't think we should do that," I said.

He hesitated, looking to Herr Lauten. I looked as well, only to see that the man was already digging through a different box himself and was even pulling things out of it. He held up a weaving, and even though this felt wrong, I couldn't help but gape at it. The colors were Plain: blue, forest green, maroon, brown, and black. It featured two stars, side by side, with three larger stars above them. That larger star in the middle seemed fractured somehow, as if it were about to implode. The image was similar to one I'd seen in the gift shop but far more disturbing.

Putting that one back, he pulled out another. It showed a flower garden, almost my garden, with petals flying up in the air as if the flowers had all exploded. Silver pieces of a windmill soared above the flowers into a dark sky.

"I really don't think we should go through her things without her permission," I said, stepping toward the door. I knew it was our windmill. And I was pretty sure the three stars represented Giselle and her sisters, and the smaller ones, Lexie and me. And the garden was definitely from home. I felt as if we were stealing something from her.

"All right," Herr Lauten said, returning the wall hangings to the box and sliding it back onto the shelf.

I pushed opened the door quickly, and nearly knocked it into Giselle. She bounded backward. "I saw the light and wondered who was in here."

We all must have had guilty expressions on our faces because then she said, "What's going on?"

"We were looking for the letters," I said.

She shook her head. "Well, I know they are not in here. I reorganized this whole shed a few months ago."

I nodded.

"Did you look at my weavings?" She was staring at me.

I must have blushed because she put her hands on her hips and said, "Well?"

"Two of them."

"That's all? There are close to thirty." She stepped around me.

"I didn't think we should go through your things."

She must have been able to tell that the plastic box Herr Lauten had gone through wasn't pushed back all the way because she opened the box next to it and held up a wall hanging of abstract dahlias, again three and then two. She held up hanging after hanging, and over and over there were similar sets of objects. Stars. Suns. Moons. Flowers. Trees. Finally she held up a hanging in the colors of a traditional Amish quilt with small squares, but each square had been woven as a separate jagged piece that looked as if it had been torn. "This is the last of my early work," she said, looking directly at me again. She glanced at the plastic boxes. "The other weavings are early versions of commissioned work."

I thanked her for showing us, realizing how far from Plain she was. A member of my community would never draw so much attention to themselves over something they had created. I also was surprised, when she wouldn't talk to me about the past, that she would so willingly bare her emotions through her art. That's what I thought about as Daniel and Herr Lauten headed up to Amielbach and I followed Giselle back toward the cottage.

After dinner Giselle retreated to her studio, while Morgan, Christy, and I cleaned the kitchen. I told Morgan about Giselle's artwork in the shed. She was appalled.

"She's storing her weavings out there?" she cried. "Between the temperature fluctuations and the humidity, they'll be ruined!" Morgan put down her dishtowel and marched toward the hall. A moment later, she and Giselle hurried out the front door. Christy and I kept working on the dishes.

Morgan returned after a while carrying two of the boxes. "She's consolidating them. Getting as many as possible in one box. We're going to cram them into her studio for now."

Back and forth Morgan went until she returned with Giselle, both loaded down with more. Altogether, they had brought in nine boxes. It would be a wonder if Giselle was able to move around in her studio at all now. I didn't say anything but turned back to scouring the sink. After I'd finished, I suggested to Christy that we walk up to Amielbach and see if her *daed* had arrived so she could tell him goodnight.

As we headed up the pathway, I felt overwhelmed with the complexity of everyone I was around. Each person seemed to have issues. Giselle and her past. Morgan and her future. Christy and death. Will and his family. Me—with more than I could count.

I sighed. Except Daniel. He was the least complicated of us all. Somehow I had the feeling that all he really needed to be happy was a library full of books and an interesting topic to research. The question was where a wife and children—correction, child—would find room to fit into that scenario.

THIRTY-TWO

Christy and I found Herr Lauten, Daniel, and Will sitting around the table in the dining room, finishing up a hearty stew.

"We're bemoaning our plan," Herr Lauten said. "At least Daniel and I are."

Will shrugged. "I just said if it's God's will, the waterfall and caves will be saved."

"But you heard the judge," Daniel said. "If we can't find that agreement…" His voice trailed off.

Herr Lauten looked just as forlorn. "It's ridiculous," he said. "The hydro plant is as good as done. Instead of the melody of the waterfall, I'll have the constant hum of turbines."

"At least if we had those letters, we might stand a chance," Daniel said. "But where could Giselle have put them?"

"The landfill. The secondhand store. The burn pile. Who knows?" Herr Lauten threw up his hands. "I had no idea she didn't care about such things when she arrived."

Glancing at Christy, I saw that she looked extremely tired, and I suggested that we get on to bed. Instead, she asked if she could move back up here so she could stay with her *daed* instead of at the cottage with me.

"Sure," I told her, adding that I would go down to the cottage and retrieve her things. Daniel said he would go with me. We hurried on our way, me fretting over Christy, wondering if perhaps the tour of Zurich was too much with all the talk of martyrdom and death.

Daniel was still obsessing about the letters. "Have you looked all through the cottage?" he asked. "High in the cupboards in the kitchen? That sort of thing."

I hadn't. I'd relied on what Giselle had told me. "I think she'd know if the box was anywhere in her house. Every room except her studio is extremely sparse and organized."

"Can you ask, though, if you can look?"

"I'll try," I said, though I knew Morgan would have better luck asking than I would.

When we arrived at the cottage, neither Morgan nor Giselle was in sight. I assumed they were both in the studio. Quickly, I packed Christy's bag. I knew it was perfectly natural for her to want to be with Will, but I would miss not having her with me after spending so many days with her. I pulled her bag out into the hall and into the entryway, and then I turned the handle around for Daniel. Our fingers brushed as he started to take it, but instead of pulling away, he clasped my hand. "It would be so perfect if it all comes together."

"*Ya*," I answered. "If only we can find the agreement."

His blue eyes focused on mine. "I meant more than that." He squeezed my hand. "I meant if you could stay here. If we could get to know each other. If we could—"

"Ada?" It was Morgan's voice, coming from down the hall. "Is that you?"

I pulled my hand away from Daniel. "*Ya*. And Daniel, but he is just leaving."

She practically skipped down the hall. "Oh, look at you two," she gushed.

My face grew warm, but he smiled.

"Hey," he said, as an afterthought. "Morgan, have you looked through all the cupboards and closets in this place?"

It was her turn to blush. She lowered her voice. "As a matter of fact, I did, tonight when I was fixing dinner. I'm so taken with all of this. The boxes. The letters. The journals. The mystery. I decided to look just in case…"

"And?"

"Nothing. Nada. Nil."

Daniel's face fell. "Where could they be?"

Morgan shook her head. "Who knows? I tried to get Giselle to talk about them this evening, but she gave me the cold shoulder. That's why I came out here."

Daniel told us goodnight, and I stepped out of the cottage with him. He gave me a quick hug and then started up the path.

The next morning I didn't see Giselle at all. By the time Morgan and I left the cottage, she still hadn't emerged from her closed bedroom door, which I assumed meant either she was still asleep or she was working in her studio.

When we arrived at Amielbach, we went straight to the dining room. Daniel was already there, and we joined him at the table. He talked about other locations we could look for the important documents. "Abraham lived in Bern before moving to Amielbach and sometimes went there on business. Maybe he left the agreement there, in a bank or a government building."

It sounded like a long shot to me.

"Or maybe Thun. There was a lot of legal activity there involving the Mennonites. Imprisonments. Trials. That sort of thing."

I wrinkled my nose, but he didn't notice. "Or maybe it's in his hometown of Frutigen."

Oskar came in at that moment, bearing mugs and a pot of tea. We thanked him for the kindness as he served us.

"Do you think he traveled there very often?" I asked Daniel.

He shrugged. "Maybe he mailed them back. For safekeeping."

"That seems like a bit of a stretch," Morgan said. "But we wouldn't have anything to lose. It's better than sitting around doing nothing."

Oskar paused at the doorway before going back into the kitchen. "Do you folks not yet realize that this whole thing is a pipe dream?" he said. "You were caught up in an old man's delusions. That's all." Shaking his head, he continued on without waiting for a reply.

"Pipe dream or not, I for one am having the time of my life," Morgan said to Daniel and me.

I agreed, but the situation wasn't without its stresses, especially with

Alice being ill and the uncertainty over the missing agreement. I also didn't have the financial stake in the situation that the Gundys and the Lautens did—or that, ultimately, Daniel and George did either.

The endless sunny weather had finally come to an end. The morning was overcast, and as we traveled to Bern we drove in and out of fog.

"Abraham Sommers was a local councilman for a few years before Elsbeth left," Daniel explained along the way.

I still found it odd that Daniel knew far more about my own ancestors than I did.

"He resigned after that. He might have still come to Bern on official business from time to time, though. I think it's worth looking at the council chambers."

Christy had decided to spend the day with Will, and although it seemed odd not to have her with me, I looked forward to a day with just Morgan and Daniel, being with my new friends, totally focused on our search. Morgan drove and I sat up front beside her, with Daniel in the back, poring over yet another one of his books.

Once we reached the city, Morgan parked the car, and we headed to the council chambers immediately, only to find that the archives' office would be closed for two hours. Back on the sidewalk, Daniel pulled some papers from his pack and said that while we were waiting we could walk through the tour he'd been designing.

"We'll need to backtrack through the old city to the first stop," he told us, eyes glowing with excitement. "Come on! Let's do this in order."

He turned and started walking. Morgan and I glanced at each other, both of us bemused at his excitement, knowing we had no choice but to follow along.

Daniel said we'd begin our tour where the main gate to the city used to be back in 1350. Located near the site was the Church of the Holy Ghost, a Swiss Reformed church that was built long after the Anabaptist movement had started. We didn't take time to go inside. Instead, we stood on the street looking up at it for a few minutes and admiring the structure. Then we started on down the Spitalgasse, the street that led into the heart of the city.

We passed two corners, one that Daniel said used to be the site of a prison where male Anabaptist followers had been held, and the next where women followers had been held. Realizing that this was to be a very martyr-heavy day, I was thankful Christy wasn't with us. We walked from site to site, taking in an open market, the domed parliament building, a street of banks, a section of the original city wall, and the *Zeitglckenturn*, a tower with a clock built in the 1520s with performing animated figures. Christy would have liked seeing this very much.

I stared at the long hand as it ticked away, realizing that the clock was as old as the Anabaptist movement itself. Daniel explained that clocks across Switzerland had been built with money the government collected from confiscating Anabaptist land. "Not this one, but many others."

"Oh," Morgan said, "that's so sad."

Our next stop was the Münster Cathedral of Bern. With a 300-foot steeple, it was a landmark in the city. Inside, the colorful stained-glass windows cast jewel-tone reflections on the floor and across the pews. All the while I kept my eye out for a bench or a box or panel that Abraham might have carved. Surely, if his work had made it to Zurich, it could be in Bern too. We followed a narrow staircase to a rooftop viewpoint. From up there, we could see the cathedral gardens below, rows of houses, and then the River Aare.

"More than forty Anabaptists were martyred in Bern," Daniel said. "Some drowned. Others beheaded." He went on to describe all manner of torture until Morgan put her hands over her ear.

"Stop," she cried, looking and sounding not unlike Christy.

"What?"

We both glanced her way, surprised to see that there were tears in her eyes. "I don't want to hear it. Enough!" After that, she turned and hurried down the stairs.

Startled, Daniel and I just looked at each other.

"Is she okay?" I whispered. "Maybe I should go to her."

He hesitated and then shook his head, saying he would do it instead, explaining that if he was going to be giving tours, he needed to get used to handling things like this himself. I agreed, and soon he was clomping down the stairs after her.

I followed along much more slowly, giving them a moment to talk. I had a feeling I knew what was going on, that it was a matter of us having been raised Plain and Morgan having not.

As a Mennonite and an Amish, Daniel and I had grown up with stories of martyrs. It was what made us appreciate the separation of church and state. It kept us loyal to our faith. It taught us to willingly make our own small sacrifices. It emphasized tradition. But maybe it also numbed us a tad. Maybe to Morgan the martyrs were more like real people and not just old, familiar figures from the stories.

When I arrived at the bottom of the stairs, Morgan and Daniel were across the hall, under a grouping of stained-glass windows, deep in conversation. Her hands bounced around as she talked. I thought of her love of art and beauty, of her concern for the environment. I liked it that she felt for our martyred ancestors, even though they had died five hundred years before. She was a person of passion, that was certain.

Daniel snagged one of her waving hands in his, and she leaned toward him for a moment, as if surrendering to something he'd said. Even from a distance, I could see his face soften in a way I hadn't seen before. I gasped. Maybe Morgan's passion was what Daniel needed to get past his arsenal of historical facts.

Rolling that around in my head, I realized something even more startling: The thought of them as a couple didn't make me jealous in the least.

Next, we stopped at a pit where two bears lived. Daniel explained that Bern meant "bear" and they were intended to be mascots for the city. Looking down at them, I thought it seemed kind of cruel. They were wild animals used to vast forests, now living here in a space smaller than some people's living rooms.

"It's no worse than a zoo," Daniel said.

"I've never been to a zoo."

"They are awful places," Morgan said.

Daniel shook his head. "They're fine. You learn so much about animals that way."

"Yeah, captive animals," Morgan retorted.

I thought about meeting Morgan's father in the Basel train station and how he'd referred to us as strays she'd picked up. I hadn't seen that quality in Morgan on the ship, but the more I came to know her, the more obvious it was. She had a heart of empathy. Maybe that was why Giselle responded to her.

After that we returned to the council chambers and Daniel spoke quickly with the archivist, only to be met with a wave of a hand and a quick dismissal. As we walked down the corridor and through the heavy wooden doors, Daniel explained the archivist had said any documents concerning a Wasserdorf councilman would be kept in the district, not Bern.

Daniel's face was drawn and he was quiet on the way back to the car. I knew the responsibility of the search weighed heavily on him. Fabric in the window of a shop caught Morgan's attention, and we followed her inside. She had been looking for a gift for her mother, and the scarves in the display caught her attention. "They are handwoven locally on an actual loom, just as it was done centuries ago," the clerk said.

"Really?" Morgan fingered the work. "How many artisans do you represent?"

"Ten or so. Maybe close to fifteen."

"Are you looking for new work?" Morgan stepped away from the scarves.

"Always," the woman said.

"Because I know an amazing artist. Giselle Lantz. Have you heard of—"

The woman cut her off. "Giselle? I already carry her work. It's over here."

We followed her to the back of the shop. Sure enough, the wall there was covered with Giselle's weaving. Instead of the Lancaster County themes, these pieces focused on Switzerland—abstract mountain peaks, forests, meadows, edelweiss. I stopped in front of the last one. It was the waterfall with the cave visible in the back. The water looked like shards of broken glass, though, and two shadows appeared in the cave. I shivered. Daniel placed his hand on my shoulder. "Your aunt seems a little twisted," he said.

Morgan shot me a confused look. She must have assumed I'd told Daniel by now about my other, more significant connection to Giselle.

"Has she said anything about the waterfall to you?" I asked Morgan.

She shook her head.

"I saw her walking across the property from there the other day," Daniel said. "It was early morning. The sun was just rising."

Flabbergasted, I started to say, "If Giselle can visit the waterfall regardless of the surveyors, then why can't I?" but I stopped myself. I didn't need anyone's permission. I decided I would go tomorrow, surveyors or not. I wasn't about to come all this way to Switzerland for the sake of a waterfall, only to miss ever actually seeing it in person.

Morgan decided to buy one of Giselle's pieces for her mother. Not the waterfall, but the abstract of the mountains. "It will look good in her office," she said with a shrug.

As we walked the rest of the way to the car, we all agreed to go to Thun to see the castle and then, for what it was worth, on up to Abraham's hometown of Frutigen. Whether we managed to turn up any important documents or not, at least we'd get a closer view of the Alps. It was just too bad we hadn't gone when the weather was so good. I hoped the clouds would burn off and we'd be able to see the mountains.

It only took about half an hour to reach Thun, and as Morgan drove the shroud of clouds around the mountains did ascend. "The Jungfrau is just beyond those peaks." Daniel pointed out the window. "And the Eiger." The beauty of the mountains, one after another after another, topped with jagged glaciers and faced with granite, left me breathless. I'd thought the Rockies had been spectacular, but these were magnificent.

We parked and then walked down a narrow cobbled street. The castle was made of stone and stucco and the roof of red tiles. We entered a great hall with weapons and armor on display. Daniel went looking for the records office, while Morgan and I took our time touring the whole place, looking at the suits of armor.

She took photos as she spoke. "So how are things going between you and Daniel?"

My heart raced a little. "I'm not sure."

"I was right on the ship, wasn't I? He's definitely interested in you."

I didn't respond.

"What's holding you back?"

"I'm not Mennonite. He's not Amish."

"But close enough, right?"

I shook my head. I could see that to Morgan, it would seem to be. But pursuing a relationship with Daniel would mean giving up everything I knew. "He wants me to stay in Switzerland to help with the tours."

"So I heard." She grinned. "That would give you a chance to get to know him better."

"*Ya.*"

"So would you stay now and not go back with Alice?"

I shook my head. I couldn't do that. It wouldn't be fair to Alice and Will. Nor to my *mamm* and *daed*.

"It would make more sense," she said. "You could apply for a work permit here. It would save you the cost of the flight home and back."

She took a photo of a display of swords. "So do you love him?" she asked.

Love him? I wasn't sure, especially after seeing the two of them together in the cathedral in Bern. "Maybe I could learn to love him," I said.

She turned toward me at the end of the great hall. I noticed another tourist staring at us. We must have been quite a sight to others—a young American woman with long hair halfway down her back, wearing jeans and boots, with another young woman in a *kapp* and apron, looking as if she might be from a century or two before, but not quite.

Morgan reached for my hand. "Do you think it was by chance we all ended up on the same ship?" she asked.

"Of course not," I answered.

"I don't either." Her gaze fell past me. "I've been praying again, for the first time since my grandmother died, kneeling at night before I go to sleep, the way you and Christy do, asking God to show me what He has for me."

"His plan for you, *ya*?"

She nodded. "And I pray for Alice and for you and for Giselle."

I squeezed her hand. "Thank you," I said. "I've been praying every night for you too."

Before she could respond, I heard my name being called and turned. Daniel appeared to our right. "Come with me," he said, motioning back down the stone stairwell he'd just climbed. "I found the dungeon, and have I got a surprise for you!" He gave me a wink, eyes shining with excitement, and then he started back down.

Morgan gave me a little push. "See," she teased.

I yanked on her hand, and we followed Daniel down the stone stairs that led to a long hall. At the end was an open door. Daniel motioned for us to follow him, and we made our way down a wooden, open staircase that led into a dark, cavernous room. Columns made of cut stones contrasted starkly to the cellar-like walls of rocks. We ventured across the cold floor toward a rope strung in front of an area between two poles, which Daniel climbed over. I smiled, shrugged, and did the same, lifting my dress a little and then smoothing it back down again on the other side. Morgan followed me.

"Is this a dungeon?" I whispered as we moved forward, wondering why no bars or cells were here. It was just an open space, our voices echoing against the bare stone walls.

"They would use irons to secure people if needed. But there's only one door out." Daniel pointed to the staircase. "And it was guarded. At other castles, such as Trachselwald, they were held in cells. But here it was one big open room." Daniel went on to explain that most of the Anabaptists held here were imprisoned more than three hundred years ago.

"In general, captives often carved their names into the stone walls. Such was the case at Trachselwald Castle," he said. "And here at Thun." He shone the flashlight to the far corner. Sure enough, it was covered with scratches of names and dates.

"Anabaptists, from time to time, were imprisoned here, even after most of the Amish had fled," he continued, holding the beam of his flashlight on a name at the edge of an especially large river rock. "And then much later, a certain man was imprisoned. A man related to you."

"Who?"

"His name was..." He wiggled the flashlight around and then settled it again on the same spot, exclaiming, "Ta-da!"

I stepped closer and read the inscription. *G. Gingrich, 1876.* I gasped. Elsbeth's husband. Abraham's son-in-law. My great-great grandfather.

Thirty-Three

I t has to be him," Daniel said. "The date works."

"I wonder why he was here?" I touched the inscription with the tips of my fingers.

"My guess?" Daniel said. "Resisting mandatory military service. As a Mennonite, he would have refused to serve, which at that time could have landed him in the dungeon. We're definitely putting this on the tour."

"What about his family? Were he and Elsbeth married by then?"

Daniel thought for a moment and then shook his head, reminding me they had been married in 1877, just before leaving the country. "No, in '76 he was still a widower with two small children, and Elsbeth was just their governess."

"Think she took care of the kids while he was in prison?" Morgan asked as she snapped another photo. "That must have been one big whomping child care bill!"

Daniel chuckled at her joke, but I was far too disturbed to laugh. A widower and father ripped from his family and thrown in jail? That would be like Will getting forcibly separated from Christy and the twins and then being locked away. Horrible!

On the other hand, Gerard and Elsbeth had fallen in love at some point, probably after he was released from here and they were preparing to emigrate. Given how things had turned out for them, at least their tragedy had turned to triumph in the end.

It was late afternoon by the time we drove to the village of Frutigen. It looked like a Swiss postcard tucked against the Alps, surrounded by green fields, the church steeple in the middle of the village towering over the multi-century old buildings, the entire scene framed by mountains. Truly, it was picture-perfect. Morgan parked the car on the outskirts of the town, and we got out and walked through the stone city gate. The buildings were made of wood and stucco. It appeared that many of the shops had residences above them. Behind the village rose green hillsides that soon gave way to the mountain peaks.

"There's no way to know which house Abraham grew up in," Daniel said, shaking his head, "but at least we know for sure that this was the town."

We stopped in front of a clock tower made from stone. Nearly every village we'd been through had a clock, and I wondered if this one, too, had been financed by the confiscation and sale of Anabaptist property. Next we walked over to the church. Its steeple rose toward the pale sky.

"Let's see if it's open," Morgan said.

We followed her up the stairs. It was unlocked. We stepped inside. The sanctuary was small, with no stained glass and no ornate carvings. A simple wooden cross graced the front.

As we looked around the hallways on either side, I again hoped for some sign of Abraham Sommers' work, wondering if he'd started carving as a teenager when he still lived in the village.

We never spotted anything, but this was still a charming little town. Morgan took photos right and left as we walked down the street. When we passed a delicious-smelling bakery at the edge of the village, we all paused to inhale.

"Coffee, anyone?" Morgan asked, eyes twinkling.

"None for me," Daniel replied, "but I bet there's a *krapfen* in there with my name on it."

Smiling, we all turned toward it. The building was three stories high with green shutters at each window and a ribbon of smoke coming out of its chimney. The proprietor met us at the door and, speaking in English, said they were about to close, but he would serve us. We chose streusel, almond cookies, and several *krapfen*, which turned out to be a deep-fried pastry. Daniel insisted on paying, and while he did, I moved around the side of the counter. There, above a closed wooden door, was a small carving. I stepped closer. It was a meadow with a mountain behind it, crowned with a ring of clouds. It was the same mountain as in the carving in the ballroom at Amielbach, I was sure. And the steeple in that panel could easily be a depiction of the church here in Frutigen. I squinted and leaned closer, my head tilted upward. The group of figures standing in a semicircle in the meadow weren't in the carving at Amielbach, I was sure of that, but the style of the carving definitely appeared to be Abraham Sommers', although it appeared more primitive than his work at Amielbach.

Morgan was behind me now, snapping a photo. Daniel joined us, the bags of goodies in his hands. "Wow." He crowded next to me. "I didn't expect to find anything of Abraham's. I thought he would have been too young when he lived here."

Before I could say more, the baker came up behind us.

"There's a story behind that carving," he said, "but I can't remember it." He sighed apologetically. "My father-in-law is upstairs. I will ask him."

We stepped aside and he passed through the door. Morgan zoomed in on the carving with her camera. Another customer entered the shop and Daniel spoke to him in German, telling him the proprietor would be right back. The customer waited for a while and then left.

Finally the door to the upstairs opened and the baker returned, holding the arm of an elderly man. The old man was tall, well over six feet, with a bald head fringed with snow-white hair. His blue eyes were clear, and the bones of his face jutted out like cliffs on a mountainside.

"This is Christian Sommers," the baker said.

My mouth dropped open. Sommers.

Daniel glanced at me and then stepped forward and reached for the man's hand. "How do you do?" he said.

"*Hallo*," the old man replied, and added, "my English is not very good anymore." It sounded perfect to me.

Daniel introduced Morgan first and then me. "We're interested in the carving. We're doing research on Anabaptists in the area, on a man named Abraham Sommers in particular." Daniel grinned. "It looks like we came to the right place."

"And you are Anabaptists?" Herr Sommers asked, looking at me as if he hadn't heard what Daniel had said.

"I'm Mennonite," Daniel answered, and then motioning to me said, "and Ada is Amish—and a descendant of Abraham Sommers."

"Ah." He turned toward me. "You are the most conservative, *ya*? With your *kapp* and apron. Your people drive horses and carriages still?"

I nodded.

He smiled and then stepped forward and turned, so he could see the carving. "That was done by my father's great-great uncle. And yes, his name was Abraham Sommers."

"No way!" Morgan cried. "If his father's great-great uncle was your great-great-great- grandfather, then that makes the two of you..." Her voice trailed off as she looked from me to Herr Sommers and back again. I could see that she was trying work it through, counting off with her fingers as she mumbled things like, "...second...third...twice removed..."

"Cousins," the younger man said finally, causing us all to laugh.

"What can you tell us about Abraham Sommers?" I asked the old man, eager to hear whatever he might say.

Eyes twinkling, he replied that Abraham had been the youngest in a large family. "The parents both died and the older children raised him. But then they split on religion when the oldest brother joined the Mennonites. He was very vocal about his beliefs and tried to get the others to join as well, but most of them stayed with the Reformed Church instead, including the brother who ran the bakery."

"This bakery?" I asked.

"Yes," the younger man replied. "It has been in the family for three centuries."

Behind me I could hear Morgan sigh. Three centuries of my family history was right here, under our feet and all around us. Incredible.

"Eventually the authorities grew suspicious of the oldest brother, thinking he was probably meeting with other Mennonites in secret. Once they had proof of it, they arrested him and took him to Thun and put him in the castle."

So another of my ancestors had spent time in the dungeon too.

"Then soon after that, young Abraham went into the military. Sadly, when his time was finished, he chose not to come back home at all but instead made a life for himself elsewhere."

"Why did he do that?" Morgan asked.

The old man shrugged his shoulders. "No one ever knew. It does seem odd, does it not? A young man completing his military service, and then simply staying away for the rest of his life?" He shrugged again. "It is a mystery. My guess was that he had been so heartbroken at the imprisonment of his oldest brother that he could not bear to live here without him. They were both artists—young Abraham showing talent as a carver, and his oldest brother already an accomplished weaver—so perhaps they shared a special bond. Whatever his reasons, Abraham never returned. As the story goes, when the family realized he was not ever coming back, they hung this old carving he had done right here in the bakery, and here it has hung ever since."

"Wow," Morgan whispered, echoing my thoughts exactly.

"Do you know where Abraham went when he left?" Daniel asked.

"No idea at all. Though, now that I have met you," Herr Sommers said, gesturing toward me, "I have to wonder if maybe he emigrated to America. Do you know if that was the case?"

We shook our heads, explaining that Abraham had ended up living near Langnau. His daughter, Elsbeth, had been the one to emigrate to the U.S., continuing the family line that eventually led down to me.

"I see," the man said, nodding. "Well, whatever the reason for Abraham's turning his back on Frutigen, all I know is that the other siblings were devastated when their family broke apart at each end—the oldest brother carted off to the dungeons, the youngest disappearing to who knows where. Even several generations later, my aunts and uncles were still mindful of that sad, sad story."

"Thank you for sharing it with us," I said earnestly.

The man reached out his hand to me and I took it. "You are welcome. It is nice to meet you, cousin," he said. From the smile slowly spreading across his face, I could tell he was enjoying this as much as we were. I had a feeling he was also getting a kick out of having an Amish woman as a relative. Little did he know how many more there were of us back home.

Morgan asked the man if she could take his photo. He said only if

I were in it too. I agreed but turned my head to the side just before she pressed the button.

We thanked Christian Sommers and his son-in-law profusely and then hurried back through the streets of Frutigen. The sun was low, and a cold wind blew through the valley. Clouds scudded across the mountain peaks, covering them up as we walked. By the time we reached the car, my face and hands were icy cold.

We had an hour's drive or more before getting back to Langnau, and I started to feel anxious about being away from Christy for so long. I hoped she'd been a help to Will today.

"Isn't it interesting," Morgan said, "that one of the brothers was a weaver?"

"It was pretty common back then," Daniel said. "I came across information in my research. The farmers could grow flax in the summer and then process it and weave it during the winter. That is, until the textile mills opened in Bern in the mid–eighteen hundreds. That put an end to the bulk of the weavers' trade."

"I didn't mean that," Morgan said. "I meant because Giselle weaves."

"Lots of Amish and Mennonite people work with fabric. It's an acceptable art form for Plain people." Daniel always had an answer.

Morgan shook her head. "I still think it's interesting."

Alice was sitting up in bed and appearing to feel much better when we arrived back at the hospital. She had a little bit of color in her face and her forget-me-not blue eyes were brighter than they had been in days. George was there too, keeping her company while Will and Christy were having dinner.

"The doctor said we can definitely fly home soon, maybe even by the day after tomorrow," Alice said.

"Depends on what's available," George added. "I told Will I'd help him book the flights when you're ready to go."

The day after tomorrow? I tried to look pleased for Alice's sake, but I wasn't, not at all. There was still so much I wanted to do here. Find the missing agreement. Hear the judge's final ruling. Explore the waterfall. See more of Switzerland. Make up my mind about Daniel.

If I really did decide to be courted by Daniel, I would also need to talk to Giselle about living with her when I returned. In fact, I realized, that was one conversation that should happen sooner than later. Depending on her answer, the big plan he had proposed might not even be possible.

After glancing at Daniel, I asked Alice if she knew where I might find Giselle.

"I'm sorry, dear, but I haven't seen her all day," Alice replied. George added that he hadn't either.

"She's probably been in her studio, working on that new piece," Morgan suggested.

That sounded likely to me, and suddenly I was eager to get going. Before I could decide about a future with Daniel, I needed to know if the basics of such an arrangement could even work.

We were just leaving when Will and Christy returned from dinner. Will wanted to stay longer, but Christy was looking pretty tired, so I suggested she ride to Amielbach with us.

"Thanks, Ada," Will said with a grateful smile, looking pretty tired himself.

George said he would stay until Will was ready to return to the inn, so Daniel, Morgan, Christy, and I headed toward the car, with Christy and Morgan leading the way. When we reached the parking lot, I slowed my pace a bit until the two of them were out of earshot. Then, turning to Daniel, I lowered my voice and told him I needed a favor.

"From me?"

"Yes. When we get to the cottage, I'm going to talk to Giselle about coming back to live with her. I want to have that conversation in private, so I'm wondering if you would mind keeping Christy occupied for a while. Maybe you and Morgan can talk her into playing a board game or something."

"Oh! Absolutely!" Daniel replied, his face lighting up in such a broad smile that I realized he had misunderstood. He thought I had already made my decision, and that my conversation with Giselle was after the fact. I came to a stop there in the middle of the parking lot and, after a beat, he did too.

"Don't get the wrong impression," I said gently. "I haven't yet decided about us courting. I'm just exploring the possibility for now."

"I see," he replied, his smile fading a bit. "Well, if you do, and if Giselle says you can live with her, then you should just stay and not go back to Pennsylvania with the others at all."

I gaped at him for a moment. "I would still have to go back home first, regardless."

"Why?" he asked, sounding like a petulant child.

"I can't bow out of my commitment to take care of Christy, not to mention that I would never be so disrespectful to my parents." Suddenly, I was feeling kind of petulant myself—and more than a little defensive. "Don't forget, Daniel, that I have a whole life back there. Affairs I would need to settle. Possessions I would have to pack. Friends and relatives who deserve a goodbye from me in person. If I'm really moving to Europe, there's a lot I have to do first."

"Seriously?" he asked. "The way I see it, you have no job and no boyfriend. You haven't joined your church. What's to miss? You should just stay."

I stared at him, incredulous. His words may have contained some truth—okay, maybe they even closely echoed words I had said to myself recently—but in that moment I realized how wrong he was. How wrong I had been.

In the distance I could hear the sound of car doors opening and then closing, and I hoped Morgan was adequately distracting Christy from our discussion out here. Breathing in deeply, I asked myself why I was having so much trouble accepting the one thing I'd thought I had wanted most, an exciting future with a man who said he cared for me. Then again, if he really did care, wouldn't he know that what I needed right now was patience, not pressure?

"Listen, Ada," he said finally, stepping closer and taking my hand. "You do what you think you need to do. I'll try to back off a little, but I can't wait around for your answer forever. Make up your mind soon, okay?"

I closed my eyes, wishing that the touch of his hand made me shiver the way Will's did.

"I'll try," I whispered, opening my eyes and giving Daniel a reassuring smile.

Then I let go of his hand, turned, and walked the rest of the way to the car, wondering if I could ever learn love anyone other than Will Gundy.

When we reached Amielbach, the others stayed up at the main house to look for a game while I headed down to the cottage to talk to Giselle. I went straight to her studio, but she wasn't there. In fact, she wasn't anywhere.

Looking around at the whole cottage, I could find no signs that Giselle had been there today at all. No dirty dishes. No books left out. Nothing out of order anywhere. Her car was still exactly where it had been this morning. Yet her heavy coat was missing from the rack by the door.

Where is she?

Sometimes God impresses us, puts a feeling in our gut to let us know something is wrong. That's how it was for Aunt Marta when she rescued Lexie from the creek all those years ago. That's how I felt right now. Somehow I just knew that Giselle was in trouble, and it was up to me to help her.

Heart pounding, I left the cottage and ran all the way up the main house. When I got there, I tried to explain that Giselle was missing, but the others didn't seem nearly as alarmed.

"She came by here this morning," Oskar said, shrugging. "She talked to Father for a few minutes and then left, saying she needed some fresh air."

That didn't help much. She could be anywhere. And maybe she'd been gone all day, or maybe not. She could have come back to the cottage and then gone out again.

"Father's in his study. He might have an idea of where she went."

Daniel led the way down the hall, with Christy right behind him. He knocked rapidly and a faint voice welcomed us in.

Herr Lauten was at his desk, but he looked as if he'd been sleeping.

I stepped forward and asked him about Giselle.

He shifted in his chair a little. "Yes, she did stop by this morning. And she was upset. I told her Amielbach was about to change forever. That seemed to upset her even more. Then..." He took a deep breath. "Well, I said something I shouldn't have. I told her if she'd kept track of that box, we'd be in better shape." He stopped.

"And?" I stepped closer to the desk.

"She said back then the box was the least of her worries." He gripped his cane with both hands. "I'm afraid I hurt her—even though I have no idea what she was referring to."

"She was referring to me." I turned to face Daniel. "And my sister, Lexie. Giselle is our birth mother," I said, looking back at Herr Lauten. "She gave us up and moved to Switzerland. Lexie was adopted by a couple from Oregon, and I was adopted by my Aunt Klara, Giselle's sister, who became my mother."

A wave of shock passed over Daniel's face, and Herr Lauten turned a sickening gray. "Poor Giselle," he said, standing. "I had no idea. She wouldn't bring harm to herself, would she?" He looked at me and then at Daniel and then at Morgan. I looked at Christy, wondering if she realized what Herr Lauten was alluding to.

But the truth was, none of us really knew what Giselle might do. "Let's get flashlights and go look for her," I said, whispering up a prayer, apprehension gnawing at my gut.

THIRTY-FOUR

As it turned out, Daniel didn't think we should go look for Giselle at all, at least not until the next day. "She's a middle-aged woman. She's probably at a friend's house."

"Don't you think we should at least call the police?"

"And tell them what? There's nothing suspicious about her disappearance. If she doesn't show up in a couple of days, then they would get involved..." His voice faded away.

I turned toward Morgan. "He's right," she said, shrugging her shoulders.

Oskar was already back in the kitchen, and Herr Lauten was shuffling down the hall to his study.

Christy said she was tired, and so she, Morgan, and I decided to head down to the cottage. I was miffed at Daniel for not wanting to help find Giselle and quickly told him goodnight.

As we walked down the steps of Amielbach, I said, "I can't imagine her staying out in the cold like this."

"Who says she's in the cold? Maybe she has a boyfriend we don't know about," Morgan said. "Or maybe she barhops."

I couldn't imagine either.

A half hour later, Morgan and I were in the kitchen when we heard a knock at the door of the cottage. I ran to it and swung it open in relief, expecting Giselle. But it wasn't her—it was Will.

"Hey, Ada," he said, a little out of breath. "George and I just got back. Oskar told us what was going on. You're concerned for Giselle's safety?"

I nodded, hating how much better I felt just knowing he was here. I invited him in, but he shook his head, remaining there on the porch.

"We know Giselle struggles with depression," I explained to him from the doorway, keeping my voice low. "What if my coming to see her has made that worse?"

He couldn't answer the question, but at least he didn't try to soothe me with empty reassurances. Instead, he simply promised to pray for her—and for me.

"You must think my family is such a mess..." I said, my face growing hot. I couldn't imagine what he thought about me or my past or my parentage.

He didn't reply for a long moment, and when he did, his words surprised me.

"To tell you the truth, Ada, I've been thinking a lot about Giselle and what she went through way back then," he said, his voice soft. He cleared his throat, shoved a hand in his pocket, and smoothed the brim of his hat. "Actually, do you have a minute?"

"Sure," I said, pulse surging. I glanced toward the kitchen, where Morgan was busily making tea, and then I stepped out onto the stoop and pulled the door closed behind me. Will and I took a few steps up the brick pathway and then stood facing each other. His brown eyes were tired but kind.

"Of course, when all that happened I was just a boy and had no idea what was really going on," he continued. "Though I knew my *mammi* was very concerned for Giselle, I didn't know the full story about all of that until recently."

I nodded, embarrassed but in a way also relieved that it was now out in the open between us. I'd already suspected he knew, but now that had been confirmed.

"Anyway, I guess I just wanted to say that your family is not alone in these problems."

I knew that. "I appreciate it, Will. All of your family has been so supportive of us through the years—"

He shook his head, his beard swaying a little with the movement. "That's not what I'm saying. My family has gone through a…similar problem."

The way he said it, I knew he meant a child had been conceived out of wedlock. I tilted my head. His family? The Gundys? Surely not his sister, Hannah.

"All families have their problems," Will said. "Jesus said in this life we will have troubles. No one is immune." He met my eyes.

Maybe he sensed my confusion. He exhaled and then said, "I can't give you the entire story because, as with most stories, it involves others, but it was Lydia. While we were courting but before we married."

Lydia? I never would have guessed.

"She had a baby out of wedlock too, a baby who wasn't mine." His voice was heavy with sadness. "And even though she moved forward with her life, her grief over that never left her. I see that same emptiness in Giselle. But even though it's hard, I think knowing you will help her in the long run."

I asked what happened to Lydia's baby.

"The father was married, and Lydia allowed the child to go to him and his wife."

"The wife knew?" I couldn't imagine.

He nodded. "She's a very good woman. A strong Christian. She didn't take out the sins of her husband on the babe. They're divorced now, and she has full custody."

So not only had Will's family dealt with a child conceived out of wedlock, but giving up that child for adoption as well! And to think I'd thought he came from the perfect family without anything worse than a little white lie or some such thing.

"Who knows about this?" I managed to stammer.

He shook his head a little as if trying to decide to answer or not. Finally he said, "Your Aunt Marta knows. And your sister. But, Ada, that's all I can say on this—for now. The main point is I know how Lydia suffered from the loss, and I know Giselle must suffer too."

I tried to soak in the information without growing too curious. I focused on my own story. "Perhaps she feels that loss with Lexie," I said, "but I don't think she does with me."

Will's expression was kind. "She had more time with Lexie. That's all. It has nothing to do with who you are."

I looked up into his compassionate brown eyes for just a minute and then quickly glanced away, overcome by the cold.

"I've kept you out too long." He gestured toward the pathway.

We didn't speak as we walked the few steps to the cottage, and when we reached the door he said a quick goodbye and turned to go.

"Thank you, Will," I said, and he turned back toward me. "Thank you for telling me about Lydia."

He nodded and then disappeared into the night.

I woke quite a while before dawn and crept into Giselle's room to see if she'd returned. Her bed was empty, just as it had been last time I checked. I entered the studio. I knew she wasn't there because it was dark, but still I flipped on the light and looked around. The plastic boxes she and Morgan had moved from the shed were still in the middle of the room. The weaving on the loom was the same as a couple of days before.

I stepped toward the back wall, to the weavings hanging there, my eyes falling on the one of the Amish woman with the three little girls. Before I'd only focused on the people in it. Now my gaze was drawn to the terrain. Rather than the lush farmland of Lancaster County, these Amish were standing on a rocky hillside, with a waterfall nearby. Moving closer, I decided that it was supposed to be the waterfall next door, on the Kessler Tract. I thought of Giselle's weaving in the shop in Bern with the same waterfall. Now here it was again: the waterfall. It was a recurring theme in her artwork.

Then it struck me. What if she'd gone to the waterfall earlier, to sketch or to think or to explore? She could have gotten injured there and been unable to get back. It wouldn't hurt to check.

A few minutes later, dressed and bundled in my down coat with a gloved hand gripping a flashlight, I ventured out into the night. I had left Morgan and Christy a note, saying exactly where I was going just in case I hadn't returned by the time they awoke. As I reached the creek, snow began to fall, big white fluffy flakes that floated slowly from the black sky.

Daniel had pointed out the lone pine, far down from the tree line near the waterfall, where he said rocks went across the creek. I stopped at the bank near there and shone the flashlight around. The snow melted as soon as it hit the water, swallowed in an instant. There were several boulders—but they didn't look like a bridge. The creek was wide, at least twenty feet or more. I hurried along the shore, toward the waterfall, bouncing the beam of the flashlight across to the other side. A few yards beyond the tree, I stopped. There were several flat rocks, one after the other. If I had a sturdy stick I thought I could cross. I hurried back toward the tree, hoping to find a fallen branch. On the far side, under the edge of the canopy, was a small one. I broke off the twigs and then held it firmly. It came to my shoulder and was the right size for me to grip. I hurried back.

Stepping from the bank, I planted my foot firmly on the first stone. I had to stretch to get to the next one and the next and most of the others. I concentrated on each one, determined not to slip. The leap to the far shore was by far the worst. I stood on the last stone, both feet planted firmly. The snow swirled around me now, big, heavy, wet flakes, coming down faster, like powdered sugar out of a sifter. I took a deep breath and lunged forward.

I almost made it.

My left foot landed in the mud and slipped backward into the freezing water. I jerked it out, scrambling up the bank, sloshing up to the field. I stomped around, trying to force the water out of my shoe but it only squished around, freezing my foot. The best thing to do was keep moving. The hem of my dress was wet too, but at least all of me wasn't soaking. I decided to keep the branch as a walking stick.

I made my way over the uneven and rocky ground, trying to remember what it looked like in the light. The foundation of the house should be ahead. I waved the flashlight back and forth, finally finding it to the left. I redirected myself and skirted around the cornerstones. The terrain began to slope upward. The ground was covered in a dusting of snow now, and I stumbled a few times over invisible rocks jutting out of the soil.

I directed the light ahead, toward the waterfall, trying to figure out the best route to the cave. As I approached it, the mist of the spray mixed with the snowflakes, and the roar seemed deafening in the darkness. I could see that a trail half circled around, still bare of the falling snow because of the spray from the water. In another half hour I thought the path might be icy, though. I turned my face away from the spray and stayed to the edge of the trail so I didn't get overly wet. A minute later the beam of the flashlight was on the open cave ahead. I stepped inside, leaving the roar of the waterfall but feeling as if the blackness might swallow me. Even with the flashlight, it took a moment for my eyes to adjust. There was a fire pit that looked fairly fresh. Probably used by youth from Langnau or Wasserdorf. The cave was quite deep, and I began to wonder how many bats or other creatures might live in it. Now I was waving the beam around wildly.

"Giselle," I managed to croak, softly at first and then louder until I had worked up to an all-out yell. "Giselle!" My voice echoed in the cave, over and over.

When it stopped I heard a faint voice call out, "Ada!"

At last.

"Where are you?" I pointed the flashlight to where I thought the sound came from.

"Ada!" The voice was louder now.

I stepped farther into the cave, bouncing the light to where I thought the voice was coming from, skimming across a pile of rocks that looked like steps but stopped in midair. I pointed the light up straight above them. Sure enough, an opening to another cave was just above.

"Giselle!" I shouted again.

"Up here!"

I dropped my stick and scrambled up the pile of rocks and reached toward the opening of the cave. If Giselle, who wasn't any taller than I was, could make it, I could too. My hands landed on the opening, but I couldn't feel anything I could hold onto to hoist myself up.

"There's an iron rod on the right-hand side," she said.

I felt around and found it. It was a single, vertical rod that felt secure, as if it had been anchored in the mountainside. I edged the flashlight onto the lip of the cave and then pulled myself up, scraping my leg as I did.

"Where are you?" I was on my hand and knees now, but when I shone the light above me, I realized this cave was nearly as tall as the one below.

"Back here."

I stood and made my way over the rocky bottom of the cave. At first it looked as if Giselle were resting. Her back was up against a rock. She had on her heavy coat and hat, and a backpack was beside her.

"My flashlight died," she said, as if that explained everything.

"And you couldn't leave the cave without it?"

She shook her head. "It's my foot." She pointed to it, but I couldn't see it. "I was coming back here to sit and slipped. My foot got wedged between two rocks, and then the bigger one slipped, pinning me in."

I'd reached her now and handed her the flashlight. "Hold this," I said. "I'll lift it."

"I don't think you can—"

I tried my hardest. The rock was bigger than it looked and much heavier. I couldn't budge it.

"Are you in a lot of pain?" I asked.

She shook her head. "My foot's gone numb."

That didn't sound good. "I'll go get help." I reached for the flashlight.

She nodded but didn't hand it over.

"I can't get help without it," I said gently.

She extended it to me. "Hurry back."

I said of course I would and went back to the lip of the cave and lowered myself onto the staircase formation, my feet flailing to find a footing until they kicked against the rock and then settled on the top step. When I reached the bottom, I grabbed my walking stick and kept on going.

My heart raced as I hurried out of the cave. I'd found her! I breathed a prayer of thanks. She hadn't tried to harm herself, as I had feared. But nonetheless, she was harmed.

"Be with her," I prayed. "And help me as I go for help." I still had to cross the creek again. If something happened to me, no one would know where Giselle was.

Thirty-Five

I slipped on the wet trail coming around the waterfall but steadied myself and kept going. In just the time I'd been inside the cave, the ground had been completely blanketed in a layer of white. As the trail disappeared, I forged ahead in the heavy snow, my feet growing wetter by the minute. I passed by where I thought the cornerstone of the house was and started veering toward the creek, shining the flashlight in the direction of the tree.

I squinted through the falling snow. It looked as if there was a light bobbing in the distance. I focused on it, bouncing my beam around, hoping to draw attention to myself. There were two lights and they seemed to be heading toward the natural bridge too.

"Giselle!"

"It's me, Ada!" I shouted back over the rushing sound of the creek.

I could make out two figures. In a moment I realized they were Daniel and Will. I exhaled deeply.

I reached the bank first and waited, relieved I wouldn't have to cross it to find help. "Giselle is in the cave," I shouted. "She's injured."

Will cupped his hand to his ear, and I realized he couldn't hear me. I motioned for them to come to me, shining my flashlight over the rocks. Daniel had crossed before, but surely never in the dark.

Will reached me first. "Are you all right?"

"Fine," I answered as Daniel joined us. "But Giselle's stuck in the upper cave, pinned by a rock."

As we hurried along, I asked how they had known to come out here. Will explained that he couldn't sleep and was standing at the window of his room when he'd seen a light. Thinking maybe it was Giselle, he had woken Daniel.

"I could tell it was across the creek," Daniel added. "I never thought it would be you. What were you doing out here?"

I told them about noticing the waterfall on the weaving and deciding to follow my instincts.

"Good instincts," Will murmured.

"That upper cave is quite the trick to get into," Daniel said.

I agreed. "And I couldn't budge the rock pinning her foot." Then it dawned on me that my walking stick might give Will and Daniel the leverage they would need. I held it up. "This might do the trick though. As a lever."

Daniel led the way past the now-invisible foundation, up the trail to the waterfall, and behind it into the cave. When we reached the formation, Daniel said I could wait below. He placed his flashlight on the edge, found the steel rod, and then quickly swung himself up over the lip of the upper cave. Will followed his example. I handed my stick up to Will and told him Giselle was toward the back.

They called out her name as they walked, and I could barely make out her soft reply. I waited a few more minutes, pacing and praying, and then I hoisted myself back up into the cave to join them. I couldn't take it anymore. When I reached them, I could see that Daniel and Will were trying to move the rock.

"It's so hard to get a hold of," Will said, bending down, his big hands wedged down between the stones. I'd seen him lift a tractor wheel as though it were a child's tinker toy. I just knew he could take care of this too.

The soft sound of the waterfall caught my ear, and I thought of the Anabaptists worshipping here centuries before. I could imagine the melody of nature mixing with their own musical voices, echoing off the rock walls. Perhaps my ancestors had sung hymns in this very cave that we continued to sing today. Surely Alice's ancestors, and Will's, had met here too.

I breathed in deeply, realizing that it was just as lovely and peaceful as the cathedrals we had visited. I felt a warmth, even in the cold, an overwhelming sensation of "The Spirit talking," as *Mammi* would say. This was a holy place, paid in part by the blood of the martyrs.

Will's voice brought me back to the present. "There are some small rocks down here," he said. "If I could get them out..."

"I could try," I said, taking my gloves off my hands. Slowly I worked a small rock out and then another and another.

"Let me try the stick again," Will said.

I stood and he shoved it into the hole and leaned back, pulling the fat branch. The rock shifted a little. Daniel stepped forward and began pulling too. The rock rose some more.

"Hold it," Will said to Daniel. He bent down, reaching as far under the rock as he could. He planted his feet and lifted, getting the rock up far enough so that he could roll it up onto the others and away from the hole.

"Got it!" Daniel cried.

I sucked in my breath and held it as Will squatted and felt Giselle's leg and foot. She winced as he did. "I had a horse who fell on a trail and a rock rolled over her foreleg," Will told her.

"Did you have to put her down?" Giselle asked.

"No." Will met her eyes. "But I might not be able to say the same for you."

Despite her fear and pain, she smiled at his attempt at a joke.

His face growing serious again, Will felt around some more, asking about the pain. She said her leg and foot were numb. Will lifted her pant leg and pinched her skin.

She winced, and he laughed. "That's a good sign," he said. "But I don't suppose you're going to be able to walk back home, are you?"

She shook her head. "You're not going to be able to get me out of here."

"Sure we are."

In a minute Will had Giselle on his back. He moved across the rocks gingerly, taking care with each step, his arms linked around Giselle's legs. Daniel walked ahead with a flashlight and I walked beside them, my stick in one hand, shining my light where Will needed to step, practically holding my breath until we made it to the mouth of the upper cave.

"Now what?" Giselle asked.

Daniel helped her off Will's back, and then I stepped close so she could put her hand on my shoulder.

"I'll go down first," Will said.

Daniel looked a little surprised as Will shone his flashlight down to the lower level and then jumped. After a moment, he called up from below.

"Giselle! Scoot to the edge."

She followed his instructions. I peered down at Will. His flashlight was on the ground, and he had his arms raised. "Let yourself drop down," he said.

I pointed the beam of my flashlight so Giselle could see. She scooted to the very edge and then stopped. "Are you sure?" she called down.

"Yes," Will answered. "I promise I'll catch you."

In a jerky motion she propelled herself off the ledge, but before I could even register the action, Will had caught her. He lowered her down, and she balanced on her good foot. I tossed the walking stick down, and Giselle leaned against it.

"Now you, Ada," Will said.

"No," I protested. "I can come down the steps."

"This is faster."

Either way was unladylike in my dress. I decided to get it over with as soon as possible. After tossing my flashlight down to Will, I tucked my skirt around my legs and quickly sat.

Below, I could see him raising his arms up for me, illuminated by the beam of Daniel's light. The moment stretched out as I gazed down at his safe, familiar face.

When I scooted off the edge, the moment stretched out even longer. I was falling and unafraid. Then he caught me, his arms gently slipping under mine. He held me for just a fraction of a second longer than he should have, and then he let me go.

"Thank you," I stammered, stepping away. I took the flashlight from Giselle and turned it toward Daniel.

His face was solemn, but then he smiled and turned his gaze from me to Will. "Do you plan to catch me too?" he joked.

Will laughed and stepped aside, and in a moment Daniel jumped, landing on his feet beside us. I avoided his eyes.

The two men made a seat with their hands and scooped Giselle up. I led the way out of the cave, holding the walking stick and my flashlight. As we veered to the right, away from the falls, a gust of wind blew through and the spray came toward us. I ducked as a splash of water soaked the side of my face and coat.

Daniel chuckled. "You've been baptized."

I didn't share his amusement as I swiped at my icy face. But as we retraced our steps down the slippery path, I did wonder if the Anabaptists had baptized each other in the waterfall.

I realized that the day was dawning, so I turned my flashlight off and slipped it into my pocket. There were now several inches of snow on the ground, and more still falling. My already soaked shoes grew even wetter as I broke the trail, and between that and my wet clothes, I began to shiver uncontrollably.

When we reached the creek, Will and Daniel let Giselle down, and then Will hoisted her onto his back again. Daniel crossed first, and then Will started over, slow and steady, deliberately jumping from rock to rock. He stumbled a bit just before he reached the other bank but caught himself and stopped. I took a deep breath, as I imagined he did too. He hoisted Giselle up a little higher, and then in a single leap he landed on the other side. I meant to follow him, but I couldn't. The cold and fatigue of the night had finally caught up with me.

Giselle slid off Will's back, and Daniel steadied her. Will looked at me and then bounded back onto the first rock. "Ada," he called out. "Are you all right?"

I couldn't answer. I tried to shake my head but my whole body shuddered against the cold.

Will leaped the rest of the way across in a single, fluid movement. "Come on," he said. I dropped the stick but couldn't budge. He unzipped his jacket and wrapped me up inside of it, pulling me close with his arms. I leaned against him until the shaking stopped and I could get a normal breath.

"Now, climb on my back," he whispered gently.

"No, I'm fine. I'm not the one with the injury." I pulled away out from under his coat and then gasped at the cold air that immediately rushed in where his warmth had been before.

"Just climb on my back and hold on, Ada. I'll get you there."

No longer resisting, I slid around behind him and he hoisted me up.

"See?" he told me. "You're as light as a feather."

Leaning forward, I wrapped my arms around the front of his shoulders, palms flat against the rock hardness of his chest.

With his first step, my hood draped back, and the snow fell against my *kapp* and face. The flakes were coming faster and faster now. Will had to be getting tired, but he was still sure and solid. I bounced as he landed on each rock. He would pause a moment and then leap again. I kept my eyes on Giselle and Daniel on the far bank, not daring to look down. As we got closer, I could see that her face seemed to be softening with each step. By the end her eyes met mine with a wistful smile. Will's last leap landed us on the bank, and I slid to the ground quickly, still shaking.

"You're freezing," he said.

"We're almost there," I answered, my teeth chattering. "I-I can make it."

The men made a chair again for Giselle, and we hurried as fast as we could, cutting down toward the cottage. When we reached it, I stepped ahead and opened the door quickly, my hand shaking on the knob.

"Morgan!" Will called out. "We need your help." He turned toward me then. "Get out of your wet clothes and into your nightgown. Then crawl into bed beside Christy. Morgan can climb in too."

I stumbled into the entryway after the others.

"Let's get Giselle in her room and straight under her blankets," Will said to Daniel. "She's not soaked like Ada."

I stepped into the office, and by the light of the hall grabbed my long underwear, fuzzy socks, and warmest nightgown. Then I closed the door and quickly changed, shaking nearly uncontrollably as I did.

Sliding in next to Christy I grabbed the extra blanket off the end of the bed, and pulled it on top of myself. Then I urged her in her sleep toward the wall, gently, so I could share the spot already warm from her body. I stayed as close to her as I could without waking her up, hoping Morgan would get here soon.

"Ada?" Morgan whispered. I turned to see her standing hesitantly in the doorway. "Will told me what happened. He said to come climb in next to you and help you get warm." She pulled the door shut behind her and moved toward the bed. "I put on some water for hot tea," she added. "That might help. But shouldn't we get you in a hot bath or something?"

Blinking, I could barely make out her features in the faint morning light.

"N-no," I said, my teeth clicking together. "This is the b-best thing to do r-right now. Though the t-tea is a good idea also."

Sliding into the narrow space behind me, Morgan positioned herself as I directed, pressing against my back and using her arm to warm my shoulders.

"I get it," she giggled, "Christy and I are making an Ada sandwich."

"*Ya.* The b-best way to recover b-body heat is to add s-some more b-bodies."

We were quiet then for a few minutes as I slowly felt myself thaw out. Soon the chattering of my teeth had stopped, and I almost felt human again. Glancing over my shoulder at Morgan, I noticed a strange expression on her face and I asked her what she was thinking.

"That I guess I should have realized that the Amish would know how to get warm. Without electricity or a gas line or anything, your houses must get plenty cold."

I was about to explain how we heated our homes without using public utilities when a soft knock was heard at the door, and then Will stepped inside.

"How are you doing?" he asked.

"Much better."

He nodded, pleased with my answer, and then he told Morgan that the water had boiled before he disappeared again.

She slipped from the bed to go make tea, and a few minutes later she returned with a mug in her hand. I scooted up just a little, pulling the covers up to my chin, and took it from her.

"Oh, Ada." I couldn't make out her eyes in the dim light, but her voice sounded as if she was fighting back tears. "What if something had happened to you?"

"It didn't," I said. I sipped the hot tea and sighed as warmth spread inside of me too. "Though I guess it was pretty stupid of me to go out there alone."

"You can say that again."

I heard Will's voice in the hall, and then Morgan slipped out to join him. Putting my mug on the end table, I wiggled back down under the covers. After a while the door opened all the way, and Will stood there again.

"How's Giselle?" I asked.

"She's is in a lot of pain but warming up. We're going to take her into the hospital in just a minute. Do you think you need to come along and be seen by someone too?"

"No, I'm fine," I told him. And I was.

"Let's check your extremities, just to be sure."

Humoring him, I climbed out of the warm bed and came to the doorway, holding out both hands and then each foot in turn to show that they were all bright pink but nothing more. "See?"

His eyes went from my hands to my face and lingered there. I was still freezing, but the shiver I felt in that moment had nothing to do with the cold.

I wasn't sure where Daniel had gone, but guilt surged through my veins as I broke my gaze with Will. "I...uh...I'd like to see Giselle before she goes," I said. Then I stepped back to the bed, grabbed the extra blanket, and wrapped it around my shoulders as I headed to her room, moving past Will without looking at him.

"Ada," Giselle said as I came through the door. Her ankle was propped up with a pillow, and she was covered with blankets and quilts. Her stocking cap was off, and her hair stuck up around her head like a halo.

I stopped beside her bed, and we talked about her ordeal for a moment. Then I asked why she had been in the cave at all.

"I used to go there when I first started weaving. I would take a sketchbook and work out my designs by flashlight. Sometimes I would explore. It was the one place I'd let myself remember." She took a deep breath. "I used to go to the Mennonite church too. The cave and the church." She shook her head. "But then I made a vow that I didn't want anything to do with the past anymore. It was too hard. I couldn't get my mind to leave it once it landed there. So I stopped going to both places for years and years—until yesterday. I thought I'd sit and sketch by my flashlight for a while and then go down to the church."

"Why?"

"Because I finally remembered what I did with the letters. I took them there, years ago."

"To the church?"

She nodded. "In the back room. I think." She shrugged. "I was in such a fog back then, but I feel as if I remember carrying in the wooden box when no one was around and sliding it into someplace dark and tight."

"Where, exactly?"

She shrugged, eyebrows lifting. "I wish I could tell you, Ada. I hadn't thought about those letters in all these years. It took me a while to recall that I used to go down to the church at all."

A rustling sound was heard in the hall, and then Daniel and Will were at the door, excusing themselves for interrupting.

"We should get going, Giselle," Will said. "Daniel and I are going to carry you to the car, and then Morgan and I will take you to the hospital." He directed his attention to me. "And you need to get back in bed."

In a quiet voice, I asked Giselle if she would tell Daniel what she told me. She nodded that she would. I brushed past the two men, holding the blanket tightly.

Christy stirred again when I crawled back in beside her, but she didn't awake even though the morning light was now streaming through the window.

I was no longer cold, but for some reason I began to shiver again. I wrapped myself more tightly in the covers and closed my eyes. As I drifted off, I couldn't be sure what was making me tremble. The thought of what would have become of Giselle if I hadn't checked the cave?

Or the memory of my body wrapped around Will's, leaping fearlessly into the night?

Thirty-Five

The sound of knocking woke me. I wrapped the blanket around me again and went to answer it. Daniel stood on the stoop, his hands in the pockets of his jacket.

"It's melting," he said. Sure enough, the eaves were dripping and the pathway was slushy. Still, the landscape looked like a winter wonderland. I breathed in the crisp mountain air.

He nodded up the hill. "George said he'd give us a ride to the church so we can look for the letters, and then he'll take Christy on to the hospital." He went on to say that George had talked to Will and Giselle's ankle was broken, but at least she wouldn't need surgery. The doctor would cast it sometime this morning.

Smiling in relief that Giselle's injury wasn't as bad as it could have been, I said that Christy and I would come up to Amielbach as soon as we were ready.

As I started to close the door, Daniel blurted out, "Alice is being discharged, so George is making arrangements for you to get home." His words came out in a tumble, and then he turned and headed back up the path before I could even respond.

A half hour later, as George drove us toward Langnau, he told us he'd finished making our flight arrangements. "You leave tomorrow afternoon."

Christy began to chatter excitedly about going by plane, but I could only stare out the window in silence. Not only did I have to make a decision in the Daniel matter, but we also had to find the property agreement and get the judge to clear the title by four o'clock today. Time was running out, in more ways than one.

George dropped us off at the church and we hurried into the office, where Daniel explained our predicament to the secretary. She led us back to the library room we'd seen on our tour and told us to feel free to snoop around.

Once she was gone, Daniel reminded me that he'd spent quite a bit of time in the library last summer, looking through the church registries and other records, and he hadn't seen a carved box or come across a stack of letters. He would have remembered. Which meant Giselle must have hidden the box well. He pulled a step stool over to the shelves at the far end of the room and started looking on the top row.

"Try to think like Giselle," I said. I looked in all of the cupboards under the windows. They were full of cardboard boxes of manuscripts.

"I went through all of those," Daniel said, moving the ladder to the next set of bookcases.

"Maybe it's in one of the other rooms," I said.

Daniel groaned. "It could be anywhere." There was a gap between the floor and the bottom of the bookcase Daniel was in front of. It was definitely big enough for the box to fit under. I grabbed a ruler from the main desk, went to the first one, and knelt down on the floor, scraping it under the edge. I didn't feel anything and scooted forward a little. When I was almost at the end, I brushed up against something. Getting down on my stomach, I wiggled the ruler further under the shelf, thinking maybe it was a book. It was wedged in pretty tight. I reached in with my hands and felt carvings on each side.

"Ada." Daniel was looking down at me. "What are you doing?"

"There's a box under here," I said. "A carved box."

As he got down on the floor beside me, I inched it back and forth until I pulled it free. The carving on the top was of the bakery in Frutigen with the Alps towering above it. Another of my ancestral homes.

"Open it," Daniel pleaded.

I lifted the lid. The box was full of letters. Tears stung my eyes.

"I'll skim through it for the agreement."

It only took him a minute to declare it wasn't there. "But this is still better than nothing," he added. "The letters might make some references to the agreement or maybe have information about where it was hidden."

He slipped into a chair with the whole stack and dove right in. I wasn't sure how much time we had, so I excused myself and went down to the office to use the phone.

I called Alice's room and got Will, who said that, between Giselle's cast and Alice's paperwork, they wouldn't be finished for at least an hour or two, maybe more. He asked if we wanted George to come to pick us up, but I said no, that we'd stay here a while longer and then just walk to the hospital. It wasn't until we hung up that I realized I'd forgotten to tell him about the box.

Back in the library, I found Daniel exactly where I'd left him, at the table, intently poring over the letters.

After I sat down across from him, he said the first letter was dated May 8, 1877, and the return address was *Crossing the Atlantic.* In the first letter Elsbeth wrote about her stepchildren and how at first they were hesitant around their father after having been separated from him for the two years he'd been in prison, but they were warming up to him. There wasn't any adjustment for them toward her being their mother because, as their governess, that was what they had come to think of her as anyway. She wrote that she was looking forward to their new life in Indiana, and she hoped her father would change his mind and soon sell Amielbach and join them in America. She also asked that he please accept the fact that she loved Gerard Gingrich and was married to him and would be for the rest of her life.

"Nothing about the agreement?" I asked.

He shook his head and went on to the next one.

It detailed their arrival in New York City and their journey west. When they arrived in Adams County, Indiana, they were welcomed by the other Swiss Mennonites there who had arrived two decades earlier. The people already had vast farms and were making good livings. An older, wealthy couple took Gerard, Elsbeth, and the children into their home and offered the young family a loan to purchase land. She was optimistic about their future.

By the end of the first year, the family had a farm with a house and a big barn—and another child. Elsbeth wrote that her stepchildren, who were now ten and twelve, were attending school but she was still helping them with their studies as both were very bright and needed to be encouraged to make the most of the gifts God had given them. She wrote that she was doing all she would have been doing as a governess for the family, and much, much more. She was far happier than she could have ever imagined being—except for being so far away from her beloved father and missing the mountains, hills, and valleys of her homeland.

While I found my great-great-grandmother's epistles fascinating, I realized none of them was probably going to have any information about an agreement between Abraham Sommers and Ulrich Kessler.

Daniel zipped through several more, saying every couple of years another baby was born, and it was obvious that Abraham had written in his letters that he was worried about his daughter. Elsbeth assured him her health was fine. The older two children grew up and left home. The younger ones began school. More kept coming. Gerard was a hard worker and was growing wheat and raising dairy cows, and with the help of his sons, he kept acquiring more and more land. None of the sons wanted to return to Switzerland to live with their grandfather as he had requested.

Daniel looked up at me. "She wrote that for all his talk of family being most important, she would think that her father would have come to join them."

Without waiting for a response from me, his head dropped back down, and then he explained that in 1889 she wrote that she was still waiting for her father to visit, as was the rest of his large, extended family. In 1890 her ninth child was born and she named her Sarah. I was pretty sure that was *Mammi*'s mother.

Daniel kept translating the letters one by one. He announced when he was on the next to the last one, and translated that Elsbeth referred to Abraham's letter "explaining everything." This must have been the letter he referred to in his diary when he mentioned his transgression. She said it was upsetting, but of course she and Gerard forgave him. She also said they had a much better life in America and all of their children had opportunities in Indiana they never would have had in the Emmental. It was God's will for them to leave, and it was obvious He used her father's ill motives to help speed His will. She would write to Marie and tell her about the agreement, in case her friend's father had only told his older sons, not his youngest, his only daughter. But she couldn't imagine her friend traveling back to Switzerland now to claim her land.

Then she said she didn't want her children to know what their grandfather had done, so she hid his last letter in the bottom of her carved box.

"Wait a minute," I said. "What was that last bit?"

Daniel looked down at the letter as he said, "She says she doesn't want her kids to know what he's done, so she's hidden his last letter in the bottom of her carved box."

"Which box would that have been?" I asked. "We have three of them now. The one *Mammi* gave to Lexie, the one *Mammi* kept, and the one Herr Lauten had given Giselle when she first moved here."

"It seems as though she's talking about the one from your grandmother with the farm scene."

I started to stand.

"Wait. Let me read the last letter," he said. "It's not to Abraham. It's from Elsbeth to Caspar Lauten."

He returned his gaze to the stack of letters and began to translate. "She writes that she is grieved her father didn't receive her last letter before he passed and wasn't assured of her forgiveness." Daniel continued reading and translating, saying Elsbeth agreed to the arrangement her father made with the Lautens to stay at Amielbach, pay the taxes, and maintain the property. In time, she said she would choose one of her descendants to inherit the property. "She also said she hadn't heard back from Marie, but at least her friend knew about the contract and could choose to do what she wanted."

Daniel folded the letter. "That's it."

"Let's go," I said, jumping to my feet.

We stopped by the office and he spoke with the secretary in Swiss German. She responded, he thanked her, and off we went.

"She said they'll never miss what they didn't know they had," he explained.

As we hurried along the slushy side of the road on the outskirts of town, I brought up Giselle, asking if he was surprised to find out she was my birth mother."

He nodded. "It's quite a story you have, Ada."

Determined that he know everything, I told him about Lexie and how both of us had the same father, an older married man, and how Giselle relinquished us when Lexie was two and I was a newborn.

"But your grandmother is your biological grandmother, right?"

"Yes. Giselle's sister Klara and her husband, Alexander, legally adopted me. They are my parents."

He sighed in relief. "I was afraid maybe you weren't a blood descendant of Abraham Sommers."

I wasn't sure why that mattered but didn't take the time to ask, because, speaking of blood, I had something else I needed to tell him.

"There's another thing you should know," I said. "I have a blood disorder. Hereditary spherocytosis." If he wanted to get closer to me, he might as well know the biggies to start with.

"Excuse me?" Daniel turned his head toward me, the box clutched tightly to his chest.

"It's abnormally-shaped blood cells. It causes hemolytic anemia."

"Is it fatal?" His voice was hesitant.

I chuckled. "No. I used to have transfusions, that sort of thing. But I've been much better the last several months."

"But it's hereditary?"

I nodded.

"So kids are out?"

"Not necessarily."

"But you wouldn't want to pass it on." We'd reached the sidewalk, and he was moving more quickly. A woman sweeping her front steps froze as we passed by, her eyes glued to me.

Ignoring her, I struggled to keep up with Daniel's pace. "My life hasn't been so bad..." My voice dropped in volume with each word. I was really thankful I'd been born, regardless of my disorder. That was when it dawned on me. Daniel would be happy not to have children at all.

THIRTY-SEVEN

Two hours later we caravanned up to Amielbach in the two cars. Daniel sat in the front of Morgan's car, and I sat in the back with Giselle, whose badly broken ankle was now set in a fresh cast.

She held the box in her hands but gave it back to me when we approached the estate. "Will you come inside while we look for Abraham's last letter?" I asked her.

She said she would as long as she had help up the stairs.

When George arrived with Will, Alice, and Christy, Will assisted Giselle up the steps. In no time she was inside Amielbach, using the crutches from the hospital to make her way down the entryway. I stayed back and walked with Alice, who took it slowly but seemed steady on her feet. Even so I held her good elbow as we walked. The nurses had had her out in the halls the last few days, and she seemed to be regaining her strength.

Morgan had called Oskar to tell him we were all coming, and he'd prepared lunch, a traditional Swiss meal of Raclette cheese with potatoes, pickled onions, and prosciutto. I settled Alice in a chair, while Daniel hurried down the hall to Herr Lauten's office. He appeared a few minutes later with the box from *Mammi*, the one with the farm scene from Indiana, in his hands. Herr Lauten was at his side.

Once they reached us, Daniel turned the box over, searching for a false bottom I presumed. When he found none, he put the box on the table where I was sitting and took out all the letters, handing them to me. Then he picked at the floor of the box.

Morgan pulled a file from her purse and handed it to him. With it he pried up a thin piece of wood. Though the box did, indeed, have a false bottom, I could tell by the way his face fell that the small space inside was empty.

"You've got to be kidding," he whispered, dumbstruck.

Then he looked straight me. "Where do you think the letter could be?"

I shrugged. Perhaps at *Mammi*'s. Maybe in Indiana. But most likely it was long gone. "We should try the other box," I said, pushing away from the table. "I'll go get it."

I hurried through the entryway and down the front steps to the pathway, and then to the cottage. Rushing to my things, I opened my suitcase and dug out the carved box, quickly lifting Christy's schoolwork from it.

"Ada?" Will called my name. "Do you need some help?"

I went quickly from the room, the box in my hand. He was standing in the open doorway.

My fingernails were long enough to pry up the false bottom. As I lifted it, Will reached in and took the thin piece of wood from me. There was no agreement inside, but there was a letter, safe and sound. I snatched it, wondering if it could possibly have the clue we needed.

Will smiled and took the box, slipping the bottom piece back into place. As we hurried up the pathway he said, his voice flat, "Your Daniel will be so pleased."

I winced at the word "your." What had Will observed?

I must have given him a confused look because he continued, "Daniel told me last night that you two are thinking about courting when you come back to Switzerland."

"He said that?"

Will nodded toward Amielbach. I shifted my gaze. Daniel was coming toward us.

We all settled back down at the table. In no time Daniel spread out the letter, but Herr Lauten nudged in beside him, saying, "Would you allow me? I may be an old man, but I believe I might be a tad faster at translating."

Daniel agreed, but I suspected it was with reluctance.

After a few minutes, Herr Lauten's face broke into a broad grin. Pulling the glasses from his nose, he looked up at us and said that while we would be very interested in the entire letter, for right now the ending was the most important part.

Sliding his glasses back on his nose, he translated as he read:

As far as the Kesslers' property, I have kept it safe these many years, as promised. The deed was filed with the land register, but the agreement has been put in a safe place; Caspar Lauten knows where. I hid it past where the goats graze, before the waterfall and mountaintop.

I will await your reply with love and deep affection.

Your father,
Abraham Sommers

Herr Lauten looked up in triumph, taking off his glasses. Alice gasped, Morgan began to clap, and Christy put her fingers in her mouth and whistled, a skill I had no idea she possessed.

"Finally!" George exclaimed.

"The waterfall is on the Kesslers' property." Daniel's voice was full of enthusiasm. "And we know for sure that goats did graze there."

"Abraham must have hidden the contract there, in the house," Morgan said.

"The house that was torn down?" I asked, unable to keep the dismay from my voice. If anything of importance had been hidden somewhere inside, it no doubt would have gone unnoticed amid the rubble when it came down. I said as much to everyone now.

We were all silent for a moment, lost in thought.

"Perhaps a man who was fond of false bottoms and such would have created a way to hide it in the foundation itself," Herr Lauten finally offered.

It sounded like a stretch to me, but the others were more optimistic.

"There are shovels in the shed," Oskar said. "I'll get the key." I was surprised at his interest but pleased just the same.

Will stayed with Giselle and Alice while the rest of us hurried to the shed, then crossed the creek, and marched up to the foundation. It was much easier traveling than it had been the night before. The sun was shining. The snow had all melted. The Bernese Alps range glistened in the afternoon light.

Daniel and Oskar started by digging up the corner stones, while Morgan, Christy, and I turned over river rock that had been part of the foundation. I couldn't comprehend why Abraham Sommers would leave it here, not when he seemed to be so exact about other things.

"Past where the goats graze, below the waterfall and mountain peak," I recited.

"You can't even see a peak from here," Morgan said. "Just the range. I think it's somewhere else."

Soon, the sun slipped behind a cloud and the afternoon grew chilly. Christy hadn't worn her coat and said she was going back. I didn't want her to cross the creek by herself and said I'd go with her.

When we reached the dining room, Alice was telling Will about the ballroom on the third floor, saying that Christy had shared how much fun she'd had up there a few afternoons ago.

"Do you want to see it?" Christy asked her *daed*.

"Sure," Will ventured, and Christy took his hand, pulling him to his feet.

I sat down as they left the dining room, imagining the two of them sliding across the wood floor. After a while there was the sound of footsteps in the great room.

"It's worth checking out." It was Morgan's voice.

Giselle hobbled out of the dining room and Alice, Herr Lauten, and I followed.

Morgan was standing in front of the floor-to-ceiling carving. "Look. There are goats. The waterfall. And a mountain peak." She was right. The mountain looked like the one above Frutigen, not like any near here.

Daniel got down on the floor and ran his hand along the base of the carving. "I don't feel anything," he said.

Past where goats graze, beneath the waterfall and mountain peak.

Heart suddenly pounding in my chest, I turned on my heel and hurried toward the open staircase, racing up it and then down the hall to the third-floor stairs. By the time I reached the carved door, with the goats and shepherdess, to the ballroom, I was certain I was right. When I opened the door, Will and Christy were sliding in their socks across the floor.

Will froze when he saw me. "What's wrong?"

"I have a wild idea." I fixed my eyes on the waterfall out the window and then to the carving of the mountain.

Will followed my eyes and then started to laugh. "I bet you're right," he said.

He motioned me to the carving, and I began running my hand along the bottom of it. Sure enough, there was a latch. I opened it quickly and I reached inside, pulling out a packet. "Let's take it down to Alice."

THIRTY-EIGHT

Christy held the packet high as she sashayed through the great room on the way to the dining room.

"What do you have?" Morgan asked.

"What Daniel's looking for," Christy teased.

He was still on the floor, and he jerked his head up, bumping it on the carving.

"Come on," Christy said. "*Grossmammi* gets to open it."

Alice's eyes filled with tears as she took it. "Could it be?" she whispered. She carefully slid her finger under the seal and pulled out a document, handing it to Herr Lauten.

He read it quickly and then kissed the paper.

"Ladies and gentlemen," he said with a grand sweep of his hands, "I present to you the original signed agreement between Abraham Sommers and Ulrich Kessler."

We all cheered, clapping and whistling and praising the Lord.

But the clock was still ticking, and we knew it. Now that we were in possession of the one thing that would save the day, we had less than an hour to get it to the judge, have the title cleared, and present it to the land and property commission. I wasn't sure we could pull it off.

Our cheering turned into a frenzy as Daniel and Morgan and Oskar tried to figure out who would ride with whom and what was the quickest way to get there. Then Herr Lauten quieted them with a loud whistle and a wave of his hand, saying, "Please, folks, settle down. I've got it all worked out." Once the noise died down, he went on to explain that he'd contacted the lawyer the moment we found the clue about the agreement, and that she'd rounded up the judge and the notary and they were all on standby, ready to come out here to Amielbach the moment we gave them the word.

"But why?" Oskar asked. "I can't imagine that those people make a habit of paying house calls."

Herr Lauten smiled. "That is true, Oskar. This is not exactly the norm. But given the frail state of Alice's health," he said, giving her a wink, "compounded by poor Giselle's injury, it was not hard to convince them that these were special circumstances indeed. As I told Betsy Holt on the phone, our Amish friends came thousands of miles to clear this title. Surely she could convince the judge to drive ten miles up here from Langnau to see it through."

As we waited nervously for everyone to arrive, Herr Lauten asked if we'd like to hear the rest of Abraham's message, the letter from the hidden bottom of the box that had given us our final clue. I felt bad that in our mad search for the agreement we had forgotten all about that. We settled in around Herr Lauten now as he pulled it out and carefully unfolded it. Then he slipped a pair of glasses onto his nose, cleared his throat, and began reading, translating for us as he went.

My dearest Elsbeth,

I have a confession to make to you. I am ashamed of something I did years ago, before you left, a sin that has tormented my soul ever since.

To explain this sin fully, I must go back to the time when I was just fifteen and still living in Frutigen with my family. I used to join my oldest brother and his flock in the meadow above the village and listen to him preach. I was proud of him, though I was never brave enough to join the Mennonites myself.

Acting without thought of ramification, as young men are wont to do, I made the grave mistake of creating a carving, one that showed my brother and his group of believers worshipping together in the meadow. I was still just learning my craft at that time, you see, and I never thought the picture would serve as anything other than eventual kindling for the fireplace. I did not know that an uncle of mine had taken a fancy to it and hung it in his workshop behind the bakery. I only found that out when I learned what happened next. The constable came across that carving and clearly recognized the meadow and the people who were depicted there.

I had lost my parents, as you know, and the family I had left meant everything to me—especially my oldest brother, who had been like my second father. Because of my carving, however, he was captured and imprisoned in Thun, along with many of his flock. I never meant to tell anyone about their secret worship, but through my ignorance and thoughtlessness, I shared more than mere words could ever convey.

I left to serve my time in the military soon after

that. While I was gone, my brother was released from Thun and he quickly emigrated to America. Knowing this, when my military service was done, I did not return to Frutigen at all but instead worked in Bern. There I met Franz Amiel, your mother's father. He commissioned me to come to Amielbach and work. He had enough projects to keep me busy for a long while, and that is where I fell in love with your mother. Her father was not happy about us marrying, and so I went away, but when he died a few years later I returned. I was older than your mother by fifteen years, but I was the healthier by far. Soon after you were born, she died.

My brother's imprisonment had sorely tested my faith years before, but it was when Tresa died that I knew God had left me for good.

I did my best raising you. I saw that you were baptized in the Swiss Reform Church. As the years passed, the delight I took in you outweighed the sorrow and guilt I still carried about what I had done to my brother and the grief I felt for my late wife.

Our lives would have continued along happily had our neighbors not been Mennonites. As children, you and Marie Kessler became inseparable, crossing the creek to be with each other multiple times a day, playing at the waterfall together, sharing stories and the things of girls. Her tellings of the early

Anabaptists touched you, and your tender heart grew sympathetic to their cause. When you were a young woman, the day you came home, after Marie had been baptized, to be exact, I feared I was losing you to their faith.

Then you took a job as a governess for the children of a widower in their congregation, a Mennonite man. This was never a life I would have chosen for you. I could see that you were falling in love with him. Knowing the fate that had befallen my brother, I could not allow this same fate to curse my only child.

I was a councilman in Wasserdorf at that time. When the military exemption for the Mennonites was lifted, I secretly encouraged the constable to enforce it, thinking that such pressure would lead Gerard to emigrate. Instead, he was arrested and imprisoned—and in Thun, no less, in the same dungeon that had held my brother all those years before. Now I bore the weight of two men, both imprisoned and tortured for their faith, directly due to actions of mine.

Even so, I held on to the hope that once Gerard was released he would quickly emigrate, just as my brother had done years before. Eventually, you would forget him and move on with your life, and forget your attraction to the Mennonite faith as well.

Then I was approached by Ulrich Kessler, who

had just learned that his sons were about to be arrested. Wishing every Mennonite in our lives to be gone for good, I urged the distraught Ulrich to take all of his children and emigrate to America before that could happen. As you know, he was a man with deep ties to the land, one who felt an allegiance to the Anabaptist history associated with the waterfall and caves that were under his care. He was so reluctant to sell the land, in fact, that I offered to buy it from him at more than a fair price, all five acres, just so that he would have the financial means to relocate his family to a new country.

When that still did not convince him, I proposed an associated agreement, one that would limit my freedom to sell the land to anyone else. He desperately hoped that the climate against the Mennonites here would soften eventually, at which point he or his children would be able to return. With such an agreement, he was able to sell me his land and yet at the same time cling to that hope. Thus, finally, he agreed to the sale.

Once the deal had been done, the land purchased, and the agreement tucked safely away, Kessler began making plans to leave for the United States. I learned of other Mennonite families who were also planning to go, including Gerard himself, who was soon to be released from Thun. Offering many of them private encouragement, financial aid, and more,

I did all that I could to see that the whole lot of them left Wasserdorf forever. All was proceeding according to plan.

Until that plan backfired miserably. In secret, knowing I would never approve, you married Gerard as soon as he was released. You made plans to leave with him and his children. Then you told me what you had done and bid me a painful goodbye.

As you know, I was bitter for a long time after that. The magnitude of my grief and anger were exceeded only by my guilt at having been the agent of others' pain and of my own demise. Only now have I finally confessed my selfish sin to God. And now, with this letter, I confess this sin to you too.

The first time I betrayed a godly Mennonite by accident. But the second time I betrayed one on purpose. I pray you and Gerard can forgive me. Please know I am the one who has lost the most. The guilt over these actions has kept me from coming to you for many years, even though I have long wanted to. I am ready to make that voyage now, if you will have me. But if you no longer want me to visit you in Indiana, please write and tell me not to come at all. I will understand. But for the grace of God, I do not deserve your welcome or your love.

As far as the Kesslers' property, I have kept it safe these many years, as promised. The deed was filed with the land register, but the agreement *has been put in a safe place; Caspar Lauten knows where. I hid it past where the goats graze, before the waterfall and mountaintop.*

I will await your reply with love and deep affection.

> *Your father,*
> *Abraham Sommers*

When Herr Lauten finished reading the letter, there wasn't a dry eye among us. So much guilt, so much regret, so much pain. I was reminded, yet again, of all the suffering that had come before, and I was grateful for the life I had and the freedoms that came with it.

Our mood was somber as our guests arrived, and we all headed into the dining room for the clearing of the title and the sale of the land. Word had spread, calls had been made, and in the end even more people had come along than we had expected, including Herr Lauten's banker, a notary, a transcriptionist, a newspaper reporter, three representatives of the land and property commission, members of the historical committee, and more.

The judge, the notary, and the transcriber sat on one side of the table, and Betsy Holt, Herr Lauten, Alice, and I sat on the other. Behind us stood everyone else, including the land and property commission officials, who had apparently agreed to come along so that if all went as planned, they could officially terminate their intentions to install a hydro plant on the property next door.

Fortunately, after reading through the agreement, both the judge and the lawyer felt it was sound. The other stipulations regarding the sale of the land were easily met by those of us who had gathered here, primarily having to do with order of inheritance, process of sale, and the intention that no expiration date be attached to the arrangement.

Finally, the judge looked up from all of the paperwork, focused in on Alice, and addressed her solemnly in English.

"As a direct descendant of Ulrich Kessler, how do you hereby exercise your rights with regards to the land described in these documents? Do you choose to purchase the property for the amount stipulated in the agreement?"

Alice nodded, but the transcriber asked for a verbal reply. Alice cleared her throat and said, "Yes. I would like to buy it."

"Very good," the judge said. "I am hereby clearing this title of all attachments and infringements. It may now be sold."

That caused a flurry of activity as the necessary documents were gathered and slid in front of me and then her for us to sign. We signed and signed, and when all was said and done, Alice quipped, "Now that my name's on the bottom line, I suppose I should ask how much I'm paying for it."

Everyone laughed, and only then did I realize that one of the men behind us was tapping away furiously on a calculator. He had to convert currencies between Swiss francs and dollars, both in 1877 and now. When all was said and done, he gave us the option of two prices. The agreement had specified that the property be sold back to the Kesslers for the same price Abraham had paid for it, but it didn't say whether that amount was to be adjusted for inflation or not.

"Let's hear both," Daniel said, his eyes sparkling.

"Very well," the banker replied. "If we adjust for inflation, Alice Beiler owes Frannie Lantz four hundred thousand eight hundred sixty-two dollars and fifty nine cents."

"And if we don't?" I asked, swallowing hard at such a massive amount of money.

"Then she owes you just sixteen thousand twelve dollars and four cents."

For some reason, everyone looked to me as if I had a decision to make.

There was no decision here. I knew exactly what my grandmother's intention was. She had all the money she needed, gained from the sale of Amielbach twenty-four years ago. Now it was Alice's turn to secure a nest egg for herself and save her family's business. Though her profits wouldn't be nearly as large as *Mammi*'s had been, I felt sure the amount would be big enough to carry the Gundy family company through their current hardships and into brighter days.

Smiling at Alice, I held out a hand and said, "That'll be sixteen thousand dollars, please."

Again, they all laughed.

Once we'd finalized that sale in every way, it became Herr Lauten's turn at the table.

"And now, dear Alice," he said, "I would like to make you an offer for your land. Would you sell it to me, please? Against the advice of my Realtor, and despite the current market value, for the sake of Amielbach and as compensation for all that you have been through, I am prepared to offer you five hundred thousand American dollars for the Kessler property."

Tears filling her eyes, Alice looked over at him and smiled. "Herr Lauten," she said, "you have yourself a deal."

Everyone cheered, talking at once. Soon the property had been sold to Herr Lauten and the historical committee had secured a guarantee of the protection and improvements of the land as an important historic site. Beyond the fact that Herr Lauten had preserved forever the beauty and ambience of his inn, I knew Daniel and George were also winners, having made great strides in assuring the success of their future tour company that would take advantage of both.

My heart was very full. Overwhelmed by the enthusiasm of the well-wishers that pressed in on me from every side, I sought out a friendly face in the crowd. I looked to Morgan, who was high-fiving Daniel. I looked to Christy, who was hugging her grandmother. I looked to Herr Lauten, who was shaking hands all around and then embracing his son. I even looked to Giselle, who was speaking animatedly with the reporter and clearly talking about herself.

Then I looked to Will, his gaze catching mine across the crowded room. In that moment, his gentle smile was filled with gratitude, even as his eyes were filled with tears.

THIRTY-NINE

Much later, after all of the guests were gone and Giselle and Alice were settled in the cottage, sitting in the living room with Christy and Will, I went looking for Daniel. It had been a crazy afternoon, but now that we'd all had time to recover a bit, the mood was calmer and happier than it had been since we'd first arrived five days before.

I finally found Daniel in the dining room with Herr Lauten, Oskar, and Morgan. Now that the waterfall had been protected, Herr Lauten was eager to finish the renovation and open his inn. At the moment, the four of them were talking about the gift shop and what they could add to emphasize its Anabaptist connection.

I joined them, listening as they discussed selling Amish-made quilts, wooden toys, and other fine crafts. Daniel had his laptop open and was clicking from site to site, showing the others examples.

"These sell well in the U.S.?" Oskar asked.

"Oh, yes," Daniel said. "The Amish are known for their craftsmanship. These things sell like wildfire."

I was glad to hear of their plans, and I knew several Amish craftsmen back home who would be happy to have a new outlet for their work.

After a while the conversation waned, and Oskar said he had work in the kitchen to finish up. Herr Lauten said he needed a cup of tea and followed his son. Morgan swiped a strand of hair away from her face and smiled. "I'll leave you two alone," she said, standing. "I think I'll see what's going on down at the cottage." She yawned. "Or maybe just go to bed early." Her hand fluttered in a quick wave as she left.

"We should talk," Daniel said to me, looking me in the eye. "Have you spoken to Giselle about coming back and living with her for a while?"

"Not yet."

"But you still intend to do it?"

"I'm not sure."

His face fell. "Will you tell me tomorrow, before you go?"

I nodded. I owed him that, at least.

He didn't seem distraught for long but was soon talking about the tours. "George has some great ideas about how to incorporate you." Daniel went on to explain that they intended to market their business to high school trips and to families as I suggested. "You could do the children's programs," he said. "You'd be so good at that."

I loved the idea of it. I imagined preparing the scholars before we visited different sites. Having handouts and coloring pages for them, that sort of thing. All the while, traveling all over Switzerland and maybe to Germany and Italy too. It sounded like a dream come true. And yet much of my yearning for adventure had been satisfied by this trip. What if I returned home and realized I didn't want to leave ever again? "I'll think about it," I said. "I'll talk with Giselle."

Daniel went on a little while longer in his excited way, but soon he was yawning too. I said I was going to head back down to the cottage and would see him in the morning before we left.

I prayed as I made my way down the pathway, asking God what I should do. Back in Lancaster County I would become an old maid. In Switzerland I would have adventures and excitement and the possibility of marriage. It wasn't that I was in love with Daniel—although I definitely liked him—but there was the possibility I would come to love him.

Even if I did, though, chances were we would never have children of our own. I would enjoy teaching the children on the tours, but I would only be acquainted with them for a week, not part of their lives for years and years.

When I reached the cottage, Will and Christy were just leaving. "Morgan will give us a ride to the airport tomorrow," he said. "Be ready by ten." He paused, and for a moment I thought he had more to say, but then he blurted out, "Thanks again, Ada. Good night."

Christy gave me a quick hug and in no time the two were hurrying up the pathway.

Though it was early evening, it had been a very long day, and all of us were tired and ready to settle in for the night. But first I had to speak with Giselle. I couldn't wait any longer. There was no guarantee I'd have the time or the opportunity to talk to her in the morning.

When I knocked on her door, she beckoned me in. She was sitting up in bed on top of her quilt, her foot propped up on a stack of pillows. She wore her bathrobe and her hair lay flat on her head, as if she'd had a shower. She had a sketchbook and a pencil in her hand.

I told her I needed to talk with her, and she motioned for me to sit down.

"George and Daniel want me to come back to Switzerland and help with the tours," I said.

"That's what I heard." She placed the sketchbook between herself and the wall.

I gave her a questioning look.

"Morgan told me," she said. "Just now."

I nodded, feeling relieved. The fact that she already knew made it easier for me to press on.

"I'm not sure what I'll do," I said. "But if I did come back, could I stay with you?"

She squinted and the lines around her eyes became more pronounced. "It depends."

"On?" I expected her to bring up *Mamm* and *Daed* and their wishes. Or maybe *Mammi*.

She continued. "On how honest you're being with yourself."

"Pardon?"

"Morgan also said Daniel wants to court you. She seems to think that's a great idea, but I'm not so sure."

I knew I was blushing.

"Have you heard this saying?" Giselle shifted a little, sitting up straighter. "Enjoy today because it won't come back."

Mammi used to say that to me. I nodded.

"There's nothing wrong with studying the past, but you're someone who embraces the present. I see that in you. The way you interact with Christy. The way you've made friends with Morgan. I think Daniel's obsession with history might weigh you down." She took a deep breath. "And I know I'm meddling, which I never do, but I have to this time. Ada, I saw love last night coming across the creek, and it wasn't between you and Daniel."

I was sure my face was beet red now. "Will's courting someone else," I stammered.

"I'm not just talking about your feelings for him. I saw love in his eyes too."

"No," I said. "He loves Leah." Giselle was in excruciating pain last night. She had no idea what she'd seen.

Her face softened. "Well, believe me, I know what love isn't. Regardless of what is going on with Will, please promise me you'll never commit to someone you don't love."

I wrinkled my nose. How could I promise her that?

"I have one more thing to ask." My heart began to race. "I…I need to know the state of your soul."

She chuckled and then said, "*Mamm* put you up to this, right? 'Cause she's asked me that in nearly every letter she's ever written to me."

I nodded and then added, "But I'd like to know too."

Her face grew more serious. "Day before yesterday, the answer would have been that it was the same as it'd been for the last twenty-six years. But yesterday in the cave, I prayed for the first time, I think, since I left Lancaster County. And God answered me." She paused for a moment, her eyes meeting mine. "I prayed again, as I watched Will carry you across the creek. And, Ada, I'll keep praying for you. Tell *Mamm* that. Tell her…" She shrugged. "Tell her I'm better."

She picked up her sketchbook again. Clearly it was time for me to leave. But I sat there still. After a moment, I asked if I could see what she was drawing. I wanted it to be me and Will in the middle of the creek, the snow coming down on top of us. That was the drawing I saw in my own head, that one I wanted to see on paper.

Giselle turned the pad toward me. It was obviously a self-portrait, but she was much younger. She was dressed Amish and was holding a tiny baby in front of the cascade of a waterfall, but the background was my flower garden back home with the windmill to one side.

Tears filled my eyes, but before I could say anything she waved me away and said, "Let me know in the morning what you decide."

I rose early, slipping out of the futon bed next to Alice and dressing quickly. The morning was overcast but much warmer. There would be no snow today. I walked toward the creek. The Bernese Alps were hidden in the fog, and a mist lay low across the Kesslers' property, all the way to the waterfall.

I thought Daniel might be in the dining hall, so I headed up the path, but then I detoured to the pine tree, sinking down against its gnarly trunk to the dry ground beneath its branches, settling in between two roots.

Giselle was right. I didn't love Daniel and he didn't love me. Sure, he loved the idea of me. The Amish girl with the historic past, the Amish girl who could give tours, the Amish girl who could attract more business. But that wasn't me. As Giselle had said, I lived in the here and now.

Besides, Lancaster County was my home. There was nowhere else I wanted to live. This trip had turned out to be the *rumspringa* I'd never had and so much more. I'd had to cross the ocean to discover myself, and now I was ready to return in faith, knowing God had something planned for me and I would simply need to trust.

I left the tree and resumed my journey up the path and up the steps of Amielbach.

Daniel was in the dining hall and was so absorbed in what he was doing that when I asked him to come outside with me he hesitated.

"Please, Daniel," I said, my hand on my hip.

We ended up on a bench in the shade of a willow tree. "I'm not going to come back," I told him.

His ran his hand through his hair.

"It's not the right thing for me," I added.

He nodded a little and then asked what made me decide that.

"Lancaster County is home," I said. "It's where I belong." I had wanted us to talk outside, where we could speak frankly in private, but now I realized there wasn't much for me to say. I told him how much I had enjoyed spending the last two weeks with him, and I was thankful for everything he had taught me. We said our goodbyes, and I started back toward the cottage, but then I turned. Daniel was walking toward the entrance to Amielbach. His steps were slow, but he didn't look back.

My gaze rose. There was someone in a second floor window. It was Will, watching me. I only saw him for a second. Perhaps the light changed. Or maybe he stepped back. But in a moment he was gone.

I hugged Giselle goodbye, careful not to bump her crutches. As we stood next to her weathered fence, she glanced toward Will and asked me in a whisper if I was coming back.

"No," I replied, hoping she could tell just from my expression that I had already broken things off with Daniel. "You'll have to come see me there. Come see all of us."

Her eyes glistened a little. "Perhaps."

We hugged again, and as we pulled apart, I said, "You would really like the woman Lexie has become. I hope you'll have the chance to meet her someday."

"Maybe I will," Giselle said, wiping brusquely at her eyes. After a moment, she added, "Would you give a message to Klara and Alexander for me?"

I nodded, waiting.

"Tell them…" Her voice trailed off for a moment, and I realized how uncomfortable and fidgety she suddenly seemed. She cleared her throat and started again. "Tell your parents they did a wonderful job raising you."

Startled by her words and deeply touched, I could only nod lest I burst into tears. It wasn't exactly hearts and flowers and open arms, but it was more than enough for me.

Daniel came down the steps of Amielbach as we all gathered to leave. He shook Will's hand and then stepped close to me. "Keep in touch," he said softly.

I nodded and thanked him again for everything.

A moment later he was talking with Morgan, making plans for her return. Seeing the way she looked at him, I realized I needed to let her know that I was completely out of the picture as far as he was concerned. She could deny it all she wanted, but I had no doubt she had feelings for him—and that he could easily learn to love her in return once he admitted to himself that he'd never really been in love with me.

Herr Lauten and even Oskar were sad to see all of us go. Herr Lauten asked that I give *Mammi* his regards and thanked Alice and me both, yet again, for all we had done to save the inn and to preserve history. In return, we thanked him for his hospitality and for his incredible generosity.

"Oh, and I have a little surprise for you folks before you go," Herr Lauten said. "Giselle and I do, actually." He held Giselle's box in his hand, the one with the Frutigen bakery carved on the top. "We started wondering if it had a false bottom too." He opened the box. "Sure enough it did." He took out a few papers. "These."

I took them in my hand. They were elaborate drawings, obviously done by a very gifted child, of the farm scene from Indiana, of the carving on *Mammi*'s box. On the top corner of the first sketch was a note.

I looked up at Herr Lauten. "Who's it from?"

"Elsbeth. She said her daughter Sarah inherited her grandfather's artistic talent. Elsbeth asked if he could carve a box based on her drawings as a lovely surprise for the girl."

I held the fragile sheets of paper tenderly, cherishing the thought of my great-grandmother. Abraham hadn't done the carving merely from the information gleaned from letters. He'd done them based on the renderings of the granddaughter he'd never meet. I turned toward Giselle and blurted out, "May I keep them?"

"Please do," she replied easily, and I was reminded that no matter how far she had come in the past week, she would probably always choose to distance herself from our family's history.

Looking down at the drawings, I couldn't help but wonder why Abraham had hidden them in the bottom of the box in the first place. I was thankful he did—otherwise they might have been lost forever—but it seemed unlikely he put them there for the sole reason of safekeeping. I marveled again at the mysteries in my family.

"Ada," Giselle said, nodding toward the box in Herr Lauten's hand. "I would also like you to have the box itself."

I stepped back, shaking my head. "You should keep it," I said, a little louder than I meant to.

"No. You've seen the Frutigen bakery. It means something to you."

Herr Lauten extended it to me, and this time I received it graciously. For a little while, until I reached Lancaster County at least, all three of the boxes would be in my possession. I was deeply honored.

Will said he would take one of the boxes onto the plane, and Alice and I each managed to squeeze the other two into our carry-on bags. Then we said our final goodbyes and drove away. Will settled into the front seat beside Morgan while in the back, Christy leaned against me a little. Alice, leaning toward the door to protect her arm, exclaimed over the beautiful countryside. The fog lifted and we could see the mountains. I thought of Elsbeth leaving Switzerland for good and how it must have pained her. I felt a lump growing in my throat.

At least when she left, it had been with the man she loved, the man she was married to. I, on the other hand, was leaving with the man I loved, but I would never marry him. Elsbeth knew she'd be the mother to the children in her care for the rest of her life. I knew I would never be the mother to the children I loved.

I blinked away my burning tears, trying to redirect my thoughts. Outside, a farmer steered an old red tractor over an emerald green field. A creek bubbled along next to the road. Smoke rose from a cottage on the hillside.

I closed my eyes. I was going home.

FORTY

I cried when I told Morgan farewell at the airport.

"We'll see each other again," she said. "I'll come to Lancaster County someday."

She promised to write letters—the old-fashioned way. I tried to return her copy of *Jane Eyre*, saying I could get it at the library to finish, but she insisted I keep it. "Finish it," she said. "And when Christy is older give it to her."

We couldn't thank her enough for all of her help.

"You were our rainbow after the storm," Alice said, alluding to a Plain proverb. "Our true friend, indeed."

Morgan modestly said it was nothing. As she hugged me, she added, "I'll be praying for you. Every night. That you'll soon know God's plan for your life."

"Thank you," I answered, and I assured her of my prayers for her also. Then I told her I wouldn't be coming back to Switzerland.

"What?" she gasped softly. "What about Daniel?"

"He knows. I told him this morning."

She studied my eyes for a long moment and then said, "Are you sure?"

"He's not the man for me," I answered, shrugging. Then I winked. "Though I do know someone he might be the perfect man for…"

From the shy tilt of her lips and the vivid red splotches on her cheeks, I knew she understood that I was giving my permission—and my blessing.

"We'll see," she whispered, hugging me again.

Inside, the airport was incredibly intimidating, but Will acted as though he knew what he was doing. The rest of us simply followed his lead, showing our passports when we checked our bags and then again as we entered the security area.

Alice was scandalized at the thought of giving up her shoes, but Will was patient and gentle with her, explaining that she'd get them back in just a minute, as soon as they'd been X-rayed.

Sure enough, after we'd all passed through a metal doorframe one by one and received an approving nod from the man in uniform there, we returned to the conveyor belt where our things were just emerging from the machine. Christy and I were both wide-eyed at the speed and efficiency of it all.

With Will again taking the lead, we found our gate, sat in a row of chairs, and waited there, much as we'd waited together for the train trip that had marked the beginning of this entire journey. As we did, I couldn't help but think about how much had changed since then, how far we'd all come in our own ways. Glancing at Will, I realized that our time together in Europe had bonded us somehow and only served to make me love him more. With all we had been through, how was I ever going to get over this man now? I turned away, telling myself that somehow God would give me the strength. Certainly, I would never be able to do it on my own.

When it came time to board the plane, I put thoughts of Will from my mind to focus on this new, final adventure, one I had never dreamed that I would experience in my lifetime. Once I got home, I'd have to be sure and tell the cows, "Flying! Can you believe it? I was flying!"

Soon, we were in our seats, my stomach roiling with butterflies as I buckled up. Will and Christy sat on the left, beside the window, with Alice and me across the aisle, in the center section. As the plane took off, Alice gripped my arm, her face aglow with a broad grin.

Will and Christy were both glued to the window as we soared up into the sky. I was just happy to realize that even from where I sat, I could see out somewhat as well, especially when the plane tilted a bit, giving us a full view of the city below. Gazing down at the incredible sight, I gasped.

"I guess that's what you call a bird's eye view," Christy quipped to her father.

I smiled, thinking we were likely too high for birds. No, to my mind, this was a *God's* eye view—His whole, big beautiful world glittering below, a testament to His glory and a delight to His own eyes.

After we'd been airborne for a while, I took out *Jane Eyre* and settled in to finish it. Soon I could hear Christy telling Will about the book and how we'd been reading it together. She began recounting the entire plot, not just the parts that had been read to her but the full overview Morgan had relayed in trying to interest her in the story. I was pleased with the enthusiasm I could hear in her voice. Maybe she'd learn to love reading yet.

Later, I put the book away and turned my attention to Alice, who had barely moved since the flight began. I asked her if she was okay, and in response, she simply nodded and grinned from ear and ear. Will leaned toward us and said if he didn't know better, he'd think she'd planned everything on purpose just for this flight home. We laughed, but long after that, his word kept ringing in my ears: *home*.

Home. Where Leah awaited. Where life would go on.

Where I would have to give Will up, once and for all.

By the time we landed in New York, Alice was exhausted. A wheelchair was waiting, and soon we were on a shuttle bus to a hotel. The next morning we took a taxi to the train station and then traveled on toward home.

By the time we reached Lancaster, we were all exhausted. *Daed* was at the station with a van and driver to meet us, and we dropped Christy, Will, and Alice off first. The twins, followed by their aunt, ran out the back door of the house as soon as the van stopped. They must have been looking for us.

The little ones were yelling for their *daed*, dashing across the grass, their little braids bouncing against their collarbones along with the ribbons of their little *kapps*. Their feet were bare even though it was cold. Will jumped from the van and scooped them up, followed by Christy. All four of them hugged for a moment until Mel squirmed down and called out my name.

As my *daed* helped Alice down, Mel slipped around them and into the van.

"Ada!" she yelled again. I lifted her to my lap and hugged her.

"Come on." She took my hand and led me out of the van after Alice. Matty wanted a hug too, and I lifted her. As Christy wrapped her arms around me, I thought of how aloof she had been with me until Alice fell ill. I squeezed her tightly.

Will invited us in, but *Daed* said he needed to get me home. He said there were two women waiting for me who wouldn't forgive him if he dallied.

"I understand," Will said, chuckling. But then he invited us to come back the next afternoon, and to bring *Mammi* with us if she was up to it. "Alice doesn't want Ada to have all the fun sharing her stories. She'd like to tell Frannie all about it as well."

As the driver neared the highway, a buggy turned down the Gundys' lane. It was Leah Fisher, waving at us, a big smile on her face.

I waved back, barely, reality smacking me in the face. Of course she would be there, eager to welcome home her future husband. Feeling nauseated, I decided that when the time came the next afternoon to visit, I would find some way to get out of it. If I couldn't have Will for myself, then I couldn't be around him at all, at least not for a while, not until the hole that had been ripped through my heart had been given a chance to heal.

To keep from crying, I simply closed my eyes and emptied my mind until the driver turned down our own lane. To the right, the corn had been harvested and all that was left was stubble. To the left, the cows grazed in the pasture, lifting their heads as we passed. The trees along the creek were completely bare, making the dark green of the fir trees in front of the white house stand out even more. *Mamm* stepped out onto the porch as the van pulled to a stop, pulling her cape tight with one hand as she hurried down the steps, a smile on her face. I climbed down into her arms, and she held me tight, not saying a word.

Daed paid the driver and then took my bag from me. While he headed into the house with it, *Mamm* and I started down the walkway to the *daadi haus*. "She's been beside herself the entire time you were gone," *Mamm* said. "Thinking about you, distraught over Alice becoming ill, worried about Giselle."

As soon as we opened the door, *Mammi* started struggling to her feet. I hurried to her, helping her the rest of the way up, and then hugged her, her weathered face against my own.

"How is Giselle?" Her voice was but a whisper.

Daed joined us, and the four of us sat down and I told them everything—about Morgan, Giselle, the property, Alice falling ill, the snowy night, finding the deed and agreement, Daniel asking me to stay, and Giselle telling me not to.

"She said that?" *Mamm*'s hands were crossed over her chest in unbelief.

"*Ya,*" I answered. "She did."

I gave them her message about how they had raised me word for word. In response, they simply nodded, but I could tell from the way they looked at each other they were as surprised and touched as I had been.

I told them about everything except of my love for Will. I could suffer through that as long as no one knew. If I told another soul, it would become unbearable.

Mammi said she wanted to see Alice as soon as possible, and *Daed* told her we'd all been invited back for tomorrow.

As we left the *daadi haus, Mamm* said she was afraid I'd be awfully bored at home after such an adventure. My eyes fell on my flower garden and then the windmill as I told her not to be silly, but the truth was, even though I wanted nothing more than to be back, there was a lot I was going to miss.

Later that night, in bed, I finished *Jane Eyre*, choking up over the line, "Reader, I married him." Picturing Will, my heart was pierced with pain. Oh, how deeply I yearned to be able to say the same.

The next morning Aunt Marta, Ella, and Zed came for breakfast. Ella brought a platter of muffins that she'd made, and by the time we polished them off, I'd repeated all of my stories.

Ella asked to see the other two boxes, and I retrieved them from my room. I told everyone I would return Lexie's to her and would keep the one of the Frutigen Bakery that Giselle had given me.

"What about the third one?" Ella asked.

"*Mammi* wants you and Zed to have it." I handed it to her, explaining it showed the family farm in Indiana, carved from a drawing by Sarah, *Mammi*'s mother.

Ella was obviously pleased, but Zed just shrugged. I was pretty sure the box would be hers alone.

I showed her my copy of the drawing, and she examined it closely. "Did you notice the circles in the bottom corners?" she asked.

I hadn't. I looked over her shoulder.

"They look like pies," she said, grinning. "And this rectangle on the bottom margin looks like a cookbook."

The objects were small and smudged. I wasn't sure about the book, but the round objects did look like they could be pies with a sheaf of wheat drawn onto the top crust.

"Sarah was just a little girl when she drew that," I explained.

Ella's eyes lit up. "Maybe she liked to bake even then. I know I did. How cool. I guess my culinary skills were passed all the way down from her to me." Running her fingers over the carving on the lid, she added dreamily, "I'd love to go here someday, to Indiana. To connect with this place from our family's past."

The clock marched onward whether I wanted it to or not, and eventually it was the afternoon and time to leave for the Gundys' house. I'd been unable to come up with a good excuse for not going along. I was tempted to feign being ill, but that would only make *Mamm* hover again. I truly didn't think I could face Will, especially not with Leah at his side, not after everything he and I had been through together. But seeing no other way around it, I finally gave in.

Rikki wasn't pleased with being forced out in the cold that afternoon, and *Daed* had to keep urging her on. It felt as if it might snow, and I realized that if it did this would be the only year of my life I would get to experience the first snow twice.

By the time we turned down the Gundys' lane, I truly was feeling sick to my stomach. I tried to distract myself from the gathering ahead but couldn't think of anything to concentrate on that didn't involve Will.

He met us by his hitching post, and told *Mamm, Mammi,* and me that we should go on in and get warm. He'd help *Daed* put the horse in the barn.

We slipped our boots off after we entered through the back door and hung up our coats. Ella called out a hello from the dining room. I scanned the table. It was just Will's parents and Ezra and Ella. I didn't see any sign of Leah Fisher.

Will's *mamm* invited us in and got us cups of hot coffee. Alice and *Mammi* sat side by side in easy chairs that had been brought in from the living room and placed at the head of the table. The girls came in to say hello, each one giving me a hug, and then the twins ran back off to play, but Christy stayed.

We settled in at the big table and chatted with Ella, who sat across the table much too close to Ezra. After a while *Daed* came in and joined us just as Ella was explaining to Ezra all about Daniel.

"He wanted Ada to stay there and live with Giselle so he could court her," she said. "But Ada told him no because she didn't think she could ever really learn to love him."

She said this knowingly, with great authority, as if someday her poor old maid cousin just might come to know a love as deep as she herself had already found. Embarrassed and a little irritated, I glanced down the table, surprised to see a strange expression on Alice's face. Eyes wide, she was looking at something over my shoulder, and I turned to see Will, standing there, staring at me. Then the conversation shifted.

"Did you hear the news about my teacher?" Christy asked the group at large.

Whipping back around, my heart began to race.

"She's getting married," Christy pronounced, answering her own question.

And there it was, the words I'd hoped I'd never have to hear. Leah's engagement was official. I turned and looked straight at Will. Tears filled my eyes and began spilling onto my cheeks, and for a moment, I couldn't even breathe, my grief was so strong.

I had to get out of there. Unable to stop myself, I stood, my chair clattering behind me, and ran from the room.

Everything was spinning as I made my way to the back door. I didn't even bother pulling on boots or coat. I simply ran through the door and down the steps as fast as I could, not coming to a stop until I reached the oak tree.

Standing there, trying not to scream, I realized that the first snowflakes had begun to fall.

I heard the back door open and close. I stepped further around the tree, mortified that everyone had seen my reaction. Now they all knew how I felt about Will—including Will himself! Closing my eyes, I heard footsteps coming in my direction, but I didn't even want to know who they had sent out to comfort me. *Mamm*, perhaps, or even Ella, who with all the good intentions in the world would still say the wrong things.

Instead, the voice that spoke into my ear was Will's.

"Ada," he said softly, causing my sobs to start anew. "Shhh," he whispered, wrapping a coat around my shoulders. Then he knelt at my feet, sliding my boots over them, dressing me as if I were completely helpless. "We already had to warm you up once this week. I don't think you want to have to go through that again, do you?"

I opened my eyes and watched through my tears as he stood and faced me again. Jokes? He was making jokes? At the moment of my deepest pain, did he really think I might laugh or at least smile? Surely he had to understand that I might never, ever smile again, much less now. Much less with him.

"I need to explain, Ada," he told me. "I owe you that."

"You owe me nothing," I said, but a sob caught in my throat as I spoke. I pressed a hand to my mouth, wishing he would just get this over with.

"Remember last spring, when your sister was here and you fell beside her car and cut your head?"

I nodded. Though the whole event was a bit blurry to me, I remembered riding in the ambulance to the hospital.

"When I learned you'd been hurt and saw you soon after, that's when I realized how I felt about you. I…" He hesitated for a moment and then looked me in the eye and said, "I decided then that I wanted to court you."

"Court me?" I couldn't help but cry. "Then why didn't you?"

He held out his hands, palms upward, saying, "It was premature. The girls and I needed more time first."

I breathed in deeply, trying to get my emotions under control. I could understand what he was saying. Lydia's passing had still been too recent back then. But if that was how he felt about me, why had he ever allowed Leah to enter the picture later, once the timing was more appropriate? Unable to stop myself, I asked him that very thing.

"Leah was to be Christy's teacher." He shrugged. "I know she came around a lot, but I thought her interest was purely in the children, in helping out. In being a friend."

A friend. I closed my eyes. Leah Fisher had managed to insinuate herself into Will's life and then his heart without him even realizing what was happening.

"I was naive, I guess," he continued, "or at the very least unobservant. I see that now."

I opened my eyes, suddenly afraid that things had changed between them before he'd even come to Switzerland, that he'd been engaged to her the whole time. "When did this happen?" I asked, bracing myself for his answer, not wanting it to invalidate all that he and I had shared on the other side of the ocean.

"Leah came over yesterday as soon as we got back from the trip."

I nodded, grateful for that much at least.

"And she and I sat down and had a very long conversation," he added.

"She initiated it, then?" I whispered, not wanting to hear but needing to know just the same. He didn't reply, so I pressed him further. "Was it hard for her to convince you, Will? Or did she need only to profess her love for you to see what you'd been so blind to before?"

"She did make her intentions clear, yes, that's true. I was pretty surprised, to say the least."

"And?"

"And it's hard to describe the rest of the conversation without sounding…well, unkind." He peered off in the distance, seeming to search his mind for the right words.

Unkind? To rip out my heart and tear it to shreds, he was calling unkind? Before I could muster a response, he spoke.

"It's sort of like in that story you and Christy were reading."

I squinted, my mind racing. "*Jane Eyre*?"

"Yes. Christy said there was another woman, the one who was determined to marry the hero."

"Miss Ingram?"

"Right. Her. Do you remember what happened?"

"Of course. Miss Ingram changed her mind about wanting to marry Mr. Rochester once she found out that he wasn't nearly as wealthy as she'd assumed."

"Exactly," Will replied, leaning closer. "My conversation with Leah was kind of like that. While we were over in Europe, she heard about the financial issues the nursery's been having. She'd come here hoping it wasn't true."

"Did you tell her about the money from Herr Lauten? About how you can use it to increase your profits and turn things around?"

He laughed. "Why would I do that? I had no intention of encouraging her in the matter. I didn't love *her*, Ada."

Slowly, Will placed his hands on the sides of my upper arms, his touch radiating warmth clear through to my bones. I didn't understand. The way he was looking at me, holding me, the words he was saying—all were in direct contradiction to the facts.

"Can you imagine how odd that conversation was for me?" he continued. "It was rather like being told hello and goodbye in the same sentence. Not that it would have ended any other way, of course, but still."

"What are you trying to tell me, Will?" I pleaded, my heart pounding furiously in my chest. "That you and Leah *aren't* getting married?"

He smiled, reaching up and gently brushing a snowflake from my cheek. "Oh, we're getting married." He nodded, his words like a knife in my chest. Then he grinned, adding, "Just not to each other."

The world stopped in that moment. Will looked as though he wanted to kiss me, but I couldn't even breathe, could barely even stand. Taking me into his arms and holding me securely there, he told me that Leah had decided to marry Silas Yoder. "I'd say that was the right decision, wouldn't you?"

Slowly, he leaned down, moving his lips toward mine. When he was almost there, I turned away, needing to hear the words I thought I'd never be able to hear from the man I thought I'd never be allowed to love.

"And you?" I whispered. "Who are you marrying?"

"I think you know the answer to that," he said, chuckling, his breath sweet against my skin. Tilting my face back and looking deeply into my eyes, he said, "God willing, if you'll have me, Ada, more than anything in this world I'd like to marry you."

"Oh, Will," I whispered in return, "don't you know that's all I've ever wanted?"

Eyes glistening, he slowly leaned forward and then he kissed me, his lips warm and tender against mine. I wrapped my arms around his neck and kissed him in return, knowing one thing for sure: We may have crossed an ocean, but our real journey had just begun.

EPILOGUE

With Will's status as a widower, we could have obtained a special exception from the bishop and married right away. But for various reasons we decided to wait and have a regular fall wedding instead the following year. That would give my mother time to prepare, the children time to adjust, and me time to go though my classes and join the Amish church—a transition I found myself embracing with great joy.

As it turned out, Morgan and Daniel ended up beating us to the altar. They were married in the spring. She sent a detailed letter of the event, a letter I kept in my apron pocket and took out the week after, reading it over again. The pastor from the Langnau Mennonite Church, their place of worship, performed the service. She said God had done an amazing work in her and that her father, on occasion, even joined them for church. Daniel would start classes at the university in the fall, and she and Oskar were expanding the shop at Amielbach to represent even more area artists and to sell Amish quilts from Lancaster County. She was working with my *mamm* on that project.

Leah Fisher resigned from her teaching job right after her wedding, and Will and I decided it would be best for me to take it, at least until my own wedding—best for me and for Christy.

I made a point of talking with Will in detail about my blood disorder. I explained it was hereditary and any children we might have could be at risk. He looked at me intently and said, "Ada, you're having a good life, right, regardless of your disorder?"

I assured him I was.

"Then what's the problem?"

I decided there wasn't one.

Alice rallied, not enough to help Will with the kids, but she said she wasn't going anywhere anytime soon when life was so exciting. Between Will and me shuttling *Mammi* and Alice back and forth, the two friends saw each other more often than ever. Their joy about Will and me marrying was endless, and they marveled that after more than a century, the two families would be legally united. They were sure Elsbeth and Marie were rejoicing in heaven.

I joined the church in October, and our wedding was in November. We said our vows in *Mamm* and *Daed*'s house in the living room and celebrated with three hundred guests, including Lexie and James, who came from Oregon. Of course, Ella and Lexie couldn't stand beside me as that wasn't our way, but they were in the second row with all of my family. Lexie had come out a week early, and in many ways it was the best week of my life, so far. I had a sister. I was marrying Will Gundy. I was going to be a mother to three beautiful children I already knew and loved. All of my dreams had come true.

I also had a place in a community that was truly home. I had a *mamm* and *daed* who, just as they had seen to the details of raising me, now saw to all the details of my wedding, ensuring that our guests would be well fed and taken care of. Ella actually helped with that by making the cakes and dozens and dozens of cookies. My Plain cake wasn't as fancy as Lexie's, but it tasted just as good.

We invited Giselle to join us, praying she would. She wrote back, sharing our joy, but said she wasn't ready to visit—yet. She hoped we'd understand.

During the ceremony, Will's three girls were in the first row, sitting beside Alice. When Bishop Fisher instructed Will and me to kneel and clasp hands, Mel and Matty managed to escape their chairs and join us. Everyone laughed, and I turned and motioned for Christy to come forward too.

Will and I each wrapped an arm around the girls as Bishop Fisher blessed our family. Then he said, "Go forth in the name of the Lord. You are now man and wife."

Man and wife. Just hearing the words filled my heart with such joy I could barely contain it.

As the five of us stood, now united as one family, a saying of *Mammi's* came to mind: *Sometimes God calms the storm, but sometimes God lets the storm rage and calms His child.*

My new husband and his children had certainly been through some storms. Lydia's death. Financial hardship. I had been through storms as well, those of growing up and breaking free and somehow finding my way to adulthood. I had known the heartache of a love I thought would never be returned to me, and I'd born the grief of knowing I might never teach, might never have children.

But whether in storms or calm, God had been with me every step of the way, growing me through it all. What I learned was that His plan for me—and His timing—were far better than anything I could ever have imagined for myself.

Now, as I reached out and took the hand of my new husband, our eyes met, and I could see so much love there it made me shiver. As Will gazed at me, I finally understood that I really was beautiful after all, but not because of face or figure or demeanor. I was beautiful because I'd been made in God's image. How could I not be so?

"Congratulations, Mrs. Gundy," Will whispered, his lips curving into a smile.

Eyes brimming with tears, I squeezed his hand and smiled in return, knowing that I had finally, truly come home.

Discussion Questions

1. Ada often feels invisible and unremarkable. She also frequently compares herself to other women she considers far prettier than she is. Why do you think she does this? Do you feel that she has changed in this somewhat by the end of the book, and if so, what causes the change?

2. Ada has an "inner teacher." What are positives and negatives about this? Are you this way, or do you know anyone who is like this?

3. Out of the blue, Morgan shows up to stay with Ada and her friends at Amielbach. Why do you think she does this? Do you think her gesture of bringing them food (mutual aid) indicates a change in her feelings about the Amish? If so, what brings about this change?

4. Why do you think Giselle is so cold and unreceptive to Ada's presence at first? Did you expect this, or did you think she would welcome her with open arms? Was her character consistent?

5. When Daniel declares his intentions to court Ada and presents his plan for her to be an authentic tour guide, how does Ada react? Do you think his idea would have turned her identity into a caricature of an Amish woman? What would you have said in the same situation?

6. Because Daniel and Ada grew up with stories of martyrs, they aren't emotionally affected by the stories the same way Morgan is. Why do

you think Amish and Mennonites focus so strongly on their history of persecution? Why doesn't Christy want to hear about the violence or death in her ancestors' stories?

7. In his attempts to keep Elsbeth from becoming a Mennonite, Abraham brings heartache to himself, his daughter, and others—leaving him bitter and isolated for many years. What finally allows him to seek Elsbeth's forgiveness?

8. Before going to Europe, Ada thinks, *I wanted the full knowledge of what was out there, of who I might be.* What are some things Ada discovers about herself during the journey to Europe? Have you ever traveled somewhere and returned with new insights about your life?

9. At the end of the book, Giselle gives Ada a message for Klara and Alexander, saying, "Tell your parents they did a wonderful job raising you." Do you think this sentiment is true to the character of Giselle? By calling Klara and Alexander Ada's "parents," what is she trying to say? Do her words provide a sense of closure?

10. Ada desires to become an independent adult. What actions and thoughts signify this desire? Do you feel she has achieved this goal by the end of the book?

About the Authors

The Amish Nanny is Mindy Starns Clark's sixteenth book with Harvest House Publishers. Previous novels include the bestselling *The Amish Midwife* (cowritten with Leslie Gould), *Whispers of the Bayou*, *Shadows of Lancaster County*, *Under the Cajun Moon*, and *Secrets of Lancaster County*, as well as the well-loved Million Dollar Mysteries.

Mindy lives with her husband, John, and two adult daughters near Valley Forge, Pennsylvania.

❧

Leslie Gould, a former magazine editor, is the author of numerous novels, including *The Amish Midwife*, *Beyond the Blue*, and *Garden of Dreams*. *The Amish Nanny* is her second book with Harvest House.

Leslie received her master of fine arts degree from Portland State University and lives in Oregon with her husband, Peter, and their four children.

❧

For detailed family trees to the characters in the Women of Lancaster County series, visit Mindy's and Leslie's websites at www.mindystarnsclark.com and www.lesliegould.com.

A POCKET GUIDE TO AMISH LIFE
by *Mindy Starns Clark*

"I cannot imagine being any happier than I am now."
—An Amish Man

As Amish fiction continues to appeal to a huge audience, *A Pocket Guide to Amish Life* gives you a glimpse into an obscure, fascinating world—what the Amish believe and how they live. Full of fun and fresh facts about the people who abide by this often-misunderstood faith and unique culture, this handy-sized guide covers a wide variety of topics, such as:

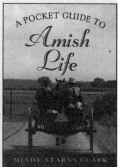

- beliefs and values
- clothing and transportation
- courtship and marriage
- shunning and discipline
- teens and *rumspringa*
- children and the elderly
- education and work

Presented in an easy-to-follow and engaging style, this pocket guide to the Amish is a great resource for anyone interested in Amish life.

Shadows of Lancaster County

by Mindy Starns Clark

What Shadows Darken the Quiet Valleys of Amish Country?

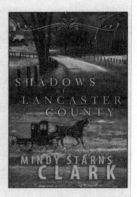

Anna Bailey thought she left the tragedies of the past behind when she took on a new identity and moved from Pennsylvania to California. But now that her brother has vanished and his wife is crying out for help, Anna knows she has no choice but to come out of hiding, go home, and find him. Back in Lancaster County, Anna follows the high-tech trail her brother left behind, a trail that leads from the simple world of Amish farming to the cutting edge of DNA research and gene therapy.

During the course of her pursuit, Anna soon realizes that she has something others want, something worth killing for. In a world where nothing is as it seems, Anna seeks to protect herself, find her brother, and keep a rein on her heart despite the sudden reappearance of Reed Thornton, the only man she has ever loved.

Following up on her extremely popular gothic thriller, *Whispers of the Bayou,* Mindy Starns Clark offers another suspenseful standalone mystery, one full of Amish simplicity, dark shadows, and the light of God's amazing grace.

Secrets of Harmony Grove

by Mindy Starns Clark

What Secrets Lurk Deep Inside Harmony Grove?

Philadelphia advertising executive Sienna Collins learns she is under investigation by the federal government for crimes she knows nothing about. Suspecting the matter has something to do with one of her investments, the Harmony Grove Bed & Breakfast in Lancaster County, she heads there only to find her ex-boyfriend dead and the manager of the B and B unconscious. As Sienna's life and livelihood spin wildly out of control, she begins to doubt everyone around her, even the handsome detective assigned to the case.

As Sienna searches for the truth and tries to clear her name, she is forced to depend on the faith of her childhood, the wisdom of the Amish, and the insight of the man she has recently begun dating. She'll need all the help she can get, because the secrets she uncovers in Harmony Grove are threatening not just her bed-and-breakfast, but also her credibility, her beliefs, and ultimately her life.

Following up on her bestselling Amish romantic suspense, *Shadows of Lancaster County*, Mindy Starns Clark returns to Pennsylvania to offer another exciting standalone novel, one full of mystery, hidden dangers, and the life-giving truth of God's forgiveness and grace.

THE WAY TO A MAN'S HEART
by Mary Ellis

Can a Loving Amish Woman Be a Refuge for a Wounded Soul?

Leah Miller, a talented young woman in the kitchen, is living her dream come true as she invests in a newly restored diner that caters mostly to locals. Jonah Byler is a dairy farmer with a secret. Having just moved to the area, can he persuade this quiet young woman to leave her adoring fans and cook only for him? Once she discovers what he has been hiding from others, can Leah trust Jonah with her heart?

Working at the diner introduces Leah to both Amish and English patrons. Though maturing into womanhood, *rumschpringe* holds little appeal to the gentle, shy girl who has never been the center of attention before. When three Amish men vie for her attention, competing with Jonah, Leah must find a way to understand the confusing new emotions swirling around her.

A captivating story that lovingly looks at how faith in God and connection with family can fill every open, waiting heart to overflowing.

The Homestyle Amish Kitchen Cookbook

by Georgia Varozza

Let a Little Plain Cooking Warm Up Your Life

Who doesn't want simplicity in the kitchen?

Most of these delicious, easy-to-make dishes are simplicity itself. The Amish are a productive and busy people. They work hard in the home and on their farms, and they need good, filling food that doesn't require a lot of preparation and time. A few basic ingredients, some savory and sweet spices, and a little love make many of these meals a cook's delight. And if you want something a bit more complex and impressive, those recipes are here for you too.

Along with fascinating tidbits about the Amish way of life, you will find directions for lovely, old-fashioned food such as

- Scrapple
- Honey Oatmeal Bread
- Coffee Beef Stew
- Potato Rivvel Soup
- Snitz and Knepp
- Shoo-Fly Pie

Everything from breakfast to dessert is covered in this celebration of comfort food and family. Hundreds of irresistible options will help you bring the simple life to your own home and kitchen.